INTER STATES
FOSSIL NATION

RALPH MEIMA

FOUNDERS HOUSE
PUBLISHING
2015

Inter States: Fossil Nation
Copyright © 2015 Ralph Meima
Published by Founders House Publishing, LLC
Cover Art by Matt Forsyth
Cover and interior design © 2015 Founders House Publishing, LLC
Paperback Edition: August 2015
ISBN: 978-0692488638

For more information please visit www.foundershousepublishing.com

Published in the United States Of America

For Mish and the kids, and a future worth fighting for.

ACKNOWLEDGEMENTS

Many deserve my sincere thanks for advice and encouragement on the decade-long path that the *Inter States* project has so far trodden. Rob Williams, source of the series' title and flag/shield logo, has cheered for *IS* since early-on, and provided valuable opportunities for promotion. My community of readers around the world has been supportive and informative, notably François Bartsch, Eve Ermer, Bob Fairchild, Magnus Nilsson, George Oprisko, Bill Perry, Beth Porch, Michel Salim, Sandy Schaudies, Mark Starik, Alex Wilson, Flemming Ørneholm, and scores more. My father Ralph and mother Barbara have been steady muses and advocates. Great gratitude goes to my publisher, Shaun Kilgore, for providing fabulous structural feedback. And big thanks also go to Matt Forsyth for his inspired cover art. You all believed in me, and this.

Finally, I salute those whose own explorations of the present and the future have been especially thought-provoking in my own project (not that I agree with them, necessarily): Ed Abbey, Gregory Bateson, Edward Bellamy, T.C. Boyle, Frank Bryan, Lester Brown, Ernest Callenbach, Fritjof Capra, Herman Daly, C. Lee Dravis, Sibel Edmonds, John Ehrenfeld, Dave Foreman, George Friedman, Joel Garreau, Ross Gelbspan, John Michael Greer, Paul Hawken, Chris Hedges, Richard Heinberg, Samuel P. Huntington, Aldous Huxley, David Holmgren, David Cay Johnston, David Jonstad, Naomi Klein, David Korten, Paul Krugman, James Howard Kunstler, Sinclair Lewis, Amory Lovins, Douglas MacKinnon, Lynn Margulis, Chris Martenson, Bill McKibben, Walter M. Miller Jr., Thomas Naylor, Gerard K. O'Neill, Naomi Oreskes, David Orr, George Orwell, Ayn Rand, Jeremy Rifkin, Karl-Henrik Robert, Ken Stanley Robinson, Mark Satin, George R. Stewart, John Todd, Naomi Wolf, and Yevgeny Zamyatin. There is a lot to make sense of, but—fortunately—also a vibrant, creative web of sensemakers.

AUTHOR'S NOTE

I did not originally set out to write a novel. In the years around 2003-2004, as I awoke to the rising chaos and corruption in American politics during the first George W. Bush administration, and pondered our growing understanding of climate change and resource depletion, I began to wonder with growing alarm about the long-term effects of bad governance, corruption, willful ignorance of science in public policy and education, and the economic stripping of the middle class. Having spent a sizeable portion of my life living outside the United States, where I witnessed cases of profound political-institutional change, I knew that things would not necessarily always stay the same in the USA—that there would have to be consequences of some kind.

At that time, I was teaching a graduate course in strategic management at the School for International Training in Brattleboro, Vermont that included a unit on forecasting and scenario planning, so I invited students to write scenarios that addressed some of the latest trends, and tried my hand as well. The results of my work were less than satisfying. This short-format futurism felt linear, uncreative, obvious, and self-important. Plus, I had once organized a "future seminar" in the early '90s in Sweden for LM Ericsson that attempted to predict the cell phone business 15 years into the future (2005), and we (laughably) completely failed to anticipate the Internet and WWW. I was therefore well aware of how inaccurate most attempts at scenario-craft tend to be.

Nevertheless, frustrated by what I felt was a lack of thorough explorations of the future consequences of current trends, I decided to embark on the deep dive of an extended work of fiction set in the future, because I concluded that its real learning/thinking value rests not on how accurate a particular prediction is, but rather on whether the people in the narrative act in an interesting and plausible manner as the future throws new circumstances at them. If we don't want certain circumstances to appear in our own future, it's useful to contemplate how to avoid them, but things are never going to turn out exactly as one expects, so the most important thing is to train one's capacity to act flexibly and resourcefully as the future unfolds. Characters in a narrative can model this.

A final note: I have been experiencing a disturbing phenomenon first-hand as I write. I call it "severity inflation" or "plausibility creep." Again and again, a fictional future situation or event (political, economic, climatological, etc.) that felt implausibly extreme to include upon first imagining—alarmist, corny, melodramatic—has, as time passed and current events piled up, started to feel increasingly tame and predictable. I don't know whether this reveals more about me or about the future. But the early chapters of *Inter States* were written well before Hurricane Katrina, Tropical Storms Irene and Sandy, Abu Ghraib, the financial crash of 2008, the Arab Spring, Occupy Wall Street, the European debt crisis, the rapid spread of the acceptance of same-sex marriage, rapid advances in space technology, and much more of both a positive and negative nature. Most of these have entailed the arrival and acceptance of a strange, unfamiliar future circumstance sooner than imagined. And I have had to go back many times to earlier chapters to "turn up the heat" because—you know what?—the future seems to be consistently arriving ahead of schedule!

INTER STATES
FOSSIL NATION

1-RECONNECTIONS

A tern dipped and swooped, riding the warm air currents as the offshore breeze hit the dunes and deflected upwards. Miles of white sand, dune grasses, and bright surf stretched away to the north and south, interrupted at short intervals by the wistful shapes of houses, mini-malls, hotels, pilings, and pavement subsiding into the hungry ocean. The October sky was a flawless azure, and the sun hot—perfect beach weather—but tourism had long since ebbed away, and the restless sands drifted alone. From a deck above the dunes, a man named Mike Kendeil sat and surveyed the Sound and the Sound-side corduroy road, a cap on his head and a bottle of water in his hand. There was a distracted tension in his manner, up on the grey, weathered deck. Good old RL, he mused. The soundtrack sucks, but the graphics are awesome. He made a circle with his thumb and index finger, and peered through it. He wanted to fly, to soar. But there he could only sit.

The hours of late afternoon passed, and the offshore breeze started to slacken. He looked out at a flock of pelicans as they repeatedly dove into the flat water, fishing. He wondered if there was any particular migration or spawning of fish at that moment, out under the sparkling surface. Fins flashed nearby in the shallow rays of evening sunshine, pushing his pondering towards a hunch. He had never been into fishing, unlike his grandfather, father, and big brother. They would ride their bikes along East-West Avenue, down to the beach, and surf cast all day—storm or sunshine—with their elaborate sinker rigs and enormous rods. It had been well over a decade since he had last seen that sight. In those days, more than a mile of houses and streets, resort hotels, and the grassy contours of the Ridge had lain between his grandparents' west-facing house and the wide Atlantic beach. Now, low billows of sand ran continuously from the encroaching breakers right across to the Sound's edge, burying everything

1

in their path. The Ridge had come apart, its millions of cubic meters of sand migrating northwards and into the Sound under the onslaught of the hurricanes and rising ocean. What was left of the Ridge provided scant shelter from the storm winds for the old family house. It would not be long now before this house, too, was lost to the dunes and then to the Atlantic, and the dwindling barrier island completely vanished.

An improvised streamer on the flagpole above the deck caught Mike's attention, flopping lazily about for several minutes before gesturing in a new direction. Festoons of insulation and loose slats of derelict siding on the nearby houses adjusted to the changed air current. The onshore breeze was kicking up as the land cooled off. He stretched his neck and back, and got up stiffly to go in. The onshore breeze would soon bring its nightly passengers—biting flies and then mosquitoes—carrying malaria, West Nile, and God only knew what else. Just coming off a six-year tour with the Army Corps of Engineers, Mike knew all about that. Even with elimlets around his ankles, wrists, and neck, he was not taking any chances.

He pulled the ragged screen door closed, and walked around the interior pulling windows shut. The air was heavy with salt and the scent of mold, but at least it was dry. As the autumn sun sank toward the horizon, he started making dinner, which at this point consisted of a handful of beans plus salt pork, rice, apples, and raisins he had bought in Elizabeth City two weeks before. When the beans and rice were simmering, he took a quick inventory of what he'd need to buy if Grandma did not show up before the weekend: more beans, rice, fruit, cheese, some milk, oats, kerosene, bacon or smoked fish, flour, sugar, candles, baking soda for his teeth (if he could find the damn stuff now). And water to refill the cans. Maybe candy and beer, if he felt like splurging with more of his remaining Army cash. And soap.

Actually, his Army savings and severance package would be good for a while, if he could lay off the satcom. The Army treated its veterans and retirees well. His credit account was replenished with a modest but reliable sum of milscrip every month, and he would never have to worry about health care. He was in a privileged position, a reward for dedicated service to the almighty Federal Government. Unfortunately, there was almost no way to spend milscrip in the rural towns and villages. They operated on a cash-only basis, and euros were the most popular. So he had to make do for

2

now. Of course, he could always blow it on Vtopia…Always. No, that was a thought to resist.

Going up to Elizabeth City would be a nice break in his solitude and abstinence. He had been at the house too long. When he first spoke with Grandma, she said she would be leaving by September 20th, and that it ought to not take more than ten days to get there. They communicated now every day or two, by email or phone. There was no cellphone coverage on the island any longer, after the phone companies stopped maintaining the cell towers. There was just the satnet, reliable but quite literally exorbitant, priced for affluent foreign markets half a world away. So, using guesswork, he tracked her daily progress on an old Mid-Atlantic/Carolinas map in the cottage's living room, imagining her path slowly wandering south.

Biking up to Elizabeth City was a major undertaking, and took around six hours. You had to walk the bike to the Point Harbor bridge before there was any blacktop to ride fast on—mostly gravel now, at that. Hauling supplies back presented a major challenge, especially if the wind was against you. There was no bike trailer at the house anymore, although Grandma had said there would be one. He wondered how he would transport two big thirty-liter cans of water without a trailer. He wondered if there was much traffic on the mainland, so he could bum a lift. He had seen boats out on the sound, but wondered how to connect with a skipper headed up to EC via the Pasquotank River route. Maybe he could bike up, find a skipper headed south, and get a ride back to Head Island. Since Nags Head, Kill Devil Hills, and Kitty Hawk had succumbed, and the bridge to Roanoke Island and Wanchese washed out, the peninsula had become deserted. There was no one to ask. Just a range of theories Mike could ruminate upon.

His remaining supplies would last no more than a week. He wished he could have stayed in Elizabeth City and waited for Grandma there. In town, there was electricity, cold beer, company, 3V, email, cellphone coverage, delicious VNET dalliances—all the urban pleasures a metropolis of 15,000 could offer—while the boredom and isolation down at the house was a challenge. But he had promised Grandma he would get there first and take care of the packing. Keep an eye on things. And she'd mischievously promised him a special reward.

It was good and dark when he finished his solitary dinner. He left the dishes and pots by the basin to wash up in the morning light, and blew out one of the two candles. He was tired, and there was nothing to do but go to sleep and awaken at sunrise. At least he was getting lots of sleep nowadays, he reflected, something the rare blessing of electric light and the siren vastness of Vtopia tended to eat away at.

Mike looked out through the cracked and taped picture window in the living room, the window that had sat behind its protective sheet-metal shutters for quite a few years before Mike's arrival brought in the light again. The dark field of view was dense and featureless. Not a single light shone. It was creepy, and the isolation was making Mike increasingly tense as the days passed.

"Frigging dream," he mumbled. It had been on his mind all day, a few remembered scenes and feelings. A dream of many visitations, with slight variations. It should have made him horny, he thought. But it only made him feel frustrated, lonely, and vaguely devastated. He rummaged around in his memory, trying to recall whether it was only a dream. He could not remember. It bothered him. He had gotten used to dreams like it, but he longed for the day when it might finally fade away, when his RDD might subside.

His years in the Corps of Engineers were almost monastic as far as RL went. A few girlfriends-for-hire hung around the bases, but the STDs held him back, and—for security reasons—contact with the civilian populations was too limited for relationships with the local girls to blossom. He had a secret affair with a female officer once—a fellow lieutenant—but that had no air to breathe in the confines of service. In contrast, the VNET always offered limitless space and endless possibilities: whole planets and galaxies of adventure. Sure, he had let it get a bit wild for a while. Slowing down had been good for him. He knew how to handle it, whatever any of his superiors might have claimed. They were just using it as an excuse to nail him. But now, for a change, he was no longer monitored.

Mike lay down on the daybed in the living room in his military fleece jacket, an old black horse blanket wrapped around him against the night air, which he knew would cool and dampen. A single candle burned, its wick crackling. He had a full belly from another good dinner of the fresh food he had bought up in Elizabeth City. The candle guttered from a stray draft. His eyes ran over the complex patterns of water stains that covered

4

the cracked wall panels. They looked like Rorschach tests, symmetrical to the left and right of the seams. He watched his T-pad beckon from the end table's surface, its tiny blue beacon level with his eyes.

"Account balance," he whispered for the tenth time that day, hoping it wouldn't hear him.

"Which account?" it promptly asked in its familiar genderless tone, its screen illuminating.

"Mil," he breathed.

"Twenty-seven thousand eight hundred and fifty nine units, and fourteen cents."

"Screw you," he intoned.

"I don't recognize that command," the T-pad said.

"Sleep," he hissed. The T-pad darkened and fell silent.

Insanity, he thought, is when you keep doing the same thing but expect a different result. Ahhh. It would be soooo easy to launch and rezz. The scrip was in his account. He had enough gear in his bag. Paradise was only a command away. But, fuck it, it wouldn't be for long. He needed that milscrip to live on.

Mike held the line yet again, successfully fighting off the temptation. He blew out the candle, and drifted off in anticipation of the freedom and pleasure that awaited him at the end of the journey, when not all roads to Rome led up a costly satnet link. Now, if only Grandma would show up.

2-A SURPRISE VISIT

Tuesday, October 16th

Mike dozed, spiraling gradually into deeper levels of sleep.

Suddenly, he started as if poked. Footsteps were coming up the wooden walkway, and voices were murmuring. Was he dreaming again? No, this was real. He rolled off the daybed and crouched, grabbing his automatic from the end table. His heart pounded. The footsteps stopped, but the murmurs went on. He crawled to the nearest window and he peered cautiously through the blinds. There was a light bobbing around.

"It's Ari Daniels, Mike," a familiar voice called hesitantly up from some twenty meters off. Ari was an old summer regular whose house lay a short distance away along the Sound shore. "Mike?" he called again. "I'm down here with Lara and Daryl. Are you there?"

Mike knew these people. He had not seen Lara and Daryl for a long time—years—but they had played together as kids and hung out as teenagers, summer upon summer. Relieved but still cautious, he crept over to the door and opened it a crack, staying low. A story below and over by the edge of their lot, he saw three figures waiting in the fog, haloed in the yellow glow of a lantern. He hesitated, trying to shake his grogginess and assess the situation clearly. It was OK. He stood up and went out onto the deck by the head of the stairs.

"Hey y'all," he called down shakily. "It's me. Come on up. You surprised me." He looked at his watch and saw it was about eight-thirty. So early! They approached and started up the stairs. Ari came first, wearing a friendly smile, a thin man in his sixties with an angular, wrinkled face. Behind him came his son Daryl, slightly younger than Mike, and then Lara, Mike's age. They trooped into the kitchen from the October night, huffing and making emphatic comments about the fog and the chill. Mike closed the door and lit another lamp, and then the candle. Ari looked at the automatic with his eyebrows raised, and shook his head.

6

"Whoa, Mike. We should have given you better warning, for our own sakes."

Mike glanced at the weapon in his hand, and quickly sliding the safety back into place with chagrin, put it away in a kitchen drawer.

"Yeah. Sorry. Well, I'm no hothead, anyway. Just didn't expect to see a human soul around here. And I was falling asleep." He rubbed his eyes and tried to smile. "Let's get some more light here." He lit another candle, which stood upright on the counter in the mouth an ancient glass cider jug, and brought it over to the kitchen table. "Sit down, everybody. It has really been a while, huh?"

"A very long time, Mike," said Ari seriously. Then he flashed his old taut smile, the smile Mike remembered down the years. "You look like a man who has seen the world!"

"Or at least a lot of Dixie," chuckled Mike. He gestured toward the table. "Here." Ari and his children, who were still standing a little stiffly by the door, started removing their coats and taking seats. "Want some tea or something?" Mike asked. They answered in the affirmative, so he lit the stove and put a full kettle on. They studied one another, savoring the unexpected reunion, noting the little changes that time had brought. Ari looked the same as always. Daryl, eyes wary, smile uncertain, looked a little gaunt, slightly stooped. Lara looked great: slim, healthy-looking, disconcertingly real.

"Hope we're not bothering you, Mike. Been meaning to get over here to see if anyone was around," said Ari. "We all got here Tuesday. I heard up in Elizabeth City that you were here." Mike reckoned for a second, remembering it was now Thursday.

"Nah, just taking it easy tonight. Been pretty lazy. I got here—what?— almost three weeks ago." Then he cocked back his head, and asked suspiciously, "Who told you?"

"Lady at the Airship Inn."

Mike laughed. "You stayed there, too?"

"Tradition," chuckled Ari. "Didn't think it'd still be there, since the drop in tourism and they moved the airship factory to Raleigh. But it was. And that girl—" Ari looked at Lara for her name.

"Annie," said Lara helpfully.

"Right, Airship Annie," Ari continued with a humorous crinkle of his eyes. "She said you'd passed through, coming down here."

7

Mike smiled. "A man certainly can't move around undetected in these parts!"

"Nope, and we heard why you're here, too," said Daryl mysteriously.

"Oh?" said Mike, raising an eyebrow.

"Yeah, from the lady herself," answered Daryl.

"Grandma?"

"Yes, she's in Elizabeth City now," said Lara, re-entering the conversation. Mike was surprised Grandma was already there. "We ran into her outside the general store. She's got quite a wagon. One bold lady, on the road like that, just her and that Latino."

"Yep. She is and she does, I hear. Already made it this far? Did she say when she'd be here?" asked Mike. "I should call her…" He paused, his attention re-set. "Latino? Spaniard. He's a Spaniard."

"Oh, OK," replied Ari. "Spaniard."

"I've never met him," Mike admitted, "but Grandma says he works for her, and that he's got a cool head and sharp eye."

"Seemed like a good guy," said Ari. "Anyway, her arrival? Tomorrow, assuming the fog burns off or thins a little," said Ari. "Didn't want to try it in the fog, late in the day, especially with the tides…"

"Good thing she didn't," said Mike. "There's nobody around in case you run into trouble. And she hasn't been here for a couple of years, and doesn't know the new terrain. Where's she staying?"

"At the Fosters', she said," said Lara. "She said Burns wrote her in the spring and said she'd better get down here to pick up what's left, or you might never see it again."

"Yeah," said Mike. "The island's disappearing faster and faster."

"We're here for the same reason," she said.

Mike looked at her in the yellow lantern light, at her wide-set brown eyes, her long, light-brown hair, and her pale, freckled skin. He'd always liked her, and had had secret crushes on her as a teen. Already married and divorced, she was. He remembered her in the last few summers before she went to college, her frizzy hair reaching almost down to her waist, her slender hips, sinewy torso, and athletic belly, always bare those summers—on the volleyball court, on a surfboard, on the sand. There had been a few times he had wanted her so much he had felt like screaming, but she always gave him that cool, sisterly look, offering no path toward intimacy, no way forward for him without acting like an idiot. And that is how it had stayed.

"Heard you're living in Roanoke now, Lara," said Mike. "From Jenny, I guess. Hon's mentioned you, too" Jenny was Mike's youngest sister, up in Fredericksburg. Honorée was his older sister, living in Washington, DC. "Still trying to fix us up!"

Lara laughed wryly. "When will they learn?" She paused, grinning sideways at Ari. "Well, I'm living in Salem, outside Roanoke. It's close to Mama's and Daddy's, and there's work there." Ari Daniels had recently retired from full-time work on the engineering faculty at Virginia Tech, and lived in nearby Blacksburg with his wife, Jessica. "I'm living with Ginny Rawls. Remember her?" added Lara.

Mike nodded vaguely. He strained to remember Ginny.

"She came down here with me a few times," Lara said. "Remember the girl with the ukulele? Tall, skinny coffee-colored girl?"

Mike laughed. "Of course." He grinned momentarily in unconcealed embarrassment. "Oh God." Ginny Rawls...

Lara laughed. "Now you remember her, right?"

"Totally." Mike coughed. So Lara was living with Ginny now. What was this? Were they just roommates? He tried to read Lara's coy face. Nothing. Their lives had been too distant for too long. There was no shared context. "So, um, what are you doing in Roanoke?" he asked finally.

"What she does best," said Daryl. "Taking care of people and animals." They all laughed at the recollection of a shared memory of Lara as a child, desperately wanting pets and "rescuing" every wild animal that crossed her path and could not run away fast enough.

"I'm a nurse at Roanoke Samaritan, and I'm also working at a huge stable operation, New Wind Farm. In Salem. They can pay me."

"You've got the skills folks need these days," nodded Mike. "What sort of stable?"

"Mixed farming and trucking draft," she said. "Everything from Clydesdales to plow ponies and buggy horses. Equine traction. We train 'em and rein 'em. And train drivers."

"How about you, Mike?" asked Ari. "We heard from your grandma that you just got out of the Army Corps of Engineers, but she didn't know where you were headed next."

9

"Well, I started with 'em in '34, right after college. Remember I was Rotsie'?" They nodded. "I thought I was headed off to one of those short regional wars, the Saudi civil war maybe. Or Venezuela. But I was assigned to construction Stateside, and the next year, the market crashed, and, well, I was glad I had a military job!" He chuckled ironically. The others remained silent, remembering. "And then Morales got elected and they set up the Coalition for Renewal, and the wars stopped, and there were all the nationalizations... So it's been energy and flood control and irrigation and water purification every since, mainly on the Federal Reservations. Peaceful stuff. Helping the population sometimes, too. And some coal logistics work."

"So, what's your rank?" asked Ari. "Captain?"

"Yessir," Mike forced a smile. "Captain. Reserve."

"Got tired of it?" asked Ari appraisingly, sensing Mike's reluctance. "Sounds like a steady job when not much is steady." He smiled at Mike through narrowed eyes.

"Yeah, well, sort of got tired of it ..." said Mike, returning smile with smile, unwilling to go into the reasons.

"That was about the best place you could have been," said Daryl. "I got laid off in DC five years ago and haven't had a steady job since... Should 'a been an electrician or mechanic—something useful like Lara—but you live and learn ..."

"What have you been doing?" asked Mike.

"Oh, gardening, trading, learning beekeeping," said Daryl with a forced laugh. "Some carpentry recently. Helping a stripping contractor. Home Guard. Living at home for now. Don't miss DC at all."

They lapsed into silence, contemplating the drab occupations of the times. To be sure, many people had jobs: monotonous, physical, resource-poor jobs. The lucky ones even got paid regularly. Most didn't lead anywhere, though.

The battered aluminum kettle started to boil. Mike got up and made four cups of mint tea sweetened with honey.

"So, your grandmother said you were going to pack up and pull out as much as you could when she gets here," Ari said inquiringly.

"Everything that's worth something," replied Mike. They looked around at the neglected interior of the beach house, its roomy open-plan common room obscured by the darkness, the rotting wicker furniture and seashell artwork silent witnesses to summer vacations stretching back across the decades. Against the walls and in unused bedrooms, Mike had stacked boxes and furnishings in preparation for moving.

"When did your grandparents buy this?" asked Lara.

"It was my great-grandparents," said Mike. "In 1955, I think. Something around then. They built it. My grandma's dad was a Washington lawyer, and everything down here in those days was dirt-cheap, really distant. Eighty-five years ago..."

"Sort of like now," said Daryl. "Dirt cheap and distant." Someone coughed. Daryl's face stayed serious.

Mike went on. "Grandma and Grandpa Jack inherited it, and this was the only place we ever went during the summer. How about y'all?" He realized he had forgotten most of their story. They were just one of the summer families he took for granted as a kid.

"My dad bought the place late in life, around 2015, or '16. They lived in Chapel Hill, and wanted a retirement home close to marinas and golf." Ari leaned back with his mug clutched between his hands. "Dad was in the IT business and moved down there from Connecticut, and they started renting at Hilton Head when I was a kid. You know, the turn-of-the-century lifestyle..." He coughed and cleared his throat. "Died of cancer a year after they bought. That summer, when he was getting chemo and living down here between treatments, Hurricane Gigi just wasted the island, and he had to sit here, a sick old man, while mom was stuck on the mainland in the flooding, and watch the roof get torn off and the windows get blown out." He looked sad. "Gigi was the first Category 5+ to come ashore. He's lucky he survived it, but..." He trailed off. "Well, we fixed the roof and the windows. Put in heavy-duty stuff. The pilings held." He looked at his children and opened up his face. "We got almost thirty more years out of it. Not bad. Twenty more than most people here."

"That's more than they got in Nag's Head and down past Hatteras and Ocracoke," agreed Lara.

"Well, it's a whole new ballgame now," said Ari. "Mountains and lakes are the places to be, if you have the means. High above sea level, away from the coast. Like Blacksburg." He stretched, signaling that it was approaching time to leave. "We're not as ambitious as you are about hauling things away, but we're down here this week to pick up the best stuff, especially the fixtures and fittings. Before the next big storm gets it.

The hardware will feed us all winter…" Ari frowned. "We planned this trip months ago, but with those big storms forming down in the Atlantic at the moment, we just might be getting down here in the nick of time! And then we had the truck, all of a sudden."

"How'd you come down?" asked Mike. "What truck?"

"We sort of borrowed a cell-electric truck, a Daimler," said Daryl. "An HFC."

"A Daimler? Nice!" said Mike with a whistle. "Borrowed?!"

"A stripper in Roanoke owes me for a lot of work. A huge hell of a lot, actually. Months. So we did a deal," explained Daryl. "Got it for a month."

"Nice one," said Mike. "Those things go for more than half a million, new. We used 'em in the Corps."

"This one's not one of the latest," said Daryl. "Ex-military DIM6, about ten years old. Stripper uses it hauling materials. I think he got it for stripping several malls for the Virginia Guard. Pretty cheap to run. Hydrogen and plug-in."

"Bet you have to ride a pretty alert shotgun on it, when you're off the interstates," mused Mike. "That'll draw attention. Hm. I could use some decent wheels, now I'm out. You get spoiled in the COE."

"I know of plenty of good wheels," smiled Lara. "But they all have four to sixteen legs in front of them." This elicited a good laugh.

"Nice payoff for all that horse obsession back when she was 10," smiled Daryl. "I could 'a cared less. Now I wish I had."

Ari stood up, and put his mug on the counter. "Mike, we'll see you again before you leave, but it's getting to be time to head home now." Lara and Daryl got up as well. Outside, the fog hung thicker than ever over the cold, wet sand.

"We should stay in touch," added Lara. "I've got to try to get back to DC again. See you all again."

"I've gotta try to get back to DC, too," said Mike, and they all laughed. "But, sure. Let's stay in touch. My email's easy." Their smiling eyes met for a hint of an instant.

Lara pulled a business card from her pocket and gave it to him. "Lara Daniels, Equine Draft & Field Traction," read Mike. "Sounds serious."

Lara smiled. "It works. Ask your grandma." They all laughed again.

"By the way, Ari," said Mike, "before you go, what's the security like around here?" Ari frowned. "How safe is it? I mean, it has seemed quiet since I came down, but, in EC and on the island, how careful do you think I should be?"

Ari wagged his head. "Oh, the usual care, but it's not a crime zone. Nobody's really around, except for a few visiting homeowners like us. Nobody squats here. No bandits. There's nobody to rob, nothing valuable. There's no fresh water, unless it rains."

"Good," said Mike. "That's a relief. We were on full alert every minute we were away from the base. I haven't exactly known what to expect down here."

Lara shook her head sadly. "And you were the guys with all the weapons and armor and fast vehicles…"

"Exactly," said Mike. "That's what the bad guys want. If I was some downouter walking the highways with my backpack, a few rags, my harmonica, and some ancient pistol, I'd have nothing they wanted."

"Doubt the downouters feel very safe, either!" Daryl was incongruously indignant. Ari and Lara glanced at one another.

Changing the subject, Mike said cheerfully, "Nice to relax here a bit. Peaceful surroundings." Ari nodded in agreement. They were all standing now. Making his move toward the door, Ari opened it, drawing a puff of the chill air into the room. "See you, Mike," he said. "Come to dinner when Florence gets here."

Mike brightened. "Sure. That sounds great."

After they said their good-byes and filed down the stairs, Mike found himself alone again. He watched their lantern bob amidst the fog until they turned a corner, disappearing from view. Then he turned away from the window, blew out one lamp, and moved a candle to the second end table at the other extremity of the sofa. "Hm," he muttered out loud. Jesus Freakin' Christ, Lara was hot, he mused. The totality of her body—its essential ratios, its slender suppleness—sent a wave of weakness through his stomach and knees. He paced around the dingy living room for a moment. I should have cylphed her, he though. Put the T-pad in some inconspicuous place and set it to holo. But she would have picked up on it, and how humiliating that would have been! He giggled wickedly to himself, and then pantomimed audibly, "Hello Miss Lara, so nice to meet you again after so long. Yes, yes. Delighted! Oh, don't mind me while I holoscan your delicious little body right here in front of your father so I can run

13

away with your cylph a bit later and cyber its brains out!" Yes, that would have gone down just great.

He sat down again, frustrated. He picked his T-pad up from the end table and placed it on the coffee table with the screen unfolded. "T-T," he commanded. "Inbox." The screen lit up, and he looked numbly at the list of received messages collected the last time he had been over the Sound where there was cellnet coverage. Gemma, Gemma, Gemma, Gemma... There were a few from Grandma and Hon, but it was mostly Gemma. The image in his mind of Lara's cylph transmogrified into Gemma's avatar: golden-honey limbed, luscious, lustrous, regal, with a mane of silver hair that flowed behind her as she moved, and firm, high breasts that rippled daintily under the light clothes she kept at a minimum.

Mike stood up again. This was getting bad. First Lara, then Gemma. His mind was swirling with sex and cyber and getting somewhere beautiful damn quick so he could relax and be himself. His eyes were now blind to the mildew stains, the dust, the powders and webs of termites and carpenter ants and spiders. He impulsively picked up his T-pad, and scrolled to the settings page. "Satnet" was off. His thumb twitched. He checked his milscrip balance again. It wasn't too bad. And, after all, it was already the 16th. He was already halfway through the month. Just a quick trip into Vtopia wasn't going to break the bank. He had this under control. Only a quick visit, for some sweet cyber and hi to everyone, but not real business, not the responsibilities that kept calling for him. That stuff could wait, *had* to wait. No, this was a quickie. And then, his thumb did it. He shuddered with relief. Satnet was on now. In a heartbeat the T-pad came alive, chiming as the messages poured down from heaven. He set it on the coffee table and rummaged around in his duffle bag for his headset, cog mesh, gloves, and other VNET gear. Here I come, he thought. Get ready.

3-GRANDMA'S ARRIVAL

Wednesday, October 17th

Flies. It sounded like flies. Buzzing. Mike's consciousness opened a crack, with difficulty. He lay at an uncomfortable angle, groggily struggling to grasp the significance of flies buzzing so insistently, afraid to move his neck, which felt stiff and threatened pain. He lifted a hand to rub the side of his head. His fingers brushed against something hard, something that was not his head. He opened his eyes with a start. His headset. His fingers had touched his headset, which had slipped off his head and was lodged under his neck against the daybed's cushion. It was on! That wasn't flies. It was people talking, street noises. He grabbed the headset and peered into one of the lenses. His avatar was still in Olia, off on the edge of a street, staring at a wall. The night's adventures all came flooding back: flying with Gemma, a wess ceremony, a quick trip to Eufoni to see the staff, and then—with Gemma's permission—a visit to the Sawin Orgies with Lishus. He pulled on the headset completely, and looked around in alarm. Passers-by laughed at him – good-naturedly, since this had surely happened to all of them at some point. He looked down at himself. Nothing was amiss. His tunic was trim. There was no graffiti on him. He glanced up at his HUD. There were messages from Gemma, Lishus, others... Then the time caught his eye. It was nearly eight o'clock in the morning EDT in RL! Jesus Christ, he thought. Still online! How many hours had he slept? When had he dozed off? He cogged open his scrip proc.

"Account balance," he panted, ignoring the pedestrians.

"Which account?" asked the proc.

"Mil," he breathed.

"Fifteen thousand two hundred and thirty-six units, and seventy-five cents." The digits flashed across the HUD.

"Oh God!" he groaned. Almost half of his monthly milscrip was gone in one night. How stupid of him, to think he could control himself and just grab a little time in Vtopia. The satnet was damn expensive. He should have completely avoided it. It was for foreigners, oligarchs.

"I don't recognize that command," the proc said through his headset.

"Fuck you!" he cursed, closing the proc, logging off, and tearing the headset from his head. Remorse and self-pity filled him like a burst appendix, rank and toxic. He fell back onto the daybed, hands to his face. Then the realization of the time caused him to bounce back upright, holding the daybed's corner post for balance. He took a deep, shuddering breath and looked out the window. The autumn fog was thinning into swirls and puffs, and bright morning sunshine flashed through the salty panes and glanced off the wet deck and railings. He groped blankly for a moment. Why did he need to be up so promptly? Then he remembered that this was the day Grandma would arrive. He almost fell back onto the bed. Grandma was an early riser, and he had wanted to travel as far as he could up the Sound road to see if she needed help driving down. He looked at his watch. Yes, it was indeed a few minutes before eight. Mike staggered over to a jug of water and took a drink, fighting nausea as he forced it down. Then he pulled on his clothes, washed his face in the basin, and made sure there was enough kerosene in the stove's tank to make tea and breakfast. He opened the deck doors to let in the fresh air. The air had a positive effect on his woozy mind. He took deep breaths. "Goddamn satnet," he thought. "That's a killer."

Out in the Sound, directly in front of the house, the fog had cleared completely. The sun rose low over the ocean behind him. Brilliantly lit in the red-golden light, some miles from him, was a huge kite-rigger in full sail, tacking north up the Intracoastal Waterway. Mike paused to take in the grand sight, blinking, and wondered what sort of cargo it was moving. Fruit, maybe? Or sugar. To the rail head at Elizabeth City, perhaps. He squinted, but could not see the flag it was flying. The ship was slowly progressing from left to right. He could see smaller fishing boats behind it.

"I'm gonna be late," he muttered, pulling on his sweater and cap, and jogging stiffly down the steps to the bicycle. He pumped slowly north on the sandy, rutted Sound road, the helping wind at his back. His whole body hurt, and his head pounded. After a few minutes, once past the main cluster of houses, he was out on the salt-marsh flats, shoved along by the gusts.

16

His heart sank. Up the road a half mile was the sight he hoped he would not see until he reached the second breach.

It was Grandma's wagon.

This was Mike's first glimpse. A John Deere, it was gaily painted in the company's trademark green and yellow. Grandma sat up in the cab, alone, the canopy pulled back and the rain doors and windshield stowed, her boots resting on the footboard. The wagon rolled smoothly toward Mike on its rubber tires. He could hear the jangling harnesses of Bill and Belle, her dark-brown Morgan-Hackney crosses. A third horse—a gray-brown paint he did not recognize—trotted behind, tethered to the tailgate. He got off his bike and gave her a weak wave. She waved vigorously back, and started slowing down. She came to a stop about twenty feet from him, right in the middle of the desolate road, and laughed merrily.

"What on earth are you doing out here in the middle of nowhere, grandson? You're supposed to either be helping me drive this team down through this wasteland, or getting me some breakfast!"

"Sorry, grandma...," Mike searched for an excuse, and then impulsively counterattacked, "Hey, wait a minute, you're lucky Ari Daniels bumped into you in town and came down to tell me the news. I'd still be sleeping!"

"Why you, you lazy boy," she laughed. "Free room and board, and all you want to do is sleep late!" She cranked back the parking brake and climbed down quickly but carefully from the cab. "You lazy little snip! Come here!"

She grinned, and he grimaced guiltily back at her, his dear grandmother, whom he had not seen since two Christmases back, when he had been up in Washington on leave. She gave him a hug. He looked down at her, hugging back. Florence Trudeau was her name, and she was Mike's mother's mother, a tough, gregarious matriarch of 72 as energetic and fit as a 30-year-old. Grandma ran a large fruit and vegetable farm in Chevy Chase, Maryland on land that had once been the golf course of an exclusive country club. She was of medium height with long, straight grey hair, increasingly gaunt as the years passed. The wrinkled skin on her face and hands was brown and dotted with freckles and liver spots. She wore a flowery wool shirt with a leather vest over it, jeans, and high boots. On her hands were leather driving gloves. Her head was covered by a wide-brimmed felt hat which Mike's hug had tilted back.

Grandma had not always been a vegetable farmer or wagon driver. Twenty-five years before, when Mike was a baby grandson and the Green Teens were in full swing, she had been the Deputy Assistant Secretary of State for Global Environmental and Natural Resource Affairs. Florence Trudeau had been and still was a woman of remarkable versatility and resilience.

"It's great to see you, Mike boy!" She hugged him again and beamed up at him. "You look more grown up every time I see you!" Then she frowned. "But you do look a bit tired. Having trouble sleeping?"

"Grandma, I, uh, no, I didn't sleep too well last night."

"Aw, well, get some more of this fresh sea air and you can take a nap later." She looked him up and down. Then she gestured with her head at the wagon. "Like it?"

Mike looked, rubbing his eyes to clear them. Grandma's wagon was a magnificent wedding of two centuries—the 19th and the 21st. It was a novel kind of wain, built for heavy agricultural and freight hauling. The frame was a mix of carbon and aluminum tubing, the sides were laminated wood, and the bed was a combination of wood planking and sheet metal. It looked light and spindly, but grandma had assured Mike it could haul four tons as long as the horsepower was there. She usually ran it with a team of two, but occasionally hauled heavy loads with six draft horses pulling.

A solar panel sat atop the cab's roof, along with a whip antenna, and LED headlights sprung like bejeweled crab-eyes from the footboard. Short ladders hung toward the ground on either side of the cab. The hub of each wheel was bright yellow.

"Nice rig, Grandma," Mike admitted. "Everyone's been telling me about it for more than a year now, so it's nice to finally see it in the flesh."

"It does the job."

"Hey!" said Mike with growing alertness. "Where's your employee? The Spaniard." He looked closely at the cab and bed. "Did you drive the rest of the way all alone?"

"Fernando? Oh, I gave him the day off in Elizabeth City. We'll pick him up on the way back. Staying at Fosters'." At Mike's dubious reaction, she added, "I know, he'd be an extra pair of hands, but he wasn't feeling well and he's been working non-stop with the harvest."

"Well," said Mike, wrinkling his brow, "Sorry I didn't get to you sooner. I thought you might stay a bit longer in town, to catch up on things, so I just got up…"

"That's OK. Let's go have a good breakfast. Didn't really want to stay around Elizabeth City for long. It's changed so much I barely knew it—quite run down, all those religious people around. They built all those levees and they have to keep pumping out half the town, but the word is that the town will be abandoned within a few years anyway, at the rate the water's rising. And there's a fear that a really big storm will seriously breach what's left of the Banks, and send the storm surge right over Elizabeth City and the rest of the inner shore. There's a dreadful, fatalistic feeling afoot. Lots of End-is-Near people."

Mike grunted.

"Juan Foster's pretty depressed," she went on. "Not much company anymore. Or maybe just getting senile. Spends all his time in VNET playing tricross word games. Burns was charming and welcoming as always. Told her to come up to stay with us in DC—move up, even. She's running herself ragged taking care of Juan, and feeling guilty and disappointed about everything." She brushed away stray hairs from her face. "Very poor now. Short of everything. I gave her a bushel of apples. But I camped in Point Harbor last night. Couldn't stand another night in EC."

Then she pointed at Mike's bicycle.

"Just put that thing up in the bed, and climb aboard."

Mike lowered the tailgate and swung the bike into the bed, which sat around chest-high. He lifted the gate up, and the hydraulics smoothly pulled it back into closed position with a hiss and click. The tethered paint chomped and blew, stepping to one side and eyeing him with its big white left eye. "That's Sherbet," she said. "Got him about three months ago." She disengaged the brake, and the wagon started rolling ever so slightly back and forth from the fidgeting of the horses. Mike stepped up onto the ladder and sat down in the seat beside her.

"You're not into the VNET anymore, are you, Mike?" Grandma held the reins ready and looked sideways at him, a hint of skepticism in her glance.

"Only when I have to." He yawned, covering his mouth, not meeting her eyes. Why had she brought this up? Was it so obvious? He went on, cutting a fine line between lies and verities. "But you know, all the Army's self-study courses and online meetings and libraries and records and everything are in there, so it's pretty hard to stay away." Grandma frowned and shook her head. "In the office," he continued, "you're in there more than half the time."

"I never wanted anything to do with it. Creepy. The Internet was more my speed. The VNET sucks away your life energy and saps your soul!"

Mike exhaled unsteadily and looked away across the horses' broad, brown backs. She shook the reins and clucked to the team. The wagon smoothly rolled into motion, the speed stabilizer instantaneously counteracting the uneven pulling of the horses until they hit their stride. Mike noted how Grandma shifted a lever from a position marked with a little picture of a turtle, to one with a running hare. He surveyed the controls, marveling that a simple wagon's cab could look almost like a motorized truck's. They rode forward into the cool, blustery breeze.

"What are the rabbit and the bunny for, Grandma?" he asked. She shot him a puzzled glance. "I mean, the rabbit and the turtle…on those levers."

She laughed, and shook her head once. "It's a tortoise and a hare, Mike."

"And…?" He waited, looking at her. "Am I supposed to know that?"

"Well, you wouldn't know this hi-tech stuff anyway. Forgive me!" She chortled. "OK, I'll tell you. The hare means free-wheeling—you go as fast as the horses want - and the tortoise is a fluid drag transmission that recharges the battery, too."

"All right. Smart." He nodded and frowned, wrinkling his chin. He summoned more focus with effort. "So, for going down a steep hill you'd switch it to the tortoise, and uphill or on a level road, it's the bunny."

"Right," she replied. "Um, hare."

"How does it know how fast the fluid drag should let it move, max?"

"This wheel over here." She rolled a wheel control on the control panel with her thumb. Numbers flashed past on a small digital display. "You set the maximum."

"Makes sense." He nodded again, and looked ahead. In the Army, he had not had to deal with animal traction. They rode in silence for a few moments.

Grandma broke it with a grand gesture at the sandy landscape. "So now we return, to pick the corpse clean," she said dramatically. Mike looked at her, mystified.

"Don't let it get you down, Mike," she continued, glancing at his questioning eyes. "I'm talking about the old house, the old life, what died here."

"It was worth a lot of money once," he replied. Not now, he reflected. With the exception of some sentimental items and viable hardware, he had found nothing of value in his weeks of waiting. Although he would never say it to his grandmother, his sense of bafflement had only grown as to why she would take off nearly a month to drive down to the old house, load up whatever remains she fancied, and then drive all the way back. To be sure, the growing season was over. But it was a big commitment of time, at a time when money and time were always tight. And it was very dangerous.

"We thought about selling once, you know."

"When was that?" asked Mike.

"Oh, back around the time you were born...sometime after that," she reflected. "The appraiser came up with one point two million. Dollars. Amazing to think about that now..."

"We sure could use that money now," Mike muttered. "In today's value."

"Grandson, a lot of things aren't worth what they used to be worth, while some of the strangest things are worth a fortune these days."

They looked ahead down the road, crowded between the advancing dunes and the edge of the shallow Sound, lined with the debris of what had once been buildings, signs, and traffic signals. This had been a thriving summer neighborhood, populated during the winter as well. The barrier islands up and down the North Carolina coast were covered with houses, hotels, commercial strips, marinas, roads, gardens, and all manner of holiday destinations. Head Island was neither tacky nor exclusive. The houses were tasteful bungalows, capes, contemporaries, mock-Victorians, surrounded by irrigated lawns and pine thickets, with little sandy gardens full of succulents and yucca plants and flowering shrubs. Cars with plates from all over the East Coast stood parked outside.

Now, it was a sandy, sun-bleached ghost town. Few houses were still used. Most were boarded up, and many were missing roofs or windows

21

from the relentless hurricanes from June to November. The gardens, trees, lawns, and cars were gone. All the houses stood on sturdy pilings; the building codes required it. But the shady lattice-work enclosures at ground level—where vacationers once parked cars and stowed beach gear—had for the most part been blown or washed away, so the houses or what was left of them stood starkly on their stilts about twelve feet in the air, unless a dune was in the process of consuming the house. Where the ocean's waves had eaten into the island along its eastern shore, what separated the intact houses from the sea was a strip of pilings, up-ended pieces of concrete walks, and asphalt driveways half-buried in sand.

"So how was the trip down, Grandma?" asked Mike. "You were pretty brief in your messages and the few times we talked."

"Oh, it was uneventful. Never pushed the team more than twenty-five miles a day. Drove in convoys when I could, which was frequent. More firepower! Took a rest day in Richmond and another in Chesapeake to visit folks. Burkhardts down there. Knew Jack."

"Hmm," said Mike, recalling his amiable grandfather. He had been dead for more than ten years.

"Hauled a load of sunflower seeds and mixed feed grain from Stafford to Williamsburg, by the way. Covered my feed bill for the whole trip."

"How did you pick up that hauling job?" asked Mike. Her work was quite unfamiliar to him. Before he joined the Army, she had been doing other things, and then six years had passed. "Was it your seed?"

"Oh, no. Not at all. You just go in to the shunt sites, and if you're a licensed hauler, which we are, and your track record is good, you just place a bid and if the price is right they email you immediately with the purchase order and the manifest. Takes seconds. Pretty efficient." She stretched her arms and yawned. "We usually just haul locally. But why travel empty when you can get paid?"

"What about the train?" wondered Mike aloud. He knew there was continuous track from Washington to Norfolk because the COE maintained it, and he had traveled it several times.

"Oh, dear goodness, child! Who can afford that!?" replied Grandma with a rhetorical chuckle. "When the lines are all electrified and we're out of this miserable depression, maybe that's how bulk commodities like feed corn will travel, but for now the train's for the rich passengers and the government. It's a real pity we're in this mess. But I can haul for a tenth of what the RF&P and the Delaware-Southern charge—maybe less. If nobody's in a hurry…"

"I've been out of touch in the Corps," said Mike. "Insulated. We rode around in cell-electrics whenever we wanted, and they're still using diesels for most of the construction."

"Diesels…," she chuckled, and putting on a fake twang, laughed. "Cell-electrics! Well, that ain't the way us civvies get around these days. You had an important job to do, and the Energy Trust to fuel you."

"The Energy Trust," repeated Mike, musing. "They keep talking about electrified railroads, but most of the engines I've seen down south and out west are coal-burners."

"I guess there's still a lot of work to be done getting systems updated. All that coal has to be dug up and then transported out to where it's needed, so I guess it's convenient to use it as fuel…" Grandma's voice trailed off, and she peered ahead into the morning breeze and the glare of hazy sunlight on the blowing sands. "You know, I just don't recognize things around here. Is that Hatteras Lane up there by that old telephone pole?"

Mike followed her line of sight. "No, Grandma. We still haven't come to Ocean Cottages yet. Another hundred yards or so…I'll let you know."

They jogged along, the horses' metal shoes grinding the sandy, crumbling asphalt with each step. The sunny street was deserted. Seagulls rocked above them, curiously following the wagon.

"My lord, is that it?!" exclaimed Grandma as they came up on Hatteras Lane.

"Yes, down there. You can turn here." Mike motioned toward the right as they approached the intersection. "Watch the drifting sand along the edge." Grandma pulled left on the reins and encouraged the horses around the turn. They straightened out on Hatteras Lane. Two blocks ahead of them rose Grandma's house, one of the few big houses still standing, and relatively undamaged. Just beyond it, the paved road buckled, and then vanished under the towering dune. Grandma's usually calm, wry expression was replaced by narrow-eyed tension.

"Well, I never thought I'd see a sight like this." She looked around her. "It's like the desert has taken over Ocean Cottages. Look at the Stapletons'." Mike glanced where she was looking. "There's hardly anything left…" The gray skeleton of a house leaned at an odd angle away

23

from the Sound, partly detached from its six main pilings. Tyvec fabric and insulation fluttered in the wind. The sound of robust surf through a gap in the dunes reminded them that this was no desert. They drove up to the foot of the walkway leading toward Grandma's house, and halted. Grandma pulled on the brake with the serrated clicking of a ratchet, and the rocking stopped. They both jumped down.

"These kids are pretty fresh, so I'll just tie them up in the shade for a while," said Grandma. Mike helped her unhitch Bill and Belle, and he then released the paint named Sherbet from the tailgate and led her across the sand to the cool grotto under the pilings. He tied her tether around one.

"We can bring down some water in a minute," said Grandma, leading the other two into the same space. Mike helped her tie them up.

"What's the security like down here now?" asked Grandma, pulling the yoke pad off Belle and patting her broad, sturdy side. "You hear anything?"

"Don't think we have anything to worry about," answered Mike. "Ari came by last night with Lara and Daryl, and said security's good here. I haven't heard of any problems from anyone, and if anyone tried to grab your horses, we'd hear all the fuss and they wouldn't get very far anyway." He lowered his voice. "I have an automatic."

Grandma nodded. "Hope you're right, but I'm inclined to believe you," said Grandma. "Heard lots of stories on the way down very much to the contrary, especially outside Richmond and Norfolk. There's a lot of thievery these days, even with the scans. I skipped an inn just south of Fredericksburg because a driver had been shot there the day before while his cell-electric truck was being stolen from right in front of him. Don't know how they can get away with this kind of thing. The police have cars."

"Desperate people," said Mike. "A lot of them…And too few police. You were on the secure highways the whole time, right?"

"Oh, yes. Well, mostly. Not completely." She nodded with a wry laugh. "But I'm too old to take any more chances than I have to. Although there are some pretty lonely stretches and you don't see state troopers as much as you'd like to."

"I'm amazed you have the guts to do what you do. Most people half your age would never try that. And just for old family heirlooms!"

"Mmm, yes," said Grandma a bit mysteriously. "Of course, Fernando's an expert shot—ex-Marine. And I'm going to feel less nervous with you riding shotgun for me as well. And we can take some shortcuts." She fussed with the horses' tack and took a step back. "Hope that was the last long haul like that I'll ever have to do, but I'm sure it will be worth it..." She took a deep breath, and smiled. "Well, I surely could use a nice hot drink right now. Before I curry off these three."

"I'll go up and put the tea water on, then," said Mike. He climbed unsteadily up the stairs, hauling on the railing, and went into the kitchen. He saw Grandma go back to the wagon and pull down a duffel bag from the cab. She wandered around for some moments, digging with her toe by the steps and a piling. He turned to his task, realizing how desperate he was for tea. In a few minutes, the kettle was bubbling and hissing. Grandma came up the stairs. The two of them sat down on opposite sides of the kitchen counter. Grandma pulled a fat loaf of what looked like barley bread from her bag, and some peaches. Her face was tight and drawn. Mike could not tell whether it was due to the fatigue of travel. He leaned back and lifted the kettle and teapot over toward the counter. He was about to put the kettle down directly on the shiny surface, and just as he was deciding to put a cutting board under it, Grandma intercepted him, uttering, "Hey, not so fast. Put something under it!" Mike laughed, his other hand already on the cutting board. "I'm a step ahead of you, Grandma. What do you take me for!?" They both smiled, and he pulled the mugs over and poured the water into the pot. Grandma's face softened. They waited for the tea to steep.

"Want some nice spelt 'n' barley bread?" asked Grandma. "Got it from Burns. Her neighbor bakes them."

"Sure," answered Mike.

She took the knife she always carried on her belt, wiped the dust off it with her sleeve, held it down on the bread, and sliced off several thick pieces. "Very tasty," he said, biting into the moist, savory bread. "Lots of energy." He was grateful for the calories. He needed to recover from his excesses. The guilt and self-reproach was fading. It was a new day. He started to feel better.

"Energy? We're going to need plenty of it," said Grandma.

4—PACKING UP

Thursday, October 18th

They worked very hard through the day, carrying the useable items of furniture, lamps, utensils, decorations, fixtures, doors, and hardware down from the house and loading them into the wagon, wrapping the more vulnerable pieces in waxed canvas. All of Mike's grandfather's paintings and his great-grandmother's woven mats were boxed up, although some had already suffered significantly from long exposure to the damp, salty air. Packed closely together and rising around six feet from the bed, the belongings only took up the forward half of the wagon. Many would not be worth much to anyone but Grandma and her family, heirlooms and mementos of the kind that accumulate in a second home over the generations. The hardware and fittings would be worth more in cash terms, sold at the open-air markets.

Everything that was too water-damaged, dry-rotten, or otherwise useless was piled on the sandlot beside the house, and in the mid-afternoon set alight and burned. Mike tended the fire, throwing new fuel on and pushing the burning fragments together so nothing would be left.

"You know," said Mike, "we don't have to burn it. There's nobody around."

"Let it burn," said Grandma, squinting as acrid smoke wafted toward her. "Burn it all."

"Should we burn the house, too?" asked Mike with a grin.

"Oh, no," said Grandma. "Not the house."

When evening came, very little was left in the house beyond what they needed for a final night's stay. Grandma and Mike unrolled a large waxed tarp she had brought and secured it over the cargo.

"Doesn't look like any rain tonight," said Mike.

"This'll keep the dew off," said Grandma. "But we should check the forecast. They were talking about a new hurricane, in Elizabeth City."

Mike could see only a smudge of her face in the thickening darkness, broken neither by moonlight nor street lamp. The air had warmed, and the slight wind was soft. The sound of surf was a muffled thunder.

"I just want to wash my hands and face, and get cleaned up a bit before we go over to the Daniels," she continued. They went back up into the house, lit the lamps, and Mike showed her the water can in the bathroom. While she freshened up, Mike turned on the radio's weather channel—cranking its dynamo a few turns to charge it—and drank a glass of water. He was tired, stiff, and feeling vaguely depressed about having to leave the beach house, which in fact had been a kind of pilgrim's sanctuary on his road from the structure, predictability, and relative comfort of military life to the wide-open randomness of the modern civilian's meager existence.

"I wonder how long the power's been off," said Grandma.

Mike glanced at her. "On the way up, the police said that the last time the power worked anywhere in the whole stretch from the Virginia line to Cape Lookout was three years ago. Only been power in a few local areas. They said that the OBX dead stretch is 180 miles long now."

"People on the mainland don't know how lucky they are. Still too many people taking electricity for granted, even after everything that's happened," said Grandma, taking a towel from her face. "Old habits die hard."

"Around five years back, when I was working out of Fort Jacob White, we were going out constantly to repair lines and substations. Power companies couldn't keep their trucks operating, even when the Energy Trust absorbed them. That seems to have gotten better, especially since the Coalition got into office."

Grandma sighed and straightened up, running her fingers through her hair—a signature habit he remembered from his childhood, a sign she was thinking out loud.

"Mike, I'm praying that the Coalition can hold together long enough to get things on an even keel. Renewables have come a long way, as well as a lot of other things, but ...," she paused as she gathered her long gray hair together, a cloth hair-tie clenched in her teeth. "But we can talk on the way home about all that. I'm worried about the political future, even more than I have been in previous crises. I suppose you know all about the criticism of the Coalition from the far right, from the Homeland people. I talk pretty often with Betsy Orman. She says Doug is very worried, but he has to keep an optimistic face to the public." Who was Betsy Orman, wondered Mike? But he let it go.

They started putting on their shoes and gathering jackets. Mike fished out the little flashlight he had managed to "borrow" when he left the Corps.

"There are Homelanders in the COE," said Mike, "and most seem reasonable, even if they are kind of harsh, but I agree with you. The last thing we need now is instability and extreme changes. We're part of the way through the Emergency. Maybe we can go all the way and come out ahead." He heard himself speaking the same way he had spoken at community forums and town meetings. But he believed most of it. Despite the continuing spread of poverty and dislocation, there had been progress since 2036.

"I think they're a lot more dangerous than you realize," said Grandma. "Zealots nowadays have all the reasons and public hysteria they need to make trouble. If you were my age you'd really feel the shock and outrage. You just might be tempted to support them..."

"What I worry about is foreign support...," muttered Mike.

"Oh, I wouldn't worry too much, and they don't need it anyway. There's plenty of grassroots ignorance and anger, if they can exploit it... Biggest foreign threat is blackmail, if anyone dared." She buttoned up her windbreaker and put on her broad hat. "Think about all the paranoid isolationism this country's capable of. It always seemed like a small minority—anti-UN, fundamentalists, racists, survivalists, free-staters, radical libertarians, what-have-you. Now their wildest predictions are coming true, never mind that it's our own stupid collective fault. No big conspiracy. But here we are..."

Mike switched on his flashlight.

"OK, Grandma. Let me hold your hand on the stairs."

"You have got to be kidding," scoffed Grandma. "I could walk down this flight of stairs drugged and blindfolded. I was walking up and down here decades before you were born!"

Mike laughed apologetically, but stayed close behind her as they descended into the inky, cricket-filled darkness. Passing the wagon, Grandma said, "Mike, shine that light over here a second." He swung the beam at the cab. Grandma opened the hatch under the seat bench and fumbled around. "Here, come a bit closer so I can see what I'm doing here."

28

Mike stood beside her as she groped into various boxes, putting dried fruits, nuts, and vegetables into a cloth bag. "Brought them for this kind of occasion. Gives the right impression."

He smiled.

"OK," said Grandma, closing the hatch. "Let's go."

5-THE DINNER PARTY

Thursday, October 18th

They had walked the stretch from Grandma's to the Daniels' house innumerable times on sunny summer days down the years. It was easy to find it in the gloom, as they worked their way around drifted sand and snags of debris. The house was the only one with lights in its windows. Up on its thicket of pilings, it formed a three-tiered octagon rimmed by decks on each level. It had once been surrounded by a lush, irrigated garden of sub-tropical trees and shrubs. The name of the house was "Aeolia"—the house of the winds. Ari's father had spared no expense, hiring a Richmond architect to design it.

They came to the foot of the main staircase. Beside it was parked the cell-electruck. A corroded ship's bell hung from a stanchion above the rail. Grandma shook the familiar clapper and the bell rang out. A door up on the second level opened, and a man was silhouetted in the startling white light of an LED lantern.

"Permission to come aboard?" Grandma called up, shading her eyes.

"Avast! Be ye friend or foe?" came an imitation pirate's voice from above.

"This is the Coast Guard speaking, and you're going straight to the brig for breaking the blackout!" yelled Grandma.

There was laughter, and Grandma and Mike ascended to the first level, their tread creaking on the rickety wooden steps. Lara was there to greet them, a long gray cardigan hanging open over an even longer light-blue knit dress. Daryl stood behind her, hulking and nondescript. The air smelled of frying onions and citronella punk. Ari came down the spiral stairs in the center of the large common room, studied and agile.

"How wonderful to see you two together again," he smiled. "It has been years since we did this!" He gave Grandma a hug. "Good thing I ran into you in Elizabeth City. I had no idea you were coming down. But I recognized you instantly!"

"You could have called," she grinned.

"We didn't remotely imagine that you or anyone else from the old days would be anywhere near here..."

"You don't expect to run into anyone down here these days, even during the 'season,'" said Lara warmly. "No one stays here. It takes so long to get here now." They all paused in the entrance for a faintly awkward instant, recollecting a shared but sharply discontinued past.

"Maybe we all received some mysterious signal," Ari chuckled, bustling. "A telepathic message! Here, I'll take your jackets."

"Oh, just throw them down anywhere," said Grandma. "I'm dressed for rough travel nowadays. Here, some produce from up north." She held up the bag of offerings. "To add to your larder."

Ari and Lara reacted in unison with delight. "Can't forget you're an urban farmer now, Flo!" laughed Ari.

"What would you like to drink, Grandma?," asked Lara. "We have a bottle of berry wine and some farm bourbon."

"Lara, I'll take a bourbon to start, neat. What *am* I saying?! Where would you get ice down here? That was a blast from the past." She laughed. "And you are looking just *gorgeous*, my girl." Lara smiled with pleased embarrassment and turned toward the kitchen. "When you were just a little girl, I knew you'd be a real belle someday. And you'll have to tell me all about your horses." Grandma gave Ari an approving look. He laughed, and gestured toward the cluster of sofas and chairs by the biggest windows, where a small wood stove creaked and hissed, filling the space with dry warmth. Beside it sat a stack of fuel liberated from some derelict house nearby.

"Come, Florence, let's all go over and have a seat. The kids will finish the cooking." He glanced over at Mike. "Wait, Mike, what would you like to drink?"

"Water's fine for me, Ari. I'll get it." Mike followed Lara and Daryl into the kitchen, while Grandma and Ari sat down. He looked around at the familiar walls, recalling visits here, summer parties, card games with Daryl and Lara and siblings and cousins. All faded and worn, but matching his memories. Memories of real people, real spaces. Real memories...

31

"Mike, you sure you don't want wine or bourbon?" Lara smiled, leaning a lean hip against the kitchen counter. She gestured at the bottles and glasses by the dry sink. "You sure?"

"The wine's awesome," grunted Daryl.

Mike smiled at them both, struggling to avoid scanning Lara up and down. Her presence was enchanting. He felt shy and almost breathless. His fingers brushed against the T-pad in his pocket. God, he thought, wouldn't she look nice as a cylph? What a catch that would be.

"Yeah, OK, wine, thanks." It came out awkward and rusty.

"Wine it is!" Lara laughed generously, cocking her head for a heartbeat as she detected his muddle. She picked up the bottle and poured him a glass. "There you go, Mike."

"Thanks," he mumbled, grinning.

*　*　*

They ate stir-fried vegetables with smoked sausage and rice, washed down with the wine, and conversation meandered freely from old stories to family news to local developments on the island and nearby. Ari and Daryl plied Mike with questions about the Corps, keen to know where projects were underway and government efforts focused. Lara was serene, smiling around in the flickering candlelight after the ostentatious lantern was turned off to save charge. Grandma was unusually quiet although pleasant, and less loquacious than her reputation normally predicted. Her journey had been a hard one, and she was happy for a break from worrying about the horses and about safety—a strain that would return as soon as they regained the road.

"So," said Ari as tea and stewed apples were served. "The old house nearly laid to rest?" His face was kind, sad, nostalgic, the deep wrinkles around his eyes deeper.

"Oh, careful how you put it," clucked Grandma. "Let's just say we won't be down here for a while and don't want to leave too many valuables in harm's way."

Ari leaned back and looked at Grandma appraisingly. "You've made quite trip down here to pick up those valuables. About a month on the road, eh?"

Grandma nodded, pursing her lips.

"That's a big commitment of time, not to mention a few risks." Ari pursed his own lips, and grimaced.

Grandma raised her eyebrows, and nodded. "Yep."

"I guess they're irreplaceable," he said with a sigh.

"Oh, yes," she said. They locked eyes and smiled. "I feel like I left a piece of my life down here—not to mention Jack's and the kids'—and I guess I just wanted to come retrieve it while I still could…"

"I know what you mean," said Ari, shifting the subject. "There haven't been many break-ins, all things considered. Coming out here must not be worth the trouble for the thieves. But I still worry a bit about the contents of this place." The Daniels' house, like most, had gradually seen its furnishings taken home, but many decorations and household items remained. "You know… A door or window blows open in one of these storms, and rain would just pour in. That already happened upstairs." He nodded over toward the ceiling on the other side of the room, where flowers of water stains and cracked molding told of intermittent leaks.

"Some folks are burning theirs," declared Daryl morosely.

"I've noticed," said Mike, in a companionable but wary tone. He had observed several burnt-out houses since he arrived, one not far from Grandma's. "I offered to burn ours but Grandma said no." He smiled ironically and Grandma clicked her tongue in reply.

"Yep, they're burning them." Daryl looked around, an expression on his face that struck Mike as a challenge. Ari forced a grin at Mike, his eyes cautious.

"This was actually one of our biggest hassles in the Corps," said Mike, deflecting the tension into a serious vein. "Burning down real estate. It's the same all over. The towns and counties want roads rebuilt, bridges, canals. Water mains repaired. But people with title to all kinds of commercial real estate and homes—rentals—can't maintain them or pay the taxes, so they burn them down to get away from the Revenue Police. Who come after them anyway. Unless they move away …"

No one spoke. Mike sipped his tea and went on. "Who's going to be left to use all that infrastructure? And pay for it? Even if the Corps rebuilt it? People are just moving on and rebuilding elsewhere, away from the flies and the heat. There isn't much in the news about this, but if the towns are gonna operate they need tax revenue, and when a building's condemned or it's nothing but ashes, zap, there goes another taxable property. And somebody doesn't have to pay taxes on it anymore."

They drank in silence. Then Daryl laughed sharply. "We're not going to do that, are we?" He looked around, and Mike felt a cool draft across his back. "We're all patriotic Americans, aren't we?" The friendly atmosphere of the dinner party was suddenly, definitively chilly. This was an unexpected twist. Mike wondered where Daryl was going with this. He had never related easily to Daryl, moody and inappropriately emphatic since as far back as he could remember. He had vague memories of silly, shrieking games with his sisters and Lara in which they ran away and hid from Daryl, who inevitably ended up crying or going to his mother to tell on them. Besides, he wondered if any of them had indeed paid taxes to the now-defunct Town of Head Island in a decade. Who would you pay? When the town government itself was abandoned!

Lara got up and withdrew from the circle of light around the table, headed for the kitchen. Mike followed her liquid gait out of the corner of his eye. Ari looked down and took a deep breath. "More tea anyone?" called Lara over her shoulder.

"Patriotic?" laughed Grandma with sharp eyes, taking up Daryl's challenge. "'Course we are, Daryl. You too, I imagine, even after a comment like that. With a retired senior member of the Executive branch, an Army captain, and a former city councilman at this table"—she nodded toward Ari—"you can bet your good name we are. Quite a stretch, going from a few local arsonists to our loyalties." Daryl's smile was frozen between his ears, his palms rigidly flat against the table.

"But asking these types of questions all the time—and I'm hearing them an awful lot these days, about serious, patriotic, law-abiding people—is NOT constructive." Grandma's passionate reaction surprised them as much as Daryl's misplaced innuendo had. "We put ourselves in this predicament, not the UN, not the EU or the Group of 12, not these ridiculous conspiracies ... And not the Chinese." She looked with perplexity at Daryl. "You ought to read about the Red Scare, Senator McCarthy, ninety years ago. There's self-interest here, cruel games, gullible ears..." She paused, realizing she had crossed an invisible line. They heard Lara banging around in the kitchen, boiling water on the kerosene stove and putting plates away. She had turned on the weather radio. Grandma adopted a bright, brisk expression. "We put ourselves in this soup and we're going to pull ourselves out of it. Together."

34

But the stinger had stung. Daryl took a deep breath and sat back, tense. "Mrs. Trudeau, you might remember me as a little kid. But I haven't been a boy for a long time... I don't, don't appreciate your t-tone..." He breathed shallowly and roughly, searching for words. Mike and Ari watched him cautiously, father and childhood friend. "Maybe I'm not some *Washington, DC* VIP, but I've gone to college and I'm not a fool... So, ah, maybe you should update your information about what's going on..."

"Hey, why don't we take a break," said Ari, seizing an opportunity to interrupt the escalation. "Let's go out on deck." He ventured a lame joke. "Check our position." He stood up.

Mike and Daryl also rose. Grandma stayed seated at the table, drinking what was left of her tea, her face red. The men headed toward the doors to the deck.

"Tense times, tricky times," breathed Ari, out in the open air. A slightly clammy breeze blew from the west—a mosquito breeze. "We've all got to think critically, follow our heads and not our hearts too much. Not believe everything we hear..." He turned toward this son. "And be VERY cautious about making accusations or insinuations, especially among friends. Everybody's trying to deal with the times the best they can."

Daryl stood beside him, tapping the rail nervously and rocking imperceptibly. "She's been a great lady all my life, but I don't appreciate being talked down to. I know she's patriotic..." He trailed off.

"Down to?!" Ari's voice rose into a pinched whisper. "You're the one who got sarcastic completely without warning, and brought in this patriotism question, a question that doesn't even belong in a gathering like this. Why drag it in?" He knew why, nonetheless. His son's poor tact and timing aside, Grandma's politics were sharply different from Daryl's, and perhaps Daryl was feeling outnumbered this evening.

"Daryl, anyway," said Mike softly, deciding he should add a mollifying comment. "This isn't about disrespect toward you, it's way bigger. Up there in DC, I imagine she's hearing different sides all the time. It's where the big political game is being fought. The election's in about three, four weeks. The Homelanders are stronger. Laugherty's popular. There's this loan, this aid package. The stakes are very high..." He closed his eyes and felt the currents of air on his face. "Grandma has always been very principled, trying her best..."

"So are the Homeland Front!" burst out Daryl. "They have principles. One is don't take shit from anybody, even when they blow up skyscrapers, poison the whole Ohio River, blow up—what?—at least fifteen US Embassies..." Ari muttered something. "And the outrage of Sanderborough! And we try to negotiate, and be nice, and have conferences with the damn Europeans and Chinese and the Caliphate... Look at us! Look at this country!" He caught his breath with a moist click, and lowered his voice. "Look at us. So you have to ask what sort of delusion the old-style Democrats and Coalition people are under. And these god-damned separatists all over the place." Daryl fought to control his shaky whisper. "So, this is *not* about me being gullible, and people shouldn't be pretending things are still normal anymore than they should be burning their houses down."

Mike looked at Daryl in the darkness, trying to follow his winding logic, and understood now. Daryl had taken sides. But was this amateur enthusiasm for Homelander rhetoric, or was Daryl a serious, engaged supporter? Daryl had always been full of bluster, prone to lectures, long-winded and rigid. Where was he now in this movement? At the core of the Homelanders and the various Brotherhood auxiliaries were hard, ambitious, violent men. Was Daryl really one of them?

"Mike, what can you tell us?" asked Ari with an air of resignation, nudging the topic away from Daryl's challenge. "What does it all look like from a military perspective now?"

"There are many who see the Homelanders as Fascists," said Mike quietly, bracing for Daryl's reaction. He could never have talked openly in this way in the COE. But Daryl was silent. Mike went on in a low voice. "Some of the officers and NCOs support them. But—and he turned toward Daryl—"many don't. The smart ones don't. I don't. OK, they appeal to our anger. But this country has gone through worse and the Constitution has survived. We just need to accept our mistakes and get our butts in gear." Mike reflected on what he had just said. Was this only self-deluded placation, or was the military still truly uninfluenced by Homelander sympathies? He honestly did not know for sure. The Front was certainly in evidence.

"Our butts ARE in gear!" Daryl laughed softly, with scorn. "Our butts are sitting in wagons and on bike seats and in saddles and they're sore, and we've completely lost our ability to project power, and we're out of gas.

36

Next, it'll be our own territorial integrity. And we're being blackmailed every day, and offered this huge international bribe. Look at this latest thing with Alaska. We can't even control our borders!"

"So what's the solution?" asked Ari. "Take away our rights and set up roadblocks, and make everybody say 'Heil Homeland!'? That would freeze any spirit left. People would rise up. I know the VNET chat rooms are running hot about this, but it'll lead to worse, not better. There is progress now. Some progress, at least."

"Progress?!" Daryl interrupted with scorn.

"We have to trust ourselves and our friends around the world," said Ari.

"There's no hostility from the EU, not even from China." Mike continued. "OK, some I-told-you-so's and arrogance and one-upsmanship. But people know the World War legends and remember the oil shock of '28. We all stood together. They owed us a great debt then." Mike heard a naïve ring in his own voice, and suddenly felt self-conscious. He was no longer in the military environment, where the only safe tone was positive and committed. He tried to lose it.

"So what are they doing for us now?" asked Daryl, his voice rising again. "Waiting like vultures."

"No, they just offered to lend us 14 trillion euros," said Ari. "Despite a lot of misgivings about our political situation."

"That's just to manipulate our election," scoffed Daryl. "You gotta remember, I was a history major—American history—and the whole period from 1600 through the 1800s was all about European powers playing games with us. Set up colonies. Burned down the White House, kidnapped seamen, funded the Confederacy."

"You studied history, but obviously not much economics. Some of that 14 trillion will go to buy dollars to stop the 'dive', tell the markets it's a global partnership now." Mike laughed. "Short–term aid. Stabilization. We can pay for our own development with the balance."

"More like a global Big Brother, and we're the bad boy," snarled Daryl. "Or it's payback time. Look, we're still a nuclear power and there are 400 million of us. All the brains, the technology. They have to take us seriously, but we have to take strong action first. Not all this talk…"

"Yes, yes, OK, and what you said is why they are going to take us seriously, without us having to wave missiles around." Mike's exasperation rose. He knew Daryl was deluded. "They take the long view. And they are ahead of us now. It's an opportunity. We can't blow it!"

"My two boys—men," said Ari, his head low, his eyes haunted and embarrassed. "These are times when friendships are tested. But don't forget all our years together…Don't forget." He turned toward Daryl, who looked down. "Don't be fooled, my son. Listen to Mike. My God. Remember your great aunt Sandra's stories from her father. The old stories about Buchenwald, about Bohemia. Remember that line from that song:

And the boys turned bright and brittle
Like searchlights and sharp metal

Ari took their elbows and pushed them toward the warm light of the doorway. "Let's keep our heads, and drink to friendship against all odds, hm?" He had had enough of this simmering conflict for now, and just wanted them to finish the evening with a semblance of harmony. His son's interests confounded and worried him.

They opened the screen door and entered single-file, Daryl last, his movements stiff. Grandma and Lara were seated at the round table, engaged in low conversation. Lara looked up at them. "That tropical depression, it's got a name now. Rhiannon."

"That was fast. Where is it?" asked Ari, stretching and rubbing his eyes as they re-adjusted to the light.

"I think they said a few hundred miles east of the Antilles," said Lara.

"Where's it headed?" asked Mike.

"Northwards, a little toward the coast of Florida. Moving very slowly, but really big."

"Have you looked online?" asked Ari.

"Can't from here, cheaply. Remember? Been having too interesting a chat with Grandma to listen to the radio, anyway." The women chuckled.

"We've been talking horses, and we might have a deal." Grandma leaned back in her chair and looked at all three men with a wry smile. "You solve all the political problems yet?" She directed a forgiving, recomposed smile at Daryl.

"Grandma, I'm sorry about my tone a little earlier," said Daryl, head low, eyes darting. Mike wondered if he meant it. "I'm worried, but I should have left my worries outside."

"We're all worried, Daryl." Grandma exchanged a glance with Ari – the practiced glance of one parent to another. "But it wasn't your tone as much as the question that surprised me, and which I just couldn't leave unchallenged."

Daryl had no taste for more argument now. He knew he would get no sympathy from the others, his own convictions aside. "Well, let's drop that. I'm sorry I raised it where it wasn't needed."

"OK, Daryl." Grandma glanced rather abruptly at Daryl, and stood up. "Mike, maybe we'd better make a move." She looked at her watch. "It's later than I realized!"

"Oh, Florence, it's way too early to think about calling it a night!" Ari gave her a beseeching smile. It truly was late, of course; the time had come to leave, but it still felt sudden.

"I'm an elderly lady, Ari, and I need my sleep," said Grandma firmly. "Mike, honey, take your old granny home. I'm too old for these kinds of shenanigans past my bedtime."

"We hardly got to hear about your market garden up there in—where?—Chevy Chase," said Ari.

"Correct," replied Grandma. "Well, you'll just have to come up and visit, and stay long enough for me to bore you to death about it!"

As they all hugged at the door, Mike and Lara connected for an instant while Grandma squeezed past. "Mike," said Lara with a sisterly smile. "I'll v-mail Honorée long before you get home, but give her a great big hug for me—like this one—and tell her I miss her terribly."

"You'll just have to come up and see her. And me, if I'm still there."

Lara looked at him sidelong with a grin. "I'd like that very much." Then she squeezed his arm, and as Ari and Grandma laughed beside them through a big, friendly, sad hug, she whispered firmly into his ear the name "Myste."

"Myste?" his lips queried.

She nodded, eyes laughing. "M-Y-S-T-E. Myste." It sounded like "misty."

He looked askance at her, an informed question mark in his eyes, hope mixed with bashful doubt.

"Rains," she added. "Myste Rains. Like from the sky. Plural."

They both grinned. Then it was down into the night and home across the damp sands to beds and sleep. Though not to Vtopia this night.

Mike would recall her smile for days, wondering if it was mainly meant for him or Honorée. Wondering what sort of invitation this was.

And wondering there they would meet, when they were back under affordable network coverage, and privacy was possible…Perhaps he would introduce her to Gemmaluna. Or perhaps not…

6-STARTING OUT

Friday, October 19th - Saturday, October 20th

Shortly after dawn the next morning, following a brief breakfast, Mike set about nailing the storm shutters back into place while Grandma harnessed up the horses—Belle and Sherbet swapping position—and made the wagon ready for travel. The air was unseasonably warm, and the breeze nearly still, as the sun rose like a bouquet of salmon roses from the Atlantic. Gulls stood stiffly on rooftops and dune fences in large numbers, all facing northeast. High in the sky was a single whip of mare's tail, hinting at a coming change in the weather.

With the final shutter secured, Mike gathered up his bags and symbolically locked the front door behind him, its futility nagging. Grandma was sitting on the tailgate of the wagon, facing aft. She looked up at Mike as he descended, and at the house behind him. Her face was somber, filled with an uncharacteristic uncertainty.

"Grandma," said Mike, "I'm all set."

"Sure, boy, good work." She remained sitting there. "That should keep the fresh water out until the salt water gets it."

"Are you all right, Grandma?" he asked.

She got down from the tailgate stiffly, a spade in her hand. "Sure. Now, there's one more thing we need from this house. It's going to take a few minutes." She took a deep breath, and let out an audible sigh.

Mike stopped, curiosity in his eyes. Hadn't they taken everything? He watched Grandma walk over to the piling to the left of the stairs. To his surprise, she began to dig in the sand at its foot: the quick, foot-assisted thrusts of an accustomed gardener. In a few minutes, when the hole was half a meter deep, she motioned to Mike. "Here, your turn." She was out of breath. "Just keep digging down on this side."

Mike scraped away the sand around the pit so he could dig deeper by standing in it. "What are we looking for?"

"Pirates' treasure." Her face revealed no joke.

"Pirates' treasure." He dug systematically, breaking into a sweat. The sand was compact and dense now, with alternating light and dark strata. He chopped downward with each stroke. "Really?"

"Really."

After a minute or two, Mike's spade hit something metallic. He scooped away more sand, lifting it to the side. A dark, rusty box appeared. It looked like a cashbox. Grandma was silent, bending over the pit. As he dug, he discovered that the box was attached to the piling with lag screws.

"OK, good. That's enough." Mike stood back while Grandma squatted down in the pit and tried to open the box. It was not locked, and the padlock latch could be moved in its hinge, but the top would not budge. "Here, Mike. Give the top a few taps with your spade."

Mike complied. Grandma tried again, struggling. Mike watched, but she appeared to want no help. With some difficulty, she finally pried the top open. In the box was a faded red plastic bag containing something round. Grandma swung it up onto the level sand beyond the crumbling edge of the hole.

"Mike, give me a hand out of here." She stood up, puffing, and he took her hand.

"So what kind of treasure is this, huh?" asked Mike skeptically, leaning on the spade handle. He was envisioning heirlooms, old coins, maybe a bronze figurine of some ancestor, perhaps even a gun. What was this little thing?

"Gold." Grandma breathed a sigh of relief, and opened the bag. She glanced around, as if the empty derelict houses were still occupied by nosy summer neighbors, and pulled back the plastic. A gold surface gleamed inside, not a trace of corrosion on it.

"Whoa!" exclaimed Mike, recoiling slightly in surprise. This kind of thing usually didn't happen in RL, he thought.

Grandma opened the stiff plastic further. Mike saw that the gold object was spherical. It was nicked and dented in a few places, and stamped with letters and a crest. "This turned up when we were lifting the house. Your mother was a baby. Nag's gold, the contractor called it. Good thing Jack and I were both here when the builders found it."

"And that it wasn't just buried deeper by the pile-driver," rejoined Mike. It was probably worth a fortune. "Do you know how old it is?"

"Well, not much more than that it was from a Dutch shipment—by the style of that crown—and that it's from the early 1700s. We did some amateur research. Used to be a lot of pirates and scavengers along this coast. You know, the Nag's Head legends. The folks they called the bankers." She was referring to the stories of how islanders would hang lanterns from horses' necks and send them wandering along the beaches to lure passing ships onto the sand bars.

"Well, there still are," laughed Mike. "Us, for instance." Grandma joined his laughter. She picked it up, hefting it in her hands. "It's a pomador." She handed it carefully to Mike.

"A pomador?" repeated Mike quizzically, with a vague recollection of the name. "Pompadour?" He hefted the gold ball in his hand, feeling its incredible density, its cold mass. The size of a small apple, it must have weighed several kilos. He gingerly handed it back to her. She cradled it with both hands, trembling slightly as she held it up.

"Well, that's what Jack and I called it. You know, *pomme d'or*—a golden apple."

It then dawned on Mike that it was in fact a representation of an apple, with an indentation where a stem might have sprouted once.

"The builders thought we took it away to Washington right away, after the guy came from the state historical society and took some pictures. But when the piles were driven we came back at night and put that box there. Of course, we could have put it in a safe-deposit box, but your grandfather was convinced we'd eventually go back on the gold standard and that it would be confiscated. *That* never happened while he was alive, of course, but then they regulated metals, and if he'd given in to me and I'd put it in a bank, all we'd have today would be a worthless Federal Gold Certificate." She dusted sand off her hands and shook them. "That was, oh, around forty years ago…"

"Grandma," said Mike. "You know what amazes me?"

"What?"

"This golden apple is worth so, so much now. Incredible. What is gold? Probably $2,000 a gram…"

"It's gone up a lot. It was at $2,300-something at White Flint under the counter, when I last checked before leaving," said Grandma.

"Right, so, if it's worth so much, then why didn't you sell it in an earlier crisis? That kind of money would have helped on countless

43

occasions in your life. You and Jack could have done many things differently... Why now?"

"Mike, there are a few reasons. First, we had a good life—never lacked for anything, really. We lived secure in the knowledge it was down here if we needed it. We could have just driven down and picked it up, once upon a time. And sold it freely! The real price of gold wasn't anywhere near where it is now, of course... Second, I think this is the last time I'm going to see this place, so it can't stay here anymore. I needed to come get it." Her face grew stony. "Third, we haven't even seen the real crisis yet. You know what I mean?" They both stood there a moment, taking in the view of the battered house and billowing dunes, the view of the Ridge, the Sound, the pit, the bag, and the golden relic of a long-vanished age of exploration, opportunity, and conquest. "But, ah," she continued, hesitating, "please keep this to yourself, but..."

"What, Grandma?" he said.

"I *really* need that money now. I won't go into it, but we've borrowed money for capital investments— in Chevy Chase and for Hon's business— and the debts are killing us." She made a disgusted face.

A sense of what the next steps involved eluded Mike. "Um, Grandma, we can't just drive home to Chevy Chase with the pomador in your backpack." It was now illegal to own gold, with the exception of modest gold jewelry, and the pomador would be discovered by the first checkpoint's scanner.

"Mike, I've been researching that problem for years, and I have a solution." She started walking toward the wagon. "Come over here." She put the apple carefully on the floor of the cab and - rummaging around in the compartment under the seat - pulled out a small object, which she held up. "Behold the poopador."

Mike stared at the cloth ball in her hand in incomprehension. "Poopador?"

"Look." Grandma opened it like a small bag and fitted it around the pomador, drawing it closed again with a cord. Mike burst out laughing. The lumpy bag was made of a hairy felt-like material over leather, and was a brownish yellow. It also appeared to have been waxed or oiled. The result looked very similar to a ball of horse dung.

"Yes," agreed Grandma. "It is ingenious. Excrementally ingenious! Hon made it for me." They both laughed. "My idea is to somehow get it down on the ground behind the horses when we're stopped—maybe with a piece of monofilament fishing line, which I also brought—and then pull or scoop it up when the scan's over and we're waved through. They won't scan the ground, which I understand produces an echo indistinguishable from gold anyway, and they're used to seeing horse poop. And they don't want you to leave it lying there."

"Grandma," said Mike mirthfully, "this is good. Really good. I've never heard of anyone trying this before." He chuckled at the novelty of sharing this sort of humor with his own grandmother. "And even though I've heard rumors about spectramag scanners eventually being introduced, I'm sure we'll only have to deal with MRI and x-ray machines."

"Is spectramag the one that can identify specific substances?" asked Grandma, a shadow of doubt crossing her face.

"Yes—spectroscopic magnetometer—but I think they are rare on the roads. We never used them. But maybe that's government disinformation."

"Well, Mike, we can discuss our exact technique on the road," she said. "It's a long way to the first checkpoint. Let's put that pirates' gold in the compartment under the seat. We'll keep it in the bag. Now, go on and drive us out of here. I'm going to stay back on the tailgate to watch it all disappear." She walked toward the rear of the wagon. The team waited impatiently. "Help me with the tailgate, Mikey," she called.

"Ah, Grandma," said Mike, a thought occurring to him. "What about Fernando?"

"Well, he'll know we're up to something, and see the poopador," she replied. "But don't worry. He works for me, and he won't know it's gold anyway."

Mike looked doubtful. "If he thought he could get a reward, he might stop working for you."

"Honey," said Grandma, "let me tell you about Fernando. He's been working for me for two years. He's got five kids—one a diabetic, and one with a bad club foot. He's saving up to get back to Spain, where he has citizenship, and where he can get the health insurance. He's making progress working for the Market Garden—maybe another year or two. He's not going to mess things up for himself just because we're smuggling something and SIF or the IHC wouldn't like it."

"You sure?" Mike had seen enough tense smuggling situations to want more assurance.

45

"Look," said Grandma. "I said, don't worry. Really. I'll tell him it's drugs. For a friend in need. I'll give him an incentive to keep quiet, OK?" She laughed. "And you do your part."

Mike raised his eyebrows. "My part?"

Grandma laughed again. "You know what I mean. You're going to be more than my left shotgun."

Mike frowned.

"My goodness, dear Lord," said Grandma, laughing ironically. "Who would have thought that in the year 2040 I'd be standing here on Head Island debating with my grandson about gold smuggling, weapons, and dirty deeds." She sighed—a bit sadly, it seemed to Mike. "All right, let's mount up."

Mike nodded silently.

When they had stowed the gold, Mike lifted up the gate and, with loud metallic clicks, Grandma locked down the buckles that held it in place. She sat down on a fender with both feet inside the bed. Mike went around, swung up into the cab, released the brake, and whistled as he shook the horses' reins. The wagon pitched for an instant and then fluidly accelerated under the team's power. Off they drove, past intact houses and wrecks, wandering dunes and sea grass, onto the main coastal highway. The sun was brightening through the balmy air and washed-away blue sky. Mike switched on the radio, and some recent Bollywood hit tinkled over the rhythmic crunch of sand and gravel in the horses' stride.

He thought about his old grandmother sitting alone back in the wagon's bed, the bed full of a life's treasures and mementos, and he thought about the gold. He had nothing to say to her, no comfort he could offer short of a grandson's silent, respectful solidarity. Grandma had played in that house as a child, built more than a decade before she was born. She had brought her beloved Jack down here as a young man just out of his teens, not long after they met. She had spent nearly every summer of her life there, bringing babies down in the Nineties, holding an engagement party there for Mike's parents... And now there was simply no way for any of them to continue using it as they once had. So own it they could, but they still had to retreat to the mainland and hope that the storms would not carry it away before circumstances improved, someday. And there was no chance of this at all, Mike knew. The swelling, warming ocean pushed in deeper with every big storm. The island was washing away under the waves, the dunes rearranging themselves daily.

They rode over the dilapidated, empty bridge to Point Harbor, and northward toward Elizabeth City, spending their first night at a nearly deserted campground south of Barco. Grandma had a last social call in Elizabeth City before they picked up Fernando and started really traveling. Coming into town bright and early the next morning—a Saturday—Mike warily regarded the boarded-up windows along Ehringhaus Street, the sandbagged doorways.

"All this storm prep's new since I was here last, Grandma," said Mike.

"New for me, too, Mike. Even just a few days ago there was much less of it. That Rhiannon must be heading this way."

An hour was passed at Juan and Burns Foster's house, a sandy wood frame house with wide screen porches on the southeastern edge of town, by the marshes and dike. Juan Foster had been mayor at one time, and the town's biggest realtor. He was an infirm, elderly man now, depressed and gloomy, but too stubborn to leave Elizabeth City. Burns, his wiry, hyper-energetic wife, nervously served tea and muffins, talking about illness, storms, leaking dikes, break-ins, and bankruptcies the entire time.

Providing a perfect signal that it was almost time to leave, a tall, gaunt man quietly walked up to the Fosters' screen porch and opened the door. It was Fernando. He carried a fishing rod, a satchel, and a string of catfish.

"Why hello, Fernando," smiled Grandma. "Look at what you brought!" She turned to Burns, saying "You were so kind to put him up," and without a pause swung toward Mike. "This is Fernando. Fernando: Mike."

Mike and Fernando met eyes and nodded, each offering a similarly reserved smile. Ex-Marine, thought Mike. Must have been a while ago. Mike stood up, and offered his hand. Fernando took it, and the men shook hands firmly. Burns was talking with Grandma about what Fernando had fixed and helped them move during his short visit. Mike regarded his new traveling companion with concealed scrutiny. He was dark, sun-leathered, a bit solemn-looking, rather than sad. He had piercing blue eyes, with dark circles below them. Mike reflected over what Grandma had said: five kids, the effort to move them all to distant safety. The vibes he got from this man were good, although he was not entirely sure.

Fernando was already moving toward the kitchen as Mike's reflection ended. Grandma was rising, smiling and chatting. Mike followed

Fernando's movement with curiosity. Through several doorways, he noted with momentary surprise how Fernando opened an old refrigerator, its light illuminating. Of course: they still had electric power here. His stay on the island had made him almost forget that many civilians continued to enjoy it, especially the further north one went. As he watched, Fernando pulled four fish from his string and put them into the fridge. A decent move, Mike thought. Neither Burns nor Juan probably got out to fish much. This would feed them for a week. Nonetheless, Mike was satisfied to see that Fernando dropped the remaining (and largest) fish into his satchel, an insulated bag he filled with ice from the fridge. He liked fried fish.

"All right, take good care...," Grandma beamed, taking Burns' hand, and sighed a long friendly ahhhh. "Time to go so soon." She leaned down and kissed Juan's forehead. Juan looked confused and Burns looked agitated and upset. Grandma hugged her with invitations to come up north. Mike and Fernando smiled their good-byes, and went down from the porch and around the corner of the house to the wagon and team, standing below a huge, squat, spreading live oak, the uncut grass to their knees, and then they were off again, back on the road. Mike was glad to leave and finally begin the real trip. Grandma reckoned it would take twelve to fourteen days, based on the trip down. That is, assuming that the hurricane did not slow them down.

7-HONORÉE

Saturday, October 20th

"Duh-duh," said the little boy, yoghurt coating his face, hands, chest, and the makeshift harness holding him in his high-chair. He pointed at the glass door.

"Doggie!" said Honorée. "Doggie!" She looked out the door at the tiny square of yard and the city sidewalk beyond, but saw no dog. The glass was cracked in several places, patched inadequately with tape that was starting to dry and delaminate. "Is there a doggie out there?" she asked distractedly.

"Duh-duh," he confirmed, and then, with a coy narrowing of his eyes and a glance to his side, he casually dropped his yoghurt spoon onto the floor. Around the base of the high chair was a mulch-field of oats, milk, apple slices, and now yoghurt. The cat lapped experimentally at its edge.

"No, Asa, shit, no!" Her delight at his emerging talk quickly turned to cursing exasperation. "You MUST stop dropping your food and things. No no no no no no NO!" Asa's face turned serious. He watched her with concern. She puffed a sigh, and took a drink of tea, trying to calm herself. "Mama works hard to make nice food for you every day, baby." She recalled a book she'd read which described birds working for three weeks without rest to feed their young, sometimes making hundreds of trips from and back to the nest every day. Three weeks ain't nothing,' birdie, she thought.

Rapid footsteps told her that Sanna was coming downstairs. She reached over and hit the button on the battered microwave kettle, and the hiss of boiling water rose to its crescendo just as Sanna strode into the kitchen, boots already on.

"Does this skirt look stupid?" asked Sanna briskly with a comic flutter of her hands.

"No, it's fine," said Honorée. "Fits you much better than me. There's a cup of tea."

"Because, look, this part sticks up like a tail!" Sanna laughed with feigned disbelief and swatted at the rear of the denim-strip skirt. "Like a turkey! It's my Saturday weird skirt." She made a grimace.

Asa examined the skirt with his mouth open, his hands absently drawing patterns in the spilled yoghurt on his high chair's tray. Honorée marveled that Sanna even had the energy to think about fashion.

"Oh, well. Beggars can't be choosers," said Sanna, distractedly dismissing the whole topic. "And choosers can't be beggars. Where's Lee?"

"He's up playing," said Honorée, standing. "LEE! LEE!" She yelled up the stairs for the four-year-old.

The thud of footsteps arced across the ceiling, and Lee came scampering down the stairs.

"Mamma Sanna is going to take you to playschool in ten minutes. Eat up, baby."

Like Asa, Lee had the fair, round, tipped-up features of his biological mother. Sanna cut an entirely different figure: tall, caramel-colored, with wavy black hair, she had grown up in Sweden with Swedish, Afghan, Ivorian, and Polish grandparents. "DC's about the only place I can live," she made it a habit of saying, "now that the American Empire has fallen. They'd never have me in Europe!" Honorée did not know exactly what Sanna meant by that, but she usually went along with Sanna's pronouncements.

"Another hurricane coming," munched Sanna, feeling for her tea as she flipped through the papers on her T-pad.

"Mmm?" prompted Honorée, pouring cereal for Lee.

"Another hurricane. They've upgraded a tropical depression to a hurricane and it's coming north. They say 2 or 3 days to hit Florida. Named Rhiannon." She shrugged. "Nice name."

"That'll put a damper on the market if it comes up here." Sanna, thought Honorée, was always thinking about great dramatic events and irrelevant technical details, while she was the one thinking about food on the table and paying the rent.

"Yup. Uh-huh," said Sanna. "Ah, a break'll be nice. The past couple of days have been really boring. Everybody's selling the same harvest crap.

50

We don't have any more honey, unless you find some quick, and we haven't done the pickles yet." She smiled. "It might be nice and cozy to stay in with tea and goodies and wait the storm out. We can go exploring somewhere fun in the V." Then she took a lingering sip, glancing sideways at Honorée. "But it won't be good for your grandma or your brother," she added darkly, "if it hits them and they're still on the road."

"I hope you're wrong and it misses them," muttered Honorée. Then her mind locked onto the first part of what Sanna had said. "A break? Is that what you think of first?" Honorée's blood pressure rose, and she told herself to back off from this one. She said nothing more, and went to work on Lee's lunchbox. Sanna leaned back, not reacting, taking another sip of tea. She chewed on a nail impulsively and looked intently at the T-pad.

"Did you know that Roger Guan is a clone?!" Sanna burst out. Honorée shook her head. "His firstling lives in China... He's an ordinary factory worker." Sanna let out a peal of manic laughter, showing her white teeth. "Talk about getting upstaged! Probably grew him for organs and the buyers let him get away. Ooops! Our organs turned into a huge VNET celebrity. Quick! Get 'em back before he dies and donates 'em to charity!" She shrieked with laughter, and then abruptly went serious as she studied the screen.

"People do that for humanitarian reasons, too..." offered Honorée.

"Yeah, right," sniffed Sanna. "For $400,000? In China? Anywhere? What planet do you live on?" Her disgusted look said it all. She put down the screen and watched the boys. Lee ate while Asa continued playing with his yoghurt. "Hey Lee." Lee looked up. "Your Uncle Mike's coming soon!"

"This day?" asked Lee with a big grin. That was his word for 'today'.

"No, soon. A few days." She turned toward Honorée, now at the sink. "When's he getting here? Didn't your mom say the 28th?"

"No," said Honorée. "She didn't know exactly. I should call them. I think they've left the beach by now. Must be in Virginia... Maybe next weekend?"

Sanna turned back to Lee, lowering her head and looking very serious. "Uncle Mikey will be here next week. Next week, or so..."

"Is that soon?" asked Lee. "After sleep?" 'After sleep' meant 'tomorrow'.

51

"No, after about ten sleeps." She put up all her fingers. "This many sleeps." Turning to Honorée, she intoned, "Great wigwam builder come to city of Big House after ten sleeps. It has been many, many moons." She then stood up abruptly, bursting out with a laugh. "Oh I am such a nasty, nasty, bigoted woman!" Lee and Asa jerked their heads back simultaneously in uncomprehending surprise.

At the sink, Honorée finished Lee's lunch, and leaned back against the sagging counter. "Sanna, remember to tell them not to let Lee nap so long."

"Right." Sanna threw on a short jacket and a cap. "And remember it's my co-op night."

"I know. It's on the calendar." Honorée fully expected Sanna would forget to mention the napping, and made a note to call them as well.

"Long day, but tomorrow's Sunday! Hey hey!" The irony was thick; Sunday meant they got to open the market stall at ten instead of eight AM, but it also meant more kitchen work. "Well, off we go, Lee. Get your lunchbox. Want anything special from the lock-up, Hon?" She pronounced it like "on" rather than "hun".

"No, I'll go out later with Asa and take the trailer."

"Kay. See you around lunchtime. See if you can find some honey. I'm totally stumped. Call the Chavezes, maybe..." She hugged her from behind, her hands sliding down around her belly and hips, and then went striding out the door with Lee holding her hand and his backpack over her shoulder, along with her market bag.

Honorée watched her go. Sanna worked hard, but her sarcasm was starting to grate. And her impulsiveness. They were semi-comfortable in their little duplex apartment, although always just about to go over the edge. There was never any spare cash around. Sanna and Honorée were both long overdue for dental work. Honorée's T-pad had just crashed and they could not afford a new one. The 'garch who owned their block was raising rents on January 1, although Honorée didn't know by how much. Neither of the boys had any winter clothes yet, and Asa, Honorée reflected once again, had never in his short life ever put on a new piece of clothing.

Every waking moment was about the business. They had had the stall at the sprawling White Flint open-air market for a year now, and had managed to expand into the adjacent spot. They sold all sorts of fresh fruits and vegetables in season, but were focusing more now on growing the pickles and preserves business, which Honorée operated from Grandma's enormous kitchen at her ramshackle old Victorian house in Chevy Chase. It was a lot of work. After a quick cup of tea, she would seat Asa on the back of her bike, hitch up the trailer, and ride off to Grandma's for a morning's pickling and canning, with Asa playing in the adjacent 3V room. Sometimes this worked out well. Sometimes, when Asa was in a wild mood, it was shattering. Meanwhile, Sanna would take their van to go store and retrieve things in the lock-up, and stand at the stall during the morning. Or she might stop by the wholesale markets in Silver Spring to pick up produce, using the van's speed and capacity.

At lunchtime, Honorée would relieve her. Sanna would then take Asa home for a long nap, do the books and process orders at the kitchen table, and later go down to the evening wholesale market to do the deals with farmers and co-ops, and order the fresh produce for the next morning. They were constantly swapping their two means of transport—the biodiesel van and the bike and trailer. The van was expensive to run, even with the food producers' subsidy, but with their tight schedules and need to move so much produce around, they thought it made sense. And Grandma was helping with the loan payments.

Scooping up the wet slop around Asa's chair with the edges of her hands, Hon couldn't resist musing more about their state of affairs. Thirty-four, and divorced from the father of her boys, she had already seen several massive changes in her life. The divorce had come through only six months before, at which time she had been seeing Sanna for about a year. Lee was born right on the horns of the crash of '36, when the dollar collapsed again. That was also the year she finished graduate school at Maryland, qualifying herself for a skill nobody had any use for now: industrial nutritionist. But with that and biology in her undergraduate background, she had a foundation for her new career because, despite the crisis, everyone still seemed to want to eat healthy food that involved pickling or fermentation. All the big chains offered it, but when energy prices went crazy and the general subsidies ended, people stopped driving, incomes shrank, and interstate trucking became prohibitively expensive. The local and regional farms and co-ops stepped into the breach, and most of them were organic anyway because it was originally the only niche they could compete in. Now, no one could buy artificial fertilizer and pesticides anyway. The chains meanwhile went out of business, despite their supposed efficiency, since everything they did relied on energy price controls. At the current price of energy, they were doomed. Their shareholders did not foresee the opportunity that would emerge from the crisis. They wanted—needed—their returns right away, but they could not get them. Now, four years later, entirely new retail concepts were popping up. But the small merchants and open-air markets were what saved the day. They had more business than they could handle.

Asa had come along two years after Lee, born when Honorée's marriage with David was already in tatters. She had not seen David since before the divorce was final, or even heard from him. A member of the walking dead, Sanna called him. A trauma case, said Grandma. Like so many people with education and a high opinion of themselves, the decline was more than he could take: going broke, losing his career, losing the house, suddenly finding himself with too much time on his hands, having to scrounge and look for pick-up jobs. No skills that anyone needed. Desperate. Honorée saw him now in the same category as her mother, and half of the people she went to school with. But as things fell apart, he grew increasingly manic and unpredictable, and then it turned out he was taking massive doses of gammahydroxyl and was dealing to pay for it. It was hard for her to have any understanding, any perspective. It was a nightmare she just wanted to escape. And then he disappeared, and it was only with the help of his parents—both decent, kind people—that the divorce could be completed. She did not know whether he was alive or dead now.

"I must call Mike and Grandma later," Honorée reminded herself out loud as she removed Asa from his chair and wiped it off. She put his helmet on and, grabbing her bag and windbreaker, hauled the struggling two-year-old out the door to the side of the house where the bike was standing. It was a sunny, breezy day, with summer humidity remaining in the warm air. "There you go, Asa-Pasa," she smiled in spite of herself, tying his harness tight. Then, dropping her bag into the open box of the trailer on top of several cases of clean pickle jars, she walked the bike and trailer to the road and stood in its pedals with her calves taut and strong until it reached a speed where she could sit down. One pedal was frozen, so she had to pedal harder with one leg and kind of limp with the other.

Turning onto Wisconsin Avenue, she passed the Cathedral and headed out toward the Maryland line in the busy morning traffic. The northeast headwind gave her extra work as she pumped uphill past Tenley Circle, but the long coast down the other side filled her with energy and renewed optimism for the day ahead. Dodging horse manure in the bike lanes, her nostrils full of the familiar, homey scents of wood smoke and autumn leaves, she spun past long rows of shops, stalls, and postage-stamp gardens lining the crowded sidewalks. Before long, the towers of Friendship Heights loomed ahead of her, and the large blocks of department stores-turned-warehouses and factories. She slowed as the traffic queued for the security checkpoint at the state border, completely forgetting Sanna for once, and idly watched the commuters around her.

8—JAKE WILDER

Saturday, October 20th

The waste paper basket grew fins and soared away into the orange sky with the hiss of a small rocket. Jacob 'Jake' Wilder watched it absently, his mind already hours ahead of this routine little task. Rising higher and higher, it shrank to a brilliant silver dot, and then with a deep boom shattered into thousands of colored sparks that drifted down toward an eternally perfect sunset. A text box flashed the message "Trash Empty". Wilder pulled off his VRI set, folded the headpiece against the visor, and slid it into his jacket pocket. He stood up, his eyes readjusting painfully to the dusty morning sunlight. He rubbed them, and looked around for the insulated coffee cup he had put somewhere before he went inworld. It was over on the window sill. He reached for it, and stood looking through the large picture window for a moment as he drank the remaining few gulps of still-warm coffee. The bright, reflective roofs of lower buildings stretched toward the river, and beyond them he caught glimpses of its slack, muddy surface. The horizon was a fence of high-rises: the square blocks of Crystal City, the slender tower above Pentagon City, the soaring needles of Roslyn, and among them, squat and symmetrical within its shaggy band of eucalyptus trees, the enormous gray trapezoid of the Energy Trust.

A group of helicopters moving toward Reagan National broke his momentary reverie. He needed to call her, and then get moving. Looking away from his window, he spoke to his office phone: "Phone—Call Christine". He glanced at his watch. He had been there for hours, but she might still be in bed.

The click and dial tone from the speaker on his desk station were followed by a ringing sound. On the screen pulsed the text "Calling". After several seconds, a woman's sleepy voice answered.

"Babe! Me. I'm still in DC, but in about eight hours I'm outta here."

The woman laughed. "Hurry up, you liar. What happened to Wednesday night?"

"I'm really sorry about that." He picked up the bat and waved it, opening the video window. Her face appeared. "This biomass bill business is very tense, very crazy. You wouldn't believe the pressure now, the stalling, the power game. I should have given you some warning."

She smiled at him. He could see she was outside on the screen porch, backdropped by a sunny display of lush green foliage. "It's OK. I understand." She was in a good mood.

"Everything OK up there? David get back safely?"

"Yep, night before last. Erin drove their trap down to the station and had to wait more than two hours because the train was late. I heard a rumor at work about protesters blocking the tracks in New York, but there was nothing on the news..."

"They never report that stuff."

She coughed and moved her chair out of the direct sunshine. He saw her body flash by before her face came back into focus. The image swayed. "There. Now I don't have to squint. Are you tired?" She picked up a mug and drank.

"Yes," he sighed. "Pretty beat. I always thought I was high-energy. But I don't have a minute to breathe, much less think."

"Are they going to keep extending the session?"

"For a little while, probably. There's a backlog of bills and resolutions a mile high, but we're never going to make it through most of them, even though most of them are really urgent. Looks like we might go to the 30th, though that's cutting it close..."

"When will I see you?" The wind blew stray blonde hairs around her face. She waved at them distractedly.

"Um, my train's at 5:15, so New York around 7:30, an hour for the transfer, Springfield about 10:00... I don't have the ticket or the new fall schedule up in front of me, but I think I get in at about 11:30." He opened another folder. "Here, wait." With a wave of the bat he opened the folder and batted it to her. "There you go." He saw her eyes turn away from the I-ball, and down toward the screen.

"OK, there it is. Yes, 11:23 pm... I'll come get you," she said. "I'll ride down this evening and buy some supplies, do some things I need to do in town. Need to stop by the vet's for Callie anyway."

57

"Thanks." That would mean a late-night ride for her, and she had work the next morning. He reflected on how amazingly simple and straightforward things always were with this woman. "What's wrong with Callie?"

"She's got a bite on her fetlock that won't heal and she's sluggish. Been like it for almost a week—running sore—in spite of the antibiotic ointment I keep smearing on. This tropical heat won't let up, the awful flies are still around, and I'm wondering if they're botflies." She waved her hand for emphasis, looking grim. "Hope that isn't it. Maybe I'm being hysterical. So, um, maybe Terri can give her a shot."

"Good luck with that." Wilder knew very little about horses and their health, an ignorance which he felt increasingly pressured to correct. "I'm going to have to go in a second." He made a wry face and shook his head. "The Energy & Transportation Committee is going to hold a hearing about the two energy bills. The pressure from the Energy Trust and the right wing is intense, but Morales's veto threat still stands for now. And I've got to do some caucusing with the Forest States Alliance. The Sunbelt keeps digging in deeper and deeper. Party lines don't seem to matter at all. They don't want to subsidize agcell; they don't want to invest in efficiency; the DO want to keep pushing ahead with ethanol and with unlimited cutting – so you get almost unanimous Sunbelt support for the FRSA as a stopgap. But what do desert and prairie states care about our forests, anyway? We've been talking to a bunch of democrats from Arizona, Oklahoma, Utah, Texas, Tennessee, Florida, but we can't come up with the deal they need. Too different on practically every other issue. They want all the scarce government spending for central wind and solar, so they can sell it for a fortune and buy up our wood."

"When are the votes?" she asked, biting into a piece of bread shiny with jam.

"Oh, not until after the election, if the motions pass in committee, and with the vetoes hanging they might not come to a vote this session, unless the leadership thinks they're veto-proof ..." He continued, "You wouldn't believe some of the stuff the Sunbelt Dems want. They live in a different universe. They might as well be Republicans or Homelanders. Most of the New England and other FSA delegations are fighting for more efficiency, for the loan package, for the WPA reauthorization, for the defense curtailment, and for the mass transit bill... And of course against OSCIA, which could break up both countries, and the Forest Reclamation and ...

you know, Forsa. What is practically every other state giving top priority?" His voice sharpened with frustration and disbelief. "The most important things for them—besides Fort McMurray—are the Heterosexual Families Empowerment Act, school communions, the Workplace Pledge of Allegiance, the Patriotic Duty Act expansion... And all the motions about "strategic disengagement". Completely unbelievable! 'Course a lot of them are also coping with the whole Aztlan thing, near-anarchy in their districts, huge migrations... But these things aren't what we need now... The mood's ugly. Some really personal attacks. Dick Cheney's famous old 'Go fuck yourself' to Leahy was nothing compared to the daily norm." He laughed, rubbed his eyes. "Homelanders are the worst. If they're bugging this, I don't care. They're fascists, pure and simple. Totally unconstructive. Like we can go on with this unilateralist fantasy..."

"Don't give up, Jake," she said softly, a tone of alarm in her voice. "I've barely met anyone who doesn't support you, sweetheart. And don't be fearful..."

"OK, OK, thanks. No, no I won't... Keep everyone up to date. Pray for me. Let's see.... We've got that town meeting on Sunday. In, um...." He found himself being pulled back into the mad pace of his legislative day and the thousand things he needed to do before he left. His attention wavered, and returned. "...In Windsor County, that's right."

"Mmm, yes. Don't worry about the details. Everything's set. Talk to you later, then?"

"Sure. I'll call when I'm on the train."

"Bye, my man," she said with a wide smile. "See you."

"Love ya. See ya." He waved the bat, and her face and the vibrant color of the leaves faded into the deep blue of the empty video window.

Moments later, the sole member of the House of Representatives from the state of Vermont was walking quickly up Independence Avenue, sweat forming on his face and back in the heavy, humid autumn heat. He crossed at a traffic light, not even glancing at the chaotic, jingling, rattling, smoking, rumbling mixture of fuel-, cell-, battery-, animal-, and human-powered vehicles that made up the sprawling capital city's endless stream of traffic. His two Secret Service bodyguards walked beside him, watchful, wondering why he never drove to these things like everyone else. Was he nuts?

9-PROKOP VULK

Saturday, October 20th

Think about everything you do, said Vulk to himself, as was his habit. Everything should be intentional. Minimize unnecessary movement. Do things in parallel, not sequentially. Optimize what you can do in one location before moving to the next. Minimize unnecessary movement and terminal time. Isolate the bottlenecks... Swinging away from the sink, he dried his face rapidly and turned to the closet. He grabbed clean underpants and a pair of socks, and in one deft motion pulled them all on. Then he quickly reached for trousers and a clean shirt, and put them on as well. In seconds, he added a jacket and a tie. The clothes in his closet were sorted by type and color. Everything looked perfect, the way he liked it. He glanced back at the bed. The girl's eyes were open. She was watching him.

He nodded in approval. "You're doing well." He gestured at the closet's order. "Nice." She opened her lips and stretched. He glimpsed her slim thighs amid the tussled sheets, and felt a thrill of renewed lust. No, there was no time for that now. He had to get to the House energy hearing. Laugherty had been very clear about that. He wasn't going, but he wanted Vulk there, to observe the subtleties of loyalty and alliance. There was no getting out of it... He glanced back at the girl's face. Suzanna, he reminded himself. She smiled secretly at his momentarily hungry, unguarded look. She knew what he was thinking. She knew she was gaining a foothold.

"I'll do a transfer," he said, regaining his tone of command. "For the coming week. Double last week's. You want tomorrow off, to go see your people?" She nodded. "But I'll see you here tonight." He looked down at her and smiled coolly. "You're good, you know." He walked back toward the bed, drawn impulsively. She had let the sheets slip further. "You're smart and you know what I like." He touched her ankleted Achilles tendon with a fingertip and drew it slowly along her calf, along the side of her thigh, across the point of her hip, over the undulations of her waist and her belly, and up between her breasts to her chin. She shivered involuntarily. "I think I'm going to keep you, um, Suzanna." He winked.

Turning to leave, Vulk picked up his T-pad, briefcase, and pistol as he passed through the hall. "See you around nine. I have to stay late," he said over his shoulder. "The place is yours all day." The door closed and locked behind him with a precise click and a whirr.

The girl leapt from the bed, drew open a curtain, and whisked on her dressing gown. Smiling to herself, she pulled out a cell phone from the gown's pocket and spoke a number. A woman answered.

"Mama," the girl said happily into the phone, "he's keeping me. You're gonna eat rich all the way to Christmas!"

10-THE HEARING

Saturday, October 20th

Above the sounds of the crowded streets, they could just discern a distant voice squawking out something through a bullhorn, and then they heard chants and drums. Davis, his senior Secret Service guard, put his hand on Wilder's shoulder. He placed his finger against his ear—over his implant—and looked down, listening. He turned toward Wilder. "Sir, protest near the Lewis Building. Completely blocked."

Wilder nodded. As they had done many times, they doubled back and took a left down Second Street. At a non-descript entrance beside a checkpoint, they ducked in, and entered its vestibule for an RFID scan. The inner door opened and they descended a flight of steps into the network of federal government tunnels, taking the pedestrian tunnel that led toward South Capitol Street. After another layer of security—this time staffed—Wilder and his two companions ascended several short stairways and gained the central atrium of the Lewis Building. Wilder strode across alone and entered the hearing room, while they took a seat in the atrium. Below them, some distance off beyond riot barricades and orange plastic fence nets, demonstrators waved flags and signs, pursuing the increasingly risky activity of public free speech.

The session chair was just calling the hearing to order. Wilder slid quietly into a seat in the inner ring reserved for committee members, and looked around at the faces present. His aides Doug and Selena were already there, at the staff table. Their eyes met, and he smiled in greeting. They both nodded back, eyes friendly but smiles restrained. Then he noticed Moriah further back, standing against one of the columns, her willowy figure exquisite among the dark suits and heavyset functionaries. She flashed him one of her frowny smiles and turned back toward the proceedings.

The large room was packed—not unusual for Energy & Transportation of late. Congressmen, the government media, and civil servants from DOT, DOE, the Trust, and various other departments and agencies settled down for the latest review of biomass and fossil-fuel policy—a tangled process that seemed to never end. They formed the usual backdrop of conservative blue and gray blazers, tunics, and go-suits—hair closely cut, beards neat, faces and hands clean. This was one side of Washington: affluent, protected, living safe and orderly lives. They were the communicators, the analysts, the clerks, the managers, the decision makers—keeping the routine wheels turning for the federal government, the oligarchs, the Energy Trust, and the other institutions of modernity and technology. The new poverty and dislocation were never far from them, but by dint of luck, connections, and endless work, they kept them sealed outside their envelopes, and some even grew accustomed to thinking they were entitled to such hermetic separation. Off they went in the mornings in their cell-electric vanpools from gated inurbs, zooming quickly onto the secure GOV-4 expressways where ordinary citizens could not travel. They worked in air-conditioned offices in an environment of organization, hygiene, and style few now enjoyed. Compared to earlier days, their circumstances could not be called opulent, but they were worlds apart from what the large majority of Washingtonians experienced from moment to moment and day to day.

Wilder continued his scan. Alonzo Crispus was there—his party and committee colleague from New York - as well as Amoroso and Dickson. Senger was at the inner table, too—a Homelander and the newest member of the committee, one of forty-six in the House from the Party for the Defense of the Homeland.

"Now let's all be aware of why we are here today," said the session chairwoman, Representative Alice Szabo, R-Ohio. She sat with a straight posture, old-fashioned bifocal glasses on the end of her nose, and looked sternly at the hundreds of people assembled. "Energy is an old story—and I often don't believe there are any remaining ways in which to tell it differently..." There was a tense, barely audible chuckle from the audience.

"Yet we know we need to keep working extremely hard on that story, because energy—biomass in particular—is presenting growing challenges to the economy and social fabric of our nation, and there is still some disagreement about the best way to ultimately meet these challenges. So we are here today to learn more about the possible positions this committee can take. We are here to refresh our memories, and to focus. We are not here to review every technology and cost-benefit analysis that's ever been done about biomass. No. This committee needs to make high-level, big-picture recommendations to our colleagues in the House next week to guide the overall direction of policy and prepare the House for the upcoming floor debates about several bills. To do that, we need the latest relevant facts and a chance to discuss and think about them. The bill in question is circulating in conference committee substantially changed from its original draft when it first came out of this committee. Some of us barely recognize it. It has traveled far..." She stopped and glared around at the members of the committee, and then out over the general audience. "Now, by high-level, big-picture recommendations, I DO NOT mean diplomatic recommendations. This hearing is not an occasion for debating foreign policy and international relations concerning Canada, the EU, the Chinese Union, or anyone else. All of us are well aware that the international loan package being discussed has certain conditions attached to it relating to energy policy, technology, and trade. And our relationship with Canada is becoming, um, complex. But, in this committee, we need to forget about OSCIA for the moment, and focus on Forsa—the Forest Reclamation and Stewardship Act—as if these other things weren't happening. OSCIA is not our ambit today. We'd be advised to leave the foreign relations dimension to our brothers and sisters on the House Foreign Affairs Committee, whose mandate *that* is. Is this clear?"

The room was silent. Several committee members nodded imperceptibly. Wilder wondered whether Szabo would win this one. Perhaps no one would challenge her. There was little contest anyway as far as the future of either OSCIA or Forsa went. The Conventionalist forces in Washington were basically invincible now. With financial resources as squeezed as they were, New Nuclear was supposedly still a decade off, but the public was at the end of its rope, which to most people meant burning whatever would burn—fossil and renewable—to power the nation through the Emergency. Although a few voices might object—Wilder's included— the effect of this hearing would essentially be one more rubber-stamp for the Conventionalist agenda. Szabo was running process for process' sake.

She's got a sentimental nostalgia for open democracy, laughed Wilder to himself without mirth. Crispus glanced at him and shook his head slightly, probably thinking the same thought.

"Conferring with the Speaker, the party leadership, and our committee chairman the Honorable Boyce Menninger from Texas," she nodded sideways at Menninger, "it became apparent that our task today is two-fold: to review today's key biomass-related policy questions—short-term and long-term—and to reach a qualified consensus about what to recommend in terms of its impact on US economic recovery, future energy options, and protection of environmental quality and natural resources. The third major piece of energy legislation in development, the Energy Assurance and Development Bill, while very urgent, is still a very unfinished work, despite the claims of some about their own versions. We will *not* debate it. The EADB will remain in process in this committee, and be taken up in a future hearing at the appropriate time."

The Homelanders are already circulating their own version, thought Wilder gloomily. They know they have already won this round.

Alice Szabo's fabled pert confidence seemed to sway for a moment. "So, to be totally clear, it is my position as chair of this meeting that we leave EADB alone today as well. Our priority is providing the House with an objective determination for the most immediate bill at hand: Forsa. I trust there are no objections."

She glared around, and continued. "So, do I have a motion that we proceed straight to this session's invited speakers, forego committee members' prefaces, and leave time for discussion later?" Someone mumbled "So moved," but Wilder did not catch who this was, and could not be bothered to glance at the screen. "Do I hear a second?" asked Alice Szabo. Crispus raised his hand and muttered, "Second." "Motion seconded by the Honorable Representative from New York," said Alice Szabo. "All in favor?" A scattering of yeas briefly erupted from the committee members. "All opposed?" The nays were distinctly louder.

Szabo frowned. "The nays have it. We will start with prefaces," she intoned wearily.

Into the pause spoke Elijah Semmel of Florida: "Madam Chair, I move that the preface period be limited to sixty minutes, with 3-minute maximums per speaker." Maureen Santiamo-Cooke of Arizona raised her hand and seconded it.

"All in favor?" asked Szabo with a grimace, foreclosing any discussion. The yeas were loud and long. "Opposed?" Wilder called out a loud nay, but he was clearly in the minority. "The motion carries," said Szabo, banging her gavel. "Sixty minutes and three minutes." There was a murmuring in the outer reaches of the hearing room. This was what many journalists and lobbyists had come for. The president had clearly indicated she would veto Forsa and OSCIA if handed to her this term. Would her opponents in Congress humiliate her with a double veto override during the waning days of her term, after the election, regardless of its outcome? Figuring out where members of Congress stood on these fateful bills was one of the biggest games in town now. Whether one praised or abhorred Congress, attention was rapt among Washington-watchers. At this moment, most eyes were on this key committee.

Chairwoman Szabo turned toward Crispus, the committee's secretary. "Secretary Crispus, please summarize the bill in question." Her face had become hard, undecipherable.

Alonzo Crispus took the floor. In his deep, Brooklyn voice, he ran through the major points of "Forsa," the FRSA. Wilder listened with the mixture of resignation and disbelief he had been unable to shake since he first heard the infant versions of these proposals a year before. The FRSA had been sponsored by a large group of conservative congressmen in both houses from districts that were primarily either urban or arid or both, i.e., short of forest cover. It was aimed at easing short-term fuel shortages for building heating and cogenerated electricity by opening all publicly owned forests (federal, state, and local) to extensive cutting for fuel wood production "until new energy regimes can be implemented," with highly streamlined permitting that the Energy Trust would control at the federal level. Most legislation relating to protection of endangered species, watershed protection, and other aspects of forest conservation would be suspended when a FRSA permit was obtained. It would also make it a federal crime for any state, local government, or citizens' group to attempt to slow or halt "expedient fuel wood recovery" or distribution of the resulting fuel wood, once permitted. A major fear among opponents was that the FRSA would be in force long enough for widespread deforestation to occur. Supporters dismissed these worries as unwarranted and hysterical, arguing that "only" 15-20% of US forest cover would be sacrificed while the New Energy Regime was brought into existence—far

66

less than the loss of forest cover in the late 1800s and early 1900s. Yet, Wilder reflected, when supporters waved that estimate around, they were silent about the additional estimates that the forests near population centers, such as those in northern California, the Pacific Northwest, and his own Green Mountains might see half of the forest cut down in the decade during which this transformation would supposedly take place. If it did in fact only take that long... Or even happen. And then there were the objections that this would degrade an enormously important carbon sink, although few cared much about that argument anymore.

What Wilder also worried about was the radical step this would represent in the further centralization of decisions traditionally left to the state and local governments. It meant that biomass, along with fossil fuels, was being essentially federalized, suggesting that biomass might even be absorbed under the Energy Trust. It was unimaginably hard-hearted, unfathomably short-sighted. Wilder wondered whether the Energy Trust was quietly revealing pessimistic forecasts to the feds about reserves of oil and gas, and telling them it needed to get its hooks into biomass now. This was of course what the conspiracy theorists' gossip now assumed. And the only thing that kept the federal government in control of the coasts, airways, rivers, and interstate highways was its lock on oil and gas. To the casual observer, they seemed to have plenty of it. The skies over Washington and other federal reserves were always full of helicopters, and between all the trucks, C-230s, Coast Guard cutters, and everything else with an engine that the feds operated, things seemed to be OK. But were they? No, of course they were not.

Wilder's constituents hated Forsa. He knew exactly how they expected him to vote when it came to that. But this was not surprising for inhabitants of a rural state with much of its timber still standing.

Morales had promised to veto Forsa, reflected Wilder. She was holding the line on all these fascist offensives on the energy front. Wilder shook his head imperceptibly, musing over the stress she must be under. Morales had also condemned Fort McMurray and OSCIA as extremely dangerous, irresponsible thinking. A Homelander senator threatened her with assassination if she did, and was suspended from the US Senate as a result.

Crispus ended his summary, a look of distaste on his face. Alice Szabo leaned forward. "Thank you, Congressman Crispus. We will now move on to the prefaces by committee members." She smiled over at the sergeant. "The Sergeant-at-Arms may start the clock when ready."

"This is fascism! This has to be stopped!" A man's voice barked out sharply from the gallery, and then yelped into silence. Wilder turned around, straining his neck to see. There was a disturbance near one of the exits as security hustled someone out. His PDA vibrated in his coat pocket. He pulled it out. It was a brief text message from Selena. "That was Broadman!" It was no demonstrator, then. Wilder shook his head. Broadman was a respected 3V journalist from Global Centrum. This outburst would mean the abrupt end of his career. Would anyone pick up this story, about Broadman's final three seconds of fame? He wondered.

Up on the wall, the speakers' queue already had a dozen names as committee members clicked bats and watched their screens. The first ten slots were determined by lottery according to this committee's custom. Wilder had the fourth slot.

The speakers were mostly from southern states, Wilder noted. Freshman rep Santiamo-Cooke was first. A poised, meticulously groomed former state attorney general, she was a hawk in foreign affairs and a part of what Wilder thought of as the utmost pinfeather of the Republican right wing. Her domestic energy and transportation policy positions were diametrically opposed to those of the Forest States Alliance. She was a Homelander in all but name only.

"The clock has started, Madam Chair," said the Sergeant-at-Arms. A digital stopwatch was now on the screens, its second-hand ticking forward.

"Congresswoman Santiamo-Cooke, you have the floor," said Alice Szabo, settling back in her chair.

"Colleagues of this Committee, esteemed guests, and dear audience," began Maureen Santiamo-Cooke. "I am very grateful that this hearing has been called today. Our great nation is experiencing a time of testing, of tempering, and energy remains at the heart of the challenges we continue to face. We are called upon to re-think things. We're called on to learn from past mistakes. And we're called upon to shed every shred of regret, sentimentalism, and discarded, romantic dreams, and look the new challenges squarely in the eye. I look forward to the wisdom our invited guests can bring to the committee today, and to your help in the nonpartisan passage of a forests reclamation bill which the whole Congress can accept. I am confident that your advice will lead us towards a solution to the energy crisis which answers tomorrow's questions, not yesterday's; which rewards new potential, instead of subsidizing outmoded industries and lifestyles; and which—importantly—preserves our nation's independence and right to self-determination…"

There were several sarcastic laughs in the gallery.

Santiamo-Cooke's expression grew sharply determined "… our self-determination, so help us God! That is all." She sat back in her seat. There were more snickers and talking.

The Chair rapped her gavel on her desk. "There will be order in this hearing room. Respectful silence. Sergeant, take measures to see to it that order is maintained! And let's not follow the example of the Honorable Representative from Arizona and start mixing foreign policy into this. I urged this committee to steer clear of foreign policy, whether it involves Canada, the CU, or the EU. That is not our mandate. Let us focus on domestic biomass and how to get it and use it." Santiamo-Cooke pursed her mouth and looked with irritation toward the ceiling.

"Now," Szabo went on, "Congressman Semmel, the floor is yours for up to three minutes."

Elijah Semmel, a small, wiry, tanned man with oddly wizened features for a man in his forties, stood up and gestured around the room. "I'm very pleased to see such a large crowd here today. Even most of the honorable committee members themselves have joined us…" A chuckle crossed the room. "Y'all's being here indicates what an important topic this is, all this business about energy policy, energy efficiency, how we're going to fuel our cars, cool our homes and offices, keep our economy going."

The economy isn't going, thought Wilder. And Semmel forgot to mention *heating* our homes.

"Now, being from the Sunshine State, I'm especially conscious about Florida's role as one of the major future engines of our nation's economy. We were a very competitive tourist destination, and will be again. The world used to always come to Florida, and get top value. We have banking, internationally oriented services, agricultural exports. We Floridians care very much about what the world thinks of us. The berms and dikes are working out just great. Florida is open for business!" There was a ripple of applause from his party-mates.

The world, thought Wilder, isn't living the high life that once allowed it to travel to resorts in Florida, and there's little sign it will anytime soon.

69

"But being a Republican," Semmel went on, "and the proud son of a small business owner, I also know that what this country needs right now is the biggest bang our few bucks are going to get us, and I'm telling y'all that insulating some homes up north, converting town energy systems, and installing some more windmills and small hydro plants just isn't going to provide that bang. On top of that, charging off into the hydrogen future—sure, Florida's got more sunshine than we know what to do with!—but hydrogen is the kind of risky gamble that I just don't believe a responsible government should support. The prosperity of this nation—all of our businesses, non-profits, and local and state governments—is hanging by a thread—a thread!—and don't you worry, Madam Chair, I'm not going to get into foreign policy issues right now, oh no – but we cannot afford to use the few resources that are ours—ours entirely—to prop up industries and communities ripe for radical restructuring while the most viable businesses and regions remain starved of the energy supplies and investment they need—the very same private enterprises that can do much more than the government—bless us—to come up with the innovations and organize the activity to move us out of the crisis. On top of that, we can't go throwing scarce energy resources down pardon-my-French rat holes when the economic dynamism of Florida—the motor of the Southern economy—relies on keeping all the pumps going and the levies dry as the sea level *adjusts*. We just cannot do that. That's why I'm putting all my support behind the Conventional Option and the FRSA as currently drafted. We know this technology. We've got all the expertise and competence right here in the USA. And it will drive growth that eventually lifts all boats, without subsidizing rust-belt industries and the communities that mistakenly cling to them, at enormous opportunity cost and real social and political hazard, and refuse to migrate their labor forces to more responsible parts of the country!" Semmel looked around with an intense stare, his eyes wide-open and dramatic.

Responsible, mused Wilder. That old code word. Now it's irresponsible to live where there's winter? Yet here it came again, as Semmel resumed...

"Responsible use of North American biomass and oil—as enshrined in Forsa and OSCIA—will bridge the gap to get us to the New Energy Future. Irresponsibly keeping forest resources away from wise use, and irresponsibly promoting romantic eco-lifestyles in places too cold for large

70

populations, is criminal. Criminal! I believe Florida's position is clear. I thank y'all for your time, and for coming. I look forward to hearing from the experts."

Two more short prefaces followed—tense, partisan, skirting the foreign policy debate without actually plunging in. The audience followed the representatives' language closely, responding with faint laughs, sighs, and hisses, feeding the charged atmosphere. The code-words flowed: responsibility, caution, affordability, competitiveness, autonomy, national sovereignty, realism... Wilder listened critically, motionless, moving his eyes but not his head. At first, somewhat enamored of rhetorical theater, he had the impulse to prepare an elaborate preface. Then, on reflection, since this was the first time the whole committee had been assembled for half a year, he decided to make a shorter, terser statement, and then hang back and observe positions and arguments. Anyway, he thought, these prefaces are just opportunities to posture and get sound-bites into the media feed, and will not have much bearing on the actual hearing. The real oratory would begin when the bills made it to the House floor.

Then it was his turn. Nodding to Alice Szabo and his staffers, he adjusted his posture and leaned toward the microphone wand. Three minutes were his. He drew in a breath and adjusted the wand. Before him, a grim audience waited silently. In this place, Wilder knew he was among few friends.

"Good morning guests, colleagues, Madame Chair. I come from a state blessed by its very poverty, for we have no petroleum or natural gas in our ground. Moreover, I come from a region where investment in efficiency and renewable energy sources has been consistent and longstanding. These two facts have not put us in the lap of luxury today, of course. Times now are very hard. There is far more to be done. But the positions of my state and of my party are clear: Forsa is an infringement of states' rights, a crutch for the federal government's reliance on its fossil fuel monopoly, a disincentive to invest more in efficiency and downpowering, and an enormous threat to the viability of our forests—forests that capture carbon, purify our water, protect biodiversity, and form one of our most valuable assets for many other reasons. Forsa makes a mockery of the responsible legislation of a healthy democracy. I remain shocked that it is being given serious consideration by members of this Congress. It is an offensive and desperate measure with nothing but regrets as its eventual legacy."

Wilder paused. Most of the audience reacted with scattered laughs of scorn and exasperated sneers. Here and there, a quiet face met his, eyes serious and supportive. Alice Szabo pounded her gavel to restore decorum. He resumed.

"Complete conversion to the sustainable energy paradigm—SHE-WEBS—sun, hydro, eco-mimicry, wind, efficiency, biofuels, simplicity—is a strategy this nation as a whole has never embraced. Many nations have. Look at their success! Why are we stuck in this dilemma, actually considering this outrageous change in our policy toward Canada and the destruction of our forests? We have had plenty of warning. This debate has raged for seventy years. Seven decades! I think every rational argument in favor of SHE-WEBS has been convincingly mounted a million times since the first oil crisis in the 1970s. I have nothing to add that would make a difference. Talk has failed. Ever since the violent Twenties this nation has been locked into a mindless, short-sighted attempt to preserve the fossil fuel economy. We're still at it, and we're already passing plus-three degrees SGW! Since the Energy Trust was created in 2023, the very viability of the Federal Government has been bound to propping up oil, gas, and coal, and the decrepit systems that rely on them. The resources of the Energy Trust and the oligarchy have bought the US government, and not a few state governments as well. Everything outside of the Energy Trust's mandate—all renewable—has been strangled. I have it on reliable authority that ninety percent of total capital investments in energy production and distribution are still going into fossil fuels. In this day and age! In the EU, it's down to ten percent. We have literally bankrupted this country hanging onto outmoded energy and other technologies because it's in the interest of the moneyed and powerful few to do so. The economy of the United States is in ruins. Poverty and misery have reached levels far beyond the Great Depression's a century ago. Nearly halfway through the Twenty-first Century, we are re-entering the Nineteenth. Capital is scarce, to be sure, but that is not the real problem. Capital can be found, domestically or abroad. The real problem, honored members of the Committee, is that privileged interests have been running the economy of the United States like their own private plantation for several decades, and those interests are now synonymous with unelected powers within the government as well. Let us not forget who the Trustees are. They are not elected by us, nor even politically appointed…"

Wilder paused for the briefest of heartbeat moments, letting his incendiary words echo through the chamber. Despite his status as a Congressman, he half-expected to be silenced. An awful, mute suspense filled the large room. He glanced across the audience. He was almost out of time. His glance registered fleeting impressions of derision, dismissiveness, impatience, and the occasional look of encouragement. He opened his mouth to finish. Alice Szabo brought down her gavel abruptly.

"Thank you, Congressman Wilder. Fifth slot goes to Madeline Garcia of Illinois."

A bell sounded. Joe Asbrink from Minnesota leaned toward his microphone. "I cede my ninth slot to the gentleman from Vermont." The audience breathed out, shifting. Alice Szabo sighed and raised her gavel above her head. "Approved. Strike Congressman Asbrink from the queue." She brought it down with a sharp report. The speakers' list in the overhead display jumped as Asbrink's name vanished from it. "Please proceed." She sat back. Wilder directed a nod of thanks at Asbrink. Asbrink nodded back. Wilder resumed, more slowly, emphasizing each phrase.

"To me, to my constituents, to my state's delegation, and, I believe, to my friends in the Forest States Alliance and to intelligent people everywhere in this great nation, the answer is simple. Dismantle the Energy Trust. Remove the monopoly. Remove the barriers to private investment. Recognize the transformation already occurring at the grassroots..."

There was isolated clapping somewhere.

"...Embrace SHE-WEBS. Scrap OSCIA and Forsa. And give American industry and local governments access to the foreign capital they merit!"

Alice Szabo frowned and tutted. She reached for her gavel, but hesitated.

Wilder went on hurriedly. "To those of you whom Big Fossil has compromised, I say this: The interests of your masters are not the interests of this country." He drew in a breath, making contact with the hundreds of eyes meeting his. "Conventional energy is dying. We are burning up our political, cultural, and natural heritage to keep it alive for the benefit of a few. The people must see this. If we fail to retire the conventional energy regime in an orderly fashion and shift those resources to SHE-WEBS, we will fail the Revolutionary promise of America. The very survival of this country may be at stake. Our livelihoods and the vitality of our communities will be even worse off than they are today. In my home state, relations with our neighbor Quebec will chill. A federally sanctioned assault on the sacred forest of the Northeast will begin, with unpredictable reactions by the citizens of Vermont. I urge this Committee and this Congress to reject OSCIA, reject Forsa, and apply all means at our disposal to move government policy in the direction of SHE-WEBS." He breathed in, and drew himself up. "Thank you."

And then his turn was over, only a minute into the time Asbrink had given him. There was a thin applause and a thicker silence. He sat back in his seat. Moriah stole a grin at him. Dave looked down at his T-pad. Crispus caught his eye, and held it with a seriousness that almost frightened him. A smirk of derision played on the face of Senger. Wilder ignored him. But he knew few would heed his words. He made speeches like this all the time. So did a few other representatives. The media ignored them. The vloggers did not. Their words of caution and dissent were out there in cyberspace for all to read—at least, until the right-wing jambots could find them and shut them down. But few took the time. Wilder's arguments were nothing new. Ordinary people had more urgent worries.

The next speakers followed in their allotted order. Their faces and voices came and went on the main screen. The battle lines were clearly drawn. Democrats and Greens spoke of crisis, desperation, alternative energy, biofuels, hydrogen, conservation, efficiency, sustainability, resilience, the long view, international cooperation, provocation of conflict, and national unity. Republicans and Homelanders stuck to bold optimism, New Nuclear, "clean coal," oil sands and shale fuels, strategic disengagement, defense, and free market competition. The committee was as irreconcilably polarized as the nation.

Free market competition and strategic disengagement were two frequently invoked, coded expressions that Wilder seethed about, but which his political opponents in Vermont and the House regularly used with reassuring authority and devastating effect. He had traveled all around the country during the searing summer months with Hedges' presidential campaign team, and he had seen the impacts of "free market competition". Where energy costs were relatively high—in the colder northern states, in the far-flung small towns and emptied suburbs—the depression had reached depths unimaginable only five years before. Businesses and factories were boarded up, homes for sale, parks and public buildings neglected, infrastructure crumbling, and populations on the move. Once-vibrant centers like Ann Arbor and Boulder were being decimated. The automobile-propped suburbs of cities like Minneapolis, Chicago, Cleveland, and St. Louis were in a tailspin. In contrast, where winters were mild and population concentrated—especially poor, migrant populations—like Atlanta, LA, Miami, Phoenix, and Houston, tent and trailer cities had sprung up, cheap bus systems emerged, and vast fleets of bicycles, people on horseback, and horse-drawn wagons flowed through freeway systems once built for cars, carrying workers to and from the manufacturing and agricultural enterprises attracted there, despite the growing oppressiveness of the summer months' heat. And, in spite of the continuing push for more electrification, smoke hung perpetually in the air from charcoal, coal, and wood cooking fires. "Scoopers" driving high-sided wagons cruised the roads day and night, collecting horse manure to sell to the cities' belts of food, feed, and biofuel farms. Sure, thought Wilder, there was plenty of economic activity in the Sunbelt, but until something dug the nation out of its crisis, it would all continue in the vein of this hopeless low-tech subsistence activity more akin to the 19th century than what was once expected for the middle of the 21st. Whole regions were going to die a slow death by "free market" strangulation unless the federal government started a proactive policy of support and rescue, and deregulated energy.

And the power bases of the Republicans and Homelanders were exactly where the climate was warmer, the winter energy demand lower, and the growing migrant populations willing to work for almost nothing, whereas the shrinking Democratic and Green parties relied on people clinging ever more desperately to life in the northern states, trying to stay warm in the winters and preserve what was left of their historically more generous social welfare, health care, and educational systems. Where was there any hope for unity? The cultures were diametrically opposed.

And then Jacob Wilder's mind turned to strategic disengagement, and he seethed even hotter. This question had seen stalemate for months, and was now a central campaign issue. Ironically or not, depending on how you looked at it, the G-12 and World Bank had offered America by far the largest structural adjustment financing package ever assembled in the history of multilateral development aid. The Morales administration had been working overtime on the aid negotiations ever since it came into office in 2036 with an initially strong mandate to do something about the crisis. But, just as the previous administration had been brought down by its "unpatriotic" handling of the collapse of the dollar, after the world finally stopped using it and curtailed lending, it looked like Morales and her cabinet were about to be defenestrated through their own window of opportunity by critics—Homelanders in the vanguard—who wanted national autonomy above all else. The FSA was begging voters to remember the Marshall Plan in Europe and the role European capital originally had in the industrialization of the US, yet jingoist rhetoric, suspicion, and fear were spreading. Nobody cared about history.

But there was nothing "strategic" about this disengagement, thought Wilder. It was just a slogan. "Dumb, paranoid, and short-sighted" would be more apt. As his mind wandered and he watched the final speakers deliver their prefaces, he mused over how a nation gets the government it deserves, and that conditions like more energy conservation, renewable resource use, fossil energy deregulation, and regional rescue might never have been stipulated in the foreign loan package if the American government, scientific establishment, industry, and voters had been able to reach a consensus long before to take these directions themselves. But oh no, reflected Wilder. Reason, restraint, and tolerant neighborliness were less important than wild nationalistic flag-waving, self-important religious cross-waving, and terribly divisive scapegoating.

"...most grateful to be able to make a few remarks at the end of the preface period."

Wilder's wandering attention snapped back to the hearing. Boyce Menninger, the chairman of the committee, was starting up to speak. A moderate Republican, Menninger had been a rancher, lawyer, judge, and state senator before he came to Washington ten terms ago to represent the Texas congressional district that included suburbs of Austin. To Wilder, Menninger sometimes sounded like an old-fashioned southern Republican, and sometimes like a NEP Democrat. He never stopped surprising him. This was the second session in a row that Menninger had chaired this committee. Before that, he had chaired Agricultural Affairs. Menninger was a soft-spoken yet blunt man, broad shouldered and big-bellied, who was clearly among the most savvy senior politicians in DC. Wilder listened carefully, as a deeper quiet descended on the hearing room.

"I'd like to commend my honorable colleague Alice Szabo for her excellent chairing." Alice Szabo smiled politely. Menninger cleared this throat, and looked around. "Now, for all the fine words from my colleagues, and all the brave statements, and all the sneakin' around the issue of Europe and the Chinese saying they'll lend us money as long as we do what they want with it, what I haven't heard is the resolve to unite all sides and make the right decision for the whole country, now and in future generations. Sure, wait," he held out a hand, its palm flat and vertical, "I know you Greens and Democrats are thinking, Hey, wait, *I* was talking about the whole country and the future, but folks, in *my* book you weren't because your tone—as you talked about all these great technologies—kept coming back again and again to that moralizing position that we wouldn't be in this predicament if we had listened to you long ago. Or at least kept listening after the collapse of the New Energy Plan back in the Twenties, when we all fell back on security concerns. Well, that is all in the past.

"But to my Republican colleagues and the honorable party to its right," he sat up higher, and Wilder was surprised to see that Menninger seemed genuinely impassioned, not merely orating, "I say to you, that all I heard here today is what I have been hearing most of my career: that private, free capital always comes up with the best technologies and most efficient market solutions, and that the age of conventional energy is not over, and in fact cannot end until nuclear power replaces it, with fusion out somewhere on that bright horizon, because alternatives just can't meet the demand."

All eyes and ears concentrated on Menninger's face and words. The room echoed faintly with the dull tapping of fingers on T-pad keyboards.

"My compadres on the right side of the House, you are also voices from the past. If this committee, and this House, and this Congress are to belong to our future, we must not listen to you. I'm an old pol, set in my ways, but let us reflect for a moment on the reality in which these deliberations must proceed. Three aspects have struck me deeply recently, and I'm sure many in this room took note of at least two them. One is the Fort McMurray Declaration. Sorry, ma'am, but if you'll bear with me for a moment..."

Menninger turned to Alice Szabo, smiling somewhat patronizingly down his nose at her, over his glasses. She pursed her mouth and studied her T-pad, declining the invitation to protest. He nodded faintly and continued.

"So, uh, Fort McMurray. There are better ways to encourage positive oil trade relations with our dear neighbor Canada…"

There was a ripple of wry laughter at this understatement.

"It's a sign to me that the federal government needs to continue diversifying, reducing reliance on oil, gas, and coal. Not because of climate change, 'course. Global warming's not an action item any longer because our economic activity has fallen off so drastically that we're not emitting anywhere near what we used to. And what's done is done: our climate system will follow whatever curve it must because of past sins. No, it's about national security and good relations with Canada. Oil can't jeopardize those. We need to bring biomass into the national equation."

There, thought Wilder. Menninger's for federalizing the forests….

"Then there is last month's successful New Nuclear test at Oak Ridge. That's number two. We can see the light at the end of the tunnel. Very exciting."

If we can believe any of that crap, reacted Wilder. How much was just more propaganda?

"Finally," intoned Menninger, "there's a bigger reason than either of these two. Please listen to me carefully."

Congressman Menninger stood up slowly and stiffly.

"The time has come to truly shift America to the green, bio-based economy we've been dreaming of for a generation." He chuckled. "Yes, dreaming, all of us. The Energy Trust was formed for expediency, for the urgent defense of the homeland. But we-all always knew the oil and gas and even coal would one day run out, and that a longer-term solution would be needed. In New Nuclear, and in solar hydrogen, we see the outlines of the long term."

Wilder almost winced.

"But the missing piece—the bridge—is bio-based energy, and we finally have the opportunity and the need to unite around biomass and biomass-based fuels as a nation, and move forward together on this, putting all the regional tensions behind us."

This is nothing but the proverbial Picassos in the trunk, thought Wilder gloomily. Menninger's making it look all rosy and patriotic, but this is just a short-term fuel switch as oil and gas become scarcer. Like burning the furniture to stay warm. Fully exploited, even with fast-growing biomass crops, biomass would never provide more than a tiny share of the Conventionalist economy's energy. They used this rhetoric when they tried to federalize water resources in the Twenties, and it almost started a civil war in the West. Now, because Congress won't play the global carbon and renewables game, or accept the loan package, we can't get the metals we need for more solar and wind capacity, so the only short-term fuel solution is burning up the forests, either as wood or as ethanol made from cellulose...

"... the Green Teens were all about new beginnings," Menninger was saying. "Remember that spirit?"

Sure I do, thought Wilder. But since when does a Texas Republican get all sappy and nostalgic for the Green Teens!?

"Well, this is the vision I see before us now, again. A nation united, the keys to our long-term future assured, and the perfect bridge from what's left of the fossil economy to a green, ecologically wise tomorrow, using a purely indigenous resource: our biomass."

I thought fracked gas was supposed to be the bridge, mused Wilder.

Menninger smiled broadly.

"Thank you, ladies and gentlemen." He sat down to a robust applause.

Wilder let out a long, sighing, skeptical breath and stretched his arms back behind his head, closing his eyes for several seconds. A nation united? He took another deep breath, collecting his thoughts. Green? Biomass never made sense more than a half-hour's rail or truck run from its source to the boiler. Menninger and the others are talking about thousand-mile trade, by the sound of it. That will never work. This is a desperate measure cloaked in reassuring language. Who in hell could be so naïve or corrupt to go for this? Or is America going to finally fall apart in a scrap over firewood? How sad the signers of the Declaration of Independence would have been about this.

Alice Szabo had resumed talking. "For the rest of the day, we will be hearing updates from some of our nation's foremost energy experts. This is mostly review. Their positions are well-known, with all due respect." He nodded at the invited experts. "Dr. Jacob Suto will brief us on wood reserves. Dr. Arlene Nguyen is with us again to focus on biofuels and building efficiency. The team from Palo Alto will bring us the latest on biodiesel. Oak Ridge is here to talk cellulosics. Professor Morinaga and his group will preview their latest report on energy crops. But as we hear the state of the art in biomass energetics, let us not get bogged down in trying to microsolve this crisis along old party lines. Or in playing mind games with the technologies. We must escape the pull of the past, and endeavor to see a new way forward."

With these final words, Alice Szabo pounded her gavel, calling a recess of thirty minutes. A hubbub of voices swelled up into the vacuum.

Wilder stood and stretched his tense shoulders. Crispus also got up, catching Wilder's eye, and raised his eyebrows. Wilder shook his head. "This is what the Trust wants," he said in a low voice.

"There are different opinions about how to get out of this situation," said Crispus, "but the time of hedging bets seems to be over. Then again, Menninger's retiring."

"Sounds like he's interviewing for a job with the Trust," muttered Wilder. "A lot think like Menninger, but none of the FSA states will go for Forsa. We've spent decades in Vermont figuring out where the limits go with sustainable biomass energy. This is nuts."

Crispus laughed a soft, sad laugh. "The country's angry and desperate and poor, and folks want to hear about solutions. His message will sell well in a lot of places. It's got the vision, the hope, the relief in it."

"It's a pig in a poke," said Wilder. "It's the feds, the Trust, and the oligarchs making a play to extend one more tentacle of control." They walked toward the lobby in the swirl of the crowded room. "You know, I read once that in medieval Europe, there were countries where every standing oak tree was the property of the Crown. The Royal Oak. For warships and things. Otherwise, people would have cut them down to burn or build with. The penalty was death. Sound familiar?"

Crispus nodded. "There are strategies... When's the FSA caucus meeting?"

"Strategies?!" Wilder snorted, ignoring the question. "The votes look bad. It's going to pass. The main question is whether the courts are up to this. Vermonters are going to go nuts."

"You're lucky you only have to deal with, um, less than a million hardy souls up there." Crispus chuckled. He was from Lake George, only a stone's throw from Vermont, where Wilder had spent lots of time. "I gotta get the attention, love, and money of no fewer than three million of my fellow New Yorkers, and this is going to piss people off to no end. Sometimes I wonder why I do this!"

"You do it because you're a good man," said Wilder, "and a masochistic maniac."

"With a huge ego," added Crispus. "And no brains... Except the part with the ego in it." They shared the private moment of needed levity.

"If I had brains," Crispus continued, "I'd have already moved to Vermont. Plus, you've got no shortage of electricity there." Wilder nodded. The brownouts had been worse than ever over the summer just ended.

"Congressman Crispus," called a blue-suited man as he approached them. They had been following the crowd up the steps to the door of the hearing room, and now stood in the jammed atrium.

"Christ," muttered Crispus to Wilder, and turned briskly toward the man with a guarded smile. "Well, Hamid, what good luck to run into *you* here!" The two started talking about some New York political issue, and Wilder patted Crispus on the back and made an opportune escape, threading his way quickly through the crowd towards a stairwell. He needed to catch up on emails and gather his thoughts for the FSA meeting later.

"Jake," called a woman's voice as he opened the door to the stairs. He turned to hold the door for her. It was Lucy Gavarino, smiling a broad smile and sort of skipping to move out of the way of an imaginary closing door, although he still held the handle firmly in his hand. He wondered if she wanted to discuss Forsa. But this was far from her mind. "Jake, I'm so *glad* I caught you. I've got some news and need some advice."

Lucy was a member of Bart Ross' staff, Ross being the junior senator from Vermont, and a Republican. She was a babe, pretty and curvy, not long out of Yale Law School and from some wealthy farming family up near Woodstock which had raised a lot of money for Ross.

"Hi, Lucy," he smiled warily. "Let's go up to the coffee shop. We can talk, and I need to send V-mail." It was one of the few privileged places in town where you could always get top-quality coffee these days, and not pay a fortune.

"Great," she said. They entered the stairwell, Lucy first. It was bustling with ascending and descending traffic. Wilder met eyes, smiling neutrally as he scanned the passing faces, and casting furtive glances at Lucy's trim fuselage as its neatly layered muscles rhythmically propelled her up the

81

steps ahead of him. Left, right, left, right. She was saying something about how busy the morning had turned out, and how she hadn't been back in Vermont for weeks. He caught little. The stairs teemed. And then, floating down the steps past him, he glimpsed Prokop Vulk, Laugherty's chief, and in a span of nanoseconds Vulk took a good look at Lucy, dilated in approval, looked Wilder full in the face, smiled knowingly, and was instantly gone in the cascade. Wilder shuddered, and then reacted in surprise at his own reaction. Vulk was a political enemy, mirthless and cold under normal circumstances. Wilder felt a little invaded. Vulk's hint of presumption was unwelcome under any circumstances.

"That Vulk," whispered Lucy over her shoulder, slowing down for a second. "Isn't he awful!" She had sensed it, too.

They finished their ascent of the two flights, and exiting the stairwell on the third floor, passed through an automated triple-scan security lock. As he waited for her to go through first, he watched her hair through the narrow window, the clean line of her chin and cheekbones, the triangle of her back and shoulders. Still thinking about Vulk, he felt torn between appreciation of Lucy and the discretion he knew he ought to show. But when the lock's far door closed behind her and the door on his side opened to admit him, his nostrils welcomed her spicy perfume.

"So, what sort of news do you have for me?" asked Wilder when he joined her on the other side. "And did you come here especially to give it to me?" He smiled with curiosity. From around a corner came the clink of dishware and eating utensils. His stomach growled, although lunchtime was still hours away.

"I was coming anyway, to cover it for Senator Ross, but we heard you'd be here from Moriah, so he asked me to pass this on personally." The keen smile left her face. She moved closer to him, and looked around to see if anyone else was near enough to eavesdrop. "This isn't anything we'd want going out publicly yet." Her voice fell to a whisper, and— spotting a camera up on the wall above the security lock—she started walking slowly toward the coffee shop, pulling him to follow her. "Senator Ross is going to announce later today that he is leaving the Republican Party and becoming an independent."

A low whistle hissed through Wilder's lips. "Good God." They were at the entrance to the coffee shop. He rubbed his chin. "That's great news. He's pulling a Jim Jeffords." He turned to her and grinned at her serious face. "Lightning does strike the same place twice!" Her earlier smile remained absent. "Guess it was time to remind the American people that Vermont can think independently. Jeffords was, what, forty years ago." She nodded. Wilder's smile subsided into a cautious frown. "This says a lot about what's going on these days. Might give our side one more vote in the Senate, but we're still eight short of the Republican-Homelander coalition. As a protest, it's one more straw. Hope the voters listen." His smile returned. "He's doing a brave thing, and will have to ride out a storm. Let's talk about how I can help. Want some coffee?" They walked over to the counter and picked up trays. Wilder looked at his watch and saw they only had fifteen minutes before the hearing resumed.

Over hasty coffee and scones, Wilder heard about Ross' anguish over the past few months, as he came to the conclusion he could not stay with his party. The pressure was intense to close ranks with the ultra-conservatives on the international loan issue, energy policy, and their biomass and oil positions. No matter what he tried to think, and no matter what bargains he and other moderate Republican Senators tried to strike with the right wing—accelerated forest "reclamation," for example, or yielding some ground on OSCIA—they simply refused to change their stance. The Republicans seemed to have completely succumbed to the financial strength of King Fossil and the oligarchs. Moreover, some of Ross' long-time colleagues were increasingly looking over their shoulders at the Homeland Front, afraid that the ultra-right-wingers might decisively grab the upper hand in patriotic rhetoric. When the majority of Homelanders at their summer convention had voted to endorse the Fort McMurray Declaration, many Republicans had been in a furor. But a central part of the Republican energy plan for two decades had been the oil from Canada's sands and shale to "keep the cars and trucks running," and now most of it was going to China, sent there by the Russian-Canadian consortium CanNeft. The Republicans were being squeezed from both ends.

In the midst of all this, listening closely to his constituents, Bart Ross found that he no longer recognized himself in the values and policies of his party. Fiscal responsibility, small business, market mechanisms—where had these gone? Vermont was not a coal state, and had—with many states in the North and along the coasts—moved steadily ahead with renewables and efficiency for decades. Solar power alone provided almost 25% of the state's electricity. King Fossil couldn't buy a Vermont politician the way it could buy one in West Virginia, Wyoming, Kentucky, or Texas. And the threats and appeals of the Homelanders did not carry much weight in Vermont.

It was, Ross decided, time to go.

Lucy ate the last pieces of her apple scone and drank from her coffee cup. Her hand shook slightly, Wilder noticed, and up close her slender frame looked gaunt. I wonder if she's doping, thought Wilder absently. It was hard to tell these days what complex mixtures of drugs affluents took to stay mentally sharp, combat fatigue and depression, and control their weight and appetite.

"Lucy, thanks for the confidential briefing. When's the announcement?"

"This afternoon."

"Here, in DC?"

"No. He went back up north yesterday. It'll be at his family's farm outside Rochester. At three PM. Or maybe in Rochester itself."

"So, who knows about this?"

"We're briefing you, Senator Rosen, the Governor, the Lieutenant-Governor, and a few others right around now."

"OK. I'll keep quiet. Need to get used to the idea. Thank Bart for his trust." He looked at his watch again. It was time to head downstairs. "We need to go back." They stood up. Wilder recalled her other request. "So what was this advice you were looking for?"

She laughed shyly as she placed her cup in a waiting tote. "Oh that. It's political but personal too." They walked back toward the security lock. "It's just this... Let's say that maybe I'll want to run for a state office down the road. Way down." She was blushing, choosing her words carefully. "My dad and uncles are going to absolutely shit when Ross leaves the party—they've always been Republicans—and I've decided to quit as well. So has most of the staff, mind you. But if I want to have any chances, should I stay independent or join the Democrats?"

"What about us Greens?" asked Wilder as the lock's door slid shut behind him, cutting off her answer. He looked into the scanner and held his palm up against the plate, and a voice said "Wilder, Jacob, Passed," as the door on the other side opened. After he exited, Lucy entered, and gave him a silent, perplexed smile through the narrow window of thick glass until it was her turn to walk through.

"Do I look like a Green to you?" she burst out, laughing.

He studied her for a second. "Sure. Maybe a different outfit would help. Something more earthy. More Dark Hill." She feigned shocked distaste. "But I'm sure your dad would prefer that to Democrat."

They both laughed again as they hurried back down to the hearing room. Wilder decisively tore his eyes from her departing back, forcing his attention back to the day's agenda. His mind was a whirl. The issues and politics were becoming crazier, tenser, more complex by the day. And with less than a month to go before Election Day.

11-CONTINUING INLAND

Saturday, October 20th (from Elizabeth City to Sunbury)

Mile after hypnotic mile the trio drove, the salt marshes and open flats of the coastal region slowly evolving into the pine and hardwood plain of the Tidewater. With such a level landscape, the horses merely walked, never having to strain up a rise or over a bump. The autumn sun beat down on the cab's roof, hot but no longer baking. They drove westwards on old Route 158, passing an endless open-air museum of the downfall of the era of cheap automobile transportation and oil-based agriculture. On the approaches to the small towns along the highway lay vast empty parking lots and desolate shopping strips, windows absent, plastic signs splintered by the wind, and every material and appliance of value long-since stripped from the structures. Weeds and grasses, turning brown in the October winds, grew thick along the medians and shoulders, and poked up through the fractured pavement. Traffic was light. A few wagons, traps, public-service cell-electrics, and military diesel trucks moved along the highway. Evidence was everywhere of depopulation and the crash in the tourist trade that had taken most of the people away from this flat, green country.

Mike was still reeling from the previous day's revelation. He was driving. Grandma sat beside him and Fernando reclined in the bed, dozing, his ancient AK-108 across his lap.

"Grandma," said Mike in a low voice, "I just can't get that golden apple out of my mind."

"Well, you've lived with it for a day and a half. Try fifty years." She sat swiveled toward him, her left arm over the seat.

"If it's about four kilos, then it's worth something like twelve million dollars!"

"Today, yes. Though it's a bit lighter than that."

"You could've made such a huge difference in everyone's lives. Grandpa Jack might have lived longer. You could own that market garden.

86

Hon's business might be different… And we'd be in a truck, not this wagon." He was not reproachful, just amazed.

She tutted. "Easy to say in hindsight. Don't know about Jack. He wouldn't have OK'd it anyway, not for his sake… And what's wrong with this wagon? You want to walk?"

"I just can't believe this had to wait until now."

"Mike, I suppose it looks this way now. I guess, well, during most of our life it represented a big asset, but gold was only, what, maybe thirty-five or fifty dollars a gram, so it was worth something like a few hundred thousand. Certainly a lot of money, but far less than our house in Chevy Chase. In the teens, around the time you were born, you'd have spent that for a minor addition. Things were very upbeat then. So we just left it alone." She blew out a deep sigh. "No one saw the past decade coming, honey, and then suddenly it was too late to think about coming down here on a whim, and the government put all precious metals under restrictions, and we have been so, *so* murderously busy just coping the past five years…" She patted his arm with a sigh, and smiled tensely. "Plus, once it was clear I had to come down here by wagon to get it, and sell it through the black market, I knew you were the only one who could help me. So I had to wait even longer."

"I understand why you need to move it from the island."

"Yes…" She hesitated and shifted in her seat, her mouth working. "If I hadn't, it might have gone to some beachcombers a few more hundred years down the line. Or divers."

Mike lowered his voice to a whisper. "How are you going to try to sell it?"

"Not exactly sure. You can do it piecemeal. Melt it or saw it into smaller pieces. Maybe you can help me with that. 'Course, maybe there are oligarchs who'd buy it as–is, since it's a work of art, too. Though that would be very, *very* risky."

"Any particular use for the money in mind?"

Grandma laughed grimly. "Mike, I'm feeling torn. One part of me sees entirely new businesses getting off the ground now, suited to the new situation, really seat-of-the-pants. There's no cash around, so entrepreneurs are desperate for capital. When I'm feeling optimistic and forget I'm so old and so far out on the edge, I think about investing in the future. The Emergency won't last forever, right? Huh?" She nudged him. "And even climate change will eventually flatten out...maybe." She laughed at the uncertainty of that idea.

"And when you're not...?" Mike faltered. "Not so optimistic?"

"Like when I start worrying about the election and about what happens if the Homeland Front keeps growing? Or if—er, when—Laugherty wins?" Grandma's words dripped cynicism. "Like when the debt-collectors come to the gate and want to come in and talk with me?"

"Yes."

"Well, then I start wondering about next moves... I wonder about where things are going to be most stable, safest - not only for me, but for you and your mother and sisters. And Lee and Asa." She looked into the distance, her tongue working at some unseen dental task. "I sometimes think about moving somewhere safer. And taking that pomador along with us."

* * *

During one of Grandma's spells at the reins, they saw what looked like a highway security roadblock far ahead, and got ready to drop the pomador for the first time. But, as they approached, they saw it was more of a command post or roadside camp. A sign in bright orange letters identified a set of buildings nearby as a DRR hurricane bunker. Coming to it, they slowed almost to a standstill, and a woman in a North Carolina state militia uniform jogged out from a van and held up fliers, offering them to the travelers. Grandma called the horses to a halt. "Hi," said the young woman, squinting up at them and shielding her eyes with a hand.

"Hey there," said Mike, his interest aroused. In the corner of his eye, he saw Fernando lounging in the bed, watching.

"Are you planning to return east anytime soon?" she asked.

"Only if you are," said Mike with a grin. The woman directed her eyes at Grandma for a more serious answer.

She's one of the good guys, thought Mike. Like the Corps and DRR, state emergency forces were always out there on the front line, trying with scarce resources to help the needy and provide relief in a time when many people barely scraped by, with no margin of security if a storm, accident, epidemic, or other catastrophe knocked them over. Hurricane bunkers like this one were located on high ground and staffed as needed from June to November—hurricane season—with stockpiles of relief supplies and reliable means of generating electricity and clean water, and of communicating with the outside world. Although DRR ran them, and the state agencies staffed them, the Army and IHC operated out of many hurricane bunkers as well, staging firepower there for the maintenance of law and order where federal interests were at stake. Down south, Mike had seen hurricane bunkers for whole counties that could accommodate thousands in safe albeit uncomfortable and often shabby conditions.

"No," said Grandma, taking over. "We're not returning east. We're eventually headed up to I-95, going to Washington."

"That sounds wise, ma'am. We just issued an evacuation watch today. Hurricane Rhiannon may come this way. If it does, they'll evacuate the low-lying areas."

"How soon?" asked Grandma.

"Few days to a week, depending on speed and direction. If it comes up the coast, in-shore."

"We last heard it hadn't even hit Florida yet," said Mike.

"That's expected tomorrow," said the militiawoman. "It's moving fast right now, and gaining in strength. That might put it here by about Tuesday or Wednesday. And they're predicting it will reach Category Four by the time it passes the Bahamas tonight."

"We'll be somewhere up in Virginia by then," said Grandma. "Further inland."

"Stay safe, and keep checking the news," smiled the woman. She backed away from the wagon, and her attention turned to a buggy approaching from their rear. They thanked her and drove on, each wondering silently how the storm might affect them, their horses, and their cargo. Mike watched the woman in the rear-view mirror as she fell behind them, her slight figure quick and erect in her baggy uniform. He liked her look. Then she was only a distant image, and then gone.

Fernando was up on the bench with them now. Grandma decided this was the right moment to tell him about the pomador, although not the real story.

"Hey Fernando," she began. "I need your help with something."

Fernando, who had been quietly studying the monotonous landscape, turned to look at her.

"We're carrying some contraband, and we're going to be doing some funny things with it, so I need to tell you and get you on board."

89

Fernando raised his eyebrows, a smile of curiosity breaking. Mike glanced at both of them, unsure. Grandma waited.

"OK, no problem," said Fernando. "You just tell me the procedure."

"Mike and I'll do the funny business. Just keep it under your hat. It's very important—a controlled narcotic, for a friend in need."

"Oh sure." Fernando smiled and shrugged. "I know all about that. No problem."

"I'll make sure I show my appreciation," said Grandma.

"Fine. You don't have to. You already have."

Grandma laughed and patted him on the arm. "I knew I could count on you."

Fernando looked back at the landscape, poker-faced but clearly pleased to be trusted. Mike took a deep breath, unable to shake all of his doubt.

Some time later, as they rounded a long curve, with the DRR bunker long vanished behind them, Grandma and Mike resumed plotting how to conceal the golden apple at the many Army and IHC checkpoints they would have to pass through. Actually tossing the pomador was likely to attract attention, especially if it landed with a thud. The trick would be to somehow lower it into place right behind one of the team's hind legs as they came to a halt, and then pull it up again as they started off. Mike, studying the harness pole, suggested that it would be less visible (but look entirely natural once on the ground) if it came down between the horses, between their legs. They pulled over, and while the horses took a good long drink that Fernando brought them, Mike and Grandma fiddled with the assortment of screw-eyes, clips, pulleys, and wires Grandma had brought along for the occasion. After several attempts, they rigged up something they thought might work. It was simple and robust, and merely involved releasing one monofilament line and paying it out about four feet until the golden apple lay inconspicuously on the ground in its hairy brown bag.

Standing in the bright light of day, and looking from an optimal angle, it was possible to notice the ball descend. From other positions, it was impossible to see the ball's movement. Grandma and Mike took note of these angles, and agreed that some diversion would be needed at times, such as hopping down to attach the horses' manure bags or fiddle with their harnesses.

Satisfied it would work, although nonetheless nervous, they drove on.

On a long straightaway a few minutes later, as the men dozed and Grandma drove, Mike's cell phone tinkled and vibrated. He snapped awake and pulled it from his pocket, setting it on his ear.

"This is Mike Kendeil," he answered. Then he saw his sister's ID in the display.

"Hon here, Mikey. How's it going?"

"Hi Hon. I'm sorry I didn't call you from the beach. Been sort of distracted."

"Where are you?"

"With Grandma. She's driving."

"Um, can I see you? Do you mind? It's blocked."

Mike unfurled the screen and clicked the video window. "Sure. See me now?"

Honorée's brown curls and small, pointed face smiled up at him from his lap. He could see she was in Grandma's kitchen. Something moved behind her, and he saw it was the top of Asa's head as he played on the floor. He strained to catch a glimpse of the nephew he had only met once in person.

"Yes. So, where are you and Grandma now?" The picture swayed as Honorée moved her T-pad and sat down at the counter.

Mike turned to Grandma. "Hey, Grandma. Where are we?"

"Heading for Sunbury," she replied. "NC."

"We're on the way to Sunbury, North Carolina. How are you doing, Hon?

"Oh, OK. You know. Good days and bad days. Market's hard work, very hard. The boys are both fine."

"How's Sanna?"

"I don't want to talk about her right now."

Mike wondered what this meant. Hon was definitely not the fragile or fickle type.

"OK. Well, say hi if that's in order. I can't wait to see you and the boys."

"Neither can I. Um, see *you*, I mean. It is going to be great having you back up here with us. Lee's thrilled. You're all he's been talking about since I told him."

91

"How's Mom doing?" Grandma glanced over at him and rolled her eyes.

"She's OK. Well, the same. She misses you. In her way." Honorée picked up Asa and his chubby face loomed beside her. "Look, Big Boy. See Uncle Mike?" The screen shook and a dark mass—Asa's hand—suddenly flooded the picture. "Oh Christ," came Honorée's voice from the darkness, and more laughing, and then, as light filled the picture again, Mike saw a flock-like pattern of flecks scattered across the video window.

"What's that I'm seeing now?" asked Mike.

"Jam. On the i-Ball." More jostling and rustling. "Just a sec." And then she wiped most of it off and Asa was nowhere to be seen. "Anyway, I've got to get back to stuff here, and you're on the road, but I just wanted to check in." She sounded stressed.

"I'm glad you did. Can't wait to get home myself! Things are so crazy. Been so long."

"So, what, about a week?" she asked. Grandma shook her head emphatically.

"No, Grandma's saying no," said Mike, his look alternating between Grandma and the cellscreen. "Longer." Grandma leaned over and tilted the cellscreen toward her face.

"Hi, sweetheart. I'm right here. I heard everything. We're going to be at least ten days on the road—so, the 29th—unless that hurricane slows us down."

"OK."

"Everything all right at my house?" queried Grandma.

"Oh, yes, everything is normal. Except those bill-collectors." Grandma frowned at Honorée's words. "I guess you're talking to Lon and the crew all the time anyway."

"Yep," said Grandma. "All the time. They keep me posted. But, if anything happens with the trash collection this week—like they don't show up again—then tell Lon to move it down to the market garden. How are they making out without Fernando?"

"OK, I guess. Well, ask Lon. I haven't heard anything, really." She stood up and the picture swooped again. "You both take good care. All my love."

Mike and Grandma waved and smiled.

"I'll call you again tomorrow." They finished their farewells and the cell phone and T-pads were switched off and put away.

A few long hours slowly passed. Fernando took over the driving so Grandma could catch up with her wholesale trading, and Mike took a short nap in the bed. Putting on her headset, Grandma opened up her red T-pad and swung the bat this way and that, reviewing what the bots had been up to since dawn, making adjustments, intervening to adjust contracts the bots had gotten wrong, and telling Marcus to buy eighty cases of tomatoes here, sell twenty drums of syrup there, deliver this to Tyson's Corner and that to Eastern Market. Grandma, Mike had reflected earlier, always found herself in the center of things, calling the shots, and it was no different today in the fruit and vegetable business than it once was in government.

"Where are we going to stay tonight, Grandma?" asked Mike later as they entered the outskirts of Sunbury. "Camping again?" Although they planned to stay at occasional motels and inns, doing it every night for two weeks was a luxury they could not afford.

"There's a good state park here," said Grandma. "Paddock for the horses and a security fence." She had the reins now, and peered ahead toward where several trucks and wagons seemed to be stopped in the road. Behind thin clouds, the sun was approaching the western horizon. "After the stories we heard on the way down, I'm not staying anywhere without solid security."

They came closer to the stopped vehicles. Soldiers were moving around the trucks—more North Carolina militiamen—and they had set up a roadblock and gun emplacement. A soldier waved them over and walked up to Mike's side of the cab. There was no sign of a scanner. Their poopador trick would not have to be used yet.

"Halt," was the soldier's brief greeting, delivered in a Carolina mountain twang. "ID in process."

"Certainly, Corporal," said Mike.

The soldier focused nearsightedly on this heads-up display for a moment, reading the results of the RFID scan. Then he stepped back and saluted Mike. "Captain Michael Kendeil. COE, 2nd Eastern Division, 4th Battalion, Quebec Company." He repeated the procedure for Fernando. He then glanced impatiently at Grandma as he realized she was not implanted. "Ma'am, please look this way." He pointed at a retinal scanner on his helmet.

93

She looked obediently at the scanner's red target above the helmet's visor. The soldier spoke a brief command into his communicator. He then faced them both. "And, your grandmother, Mizz Trudeau." Addressing them both, he continued. "What business brings ya'll to this stretch of road tonight?"

At first, Mike had thought the soldier sounded terse, unfriendly. Then he heard it simply as fatigue.

"We're moving my grandmother's things up to DC from the Outer Banks."

"Where on the Banks, sir?" the soldier asked.

"Head Island," Mike replied. "What's left of it."

"Mind if I take a look?" the soldier asked, nodding toward the bed.

"No, go ahead," said Mike. He was used to this, but wondered why the Guard had set up in this particular place. He watched the soldier as he circled the wagon, making a complete circuit and consulting his T-pad as he went.

"Seems polite enough," said Grandma quietly.

"I'm not so sure," said Mike under his breath. "There's polite and then there's indifferent, which is rude in my book. Things are tense enough these days without guys like this driving another wedge between civilians and the Army. Makes the COE's job that much harder."

"Still, it's rare and I never saw it on the way down. The state police are usually a lot worse," she whispered.

The soldier came back to the front of the wagon along. "Just a routine check, gentlemen, and Mizz Trudeau." His manner relaxed and rang slightly confidential. "There was a railroad holdup near Ahoskie early this morning. Two men shot dead. One of the terrorists was just caught at the state line."

"Hope you catch the rest of them," said Grandma. "Was it a robbery?"

"That's classified, ma'am."

"Government train?" asked Mike.

"Classified." Almost all the trains were military, except for the Energy Trust freights and a few private passenger companies.

"We'll keep our eyes and ears open, Corporal," said Mike.

"And by the way, folks," said the soldier, his eyes directed toward the men and away from Grandma. "That sure is a nice wagon you're drivin.'"

"Thank you, Corporal," laughed Grandma. "It's mine."

After they had been waved through, Mike turned the lights on, and they trotted now in deepening dusk. "You hungry, guys?" Grandma asked.

Both men responded with enthusiastic nods.

"There's a barbeque pit at that state campground, and I hope they're open tonight. Pork and chicken. We ate there on the way down. Very reasonable, down here in hog country."

"Sounds perfect, Grandma," smiled Mike. "Want me to drive now?"

"Sure," said Grandma, and handed him the reins.

"Travel sure was different in the old days, as far as eating went, wasn't it," reflected Mike. "We must have passed twenty fast-food ruins for every open food stand we've seen. People must have been eating all the time."

"You remember all that, don't you? All the overweight people?" Grandma looked sideways at Mike, her eyebrow cocked. "It wasn't all that long ago."

"Sure, in a way, but I wasn't driving yet back then, and … well, it does seem long ago, tell you the truth. Yes, it does."

"Not to me, Mike. It's like yesterday."

"You could just pull off anywhere and find hot meals, coffee, burgers," said Mike.

"You certainly could."

"Amazing how sensitive it all was to energy prices," mused Mike. "It must have seemed unshakeable."

"People stop driving. The traffic disappears. No customers. Running a kitchen gets expensive. Food gets expensive because it's got to be shipped. Heating and lighting prices jump up. Restaurants have to lay off, and close down. People have no work, so no money to spend. It's been one huge vicious circle." Grandma sighed. "But we all took it for granted while it lasted."

"Wonder how much of it will come back once energy gets more reasonable again."

"Some. Not all. You should have more answers than I do, Mr. COE," laughed Grandma.

"I guess I'm torn between the Energy Trust's propaganda and the reality most of the time," Mike admitted. "There's nothing as cheap on the horizon as gas was once, but we ought to get somewhere in the next decade with hydrogen, and the slurry lines have been going full-tilt since coal started getting top priority at the Trust." He pulled back on the reins to slow the horses. They were approaching a large intersection. "But politicians and bureaucrats make a lot of promises…"

Grandma frowned and looked at her grandson with a mix of accord and impatience. "Yes. Look what's happened with the district heating schemes. People are burning up whole forests waiting for those… It's going to take money—which there isn't much of these days—and political will. Not fancy rhetoric and nostalgia. I wondered about it for a while, but I made up my mind some time ago that the whole nationalization thing was a big mistake. The Energy Trust looked like the only way to get capital and brains to stop what might otherwise have been a process of runaway decline, not to mention climate change. But now it's so rigid, so closed, so corrupted. How many Trustees are there? Goldman Sachs, Rothschilds, JP Morgan, Warburg banks, UBS…. I don't know, others…"

Mike looked at her, interested, trying to follow her logic.

"I don't think that Congress really has any idea of what they're up to," she went on. "But the government couldn't function right now without some sort of monopoly control over the mines, wells, refineries, pipelines, power lines, and all that…" She fixed a distant look beyond the horizon. "Where would they get the money?"

"Straight?" asked Mike, interrupting her train of thought.

"Oh, yes, sorry. Go straight. I was getting off-track. It's about another mile. On the right. We'll see the big state park sign."

They trotted along the dark highway. Candles and lamps could be dimly seen through the windows of the outlying houses of Sunbury clustered along the road, but the woods and fields spread out behind them like black velvet voids. Yet in the fields, as they drove along, they began to see the little fairy lights of dozens and dozens of vegetable farmers working in the cool of the evening, tending the intensive gardens that lined the highway after the last searing rays of the autumn sun had vanished.

Grandma was silent for several minutes. She then spoke up, quietly and deliberately. "Mike and Fernando, when I was in my twenties, my grandfather—my dad's dad, John Lambert—showed me a picture from one of those old TIME-LIFE books, a street scene in downtown Boston from long ago, maybe around 1925. If I was in my twenties, then he was already in his eighties… He pointed to that Boston scene—a modern city already, but still full of horse-drawn carts, old-style billboards, really old-fashioned, although kind of like nowadays, too—and he said, 'See that picture? It looks like history now, but I was a grown man when it still looked like that, and I used to walk down that street and go to work in a publisher's right there,' and my granddad would point to a building in the photo… 'That was normal everyday life for me,' my granddad said. 'Like it would never change. And yet, today, that world is completely gone. Nothing left. If I go to that street—Commonwealth Avenue, by the way—there are different people there with different thoughts… Nothing left.'"

Fernando nodded and let out a grunt of agreement.

Grandma turned to Mike.

"That's exactly the way I feel today," she said. Only it's even more extreme than the interval from the 1920s to the 1980s, or, no, maybe not… Just as extreme, anyway. But on this highway and going up 95 and driving around DC and Montgomery County, I look around, and I can visualize the way it used to be on this street corner and on that side street, and you know, I can see it vividly right there in my imagination—the busy traffic, the manicured landscaping, the irrigated, lawn-mower-cut lawns, the air-conditioned department stores, the smells of the cosmetics departments, the high-pitched squeak of clothes hangers on the display racks…, the fancy latte shops, the busy strip-malls—but like my granddad Lambert said, it's all completely gone."

12-TRAIN RIDE NORTH

Saturday, October 20th (evening)

After a brief attempt to read some of the materials stuffed in his briefcase, Wilder gave up and dozed, his head uncomfortable in the seat's too-vertical headrest. It was not until they were well past the Delaware River that he re-emerged from what was less than a sleep and more than resting his eyes. The work and travel were taking their toll. He was seldom this tired, at least not since the violent Twenties when everyone was pushed to extreme states of tension and overwork. He sat with his eyes closed, feeling the faint rolling rhythm of the train, trying to recapture the sense of dread that the endless random terrorism of the Twenties instilled. He shuddered. That was a dark passage. He considered. At least isolation had bought them relative peace at home. Perhaps that lay at the heart of the Right's opposition to the aid package. Although it was misplaced.

Hushed voices whispered in conversation, punctuated by the occasional pneumatic squeak of the doors as passengers traversed the car.

"Next stop, Princeton," called the PA system after a series of soft, musical tones. "Doors open on the left side of the train. Please wait for completion of security procedures." He opened his eyes and sat up, arching his stiff back and breathing in deeply. His watch said 6:52. The woman to his right started packing her briefcase. "Thank you for traveling tonight with Eastern Railnet. We look forward to serving you again." The maglev train started to decelerate, passing from evening-dark countryside into the lighted streets and commercial districts of the small city. The deceleration intensified, and then suddenly the wheels took over from the magnetic field with a slight bump and sound and vibration rose up from below. With a final lunge and coast, the train stopped. After an instant of silence, the outer doors opened and passengers began bustling down the aisle. The woman beside him stood up, and without as much as a glance at Wilder, her bags clutched close to her sides, she left the booth and disappeared. He mused. She was in her forties, soberly dressed, neat, private. Who was she, and where was she going? Returning? On a business trip? With the ER trains far beyond the means of ordinary travelers, almost everyone on board now was either government or a member of the business oligarchy, and what each person was up to was a perpetual source of curiosity for Wilder. Riding this route as often as he did, he saw some faces again and again, hers included. But most remained closed and anonymous, blank from years of crisis and distrust.

The booth was now empty save for Wilder, so he moved to the seat by the window and reorganized his reading materials. He looked at his VR glasses and thought about calling Christine, but remembered she would still be in class. A few passengers boarded the train once a greater number had disembarked. One, Wilder saw in the corner of his eye, made for his booth. He nodded in curt greeting. The man was a middle-aged diverse, dressed in the height of andrometro fashion. He wore a cream-colored top-hat, which he put on the overhead rack, and a black velvet jacket with lace at the cuffs and a dark red quinlette between the shoulders in back. As he sat down, he cautiously returned Wilder's nod, and then his face opened and he exclaimed softly, "Why, you're the congressman from Vermont!"

"Yes," replied Wilder with a guarded, unprepared smile.

"Forgive my bad manners," said the man. "I don't mean to intrude on your privacy."

"It's perfectly fine," said Wilder, stifling a yawn, thinking it really wasn't.

"It's nice to see you traveling in a public vehicle."

Wilder relented a little, his curiosity warming. "I travel this way on purpose, not concealed in limos with tinted windows and guards and KP's - like most of my colleagues."

"Excellent!" said the diverse. "And the right thing to do. Politicians shouldn't recoil from the people." He laughed quietly. "In spite of all the terrible things they've done!"

"Who've done?" asked Wilder with concealed alarm.

"Oh, well, not the people, certainly," said the man. "They're always the victims!"

"You don't like politicians, then," suggested Wilder. The outer doors closed with a hiss and whump, and the train started moving again.

"Oh, no, no, no! On the contrary," said the man emphatically. "I love them. It's my work."

Wilder frowned with curiosity and waited.

"I'm a political scientist." They looked at each other. "Sash LeTourneau's my name." That rang a bell. "Here at Princeton."

"Right. You do the policy surveys," volunteered Wilder.

"That's right!" LeTourneau beamed. "How gratifying that you know my work."

Wilder relaxed and smiled. "Sure, I use it all the time. We do – the Vermont delegation." The surveys and studies from the Princeton Public Choice Institute had been backing up Democratic and Green positions for years. This academic was on his side.

"Keep them coming," Wilder added. "God knows we'll need all the sanity and balance we can get in the coming weeks and months."

"There's more to come," said LeTourneau. "We just published the loan survey today. The demographics are the most bimodal I've ever seen. Euroamerican men under forty with less than four years of college, for example, are 90% against the loan package. Women as a whole are 60% for it, with educated women over 80%."

"What's your personal position?" asked Wilder. This was interesting data.

"Oh, I don't really care anymore, although I'm certainly for it. For anything sane."

Wilder was surprised. He did not expect that. "Isn't this sort of life and death at this point?" he asked.

The train reached maglev speed, and with a lift and a surge the noise of the wheels receded and the cabin became quiet. They lowered their voices to almost a whisper.

"For many people, it actually is," reflected LeTourneau. "Truly." He looked down. "For my relatives in Chicago, for example. Very ill, hot, but too poor to move." He rubbed his eyes. "I suppose I have come to believe that rescue isn't going to come as easy as that – Brussels and Beijing swooping in to save us from ourselves and set us on the right path. We wouldn't manage it anyway… But even if we did, it's not really what we need, what we need to go through." He looked a long, clouded look at Wilder. "You might think that this sounds like one of those detached, head-in-the-sky academic notions, but Rome wasn't built in a day, and neither were China, France, or any other old state. Our dear old USA had beginner's luck and a big treasure trove, but we have a long way to go to become a *civilisation* [his pronunciation was French], and learning collectively through our energy and economic and military mistakes, horrible as the costs may be, is a journey we can't avoid."

"That sounds very gloomy, professor," said Wilder. "Fatalistic. Not what my constituents want to hear at all."

"You're from an enlightened state," said LeTourneau. "From among a special few. Minnesota, Oregon, Massachusetts, Iowa... But this is a huge country. Attitudes are deeply entrenched. Especially after all the troubles of the past forty years, the Decades of Decline... A lot of people know nothing else. They are furious, disappointed. There is real hardship."

They sat in silence. Then LeTourneau coughed and continued: "I'm pulling out for a while, anyway. Taking a *séjour*, you know?"

"How do you mean?" asked Wilder. "Out of the PPCI?"

"In about six months, the PPCI won't even exist. Our funding has been drying up, and our president just announced we'll be folded into the Department of Statistics." He laughed with irony and shook his head. "Statistics! That'll kill it dead."

"That will be a big loss for my staff," said Wilder with disappointment.

"I think the whole money thing is a sham," said LeTourneau. "That's not really it. The president's under pressure, maybe from Homelanders. We're inconvenient..." He looked out the window. A chill ran down Wilder's spine. "You know who Rick Chen is?"

Wilder hesitated.

"The defense lawyer?" LeTourneau pressed him, in a hushed voice.

He shook his head. He was drawing a blank.

"He defended the Philadelphia Six."

OK. Now Wilder knew. The guy who ran the defense for the civil rights demonstrators who got death for sedition.

"They arrested him last week, in Atlanta." LeTourneau looked intensely at Wilder, and then abruptly out the window. Wilder had heard nothing. There had been no media coverage at all. "He was defending some journalist down there who was being sued for libel by a prominent Georgia Homelander, and the Feds got him on violation of the Truth Disclosure Act." LeTourneau chuckled ironically. "He was trying to protect his client's Fourth and Fifth Amendment rights. Some people never learn…" He clicked his tongue against the roof of his mouth.

They rode in silence for a minute

"So, I'm going on sabbatical!" finished LeTourneau, brightening up. "Right now, in fact." Wilder saw he had quite a bit of luggage.

"Where to?"

"Humboldt University in Berlin," he answered. "They've got a wonderful global political trends unit, and I've always wanted to live in Berlin and resurrect my German. And Berlin is such an amazingly liberated place these days. A city of light, an island in the darkness."

"So are you leaving tonight?"

"No, next weekend. Seeing old friends in New York first."

"Flying?" asked Wilder.

Sash LeTourneau chuckled, and then shrugged. "Trains and ships I can afford. Planes and airships are exquisitely beyond my budget." He settled back. "I used to fly a lot, but I think I'll like the ship a lot better, anyway."

"Which one are you taking?"

"The Palanga. Do you know it?"

"No, never heard of it. Sounds exotic." Jake Wilder had not left the US since military service. Not that he did not want to. But the security situation, and then the soaring prices, and now his workload made it quite impossible. And he sometimes wondered if he would be let back in, with his political views.

"Lithuanian. It crosses to Le Havre in six days, and it's fully set up for work or play the whole way. Two thousand passengers."

Wilder raised his eyebrows and nodded, a polite well-what-do-you-know expression on his face.

"Quite a few with one-way tickets, I should imagine," added LeTourneau sarcastically.

The train sped across the flats of northern New Jersey, passing through better-lit areas with growing frequency. They were rapidly approaching Newark. LeTourneau sat in silence, looking out the window. Wilder opened his T-pad, and scanned the headlines. The Bart Ross story was getting some attention, but less than he expected. So what if a senator from a small state switches sides? It did not change the overall political math. Just another small gesture of disagreement with the overwhelmingly dominant trend.

The approaching hurricane, already lashing the Antilles with high winds, was getting more press. The news was oddly quiet about the Hedges campaign, with the election so near. He wondered if Hedges would go on the offensive, despite his dwindling cash. In contrast, the criticism and defensive responses of Morales were constant, major stories. Morales was a first-term lame duck, gamely struggling onward with the loan process, which increasing numbers of Republican and Homelander politicians and pundits were blasting. One right-wing governor, Kellerman of Oklahoma, had just gone on record at this week's state-wide campaign conference with the promise that Oklahoma would declare independence and spearhead a Conservative Confederacy if Washington took the money and accepted the terms. The photo beside this news story showed a huge stadium full of thousands of supporters cheering and waving flags as Kellerman delivered this ultimatum. Other politicians and pundits on the right were demanding that the Morales administration step down as soon as the November election took place, dispensing with the customary wait until January's inauguration and swearings-in.

Wilder's eye caught Laugherty's convivial face off to the side of a photo, in the background behind Kellerman. Ah. Laugherty is everywhere the rabble is being roused these days, thought Wilder. Smart man. The anointed candidate of the Republican Party, making sure that the rising populism does not get ahead of him.

The train's speed gradually eased, and it passed through a tunnel before its final approach to Newark. Emerging on a long curve to the southeast, Wilder caught sight of Manhattan, a curtain of lights across the Hudson River. He kept meaning to spend some time there, but always seemed to be passing through with no more than an hour's layover. The city was doing well, a hive of activity, both essential to and dependent on New England and the Mid-Atlantic region. While an almost continuous stream of wagons and trucks flowed into New York City carrying food and raw materials of all sorts, manufacturing kept expanding in the lower skyscrapers and warehouses of this strategically located metropolis. Clothing, electronics, tools, books, furniture, toys, housewares, vehicles, weapons, medicine - a thousand features of daily life - were again made here, benefiting from the low energy cost of everything being in one place, plenty of electricity, the staggering expense of importing, the vast skilled population, and access to land and sea routes for export. Balancing the road traffic were ships and barges of all sorts, landing at and departing from the miles of slips along the East and Hudson Rivers. And above it all rose thousands of windmills, harvesting the reliable offshore wind. Everyone seemed to have work in Manhattan, and food. Living space was getting harder to find. Renovation and infill development was expanding the better neighborhoods across the Bronx and Queens, and Harlem's ghetto-poverty was a thing of the past. Now, everyone was poor, but in a different, respectable sort of way.

Tens of thousands of migrants from abandoned suburbs out in Jersey and Connecticut – people with education and memories of affluence – continually added to the diverse dynamism of the Big Apple. The idea of "gentrification" had been replaced with "Jersification," as New York's Green mayor Hadrian Ashanti liked to humorously quip. Misery was never far from view, of course. Competition was tough among all the new migrants to the city, who usually arrived broke. An underbelly of money lenders, con men, and petty crooks preyed on their vulnerability. But the police and enough of a decency ethic among the populace kept it in check. What contributed to the general sense of security was the New Amsterdam Dike Complex, holding back the gradually rising ocean and its spring tides and storm surges. Building started in the late Teens, and now a system of dikes, gates, locks, and canals kept the Hudson moving past the city and the Atlantic safely at bay.

The stop in Newark was brief, and in minutes they were shooting beneath the river, toward the terminus. Passengers started gathering belongings, putting on jackets, and moving toward the doors. Midway through the Giuliani Tunnel, the train's wheels took over from the field, and with a final rumble and hissing of brakes it pulled into Penn Station.

"Good luck to you, Professor," said Wilder.

"And you, sir," said LeTourneau, taking his hand. "It was a pleasure talking." Placing his other hand on Wilder's forearm, his voice dropped to a whisper and a stricken look flashed across his face. "It's up to people like you now. I... I just couldn't stand it anymore. Academia's lost its soul."

Wilder shook his hand firmly. "My job is getting increasingly lonely. We need..." His voice caught, and he hastily covered it up with a cough. "We need as many thinkers and writers like you as we can get. Stay in touch."

They looked hard at each other. And then LeTourneau bent to drag his heavy bags to the platform, jostled and jostling, where he could clip them together and activate the propulsion. The passengers flooded out of the train, sweeping Wilder along. He hurried up into the main concourse, teeming with travelers and traders. In a few hours now, he would be home. He could not wait.

13-A MEETING OF THE PLAIN WORD

Saturday, October 20th (evening; arrival in Sunbury, NC)

"All that light must be around the campground," said Grandma. "Wasn't like that coming down, was it, Fernando?" Ahead, they could see the headlights of wagons and motorized traffic coming toward them from the west, and then turning left at an intersection. By the roadside and back among scattered trees were many lights—the orange of fires, the yellow of kerosene lamps, and the white of gas lanterns and electric light bulbs. Something big was going on at the campground.

"I hope we can get a spot and something to eat here," she continued. "Preferably a cabin. Looks like some kind of festival."

"Weird they don't let you reserve over the VNET," muttered Mike.

"Most places like this are first-come, first-served."

"A wedding party, maybe?" wondered Mike.

"Odd time for one. Well, it is Friday night—pre-wedding, maybe. Or maybe it's some sort of concert, or religious thing," Grandma speculated.

They drew closer, slowing down and passing a large green and black state park sign with an arrow pointing toward the right.

"I hear singing," said Mike. They all strained to listen over the horses' tread and crunching gravel.

"Maybe it's a camp meeting," said Grandma dryly.

They turned right, merging with the entering traffic. A trap full of smiling teenage girls let them pull into the queue. After a hundred yards, they slowed to a halt in the line of vehicles waiting to pass the gatehouse. Mike pulled up the brake, dropped the reins over their hook, and sat back, stretching his back and folding his arms above his head with a deep yawn.

"God, it will be nice to get down and relax," he said.

"COE spoiled you, driving around in air-conditioned cars and trucks all the time," laughed Grandma. "Now you're walking in normal people's moccasins."

106

"We have a lot of wagons as well, Grandma, although with my work you're right, we did usually get access to the motor pool."

"Very nice for some," she ribbed him. "Very nice."

"Um, Grandma," said Mike, changing the subject, "should we get the pomador ready? We're getting very close."

Grandma looked askance at him. "This isn't a federal checkpoint, you know. All they care about is weapons."

Mike felt a faint flicker of irritation. "No, I know. But wouldn't this be a good place to rehearse? We're not going to get too many dry runs."

She cocked her head, a smile of approval on her lips. "Why, I guess you're right. Good idea."

They schemed for a moment, and decided to simply lower the pomador quickly as the horses came to a stop. Mike would release the line. That way, in case it was necessary, Grandma could jump down simultaneously and create a diversion behind the horses with the dung bag.

The minutes crawled slowly by in the stalled queue. Mike and Grandma inspected the vehicles ahead of them, standing along the curve of the entrance road. They were a varied mix. Just ahead was a rough, home-made flatbed wagon on old rubber-tired automobile wheels, pulled by a single mule. The wagon was covered with young people, laughing and talking. Ahead of that was an ancient pickup chugging what was probably low-quality biodiesel, to judge from its smoky exhaust. Next were a couple of high-slung traps, an enclosed carriage, another flatbed wagon, a motorcycle with a side car, a whole flock of bicycles with pack trailers, and some more wagons – most of them the narrow, high-sided, roofed wagons used for local deliveries and contracting called "uprights". Beyond these were a recent-model silver cell-electric car and a large green diesel van.

The vehicles trickled past the gatehouse. Mike's and Grandma's turn finally came. When they drew level with the gate, Mike reined in the horses a bit too abruptly, and they stopped walking with a burst of stomping, shaking manes, and snorting. In that instant, he paid out the weighted line about five feet, and the pomador landed quietly in the dirt and gravel between the two horses' hooves. Of the guards and others standing nearby, no one seemed to notice anything. Grandma winked at Mike from the step. Fernando was impassive.

"What's the event tonight?" asked Mike, as an approaching gateman raised an old retinal scanner toward his face. Two guards in body armor and helmets stood by the road watching the vehicles, automatics over their shoulders and stunners hanging from their belts.

"Plain Word folks are having their annual state-wide meeting. We're the lucky campground this year," smiled the gateman, faintly. "Now, if you don't mind." He held the scanner level and its blue light flashed once, with a tiny beep.

The air carried the smoky flavors of barbequed meat. "Guess it means we'll eat well," replied Mike. "How long does it go on?"

"Oh, you sure will," said the gateman, answering Mike's first question. "They started yesterday, and they'll go 'til Tuesday." The gateman scanned Fernando, and then aimed the scanner toward Grandma. "You have a lot of questions, mister."

"So do I," said Grandma pleasantly, holding her face up to the scanner with just the faintest trace of self-consciousness—a typical reaction for the older generation, Mike reflected—almost as if she were being photographed. "How many people do you expect?"

The gateman shrugged. "Thousands. We've already hit two, and they keep coming." He glanced at the scanner, and asked, "Welcome to Millpond State Park, folks. Will this be debit?"

"I'll pay for it," said Grandma, "and it will be debit, yes." Returning to the questions, she asked, "Thousands? Do you have that kind of capacity?"

The gateman ignored her, and pulled out a security screener on a stand beside the gatehouse and positioned it alongside the wagon. He studied the display on his arm for a second. Despite Grandma's assurance, Mike suddenly felt nervous at the thought of the gold on the ground in front of him. Would they notice its unusual density?

"Y'all have three legal KP's, which you'll have to check here for your visit, and besides that you're clear." He tapped a button. "I just sent receipts to your accounts. Please hand over your pieces to this man."

Mike quietly let out the breath he was holding, and glanced at Grandma. Her face was deadpan. One of the guards came over with cloth bags. Mike pulled his automatic pistol from its holster and popped out the clip. Fernando stiffly handed over his AK. Grandma rummaged around in the storage box in the middle of the dashboard and retrieved an aged MAC-C22. They handed the pistols carefully over the guard, who dropped them into a numbered bag along with the assault rifle and took them into the gatehouse.

The gateman stepped back. "Go ahead, now. Y'all enjoy yourselves. Your spot is number sixty-three—full-size wagon and team space. Cabins down there are all full, but there's tent space. Go straight down there and take a right by the shower house. And use plenty of mosquito repellent. Season's not near over."

They started up, pulling the pomador back up as the horses started. "Wasn't too bad," whispered Mike. Grandma smiled and squeezed his arm. "I think we can get that into a routine." She nodded.

"Great awakenings," said Grandma ironically as they drove into the campground moments later. "Thousands of pilgrims..." All around were tents, campers, vehicles, picnic tables covered in food, fires, bright lights, and hordes of people of all ages coming and going. The woods were full of wagons and teams. The atmosphere was somewhere between that of a summer camp and a blue-grass festival. Music seemed to be coming from all directions, some of it fiddling and guitar strumming, some of it choruses of singers. There was no uniformity of dress at all. Visitors wore everything from modern go-suits to jeans to medieval capes and jerkins. What was striking was their racial diversity, but then, the Plain Worders were known for this. They had actively fought the growing racial segregation in the religious movements, the segregation in the stockaded towns and gated villages. Their "Eleventh Commandment" was one of the things that set the Plain Word apart. Indeed, Mike and Grandma had already seen it posted on a tree back near the gate: "You shall love your neighbor as yourself, and accept men and women from every nation who fear God and do what is right." For this reason, the Plain Worders were nicknamed the "Eleveners". All the mainstream denominations and most evangelicals considered this the worst kind of heresy, a desecration of Moses' Decalogue.

They passed under a large white and blue banner strung between two trees. It read, "Evangelical Church of the Plain Word of Jesus Christ Our Savior and Guide - Sixth North Carolina State Convocation." The road pitched slightly downhill, and passed a large cinderblock shower facility. Beside the road was a hand-painted sign: "No Plain Word Accommodations Beyond this Point—Non-Convocation Guests Only." They kept going, peering around at the site numbers for 63.

"There it is, men," said Grandma. "Right next to that cabin."

In a pine grove, a row of tiny identical white cabins stood by the gravel road, all with screen porches. Most were full to bursting. Light and people spilled out of them, screen doors opening and smacking shut. At the end of the row of cabins began a row of camper spots. Number 63 was just beyond the last cabin. They eased into the space, the tired horses disorganized and floppy, and Mike pulled up the handbrake.

"Nice, Grandma. Hitching rail, pasture, the works," said Mike. "But can't we try to find you something more comfortable?" He knew that would be hard, but the idea of his old grandmother roughing it in a tent next to him suddenly seemed inappropriate. Didn't she deserve a more comfortable arrangement?

"Oh, goodness. This is nothing, boys. I can handle much worse. If they had a free cabin, OK, but let's not worry now. Plenty of chances for luxury later on." Grandma stood up in the cab and stretched.

Mike jumped down from the bench and looked around. On the other side of the road was a paddock enclosed with a rail fence, a dozen roofed stalls situated along it. Several horses stood eating from a long trough near its gate. A sign read, "Hay $70 per bale. Multi-grain feed $100 per bag. Inquire at store. Open 7 AM - 9 PM." Under the sign was a water spigot and half a dozen wooden buckets.

"Not much room for our tent," said Grandma. "We'll have to pitch it right up against the wagon." She glanced over at the area ahead of the horses under the hitching rail, and gestured, "Or up there in the mud and horse poop."

"I'll sleep up in the bed," offered Fernando. "I got a netted bivvy sack."

Mike grimaced. The wagon's bed looked like a good option, bugs aside. "Maybe the neighbors won't mind sharing their side-lawn with us," he suggested. They looked over at the little cabin beside their spot. A strip of grass a dozen feet wide ran along the cabin's left side. In the driveway were parked the silver cell-electric and the green diesel van they had seen in the traffic on the way in. Electric lights were on inside. Grandma nodded with a shrug and a frown.

"I'll go over and ask," Mike continued. He walked carefully across the grass to the foot of the steps, and called up, "Hello? Anybody home?" There was no answer, no sign of anyone. "Anybody home?" he repeated. He saw a knocker on the door and started up the steps warily.

110

As his foot reached the second step, the door opened and two men came out. They started down the steps, almost bumping into Mike in the weak light, and stepped backwards with a start. There was a brief instant of tension.

"Sorry, sorry," said Mike, backing down and away from the steps. "I'm one of your new neighbors"—he gestured with both empty hands visible toward Grandma, Fernando, and the wagon, the horses still hitched up—"and we were just wondering if our tent could spill over onto your patch a little bit. Our wagon's pretty big and this was all they had left."

Cautiously but with apparent relief, the men both smiled and said it didn't matter—no offense. "We won't need that space. Go ahead and feel free." Mike detected a foreign accent. "We'll be gone tomorrow anyway. No worries."

"So will we, but thanks a lot," said Mike, trying to sound cheerful and reassuring.

Mike and the men parted and he headed back toward Grandma, who had Belle unhitched and was starting to walk her over to the paddock, following Fernando with Bill.

"What was all that chatter about?" Grandma asked with some irritation.

"Sorry, Grandma. First, I scared 'em so I felt a little embarrassed. Things were a bit tense."

"Well, help us with these horses so we can get some dinner. Can you bring Sherbet?" She crossed the gravel road, opened the gate, and let Belle loose in the remaining free paddock with Bill, watching the other horses' reactions beyond the fence with narrowed eyes.

14-CAROLINA BARBECUE

Saturday, October 20th (Sunbury, NC)

"Should we take turns eating and watching things?" asked Mike when they had set up the tent, finished getting cleaned up, and coated their exposed skin with a new layer of mosquito repellant.

"Oh, I don't think things could be much safer here," said Grandma. "You don't usually notice it, but this state park has a good reputation for security. And I'm sure the Plain Word folks are also making sure nothing happens with all these families here. We can relax. We'll just make sure the seat box is locked. Don't want to draw attention anyway."

"I can stay back for a little bit," said Fernando. "Gotta call Maria and catch up with some things."

"OK," nodded Grandma sweetly.

"You know," said Mike, turning toward her. "I feel a lot less secure out in civ life than I did with the Army. In the Corps, there are lots of security fences and guards and MPs and all that. You're armed all the time and there's nothing unusual about it. You almost never go anywhere alone. You forget what most people are dealing with."

Fernando and Grandma laughed. "See what I mean? Army made you soft, made things seem normal and orderly. Now you're getting to see how deep the crisis has gotten. Let's go get some dinner."

In the humid darkness—it was now past 8 o'clock—the crickets and katydids still sang their summer song, but there was an autumn dryness to the rustling of leaves and grasses in the light breeze. The temperature had fallen, and it had become a very pleasant night after the bright, muggy weather that day. Mike walked beside Grandma, wearing for the most part what he had ridden in. Grandma had changed from her heavy riding clothes into a long, woven cotton dress. Her riding boots had been replaced by light shoes. Over her hair, she had modestly tied a bright blue kerchief.

112

Leaving Fernando behind, they retraced their arrival up the gravel road, emerging into a slanted three-way intersection by the shower house. The throng of people seemed to be generally drifting toward the left fork, away from the entrance road. Mike and Grandma followed along, taking in the high-spirited atmosphere and feeling unexpected relief at being among crowds again. Alongside the road, upright after upright was parked, rows of tents behind them in orchard-like glades. In one meadow, a softball game was underway under the glare of makeshift towers of LED clusters. After about a hundred yards, they came to a wide field where lantern-bedecked food stands and picnic tables had been organized. The crowd spread out as it issued from the narrow lane into the large open space. Music and cooking smells filled the air, along with the tang of citronella.

"I said there'd be barbeque here," said Grandma with delight, "but I never expected this! All this food!"

They strolled along the stands for several minutes, looking at the options: barbequed chicken, barbequed pork, half-smokes, Thai food, Chinese noodles, veggie burgers, enchiladas... and more. Other stands sold tea, lemonade, doughnuts, pies, and cakes.

"The Plain Word must be: 'Chow'," chuckled Mike quietly to Grandma.

She laughed, but cautioned, "Don't get them started, now. They take it extremely seriously." She pulled at his arm. "How about that pork stand over there, Mikey?" They were drawn magnetically toward it.

* * *

"Where're you folks from, might I ask?" inquired a friendly-looking middle-aged man as they sat down at a picnic table with their plates loaded with pork barbeque, corn bread, coleslaw, baked beans, and hush puppies.

"Maryland," said Grandma pertly and pleasantly. "And you?"

"We came over from near Rocky Mount," said the man. He motioned toward what appeared to be his wife and a pack of pre-teens. Mike heard some trace of what might be a British accent in his speech. "What's the name of your flock?"

"Oh, I guess we're what you would call ordinary guests here – just traveling through."

"Great, great," the man smiled expansively. "Ours is the Red Oak Church of the Almighty. I'm the First Deacon there."

"Nice to meet you, Mr. First Deacon," smiled Grandma, taking up her cup of lemonade.

"Ephraim Skewe's my name, Mizz...?" answered the man, prompting her.

"Trudeau. Florence," Grandma replied. "This is my grandson Mike here."

Mike nodded, mildly cautious about the attitudes and politics behind the movement, and not inclined to an extensive chat with these strangers. The man seemed to be in the mood to talk, however.

"Well, Florence and Mike, what do you make of all this business?" Ephraim Skewe waved around at the crowded tables, stands, wagons, and lights. "This gathering of the tribes. This your first one?"

"Very well-attended," smiled Grandma.

"That is the very darned least you could say about it, Mizz Florence," said Ephraim Skewe with emphasis. Mike noticed how rotund he was as Skewe sat up higher on the bench and took a drink from his cup. "I would say—and I've been with the Plain Word since early days—that this is a, um, no, an historic moment. Right here and now. We've reached some sort of critical mass this weekend, here in Sunbury. Never been near as many folks at the annual camp. Last year, we barely hit three thousand. Election's a big reason."

Mike and Grandma made vague body signals of appreciation and awe.

"And do you know how many faithful souls the Virginia Regional called together last month, in Lynchburg?" continued Skewe. "One hundred and sixty thousand! One hundred and sixty thousand faithful souls. There myself. Praise God!" He shook his jowly head. "Things are starting to get very interesting." He smiled at them benevolently. "I don't know what you folks believe in—not my business at this moment—but 'Watch This Space', as they used to say. "Watch this space."

"You have certainly put together a nice meeting here," said Grandma pleasantly. "Seems very safe and well-organized. Wonderful food." Mike was silent, wondering how to avoid being proselytized to so he could enjoy his dinner.

"Thank you, Mizz Florence," said Ephraim Skewe. "Thank you. This nice get-together is great—something we all need to keep up our work— but there is so much madness and evil at work in the world today that we're going to have to multiply our evangelism and ministries a thousand times if we're going to have any impact. You, sir…," said Skewe, looking at Mike. "What did you say your name was? And what was it you said you do?"

"I didn't say," said Mike. "My grandma did. But since you asked, I just ended active duty in the Army Corps of Engineers. And I'm Mike."

"Oh, yes," said Skewe, his eyes shining. Mike wondered what to expect. "Yes, well, Mike, you're trying to keep things together, aren't you? Clean drinking water and heat for our homes. Keeping the bridges from washing out."

"We're doing what we can," said Mike warily. Skewe's tone was not sarcastic, nor was it patronizing, but Mike detected skepticism and strong opinions.

"Sure you are, Mike. Most of you are good people." Skewe looked as if he were about to get up, but then leaned forward and put both hands palm-down on the tabletop, as if steadying himself. "But if you have a chance while you're here, come listen to the Plain Word. Whatever your faith, you have to admit that the times aren't what they used to be, and the plain truths of Jesus Christ lay bare to the bone the errors of so many of our ways, from 3V and th' VNET to drugs to GMOs and genetic enhancement therapy, not to mention abortion, homosex, sex changes, and all the things us faithful have been battling for decades." His smile was gone, replaced by a look of grave urgency. "Bare to the bone! And what we've been doing to the environment and our fellow men around the world! We were heading for a come-down of Biblical proportions, and now we've arrived at the threshold."

15-SAFELY HOME

Saturday, October 20 (evening)

Jake Wilder slept as the train crossed the Connecticut border and skimmed up the string of cities in Western Massachusetts. The foreign maglev drive was as smooth as silk, the only system of its kind installed in the United States during a bygone era of public optimism and support for bold energy-efficient, carbon-neutral infrastructure. Wilder never awakened during their brief stop in Springfield. Brattleboro lay ahead, a half-hour away. It was only when the conductor touched his arm and spoke that Wilder's consciousness returned. He sat up with a start, adrenaline clearing his mind. For a second, he was afraid he had overslept and passed his station. That had happened before.

"Brattleboro, Vermont, next station," the conductor said. She moved down the aisle and touched the arm of another sleeping passenger. From the silence, Wilder could tell that the maglev was still on. That gave him a few minutes to wake up, use the toilet, and get his things together.

It had been over a month since he was last home. Because Naegel had dropped out, he was running unopposed, so it took the heat off his campaign. Policy matters and politics in Washington were all-consuming, anyway. It was a blessing. People wanted him working, focusing on the latest threats in Washington. Since the New Haven Compact was signed, there had been an uneasy truce between the states, the Energy Trust, and the private timber companies. Only a few skirmishes had been reported. The case was slowly winding its way toward the Supreme Court. Wilder knew that there was only a slim chance that the FSA states would like the decision. And Forsa could speed things up very abruptly if it passed. What on earth would happen then? A very serious crisis would ensue—there was no doubt. When the Compact was signed, some in the media reacted as if war had been declared. He glanced at the date on his watch. Yesterday. That was the two-year anniversary of the New Haven Compact. What a wild term it had been. Wilder thought about the stress he would have faced if this had been a tight campaign, like 2038. But, then again, he would have been spending more time in Vermont, with Christine.

The overhead lights became brighter, the maglev was switched off, and the train started its rattling, hissing deceleration. There were few people left on the train, and fewer still who stayed in their seats, bound for White River/Hanover, Montpelier, Burlington, and Montreal. The guards took their positions inside the doors, their automatics ready. The doors swung open and were retracted into the car's fuselage. Dimly lit, the platform was fairly crowded, with many more passengers waiting to board than disembark—the Friday night business crowd heading home to Montpelier and Burlington for the weekend. With its proximity to Massachusetts and southern New Hampshire, Brattleboro had turned into a key regional center for trade in what people needed in the more densely populated parts of New England: firewood, charcoal, pitch, cut stone, lumber, milk, cheese, vegetables and fruit, cured meats, maple syrup, wool, and cloth. Now, with most foreign imports banned or exorbitant, and more distant US products so costly, regional supplies were very competitive. At this junction of highways, railroads, and the Connecticut River, with abundant renewable electric power and a growing bioenergy complex near the old nuclear power plant just to the south in Vernon, commercial business was brisk.

Stepping down from the car onto the platform, Wilder felt the warm, balmy October air hit him. The night was full of animal sounds, down here by the river: crickets, katydids, tree frogs, bats' clicks. Christine came at him out of the darkness, a smile on her face. They kissed and caught one another in a wide hug. The train's doors hissed shut behind Wilder, across the platform.

"How's my darling, then?" she asked. "Tired?"

"I slept most of the way after New York," he answered. "Just woke up. Feel like I left my brain on the train."

"Brain on the train, train on the brain!" Christine giggled. "Nice you've arrived this time all alone, just for me, no traveling journalists and staff."

He smiled back. "I'm tired of all that. Need to start separating private and work life a little more."

She picked up one of his bags, took his arm, and pulled him toward the steps. "You're in the wrong business, honey," she teased. "Let's get you out of here before a journalist spots you."

"Or a Homelander sniper," he muttered, immediately regretting his cynical remark. He glanced at her face. She did not glance back. They were walking through the overpass tunnel now.

"OK, no depressing stuff tonight. All right? You can save that for the campaign meetings." They both laughed at that idea. "Miss me?"

"You know I did. That was the longest month." Coming out of the station, they could see Callie standing down by the street, hitched to the trap. She was flicking her ears around, swinging her head and eyeing the pair as they approached.

"So, how about a nice relaxing drive home? We can get re-acquainted. I brought a thermos of tea and some cake the Resnicks made for the school bake sale." She opened the trap's trunk and pushed the bag she was carrying in. Wilder swung the larger bag in after it.

"Tea? From where?" he asked.

"Secret sources. If I tell you, I'll have to kill you."

"Forget I asked." He feigned exaggerated fear, but then felt instinctively uneasy as well. Only a joke, he reminded himself.

"It's from Boston. Doug Whitting was down there for weeks and brought back a load of things he bought at the dock markets."

They climbed up into the trap. Christine released the brake and Callie high-stepped away from the curb. She clicked to her, speaking softly, and shook the reins.

"How's Callie, by the way?" Wilder recalled their conversation earlier—it seemed like days ago already.

"They did a blood test and she's clean. Said it looked like a bot-fly nest, but there was no infection beyond the immediate sore." He peered ahead to see if he could spot it. "You can't see it from back here. It was pretty yucky-looking. The vet cleaned it out, gave her antibiotics, and updated her shots. Which cost a fortune, by the way. Three-hundred allens."

"Except for the cost, that's a relief," he said. "What did you do?"

"Didn't pay cash," she said. "Dean came over and we took Rambo to slaughter. The vet took some of the mutton."

118

"That was smart," said Wilder. "But could we spare him? He wasn't that old."

"Rambo?" said Christine in surprise. "He was at least eight or nine. Anyway, we have two other rams and can always stud one of the neighbors' if we run short."

"Moment of silence for Rambo, then," said Wilder. "Gave his life so a horse might live."

"Mmm," said Christine. "There's more and more to worry about with horses' health these days." She guided the trap up Bridge Street and right onto Main Street. "But lose a horse like Callie and you're really in trouble." Living in a village outside Brattleboro without good horses and the requisite trap and wagon meant you were cut off from both work and shopping. Unless you were rich enough to maintain a cell-electric or diesel.

"Speaking of creepy-crawlies," she continued, "I heard of a boy in Putney recently who was diagnosed with hookworms. Very sick."

"That's a new one."

"Hard to keep up with the changes." They leveled out at the top of the hill leading up from the river, and trotted north down the empty street. The warm night air smelled of dung, tar, hay, and wood smoke. Two cats raced across the street in the darkness.

"Want that tea, Jake?" She hooked the reins over the footboard's rail and reached down into a basket beneath the seat. "Callie knows where to go."

"Sure. Really nice touch, Chris." The trap's rubber wheels bounced along on the broken asphalt road, gravel softly crunching, and then with a bump climbed up onto new stone cobbles and assumed a quicker rhythm. "Looks like they're making quick progress with the re-paving."

"Oh," she glanced down. "Look at that. They're already at High Street. I hadn't noticed."

"The pavement was getting really bad."

"I know. Can't get asphalt anymore. Some back streets are all heaved up, even after a summer, and the mud gets awful."

"This is looking nice."

They settled back into silence. After a while, she broke it. "Jake, what's wrong? You're more than tired, aren't you?"

"Oh, yeah, well, things are crazy and tense enough as they are, you know... Had a sort of depressing conversation on the train... I met a

119

Princeton professor we've gotten help from before, a diverse named LeTourneau. He's leaving the country. And he told me that Rick Chen—you know, the Philadelphia Six's defense attorney—was arrested for breaking the new client disclosure law."

"Where's he going?" she asked. "The diverse."

"Germany."

"What, permanently?"

"Maybe. Sounded open-ended. But it also sounded like he's leaving because he's scared, because he's written enough stuff now that he feels out in the open and doesn't feel safe anymore."

"I've heard other stories like that."

"Me too."

Christine took up the reins again to help Callie negotiate a turn. "The Ghoshals went to Canada. She was Canadian, of course. And Yolanda what's-her-name, at Smith. A bunch of U-Mass faculty went to the UK. I wonder what the statistics are?"

"The media're staying away from it, so it's hard to get any overall facts. It's always been there, for years. Can't say when I first started noticing it... Thinking about it..."

"No," She yawned. "What was the rest of your day like, baby?"

They passed the next mile with Wilder's summary of the day, a day with several surprises. He talked and she listened. Once, a town trolley bus came humming up behind them, passing as Christine moved Callie closer to the right-hand curb. Few passengers rode the bus this late at night.

Within twenty minutes, they were at the north gate by the interstate exit. The gate stood open, and a guard sat in a booth, watching traffic. He nodded with familiarity toward Christine and Wilder as they slowed to pass through.

"Hello, Scott!" she called.

"Have a good evening," they heard him call back.

Although Brattleboro had no stockade or perimeter fence, they were more on their own now, out in the open country between gates. The roadway was unlit there, and there was little traffic.

"Things still safe around here?" Wilder asked. Spending time in DC sharply increased his awareness of crime.

"Oh yes, no incidents at all." She sounded genuinely relaxed about saying that. "Just the usual family tragedies. Quite a lot of nasty stories coming from further south, though. A lot of hold-ups, especially on the interstate. Stealing cars and horses."

"I'll bet it still has a long way to go to catch up with Washington."

"I hope we never do..."

"Wonder what the security situation is like down in Northampton and Springfield, and south of there?"

She shook her head. "Don't know. I'll ask Marta the next time I talk with her. Don't think it's too bad. Lots of neighborhood groups and militias. Local stockades."

"Chad Urizo has been using the Connecticut situation a lot in his House speeches. Condemns it and blames the Republicans. In Hartford and south it's like an archipelago of stockade islands but you take your life in your hands in between."

She made a little "hm" through her nose. "New York seems to be OK. Wonder why it's so rough in Connecticut?"

"Urizo calls it the 'suburban post-depopulation wasteland'. When the companies like GE fell apart, and the financial markets and insurance companies, and nobody could afford gas, all those places like Meriden and Fairfield went into free fall. The small towns and the big cities have been the winners."

She mused. "Seems like ancient history already. I've gotten so used to this life, it's hard to keep it in perspective..."

"You're just enough younger than I am, Chris." Wilder was 51. She was 41. "I was born in Eighty-nine—the year the Berlin Wall went down. I was already a teenager during the Younger Bush administrations. Drove a gasoline car, went to the malls, flew around in jets. I was in college during the New Energy Plan. I remember the boom in the late-teens. What year were you born, again, Chris?"

She laughed. "Wasn't born again! You've been spending too much time down in the Bible Belt. I was born once, and that was enough. Least that's what my mom said."

He chuckled, relaxing in her laughter. "You know what I mean."

"Ninety-nine. Don't you remember my NID number?"

"Of course." He rubbed his eyes. "Must be my tiredness." He recited her national ID number. "One-nine-nine-nine-oh-nine-twenty-one dash A-oh-six-B-L-L-ninety-eight."

"Spoken with true devotion," she laughed again.

121

"So, Chris, 9-11 and Iraq and Hurricane Katrina were all when you were a toddler. They were old-fashioned days. But those were just the prelude. And then when it all hit the fan you were passing all the milestones of adulthood for the first time. But being an adult had already settled in for me when Sanderborough happened, for example."

"I was twenty-two...I think that's really when I grew up. Overnight."

"What a welcome to adulthood." He sighed a deep, long sigh. She took his hand and held it.

They drove onward through dense woods and pastures, making for the south-east Dummerston gate. Moths and beetles spun and flopped around the trap's headlights, and a fox leapt across the road in the darkness at the far limit of its beams.

"How about this business with Bart Ross?" asked Wilder, breaking the silence.

"I know. Boy." Christine had heard about it instantly, well before Wilder called her.

"Lucy Gavarino—," Christine wrinkled her eyebrows in non-recognition, "—you know, Ross' aid...Well, she said he'd go independent."

"Really?" Christine chuckled.

"Guess that's all he told her." Wilder yawned. "Maybe she couldn't think beyond non-partisan political independent. Her family is very conservative, old-line..."

"She must have had quite a shock. Unless she was keeping it secret, too."

Wilder put his arm around her shoulders. "These are wild times. It'll send a signal to a lot of people that secession is something to take very seriously this time around." He laughed a faint puff through his nose. "Imagine a US senator going back as a member of the Green Mountain Party to a Congress he doesn't even want Vermont to be a part of... And he still has two years left in his term. Wonder if we'll still be there, then."

"Do you think the referendum will pass?"

Wilder paused to reflect. As the separatist movement had gradually gotten stronger over the decades, he had watched it with a mixture of fascination and bemusement. His party, the Greens (and the Progressives before), had never adopted the separatist position. No party had, besides the GMP, which was a one-issue party. The advocates of the Second

Vermont Republic always seemed like such an odd mish-mash of dreamers, idealists, and eccentrics, from utopian libertarians to born-again socialists. The activists were mostly professors, writers, and off-the-grid individualists. They had little apparent support in the business community or political mainstream. Chance comments now and then, however, made Wilder wonder whether there was more closet support for the GMP among the mainstream than polls and party positions revealed. The referendum to create a state convention to pursue secession was up now for the third time in a dozen years. The separatist rhetoric had gotten bolder and more caustic as it rode the enormous wave of dissatisfaction with the economy and civil liberties and states' rights.

"Maybe it will pass, but somehow I don't think so," said Wilder. He turned to Christine. "Don't you think people are going to give Hedges and the loan process a decent chance?" He heard the note of doubt and uncertainty in his voice. "Laugherty is not the guaranteed winner. There is an awful lot we have at stake in the US and our part in it. Even if Laugherty wins, right-wing governments come and go in cycles…"

Christine took a deep, slow breath. "Maybe it's because I don't have the long perspective you do, darling…" She looked into his eyes. "I mean, China and the EU might prefer to lend to smaller units anyway. I guess I worry that our stake in the USA is costing us more than it's worth… Anyway, how could Laugherty NOT win at this point?" She clicked and talked to the horses as they slowed to negotiate a small washout along the side of the road.

"Statehood sure doesn't come for free," he said quietly. "And you don't always know what you're going to get in return anymore."

16-INCIDENT IN SUNBURY, N.C.

Sunday, October 21st (morning)

Echoing through the early-morning forest, mingling with the dawn chorus, came a swell of women's voices holding a high chord in haunting harmony. The sound trailed off and vanished. A slight puff of wind moved the tent's fly. A blue jay yelled nearby. And then the haunting choir rose up again into a crescendo, shifting from minor to major key. Mike lay quietly in his sleeping bag, hands clasped beneath his head. The singing stopped, and he heard clapping and distant shouts. It was barely light.

"Doing their morning devotionals, I imagine." Grandma's hoarse voice came from deep in the sleeping bag beside Mike. "Matins."

"It's pretty amazing, Grandma."

"Nice to wake up to, I guess." She coughed and changed position, a slipping of very old nylon against itself. Mike watched the silhouette of an earwig scrambling along one of the ridgelines of the tent, under the fly. He felt extremely comfortable, neither warm nor cold. "But it's only people," added Grandma. "Not that band of angels a comin' to carry us away. Not yet, anyway."

"You're such a cynic, Grandma."

"What? Are you a convert now, too?" Florence Trudeau was secular to her core, from a long line of skeptics with Roman Catholic roots somewhere back in the past and low-key Protestantism ever since. Mike felt the same way—feeling no pull from the ever-spreading evangelical movements of the times—but he was intrigued by the faith so many people he respected seemed to display. Especially in the Corps.

"What do you have faith in, Grandma?" he ribbed her.

"Grandson, I have faith that, after some breakfast and strong tea, my back and neck won't continue to feel like rigor mortis has already started setting in. Always works."

"Ha!" Mike laughed. "No, seriously, what do you believe in?"

124

"I believe that some folks are drawn to organized religion and some aren't."

"A lot more of the former than the latter, Grandma. A lot more." Mike stretched long and deep, and listened to the avian dawn chorus rising toward its own peak. His watch beeped. He looked at it: six o'clock. "It's six," he said.

"Mmm." She sat up with a grunt. "Mike, I keep wondering about what's exceptional these days and what's just more of the same. Some of the situation is exceptional—the climate change, the Emergency, the global political situation—but all this religious upheaval is just America being America, I think. I'm no expert but our history is full of utopian experiments, tent revivals, traveling preachers, miracle workers, back to its beginnings. They've always been predicting the end of days and gathering lots of followers..." She started organizing her clothes and rooting around in stuff bags. "And you'd have to look in the history books for the details, but this isn't the first time America's suffered economic depression, political division, and upheaval... I just hope I live to see things start turning around."

"Well, there's something you have faith in, Grandma." Mike smiled. "That things *will* turn around."

She laughed, and coughed again. "Sure. OK. They will and you'll still be young enough to enjoy them. I envy you."

"If I live through whatever's coming."

"Now that's a dark thought from such a promising young man!" She looked at him with a frown. He frowned too, and shook his head.

"Sorry, Grandma. That was bad attitude talking. Baditude."

"That's right. Where's your military training? Now get out of here, go help Fernando feed and water the horses, start breakfast, and show your old Granny some consideration!" They both laughed.

Horses were seen to, and camp was quickly broken. All around them, the campground came to life as the light brightened. Screen doors smacked shut. Voices murmured in tents and called across campsites. Horses whinnied. Dogs barked. Axe-chops echoed from the kindling lots. Wood smoke snaked through the clearings. Pots and buckets banged. A baby cried down the row of cabins. Engines started in the distance, and more singing could be heard through the pine woods.

One of the campground's uniformed staff came strolling along, inspecting the activity as he passed each campsite.

"Morning," said Mike.

"Morning to you." The man looked around at the scene. He was of medium height, slightly heavy, with a nose like a pig's, but a kind mouth and eyes.

"Headed out today?" he asked.

"Yes," replied Mike.

"Well, I hope you beat the storm. Today's the—," he looked at his watch, "—the twenty-first. How long will it take you to get home?"

"A little over a week." Mike mused on the weather. "Any news about the hurricane?"

"Sure. Supposed to hit Florida tomorrow, somewhere around Miami. It's called Rhiannon now. Incredibly powerful. Apparently has missed the islands and been out at sea, but its storm surge is big."

"Hmm," said Mike. "I guess we'll head inland, maybe. Are you pretty safe here?"

"I hope so. There's a hunker not too far away. They're calling it a Category Five-plus. Only the, uh, third of its kind."

"Been one heck of a season," said Mike. "You should see what the Outers Banks look like."

"I doubt there'll still be banks left after this one comes through, given what they're saying about it," said the man, shaking his head. "Hope it goes out to sea."

Mike glanced over his shoulder, and saw Grandma leading Belle out of the paddock.

"Thanks for that update," said Mike.

"No problem," said the campground man.

"Mikey!" Mike heard Grandma calling discretely from somewhere behind him. He turned around. She was already hitching Belle to the wagon.

Mike headed back to Grandma. She raised her arms impatiently and shook her fists, but her face was smiling.

"That guy was talking about the storm," Mike said. "Starting to sound serious."

"We have a long way to go today, and you're off chatting about the weather."

"OK. If we get overtaken by a monster storm, then you owe me."

"Hm," said Grandma. "Monster storm."

"Jeezus," laughed Mike, going back to packing up and stowing their camping gear. "You are so skeptical."

"Disrespectful boy! Who brought up your mother?!" She shook her head disapprovingly. Then she laughed. "Oops. I did!"

They packed rapidly, and saw to the horses, making sure they were fully watered and that their feed bags were full. When all was ready, Grandma took the reins for the tricky process of backing up the team a wagon's length so they could exit the parking spot and get turned around. Mike stood behind the wagon to help guide it back and to warn pedestrians. Fernando stood back a ways, holding Sherbet's rope. The horses stepped gingerly backwards and completed the maneuver. Fernando attached Sherbet, the men jumped aboard, and Grandma started the wagon toward the front gate.

Coming out of the area reserved for ordinary travelers and campers, they slowed to nearly a standstill because the narrow gravel road past the turnoff was packed with Plain Worders, all solemnly moving in the same direction, back toward the meadow where they had dined the previous evening. Most were dressed in simple white and brown robes, and many were singing a low hymn and carrying cumbersome-looking crosses and icon-like displays. The lightheartedness of the previous evening was entirely absent.

Mike and Grandma looked out over the throng and waited. After a few moments, an opening appeared, and they moved out into the road they would have to share with the crowd for about 30 meters. The horses acted nervous, surrounded by so many people.

"Mike, could you get down and lead them, and try to keep folks from pressing in too close? Belle and Bill are city horses, but this is more than they're used to. Fernando, go back and see how Sherbet's doing, will you?"

Mike and Fernando hopped down, walking among the crowd and encouraging the Plain Worders—especially the kids—to give the horses some space. They rolled along like this for some distance. The singing droned. Then, the crowd halted – some delay far ahead—and Grandma called the horses to a stop. At this moment, Bill decided to urinate a large volume down among his and Belle's legs. Belle pranced, and drops splashed out among the bare legs of the crowd. People jumped back—some with yelps, some with surprised laughs. The delay lengthened.

Looking down, Grandma noticed a knot of teenagers and young women talking and glancing over at the wagon. One of them called up to her, "Y'all's supposed to be on foot, not bringin' the whole household with ya." They smirked, and a few others turned to stare. Grandma knitted her brow and pursed her mouth. Mike was trying to think of something disarming to say when the same girl continued: "And why're y'all leavin' now, anyhow? We're just startin' the praises."

"We're just starting, too," answered Grandma. "We only left yesterday and we've got more than a week of hard hauling ahead."

"And with a hurricane chasing us," added Mike.

The banter had no softening effect on the girls. "Maybe y'all ain't Christians, are y'all?" said one. They looked expectantly at Grandma.

"'Course we are." That surprised Mike mildly, but this was no time for a debate about what "Christian" meant. The dense crowd around the wagon was quiet, observing.

"If y'all were honest Christians you wouldn't be leavin' now," said a woman on the other side of the wagon. The girls laughed slyly.

"Yer heathens," shouted a girl. "Chevy Chase Market Garden," she mocked, reading the wagon's lettering. "Yer the Devil's do-helpers," she yelled, and kicked gravel up toward the horses' flanks.

"Easy with the horses," said Mike quietly, who stood closest to the girls.

"Devil's doers, Devil's doers," chanted a couple of the girls, and then the whole group chimed in. A man tried to speak with them, but their chanting grew louder and more determined. The crowd, beginning to move again far ahead, was a sea of diverse expressions: fear, curiosity, approval, disapproval. A few shook heads, and one woman smiled at Grandma and shouted up something reassuring. Others glared. For the first time since they had entered the KOA, Mike became aware of the fact that he was unarmed. He thought of their weapons, checked at the gate house. He surveyed the crowd nearest them. They were unarmed, too. All that was left were fists and feet, sticks and stones. But they did not look threatening, just poor, tired, and sullen.

Suddenly, a boy picked up a handful of gravel and threw it toward the wagon's side. The air was filled for an instant with the rattle of stones on metal and wood. Belle shied and reversed, the wagon lurching a few feet backwards and the rapid thrust of the harness pole pulling Bill off balance. The wagon shoved Sherbet, tethered to the tailgate, in the face; she reared up, stumbling. In a flash, all three horses were plunging and whinnying. Up in the cabin, Grandma struggled to stay in the swaying seat and called urgently to them, holding the reins in one hand and pulling up the handbrake with the other. The crowd fell back, children whimpering, people scrambling past one another, a few tripping and falling.

It was all over in a heartbeat. The horses quieted down, nervously blowing and looking around with wide, rolling eyes. "Shhh, shhh, it's OK now, it's OK," spoke Grandma, her face pale. Standing up now on the footboard, the canopy open, she glanced irately after the scattering teenagers, and then began looking around the wagon. Mike followed her eyes. Then he heard a woman sobbing and sensed crisis. It came from the other side of the bed. He ran around the rear of the wagon.

A man lay on the gravel road, apparently unconscious. There was blood around his mouth. Several women were kneeling next to him, one taking his pulse. The others were praying - an eerie murmuring. Although the crowd was flowing along the road again, a small group remained around the fallen man and the wagon, watching, worried. Mike ran to the man and knelt down. He was middle-aged, thin, wiry, his long beard and robe a light brown. The robe was bunched up around his knees. On his feet were sandals made of tire tread. Beside him was a wooden cross he had dropped as he fell.

"What happened?" he asked. "How bad is it?"

"You hit him!" snapped one of the women. "You backed into him."

"Did you see what happened up there?" asked Mike distractedly, wondering how injured the man was. Their angry, bewildered faces suggested they did not know why the horses had spooked.

"How is he?" queried Grandma, running to join them. She had the wagon's first aid pack in one hand. The man groaned and moved his head. He opened his eyes.

"What, what..." he started, coughing and choking slightly on the blood. The angry woman put her hands on his forehead and leant down to him, studying his mouth and demeanor.

"Accident, accident. How you feeling, honey?" she asked.

The man struggled for a second and sat up. He spat blood and saliva from his mouth, and rubbed his face with a towel Grandma handed him. Then he pursed his mouth, his tongue working, and pulled a broken tooth out with his finger and thumb. The women murmured and shook their heads. "Bust this right off," the man said in surprise, his composure returning, and not apparently injured in any other way. His face must have been in the wrong place when the tailgate lurched backwards. "Good Lord," he said unsteadily.

"Oh, I am so sorry," said Grandma. "This just shouldn't have happened."

"Well, it did, and I think you'll be owing us for some suffering," countered the woman closest to the man. They appeared to be a couple. "Millie," she called to another woman standing nearby. "Can you find a way to get the sheriff's deputies here?" The other woman ran off into the woods, taking a shortcut toward the gatehouse.

Mike's heart sank. This could take hours, all because of a stupid mishap caused by reckless behavior. Glancing around, he saw that the teenage girls had vanished. Grandma watched the man and his companions with a worried expression. "Can I get you a pain-killer?" she asked. The man nodded. She pulled out a vial of tablets and offered him one. He took it. Someone handed him a water bottle, and he took a swig. He then poured the water over his face and chin, washing away the blood, which seemed to have stopped flowing. With the help of another man beside him, he stood up. "Sure didn't see that one comin'," he grimaced, trying to make light of it.

Mike rose. "See to the horses, Mike," ordered Grandma quietly, also getting up. Mike glanced at Sherbet, who now stood calmly by the wagon, Fernando beside him. He jogged forward to the team. "You guys OK now?" he asked the horses. Reaching under the cabin's seat, he pulled out apples for the horses, and offered them with open palms. As the horses munched, he looked back at Grandma. These were undoubtedly very poor people. Their faces were weathered and wrinkled, their hands rough and callused, their eyes squinting and downcast. In the Corps, he had met so many like them: terse, anxious, disappointed people, living from day to day by a thousand tricks, trading, farming, making crafts, fishing, cutting wood, patching up old clothes, getting by. Extra money for doctors and dentists was something none had. They knew at a glance that, by

130

comparison, Grandma and Mike were rich—rich northerners with a fancy, high-tech wagon, three good horses, T-pads, quality clothes. They would want some compensation for this accident, and they knew they could get it.

The summoned sheriff's deputy joined them, jumping off a bicycle. Grandma went with him to the victim and his companions. They spoke in a small circle, voices low.

The worshipers continued streaming by, going around the wagon on both sides. They were thinning now, hurrying to catch whatever was beginning ahead. There was no tension or hostility; these people had no idea what had happened. Mike heard music and singing ahead, a lively gospel hymn. Bells rang out. He saw the small knot breaking up, and Grandma walking his way with quick steps. The deputy had already disappeared.

"Well, that's that," she muttered, fuming. "Let's get back on track."

"How did you work it out?"

She frowned and shook her head. "Hundred and sixty euros," she spat, with a sarcastic laugh. "This was just what we needed. Puts us pretty low on cash…" She sighed. "It was clearly our responsibility. Doubt they'll spend it on a dentist. And they wouldn't take dollars, even with a deputy standing there." She ran her hands over the horses and tack as she visually inspected their harness. "Good thing I had euros."

"Do you always carry them?" asked Mike. This was another sign of change during his time away from civilian life.

"No, not always, matter of fact. But the hauling I did on the way down was all paid in euros, cash, and you can't argue with euros."

"What's it at now?" Mike had not bothered to check in months, with his milscrip.

"About three, I think. It had been worse, but the election and the loan package seem to be pushing the dollar rate up." Grandma stood back and looked at the team and wagon, apparently satisfied nothing was damaged. "Wish I was as optimistic." She wrinkled her mouth, and shot Mike and Fernando a wry glance. "I'll drive, and you guys stay down with the horses until we make the gate, just in case."

* * *

An hour behind schedule, they drove out of the state park campground and onto the open road. A crisp breeze blew from the west, ruffling the canopy and the tarps over the cargo. The sky was a clear blue, with high white clouds. It was a good day for driving north.

17-WHITE FLINT MARKET

Sunday, October 21st (morning)

The weekend market at White Flint was a massive affair, centered in the vast halls of the former shopping mall, and sprawling out across the surrounding parking lots. With its location along the Metro's Red Line and major roads, White Flint attracted shoppers by the tens of thousands. Hectare-sized sections were devoted to nothing but car parts, or tools, or clothing, or books, or computer hardware. Food was a major theme throughout the market. Besides produce, vendors sold a hundred varieties of ethnic foods, some with little outdoor café tables and tiny meal tents. Musicians played, jugglers juggled, police patrolled, market wardens strolled, peddlers hawked, and whole tribes of beggars sat with tattered signs along the roads surrounding the parking lots.

Honorée trudged up the defunct escalator from the deep Metro station, Asa on her back and two heavy bags of pickles in her sore hands. The steeply angled escalator was packed. At the top, she threaded her way through the lobby and out into the bright, breezy sunlight, angling toward Rockville Pike. As she approached Area 6, she could see the crowded bus stops along the Pike: hundreds of people standing with their cloth shopping bags, milling among the rows of ever-multiplying small kiosks that sold combs, matches, flowers, cigarettes, memocubes, used smart cards, and a thousand other small wares. A trolley bus approached the nearest bus shelter, and as a crowd welled toward it, Honorée noted the ubiquitous Homelander campaign ad on its side which bemused her: "This land is your land. This land is my land. Not theirs." At a visceral level, the jingoistic politics repulsed her, but the lyric clumsiness and incorrect punctuation was somehow even more offensive. Always a dutiful student and a stickler for detail in language, Honorée resented the undertone, which seemed to be saying to her, "We're going to be crude and illiterate, but we're going to take power anyway." It was a gesture of scorn. She could not understand why so many people went along with it.

Even with her good physical condition, from so much biking and walking, Honorée was breathless when she reached their stand. It was the gusty wind as much as the sleepy boy on her back and heavy bags in her hands. Taking a deep breath, she scanned the scene. Sanna was nowhere. Behind the display bins of their stall reclined a skinny, stooped man with long hair bound in a red bandana.

"Where's Sanna?" asked Honorée in disgust, putting the heavy bags down behind the counter. Her shoulder sockets ached. "She taking a break"?

"'Ep. Uh, errand." Grackle sat up on his stool, his tattooed hands on his bony thighs. "Got some cash for you here." He held up a plastic box. "Sanna said I could have five percent."

"Is she crazy?" Honorée did not like Grackle, and wondered if he had already taken a first cut and was poised to double-dip.

Grackle put down the box, and spread his wiry arms, tufts of black arm-pit hair spilling from the sleeves of his tattered T-shirt. "Have mercy, princess. Mercy! She's been gone a long time and Grackle just wouldn't let you two fine ladies down." He smiled a sharp, chipped-tooth grin.

"How long?" Honorée kept Asa on her back. He was quiet, ready for his nap.

Grackle glanced at the alarm clock on the counter. "At least an hour."

"An HOUR?!" Honorée's quick anger came out with a barely-suppressed gasp. "Where did she GO?"

"Keine Ahnung, princess. Said nary a word." He slid off the stool and pressed back to let Honorée pass, sliding toward the walkway. "She just said she needed to go do an errand."

Honorée looked through the cashbox. "There's a lot here. Didn't she take the morning's receipts with her?"

"Oh, yeah. She did. That's just since I took over." He smiled ingratiatingly. "Sold a lot of those marmalades."

Honorée's impulsive hostility toward Grackle started to fade. "Well, thanks. You want the five percent?"

"Oh, already, um, deducted that." He coughed and Honorée's suspicion returned, vying with relief at his honesty.

"Uh huh. OK. Bye, then." Honorée frowned at Grackle and started unpacking the new pickles. Grackle laughed, and with a thumbs-up sign disappeared into the crowd. He was a market bird. Everybody knew him. He carried things for you, did errands, helped set up, hauled trash, and did pretty much anything anyone paid him to do. Normally, Honorée tolerated him well enough, but she never would have left him alone at the stall with the money. Today, she was tired and angry at Sanna, and Grackle was an easy target. He did not deserve it, she reflected. She made a note to be nicer to him next time she saw him. There were worse market birds, real thieves and hoods, or offliners who couldn't finish a sentence. The wardens never suspended Grackle, which was a good sign. Honorée heard a rumor once that, long ago, he had been a chef in one of the finest downtown hotels.

"He was OK," Mary called over from the next stall. "I've been keeping an eye on him."

Honorée looked up at smiled. "What, did you hear all that?"

"Sure. Stuff like that keeps this job interesting."

"Was I too hard on him?"

Mary tossed her head side-to-side with a frown. "A bit. But he likes you girls and most people give him a lot more crap than you do."

"I'll be sweet next time."

Honorée helped a customer bag apples and dill, and gave her change. Asa was still on her back, dozing, slumping off to one side. "How are you, Mary?"

Mary was also handling a sale. "Oh, pretty good. You know… I'm finally back in the six-day routine here again… Got my kids coming down for Thanksgiving."

"Nice. When did you last see them"?

"Been more than a year. New York's treating them well but they never get any time off…"

Customers came and went in random batches. Honorée glanced at the clock. It was now almost one-thirty. Still no sign of Sanna. Honorée's initial irritation had turned into a mixture of disappointment, curiosity, and worry. If something serious had happened, then she had no right to be angry. The cool breeze brushed her face and lifted the edges of the stall's roof tarp. It was turning into a crisp day, the first real forerunner of fall. The sky was a deep, cold blue, with flat white clouds sailing evenly across it in rows. A pulse of wind gathered and swooped over the market, causing tarps to snap and trash to swirl up in sudden eddies.

"Oh!" Honorée heard Mary abruptly exclaim. There was a crash of boxes and shattering of glass. She whirled to see what had happened. Mary was squatting down on the floor, and she could see that a stack of crates standing against the sidewall of the stall had apparently been upset by the burst of wind.

"Are you OK, Mary?" Honorée crossed the aisle between stalls.

"Sure, thanks, it was just empty jars, returns. I'll have to sweep this up." Mary dried the herbs she grew and sold them in jars during the fall and winter. Honorée reached for a broom in Mary's stall.

"Here you go."

Mary stood up. She was at least ten years older than Honorée, tall and wide-shouldered. She had only been in the stall since September. They had never gotten very personal in their conversation, in the few lulls between serving customers, but Honorée always sensed things unsaid, untold stories on the tip of Mary's tongue. She seemed nice, mature, quiet. She talked often of her children. What more was there about Mary? Honorée could not put her finger on it, but the intrigue remained.

"Thanks, honey." Mary smiled and reached over for the broom. Her eyes shifted to a place behind Honorée and her expression dropped an almost imperceptible degree. Honorée turned, thinking it might be a customer.

"So sorry, so so SO sorry!" Sanna came whirling into the stall, her black bomber jacket zipped up against the wind and her hair wild. She had an empty flat crate under one arm and a heavily loaded cloth bag in one hand. "Jesus, Jesus. Sorry to hold you up, Hunny Bunny." She spun by, kissing Honorée on the cheek and inadvertently jostling Asa, who jerked awake and let out a cry.

"Where were you, Sanna?!" asked Honorée. "It's not so much me waiting. Asa's been good. But, I mean, leaving *Grackle* here alone?!"

"Oh, that van, that van… Had to get it down to Jackson's." Sanna's face looked red under her brown skin, and she laughed nervously. "It barely started and was all funny coming up from the wholesale mart."

Honorée hesitated, strung up between irritated doubt and believing. "Why now?"

135

"Oh, had a lull, couldn't have done it with Asa. Very quick." She spread out her hands and addressed Mary. "It's our lifeline and it would have been just TERRIBLE if it broke down."

"So, um, did it cost much?" Honorée heard Asa begin to grumble behind her, and rocked the backpack to quiet him.

"Oh, nothing, nothing." Sanna shook her head with emphasis, her eyes darting around. Honorée looked at her skeptically. "They owe me favors down there and it wasn't so complicated."

"What did they do?"

Sanna froze with an earnest expression. "You know, I have *no* idea. They messed with the battery and the wires and took this little box out, and put it all back in, and it just started with no trouble." She turned sideways, her profile in silhouette, and put her hands together. "I am a woman of faith, and I have faith in Jackson's. They are, they're, like, they communicate with another plane, and they just KNOW how to fix things."

Honorée began taking off the backpack. "Right." She lowered her voice so Mary and customers would not be privy. "How much money did you leave here with Grackle?"

"None." Sanna helped her with the straps and steadied the pack.

"None?!" Honorée's voice was unbelieving. "He gave me almost sixty dollars. And some euros."

"Oh, then it was a great morning."

"Where's the rest?"

Sanna reached into one jacket pocket. "Here it is, but it wasn't a good start."

Honorée glanced at what seemed to be less than Grackle had given her. "Looks like it was a horrible morning. When did you leave here?"

"I guess, eleven, bit before." Honorée heard Mary cough and saw her watching in the corner of her eye. She decided to let the whole matter drop.

"Look, Sanna, OK. The van's key. We lose that and we're never going to find another one as cheap, and then we'll have to get into horses, which is a big step I'm just not ready for ..." She sat back on a stool and put Asa in her lap. "I just wish you'd left me a note, and I'm really, *really* not comfortable with letting Grackle fill in... And you're going to be late, and he's going to start his nap really late, if he'll sleep at all after this backpack snooze." Honorée took a deep breath, and felt the straps of her anxiety tighten around her chest.

"Hon, don't worry, don't worry." Sanna came over and put her arm around Honorée's waist. "Little breakdown in communication. But no van breakdown. Sorry." She gave her a squeeze, and smiled at a customer inspecting a jar of mint jelly. "It's brand new. Very fresh. Organic from Chevy Chase. Spearmint!" The customer, an elderly man, smiled faintly and raised his eyebrows. Sanna turned partially back toward Honorée. "And what's wrong with horses? Lovely beasts. So noble. And your grandma can tell us everything we need to know!"

Honorée ignored her remark. "Here's Mamma Sanna, Asa," she said. She addressed Sanna. "You taking him in the pack?"

"No, the van's just over by the Gaithersburg bus stop. Gotta move it soon. I'll just carry him."

Honorée handed the little boy to Sanna. Asa looked groggily unhappy, but did not cry. Handing him over to Sanna at this point in the day had become so much a part of the routine, yet it never felt natural, Honorée reflected. "See you later, baby boy." She smiled wanly at Sanna. "See you later, San. Sorry about all that. I was worried." Sanna beamed at her. "Drive carefully."

"You bet, Hon. See you at home." She settled Asa on her hip, took the backpack under her free arm, and walked jauntily off into the crowded market. Honorée watched them go. She sighed.

The crowd in the alleys between the stalls started thinning in the mid-afternoon lull. Honorée absently arranged merchandise, filling gaps with more from under the tables. Women and men shopping for families strolled with their orange net bags and gray cloth sacks. Youths with nothing to do hung out, chatting and laughing in groups. Offliners out to stock up on supplies drifted by like ghosts, pale and thin, their red eyes urgent, their body language limp.

"Hey Honorée," said Mary. "I can always watch your stand in the future. It's no problem for me here." Honorée wondered why this had never occurred to Sanna. Maybe Sanna did not trust her.

"That's a nice offer, Mary. Thanks."

"And I won't charge you a commission, either," added Mary.

"Ha," laughed Honorée. "What's the catch, then?"

"You watch mine sometimes," said Mary simply. "I'm on my own. I don't have a partner."

The way she said that, thought Honorée… Was she just saying that she had to work the stand solo, or was there more? She felt flustered, off balance.

"Sure, if we can manage that. We're obviously NOT the most reliable team around here!" Honorée laughed sarcastically.

"You seem to be the most reliable member of your team." Mary laughed too, probing. This was drifting toward topics Honorée did not feel like exploring.

"Oh, not always." Honorée turned toward a pair of women stirring a pickle vat with its ladle, examining the big, pale dill pickles floating in the brine. One of them had a large open glass jar she had just pulled from her bag. This looked like a sale. "Would you like me to weigh that jar, sister?" she asked.

The woman smiled and handed Honorée the jar. She wore a striking red wool poncho, fastened together by a bird-shaped clip at her breast. Honorée's eyes were drawn toward the clip. "Isn't that fastener pretty!" she added.

"So nice of you to say so," the woman answered. "My grandmother's family brought it from Italy. It's about the only piece of jewelry I haven't sold." She put her hand up to the clip. "I just never could bring myself to…"

18-ON THE CAMPAIGN TRAIL

Monday, October 22nd

"That's Al Conley," whispered Christine, in a break in the greetings and hurried conversations. They stood deep in the crowd gathering outside the First Congregational Church. Jake Wilder glanced where she was looking, meanwhile nodding and smiling at the polite faces all around. Conley was the new editor of the Rutland *Herald*. Wilder had never had any contact with him before, and wondered if he was recently from out of state.

"Have to get in a chat with him, come all the way down here like that," he replied quietly. An older woman Wilder vaguely recognized stepped forward out of the crowd and took his hand.

"Oh, Mr. Wilder, it's just great to see you here, in these times. We are so happy with the job you're doing."

"Thank you. You look familiar. We've met before, haven't we?" He was fishing through thin ice. Christine grinned, and he noted the look of "Be Careful!" in her eyes.

"Oh, just once or twice, years ago. I'm just one of the biddies from Windsor who raises money for the Greens in the county in our spare time." Her laugh was jolly and self-effacing. Whew, he thought. Not a VIP with a big ego. "I'm Margaret Stern."

"Your help is so, so very valuable, Margaret. We couldn't do our work without the help of many people like you." His voice was genuinely warm and encouraging. She was the grassroots, the sort of person who had helped him take his first political steps nearly three decades years earlier, the sort who had bake sales and invited strangers from nearby villages into her living room for party meetings. Margaret Stern was the sort Wilder really missed down in DC, where everyone was either dirt-poor and desperate, or playing some sort of high-stakes political or money game (which were the same, after all). You had to watch yourself with both. With Margaret Stern, you could relax and enjoy the muffin.

"This is Gladys Kapp," said Margaret Stern, indicating a slight, elderly woman on her left. That was a name he knew.

"Are you related to Roy Kapp?" he asked her, raising his voice over the growing hubbub. The lady narrowed her eyes and shook her head in denial.

"Yes, she's his mom," beamed Margaret Stern. She leaned closer to Wilder. "Her hearing is a bit weak." Roy Kapp was a state rep from Windsor, a moderate Republican. And apparently a firebrand. He was running for re-election, and was siding with the separatists, which few Republicans had dared to do until now. Wilder wondered whether she sided with the Greens, or was there for some other reason.

A burst of honking horns nearby caused Wilder to jump, still on edge about security. They all turned toward the street. But it was nothing to worry about and Christine squeezed his arm to confirm this. A man was holding up a large hand-painted sign that read, "Honk if You're Happy with Jake!" The drivers of a big biodiesel logging truck and a trap behind it had been happy to oblige.

"Let's go in," said Christine. "I haven't seen Anna yet, but we still have ten minutes." They started moving toward the steps of the faded white wooden church annex. It was a cool, dry day, a harbinger of real fall weather. There were hints of fall in the maples and big-toothed aspens across the town's common, and more red and orange starting to show on the high ridges above the valley – the advance flares of a color season that now peaked in late-November. Fall came to Wilder as a relief, after the long, oppressive summers. Release from heat, disease, mildew, insects, the violent downpours, the sense of chaos.

They crossed the threshold of the church's annex and walked over the wide planks of the worn, polished floor toward the low stage. It was a spacious hall with a high ceiling, full of battered metal folding chairs, with lots of windows at odd intervals along its white walls. Arden Sommers, the county chair for the Vermont Green Party, was waiting by the lectern along with several local volunteers. She turned to greet Wilder and Christine as they approached. Behind them, the hall started filling as the crowd swelled up the steps.

"Jake, Christine, hi," she said. "Looks like we're going to have a big turnout." She gestured out into the hall.

"Thanks to you, Arden," smiled Wilder. "You've been busy."

"Oh, thanks, but—believe it or not—we're not doing anything out of the ordinary... Public interest in this election is way beyond anything I've ever seen. They keep talking about the Age of Apathy, but this is far from it." She turned toward the handful of volunteers beside her. "Wouldn't you say so?"

They nodded in agreement. "Lawn signs, letters to the editor, chats on VNET... It's all up," said a thin man with a long gray beard.

Christine had been scanning the entrance for the primary guest of honor, Anna Cleary, and now she saw her, easing her way through the crowd with her campaign aides behind.

"Here comes Anna," said Christine. Their eyes turned to follow hers.

"Great," said Arden. "Jake, I'll introduce you right now, and then the podium's yours." Arden turned and hopped up onto the stage. She called "good morning" and "thank you" several times above the hubbub, and as a quiet settled onto the crowd, she began.

"Men and women of Windsor County, I am very happy to see you all here this morning, taking time from your busy lives to hear and talk with our guests. We are now less than a month away from what may be one of the most crucial elections in this state's and this nation's history. Especially in light of the difficulty of these times, a difficulty which strikes at the heart of our daily lives, your active commitment and participation remind me of the words of President Calvin Coolidge more than a century ago, surveying the damage of the floods of 1927:

> *If the spirit of liberty should vanish in other parts of the Union, and support of our institutions should languish, it could all be replenished from the generous store held by the people of this brave little state of Vermont.*

She paused for a heartbeat. All eyes converged and held her. Above a heavy silence echoed a few coughs and the metallic scrape of a chair against the floor.

She beamed. "Without further ado, I have the pleasure of introducing our first guest, who you all know —Vermont's one member of the House of

141

Representatives, one of only twelve Greens in the House—The Honorable Jacob Wilder!"

The crowd clapped vigorously, standing up, and a few cheers and whistles were heard, along with calls of "Alright Jake" and "Welcome back!"

Arden Sommers flashed a smile at Wilder and at the crowd as they passed each other in front of the podium. He turned toward the hundreds of faces, many framed in gray, which were turned up at his. In the front row below, he noted that Anna Cleary, looking breathless and stressed, had taken an empty seat beside Christine.

"Well, it sure is nice to be able to talk to folks in the flesh and blood, and not from behind bullet-proof glass!"

The audience chuckled. He was in a friendly district. Windsor tended to support him and the VGP, although they swung toward centrist Democrats for most other elected positions.

"'Specially way up here in the north!"

The crowd murmured with amusement. Bingo, thought Wilder, the joke being that the only county south of Windsor in Vermont was Windham—which he called home. From Windham, everything in Vermont was up north.

But he immediately adopted a more earnest tone. Folksiness went only so far in southeastern Vermont. These people supported local agriculture and Vermont's rural tradition, but few of them had ever milked a cow or tapped a maple until the past decade. Along with the farmers, mechanics, contractors, and laborers, there were erstwhile teachers, journalists, social workers, small business people, college professors, and software developers—many retired or middle-aged—who were thrown unexpectedly into hard-knuckle rural poverty by the changes of the Thirties. They were all Morales-supporters, now doubtful and confused by the direction of the country. Their humor was thin and strained these days.

"My fellow Vermonters, I only have a few things to say, because as you may know I am not prioritizing my re-election, with so much at hand in Congress, and no declared opponents..."

"Don't forget the write-ins," called a woman's voice to a few laughs.

"... I am grateful that a lack of opponents is affording me this luxury this time around, so I can focus on *your* business" (knowing nods). "No, the main event is a talk with Anna Cleary, who I have known for many years and will shortly have the honor of introducing." His eyes met Anna's, and he nodded his greeting to her. "Anna Cleary is the kind of person who can unite Vermont in these challenging times, who has both the vision and the practical talents to move us beyond our present situation. We have worked together on many issues, and I am here today to lend her my full, unreserved support and encouragement."

Wilder paused, and looked at the audience.

"Since I just got back from our nation's capital two days ago" (there were several hisses), "I thought I would take this opportunity and quickly run through several urgent items with you, let you know what I have heard, and add a few remarks."

Ten minutes, Wilder reminded himself. Keep it to ten minutes. He glanced at his watch, which he had laid on the lectern.

"First, there's the news we have all heard, about Senator Bart Ross." The crowd nodded and muttered. "I was briefed by one of his aides in Washington on Friday, and certainly understood his reasons—as reported to me—for feeling that the time had come to part ways with the Republican Party." He straightened up and grinned. "I understand his sentiments perfectly." There were a few tense chuckles. OK, no more humor now, thought Wilder.

"What I *was* told, in that briefing, was that he planned to become an independent in the time-honored tradition of the late Senator Jim Jeffords, God rest him. I believe his aide who briefed me thought that too. I received no warning that he planned to join up with..." He looked around the room, feeling a silent hum of barely-suppressed controversy, "... with the Party of the Green Mountains." The crowd let out its breath, and he sensed the simmer of many hushed conversations as he continued. The news had just broken.

"You know my position on that question, with all due respect to Senator Ross, and the position of the Vermont Green Party. I will repeat it here as forcefully as I can, and then we can debate it in other forums later on. I believe that it would be an enormous—a potentially tragic—mistake for the State of Vermont to secede from the United States of America. And I hold this position for one main reason that has nothing to do with our pride, our identity, or our history prior to 1791. Vermont has a history to be proud of, and an immensely strong identity, and that's all there is to it...

"No, it is this simple, and I think Abraham Lincoln said it best: United, we stand; divided, we fall. This country is in a very serious crisis, and it is no one's fault but our own. But it is not the first time, and the Union held together through other crises, and both our civil rights and our economic welfare were ultimately served by that unity. Being a Green, my convictions run deep that the past century has seen an awful series of mistakes made by *us*—us as consumers, as voters, as family members, as members of communities—on the environmental and energy fronts. In economic policy. In social programs. Correcting these mistakes has been my main mission in twenty-five years of politics. But blaming the situation on the USA misses the main point. None of the really big problems can be solved regionally or locally. It takes a nation, a continent. Look at how greater union, not fragmentation, has yielded new solutions for the European Union and the CU-Japan East Asian Compact. No, breaking away would cause more problems than it solves. As a US state, we are part of the political process down there in DC. People listen to Vermonters. I work with allies all over the country, issue by issue. A right-wing, fundamentalist politics is certainly at work in this country, perhaps more concentrated in certain states, but as long as there is unity and constitutional process–freedom and unity!—there is hope." He took a deep breath, and coughed. "I hope you will stand with me."

A cautious, thin applause spread through the hall, from the front to the rear. A few dozen people stood up and clapped hard, but most did not join them. He took a drink of water from the cup provided, breathed deeply again, and went on.

"I am almost out of time, and there are two other issues I would like to share with you. First, there is the matter of the international loan consortium. We realize that some very important projects are on hold here because of the financing uncertainties. As you know, I am a ranking member of the House Subcommittee on National Security, Veterans' Affairs and International Relations. We have been back and forth on this one. The Republicans and Homelanders together hold the majority, by three votes. I am afraid that there is basically zero chance that we will see a bill leave this committee during this presidency that accepts even a small portion of the aid, even with extensive restrictions. There is even a lot of debate about which committee this will end up being handled by, and that may change."

144

There were mutters of disappointment.

"And we will have to wait and see how things look after the election. I *wholeheartedly* support Anthony Hedges, and I know that, if elected— *when* elected—he will continue the work of the Morales Administration in working constructively with the international community. In other words, there is a reasonable chance that we'll see some of that money up here in the next year, and I know that means a lot to the continued functioning of our communities, businesses, farms, and schools, in spite" (and he raised his hand and voice for emphasis) "of the fantastic progress Vermont has made since the New Energy Plan—and even before—in expanding renewables, investing in energy efficiency and resilience, building the two new trunk railroads, and in accommodating the migrants who've been coming here in growing numbers."

Wilder's audience applauded, but he knew time was starting to drag, and the room was becoming slightly stuffy, at least up closer to the rafters where he held his head.

"So, men and women of Windsor County, neighbors from nearby, the last remarks I would like to leave you with before Anna takes over—the podium, as a warm-up for the Governorship..." (a few chuckles) "...are these. I believe, after having worked in this area for a long time, that Vermont will never remain on a sustainable path to economic revival, energy enlightenment, and environmental stewardship without an infusion of capital that we simply won't be able to raise internally anytime in the next decade. This is a harsh fact, but one I do not hesitate to state, despite the attacks it always attracts from the right. We can languish, or we can import capital. But the importation of overseas capital is exactly what got Vermont started in the first place, and I never get tired of reminding the Homeland Front that the EU is strong today partly because of American capital it received ninety-five years ago through the Marshall Plan, money—by the way—to bail Europe out of its own experiment with self-destruction accompanied by extreme right-wing politics and poor policy decisions."

Wilder looked around, and smiled down at Anna, who appeared relieved he had held the podium so long, allowing her to recover her composure after a rushed trip from an earlier appearance.

"So, my position, which I feel is made necessary by events, and which I have until today not made public, is that I believe that *even* in the event the White House and Congress reject this generous and historically wise lending offer, Vermont—along with most of New England, I'm assured—should move ahead and begin direct negotiations with China and the EU for assistance."

"That's secession," yelled an elderly man near the front. "Only the federal government can sign treaties!" The crowd clapped enthusiastically, yet an undertone of conversations and scraping chairs reflected the disputes over this comment.

"This is not secession." Wilder sought to meet the eyes of the man behind the yell. He raised the volume of his voice. "We have to be clear about this. There are many forms this assistance might take, including private foreign direct investment—jobs, factories like they have now in New York City, build-operate-transfer infrastructure projects like hydro dams and rail lines, and so on—and I am convinced we need to explore these avenues, even if we have to do it as a state, or in concert with our region."

The crowd was in turmoil, but a small majority appeared to approve of his position. He motioned to Anna to join him.

"Thank you very much for your attention today. I look forward to continuing these discussions, and thank you for your continuing support and ideas. Now, here is the woman you have really come here to listen to, our Lieutenant Governor, Green Party Candidate, Vermont's next Governor, and a lovely native of Castleton whom I have known all my political life, Anna Cleary!"

Jake Wilder stood aside as Anna took the podium, clapping, hearing the warm applause roll through the venerable old hall, and relieved that his time was up and that he could take his seat again beside Christine and take a long drink of the chilled cider they had brought with them for this moment.

"You didn't mention the forests," whispered Christine into his ear. "Did you forget?"

He glanced at her wryly.

"This is Anna's event," he whispered back. "Anyway, what is there to say at this point?"

146

19-TO FRANKLIN, VA

Tuesday, October 23rd

"Eight miles to go," said Mike as a decrepit sign for Franklin came into view around yet another broad bend in the flat, even roadbed of old Route 258. They had been silent for a long time, Grandma dozing at the reins, Fernando in back somewhere, and Mike numbly watching the messages from Olia pile up in his T-pad—messages he could not afford to respond to until he found a free network.

"Just in time for supper," said Grandma drowsily, fighting sleep.

Mike glanced at his watch. It was just past three o'clock. "We're making good time today," he said. The early start from the campground in Murfreesboro had been wise.

"After that story in Colerain, I'm keen to stay off the roads after dark," muttered Grandma. "Crack of dawn from now on, especially with the days getting shorter."

"When I mentioned to our battalion commander that my grandmother was driving a team down from DC with just one extra person to meet me in North Carolina, he just laughed and said she's either damn brave or living in the past."

"Oh, I'm just living in the past," said Grandma, more fully awake now. "When I was your age, a single woman—young or old—would think nothing of driving all the way from DC to Florida, or California, for that matter. Just had to lock your car doors sometimes."

"Trips were a bit quicker, though," countered Mike.

"Mmm-hmm. You know, when I was in college all the kids in the northern schools would drive down to Florida for spring break. Imagine that!" A faint smile of recollection brushed her face. She turned away from the reins and the road and looked at Mike. "One spring break, up at UNH, three feet of old snow on the ground and still very cold, a bunch of us drove to DC in some boy's family's old retired limo. Think they had a limo

147

rental company, or maybe a funeral home. Had dinner at my parents' house, and hit the road again all the way to Daytona Beach. Took nine hours to DC and another fifteen to Daytona."

"Imagine," said Mike quietly. "A limo." He pronounced the archaic word carefully. "Imagine that." Of course, there wasn't any Vtopia back then, he reflected.

"The funny part was that we had to all sleep in a two-bedroom cabin," she continued. "About twenty of us. We were all over the floor in all the rooms. All sunburned, sun-drunk after the winter in New Hampshire."

Mike was silent. It didn't sound funny.

"Some were drunk in the usual way, too… That limo broke down right on the beach. We were three days late getting back to school." Grandma was lost in reverie. "Must have been, maybe …1990."

"Who was president then?" asked Mike.

"Clinton. No, Bush the First. Simpler times."

They rode in silence for a while. The weather had become muggy and warm, windless, stagnant. The thick, brooding woods of tulip tree, black gum, sweet gum, cypress, oak, and a host of other lowland tree species seemed to slowly breath in and out, a moist respiration gradually sucking the crumbling road into the swamps. Clouds of mosquitoes followed in the wagon's languid slipstream, coming close but held a few inches away by their elimlets and the slowly smoldering punk smudges Fernando had stuck around the wagon's periphery.

Not far to the east, the Great Dismal Swamp sat like a great peat sponge on the late-afternoon landscape, its festoons of Spanish moss motionless, alligators now competing with the native caimans for a share of its rich rodent and fish life.

"Grandma," Mike mused out loud, breaking into the long pause. "Speaking of road trips—as you used to call them; in those days, whole populations could just hop in their cars and get out of the path of hurricanes, couldn't they?"

"Oh, I guess they could. Although there had to be a lot of warning and coordination so they didn't end up stuck in traffic jams as the storms hit. Sometimes, things didn't go so smoothly. There was that hurricane named Katrina back around 05 or 06 that hit New Orleans. A lot of people died because they either couldn't or didn't bother evacuating. Even back in the gilded age, some people didn't have cars..." She gestured with the reins. "Want to drive?"

"Sure." Mike took them. It would get his mind off the messages. Grandma stretched and shook her arms and hands vigorously. He resumed his train of thought. "I was thinking about those folks down in Florida now. They're pretty much stuck. My old buddies in the Corps and the Florida Guard are certainly moving them away from the shore and from areas that always flood, but that's all they can manage, with so little transportation. Pack 'em into hurricane bunkers and hope for the best."

"Not a safe place to live in these days," murmured Grandma. "No wonder all those folks have been leaving Florida, heading west. The 'Ridians."

"Do you think we should be changing our course?" asked Mike. "Maybe heading west, too?"

Grandma laughed fatalistically. "Who knows? What, we travel 20, 30 miles inland, and what if it hits us anyway? Wouldn't we feel dumb?"

"Seems like it would lessen the chances, anyway."

"Maybe you're right, Mike." She sighed. "But we add a few days to our trip as well, whatever danger we escape or don't escape, and every additional day is another day we might get held up, or lose a horse, or ..."

"Let's hope the thing veers off and goes out to sea," said Mike.

"They usually do." Grandma peered around at the lush forest. "Did you see whether we're in Virginia yet?" They were passing a billow of kudzu vine like a wave about to break on the road.

"You know," he said, "I've been wondering and haven't seen a sign, but I'll bet we are. I think the border was around half-way. Maybe the sign was covered up." He nodded at the kudzu.

They continued in this vein for some time, talking about weather, the surrounding landscape, the condition of the road, the hamlets they traversed. They passed a huge snapping turtle, big around as a bushel basket, as it was just starting to cross the road. Grandma gazed down at the impressive reptile pensively. It recoiled from the horses' hooves and wagon wheels, hissing.

"Talking about road trips and the old days, another difference just occurred to me, Mike."

"What's that, Grandma?"

"Why, the road kill!"

149

Mike looked at her, his head cocked. "Road kill?"

"All those years driving down here in the car with mom and dad, and later. Sometimes we'd take I-95, sometime we'd come this way. With all that fast traffic in those days, the animals would die in droves, get hit by the motor traffic. Especially places like this, with thick forest both sides of the road. Their instincts had no place for cars and trucks going 65 miles an hour." She gestured up the road ahead. "Every hundred feet there'd be something dead and rotting by the roadside. Skunks, raccoons, possums, frogs, coyotes, beavers, turtles, snakes, people's cats and dogs... Folks hit deer sometimes, even died in deer collisions. Up in New Hampshire we were always afraid of hitting a moose."

"Don't see that nowadays," commented Mike. "What a mess it must have been." Almost on cue, a chipmunk scurried across the road with its tail held straight up like a whip antenna.

At a crossroads, a woman in a trap drew level and tried to cajole them into buying eggs. Grandma was friendly but clear. "I'm in the food business myself, hun," she called over the clopping hoof-beats. Driving through a large village named Forks of the River (although no river was visible), they were surrounded by a group of ragged children begging for loose change. Mike hesitated—this had been a daily occurrence during his Army service, and giving meant breaking the rules—but Grandma pulled out some silvers and tossed them down.

"God bless you, Mizz," shouted two older girls in long, grimy smock dresses and aprons.

"Make for at least one better meal for those kids." She glanced at Mike.

"Couldn't do that in the Corps," he noted.

"Well, I don't do it all the time, but the kids always bother me. We ought to at least be able to feed ourselves well. Lots of land. Lots of knowledge. Lots of able hands. No water shortages here..."

"Lot of people going very hungry," said Mike. "You should have seen what I saw in Georgia and Alabama. Rich agricultural land everywhere and people practically starving in the cities. Things have looked pretty good since I got to North Carolina."

Another sign for Franklin appeared—only two miles to go—as they drove under Route 58. There was more traffic in evidence. "Let's stay at an inn tonight, Mike," said Grandma. "It's on me. We've earned it."

150

"That sounds great, Grandma. Any place in particular?"

"There's a Southern Comfort Inn I heard good things about on the way down. Old motel, with a full stockade all around it, guarded. Staffed stable. Free wifi. We'll be safe. Plus, they've got a diner. Think it's right near the center. If that's full, I think there's another one around here as well. They'll know."

With another long day together coming to a close, Mike thought about how, in a mere six days, he had spoken more with his grandmother than he had in the previous ten years. They'd covered so many topics: family, politics, the past, the future, Mike's career, fruit and vegetable gardening, horsemanship, and of course the golden apple. On several occasions, he had repeated an early question: "Grandma, are you sure you never told anyone about the gold?"

"No one alive," she consistently replied. "My parents knew. So did Jack's. Maybe Ed knew, too, but he was very discreet. Never would have gossiped."

"So I'm the only one, now?"

"Yes."

But, finally, after several days of denying it, Grandma admitted that there was one other person who she had told relatively recently. "Maryann knows now. I always felt guilty about not telling her. Of course, she never had much interest in the island, and stayed up north from college onwards, while I pretty much took over responsibility for the house once I was out of UNH."

"How did she react?" Maryann was his great aunt, Grandma's sister, who he had seen little of since he was small.

"She laughed and laughed, and said I was starting to suffer from delusions. Then, when she started to believe me, she was OK about it. Seemed perfectly accepting. Probably still doesn't quite believe me. Just humoring me... Plus," added Grandma, "I plan to give a small amount to her and Christine, as a gesture."

A gesture of what, wondered Mike? And then he suddenly realized he was starting to feel possessive of this gold—this fortune which at today's prices could completely change the lives of Grandma, him, and the rest of their immediate family. Gone would be the endless work, the physical toil, the tiring trudging and pedaling of bicycles in the summer heat and winter cold. They could completely upgrade their quality of life. They'd have decent food, a cell-electric, home security, medical care. They could live almost like oligarchs...

Grandma watched his reaction closely. He realized he was frowning. She laughed and whispered to him, even though Fernando was back in the bed and could not hear, "Mikey, don't start losing your wits over this!" Her whisper became more authoritative. "Don't start getting jealous and paranoid."

He was taken aback, but then smiled sheepishly. "Grandma, it's worth a hell of a lot of money. I guess I'm just afraid something might happen to it. It could make such a difference for us all."

"And it will," she said. "I decided to let you in on this because you've always been trustworthy, and you're the only one in our family who can make a trip like this and play the role you're playing. I've been dreaming and thinking and worrying about this gold for almost twice as long as you've been alive. We're not going to blow it. But we need to trust each other. Can we?"

Mike sat up, embarrassed and surprised. "Yes, of course."

"Good, because there're a lot of people we can't, even people close to us who have good intentions but weaknesses as well. Your mother, for example, poor girl."

"And Hon?"

"Mike, look, now you're talking like a kid. The gold stays between you and me, period. You don't tell anybody. Nobody. If I decide someone needs to know, I tell them. OK?"

Mike chuckled, shaking his head and taking a deep breath. "Yes, Grandma. I understand completely. Funny how personal family things make you forget how to think like an adult."

"Yep. Even a commissioned officer like you." She patted his leg. He fought to hide a wave of regret as he contemplated what had happened to that commission, and hoped it didn't show on his face. "Let's run this one as if national security depended on it," she continued. "In particular, two people I'm especially concerned about are David and Sanna."

"David? Has he been around?" Mike was surprised. David was a dangerous, unpredictable bundle of weaknesses.

"No, no sign of him for a long time. Hon got her divorce in absentia. But you never know when he might show up, and, I mean, he's got a criminal record now."

Mike nodded, his eyes on the team. Grandma called to the horses to slow their pace as they entered the town.

"What about this Sanna?" he asked.

"That's right. You've never met her."

"No."

"Well. Where to start? She's got this nice, breezy manner, very funny, but sometimes she's so keyed up she's manic. ADHD-type. RDD, maybe."

Mike winced.

"Seems honest, maybe," continued Grandma. "She's a full partner with Hon in the business, works hard. But I think there's more than meets the eye. Just a hunch. Vtopian, I've suspected. I'd never trust her for a second with something like this." Grandma was studying the road signs and the approaching town gate. "Here, Mike. I'll take over the driving in these close quarters." Mike handed her the reins. They stopped at the open gate. To the left and right stretched a mixture of chain-link and wooden fences. Beside the gate was a watchtower. Two policemen came up to the wagon. They both had automatics over their shoulders. Mike watched them approach, glancing to see Grandma's reaction. She was pleasant, steady.

"Evening, ma'am. Sir. Um, gentlemen."

"Evening," replied Grandma and Mike in unison. Fernando waved and nodded.

"Business in Franklin?" The senior policeman was blank-faced, official. His younger colleague was circling the wagon, looking at the exterior and at the scan imagery on his hand-held.

"Stopover for the night, officer." Grandma spoke with a friendly, polite lilt. "My grandson Captain Mike Kendeil and I are moving a household shipment from the Outer Banks up to Chevy Chase, Maryland." They waited for the usual retinal scan; this was not a Federal checkpoint, so there was little likelihood they would be using RFID or trode scanners.

"Where're y'all staying for the night, ma'am?" asked the policeman.

"At the Southern Comfort Inn, we hope," answered Grandma.

"Reservations?" His tone remained terse, formal.

"No, sir. Should we?"

The policeman smiled. His partner put away the hand-held and rejoined him. "Well, they don't look that busy right now, so you're probably fine. If they're full, I'm sure they can find y'all somewhere safe and comfortable nearby. They're all about service." He raised his hand.

"Have a nice stay in Franklin. We appreciate your business." He pointed up the road. "Fourth left, and then look on your left a block past the railroad tracks."

They rode up wide, shady streets of modest brick and wooden houses. The town looked well-cared-for. You could tell they had reliable electricity and water. There was fresh paint around. In the yards behind picket fences, children played and people worked in gardens. Horses grazed in corner lots. Pigs and goats idled in garden-side stalls. Roosters called. Wagons and carts stood parked in front of the open doors of carriage houses, and traffic rattled on the rutted streets. They passed hardware stores, grocers, farriers, a fabric shop, a dilapidated bank, a lumber yard and sawmill, a large covered electronics flea, and various open-air markets. The tang-tang of a blacksmith's hammer rang out from up an alley. A coal-wagon stood unloading outside a steam laundry, its grimy driver eying them as they passed.

"Fourth left. High Street," said Grandma. "I think we need to turn left here. The inn is right after we cross the railroad tracks."

They drove the last few blocks in the falling dusk, spirits rising as they looked forward to showers, clean sheets, and their first restaurant meal of the journey.

"There it is," said Mike. They saw the extravagant electric sign first, and then the high, ornate stockade fence. "The Southern Comfort Inn!"

Grandma let out a shaky sigh of relief. "I can finally wash my hair."

But Mike's eyes spotted relief of a different, more tantalizing kind, if he could countenance the outlay. Beside the Inn, just outside its stockade, painted on the blank cinderblock wall of a low, squat building, was a sign announcing "The Venus V-TEL." Beside its narrow metal door hung a placard on which was hand-painted the word "Vacancy." He took a deep breath. It already felt like too long.

20-BETRAYAL

Tuesday, October 23rd – Wednesday, October 24th

"Hon, sweetheart," said Sanna, after they finished dinner and began the process of cleaning up the kitchen and bathing the boys. "I'm going out with my Glover Park hoodies for a little bit. It's Shyloh's birthday—you know, the gal from Baker's—and I want to show them all I care."

"You show them you care by buying from them every day." Hon was exhausted, her temper short.

"You know what I mean." Sanna whirled around emphatically. "Don't worry, kitty. I won't go before the boys are in bed." She walked out of the kitchen with Asa, calling for Lee.

Honorée looked at the clock. It was seven, and she was behind schedule. "As long as you don't oversleep for the early wholesale!" She did not have much empathy for Sanna's restless appetite for nightlife. With the market stand and the products business, plus the two boys, there seemed to be no time at all for anything extra. *She* didn't have a social life. Thanksgiving was the next opportunity for a break, and it was still six weeks away. Going out like Sanna wanted to felt frivolous, expensive, and draining. Honorée scrubbed absently away at a greasy frying pan, fuming and wishing they had some strong coffee. And hot water.

"They're both in the tub now," shouted Sanna from the front hall stairs a few minutes later. "Do you need the kettle back now?"

"Could you PLEASE stay up there with them?!" asked Honorée, raising her voice. "You shouldn't leave them alone in the tub!" She lowered her voice and muttered, "Why does she *keep* doing that?"

"Going right back up, sarge!" Honorée caught sight of Sanna with a load of laundry bounding back up the stairs. She heard her start singing some old show tune, and then the splash of the bathwater.

At eight-fifteen, when both boys had been bathed, dressed in pajamas, read to, and put to bed, Sanna was out the door like a shot. "I'll keep my eyes and ears open for new pickle deals, puss. Won't be too late!" She mounted her bicycle, engaged the dynamo with a thump, and sped off toward Massachusetts Avenue in the muggy darkness, her lights flickering. Honorée switched on the 3V and turned toward a new pile of clothes. Two hours of ironing and folding passed, and—barely able to stand for fatigue—she dimmed the living room lights and staggered up to bed.

* * *

The sound of the kitchen door closing awakened Honorée from a deep sleep. A light went on downstairs. It had to be Sanna. She rose up on her elbow, watching for motion. Sanna banged around in the kitchen. Then there was silence. Honorée became more fully awake. Sanna did not appear. Curious, Honorée slid her legs out of bed and stood up. Not wanting to awaken the boys in the next room, she tiptoed along the hallway to the top of the stairs. "Sanna," she whispered sharply. Silence, but then she heard Sanna speaking and laughing quietly in a foreign language - Polish, by the sound of it. Was she on the phone, or VNET? It's already morning there, thought Honorée as she descended the stairs softly. Sanna stayed in touch with her wide web of relatives across Europe. Her voice came from the tiny den off the living room. Honorée passed Sanna's bomber jacket, slung over the pommel at the base of the banister, and the strong scent of hemp smoke filled her nostrils, blending with Sanna's customary perfume. Her anger started to ignite. This was starting to feel like David all over again. She came to the door of the den. The scene punched her.

Sanna was kneeling on the floor, the VRI headset covering her ears, eyes, and chin. She had taken off her top, and was writhing rhythmically with one hand on the arm of the sofa for stability, batless, since she was a fluent mindsurfer. Sanna did not need a bat any more than she needed a mouse.

She was moaning and speaking softly and urgently in Polish, breathing in little shallow gasps. A wireless I-ball sat perched on the sofa, taking in the scene for someone, somewhere. Honorée watched this for a split second, and then—in a fury of disapproval and disappointment—swooped down on the PC and pulled out the plug, smacking the I-ball into space as she lunged. Sanna froze.

"Yes," shrieked Honorée, forgetting the sleeping boys. "You're in my reality again, back in MY home! What the fuck do you think you're

156

doing?" She coughed up a sob. Sanna remained frozen, on her knees, both hands now clutching the sofa, the headset still covering her face. Honorée could not see her expression because the muscle-sensor mask came down so low.

"You stay down here, Sanna." Honorée was in control of her voice again, talking low and angrily. "Don't come near me. We'll talk about this in the morning." Dizzy, holding the doorframe, Honorée turned and quickly returned upstairs, her heart pounding.

In the bedroom, she closed and locked the door, and then, remembering the boys, she unlocked it and opened it again. There was silence throughout the house. Nothing from the boys, nothing from Sanna. She sat down on the bed, her heart still pounding. This was it, she thought. She had denied the obvious and delayed the inevitable with David for two years like a stupid fool, and now, impossibly, she seemed to be heading right back into the same kind of situation, and not even with a man this time. Tears of rage ran down her face, and her chin contorted beyond her control. But she was not going to just wait and hope this time. She was going to lay down the law and set the terms and the pace of what happened next. She wished Grandma were already back. Grandma was always wise and empathetic in tough situations, and acted fast.

* * *

Honorée did not know when she fell asleep, but when she awoke, it was getting light and she could hear Asa talking to himself in his crib in the next room. Lee was deeply asleep beside her. He often joined them in their bed in the early hours, silently and stealthily. The clock said quarter of six. She got out of bed and pulled on her bathrobe, the memory of the night before returning. Was Sanna downstairs? What next? Was Sanna going to be honest about her VNET and physical nightlife, and put it behind her? How should she respond? Could there be reconciliation? Nobody was perfect. Honorée had no taste for lies and concealment.

Downstairs, there was no sign of Sanna: no note, no mess in the kitchen, nothing. Her jacket was gone, and Honorée saw the PC was still unplugged and the VRI set lying on the sofa. The I-ball lay sightless in the middle of the carpet. Probably went to one of her friends' apartments, Honorée surmised. Sanna always just took off - walked away - when things got difficult. Or tried to turn everything serious into a joke. That was one of the things Honorée had loved about her in the beginning. Her own

157

family and their network of friends were so serious, so neo-puritan, so earnest. Sanna made everything lighter, easier to take. But the danger with levity, thought Honorée, was there were too many things in this world that just weren't funny, and they were waiting to get you.

She opened the kitchen door, which was unlocked. Something small and light caught her eye. She glanced down. It was a partly smoked joint, lying discarded next to the doorstep. Then something bigger struck her. The van! It was not in their narrow driveway, inside the garden wall. She looked around quickly. Sanna's bike was still there, on the porch, as was her own, with the trailer behind it.

Very worried now, she retreated into the kitchen, closing the door. Upstairs, she could hear Asa banging something, wanting to be let out of his crib. She needed to think this through. Maybe Sanna had gone down to the morning wholesale market as usual. They definitely needed income, and a missed day would cost a lot, spat or no spat. Who would know? Barry Johnson, the fruit guy! She picked up the phone and started scrolling through the list of called numbers. His name came up. She tapped the button with her thumb.

"This is Barry," came his deep voice over the background din of the market.

"Barry, this is Honorée Loporto, Sanna's partner."

"Hey Honorée," he answered jovially.

"Hi. Sorry to bother you, but have you seen Sanna?"

"Nope, not yet. When's she coming by?"

"Oh, I don't know. Trying to track her down. I don't know."

Barry returned, "Because I've got those four cases of nice peaches for y'all here, and we're closing up in two hours, and I can't hold 'em if Sanna doesn't show pretty soon."

"Well, go ahead and sell them if she isn't there by seven. I'm really sorry to put you out like this."

"No worries, Mizz Loporto. Hope I see her soon."

"Me too. Thanks."

"Bye." They hung up simultaneously. Honorée leaned back against the counter. She held the phone against her chest, pondering, ignoring the thumping upstairs. What to do now? Honorée's mind was a whirl of questions. She had to get Lee to preschool. Grandma was gone – no help there. Who could watch Asa if she had to go out to the stand and work it alone? She could call her mother, Claudia, but was reluctant because Asa was almost too much for her to handle. She wished once again—a futile wish—that her sister Jenny still lived in Washington. She was good with small kids. Lee and Asa loved her. And how would she track down Sanna and the van? A crash from above—Asa pulling out one of the dresser drawers—sparked her into action, her stress level soaring.

Two hours later, things were better. Claudia was there, sitting in the kitchen with Asa on her knee. Lee was at school. There was still no sign or signal from Sanna. Honorée downed a strong tea, and smiled wanly at her mother.

"You got over here so fast, I could hardly believe it."

"I was up early for some reason. Lucky for both of us." Claudia did not appear to feel lucky. "I don't usually take cabs these days—you know, so expensive—but you sounded desperate." She huddled on the chipped, faced kitchen chair, knees together, as if she was trying to avoid contact with the furniture and counters.

"I'm really sorry about all this, Mom."

A look of sympathy mixed with disdain conflicted her mother's face. "I know it's not *you*, honey."

Honorée ignored the barb aimed at her partner. "I hope this isn't anything. Just a one-time thing." Honorée had not told her mother about the night before. "We're in business together, and things are pretty hard these days... Plus, she's got the van and it will make me nervous until I know it's safe."

Asa kept trying to reach for a nearby curtain. Claudia pursed her mouth and said nothing, jiggling him absently in her lap. Claudia Kendeil was a thin, sharp-featured woman in her early fifties, with dark bags under her eyes and chestnut hair coiled in a tight bun on her head. She lived with Grandma in the big, old Victorian in Chevy Chase, where she had moved some years before when she lost her editing job downtown. Once a feisty, resolute woman – she had raised three children alone after her divorce from their father – she had become increasingly melancholy and withdrawn in recent years. She continued freelancing, mostly for old friends and acquaintances in the government, and helped Grandma with market garden paperwork and household chores. Although her mother would not admit it, Honorée suspected she was taking some sort of drug. At a deep level they could not discuss, Honorée understood her mother's

159

state of mind had more than a little to do with the fact that the world in which she had grown up and thrived had all but vanished. Gone were the charity balls, debutante cotillion dances, country club luncheons, and tennis dates with high school friends. The identity that Claudia Kendeil had fashioned securely around herself, always short of money but still able to preserve access to a world of privilege and social affirmation, had become utterly impossible to maintain.

"I'm going to call Mary, at the next stall. If Sanna's not there, then I'm going to have to go into VNET and see if I can track her down there."

"Better you than me." Claudia was no fan of VNET, after what she had seen it do to others.

A quick phone call confirmed that Sanna had not appeared at White Flint. Honorée swore in frustration—prompting a disapproving sigh from her mother—and went into the den. She plugged the PC back in, waved the bat to open the VNET V-Icle, and put the headset on. For an instant, with her eyes adjusting to the changed focal depth, all she saw was the perpetually sunny landscape of the screensaver, accompanied by the sound of wind and distant music. Unconfident with cognitrol, she settled back on the sofa with the bat in her right hand. Steering with the bat, she fought diziness as she started flying across the virtual landscape toward Menu City, laid out below her like an endless pastel grid of buildings, parks, streets, and glistening watercourses.

"Peepfinda," she said softly. With smooth precision, she dove into a wide and deep stadium, which seemed to telescope into increasing depth the deeper she plummeted into it, becoming almost like an enormous fluted cylinder. The stands were full of thousands upon thousands of people. However, instead of watching some sports event, they were all talking, writing, gesturing, staring, or doing a variety of other things, seemingly oblivious to their neighbors. Some in fact were not ordinary people at all, but an endless diversity of animals, monsters, super-heroes, historical figures, and other assumed forms. "Peepfinda ready," responded the service with a slight reverb.

"Find Sanna Nanou-Olsson, NID last four digits three-six-three-nine," intoned Honorée, clicking the button at the top of the bat with her thumb. "Found," came Peepfinda's reply. She swooped toward a lower level of the stands, and zoomed in toward a distant figure sitting talking, its legs crossed. A flashing red square surrounded the figure. As it rapidly grew larger, Honorée saw it was a cobalt blue chimera with the body of a curvaceous woman and the head and tail of a cat.

"Sanna?" she called, pointing the bat at the red square. The cat-face looked up at her and suddenly vanished. The red square continued to flash on the now-empty seat. Honorée hovered in space about twenty feet from it. "Sanna, are you still there?" She knew she was still online, lurking and listening. "Please answer me." She clicked impatiently on the square. "Sanna, come on. Talk to me. Don't just go online and drop out. We need to talk. Where's the van? What are you doing?!" Her voice rose in anger at the end. Still, there was no reply. Then, the red square vanished.

"Find same again," Honorée said.

"Offline," said Peepfinda.

"Take email dictation," said Honorée.

"Dictation ready!" Peepfinda was replaced by a smiling, vivacious Tinkerbell, flitting a few feet ahead of Honorée's avatar in the vast open space of the cylinder. Honorée started speaking. The text flew like quick little bees onto the curved surface of a bubble in Tinkerbell's hand, which expanded as the message lengthened. Honorée repeated her questions for Sanna, implored her to get in touch, and vented her frustration slightly at the difficult practical situation now confronting her above and beyond their personal falling out.

"Done. Send it." Tinkerbell and the bubble shot off into space, vanishing into a point. Honorée floated, wondering what to do next. Sanna's friends? Could she find them?

"Peepfinda," she said again.

"At your service," came the reply.

"Find Sanna's friends."

"Password please," answered Peepfinda.

Jesus, thought Honorée. What could it be? "Blue-jean queen," she tried, remembering what Sanna used for the van's personal config lock.

"Incorrect. No access," said People-finder. "Password please."

Honorée reflected for a moment. This avenue was closed. Who could she call? Sanna had plenty of casual friends, but few good ones and no relatives in the area. There was always her mother, in Göteborg—a woman with whom Honorée's contact had always been distant and cordial at best.

"Find Zenobie Olsson in Göteborg, Sweden," she requested.

"Found." After a series of rapid, spiraling drops, Honorée found herself hovering in an empty foyer in front of a Barbie-like teenage figure with a mop of blond hair, a small round suntanned face, and sparkling green eyes. She wore cutoff shorts and a white T-shirt. The Barbie looked up at her in surprise. She was clearly in a conversation elsewhere.

"Ja? Vem är det?" Sanna's mother answered in Swedish.

"Oh, hello, Zenobie, it's me, Honorée." Honorée looked down at her own form, and realized she was still using the silly mermaid avatar she had created months before. "Just a moment." She pulled down the personal profile menu and selected "Normal," instantly re-rezzing as her own holomorph.

"Oh, yes? How are you?" Zenobie seemed unexpectedly friendly. This caught Honorée off guard. In her short acquaintance with Zenobie, she had always seemed to sense either a disapproval of Sanna's lesbian life-choice, or was it suspicion that Honorée was not reliable and might change her mind about Sanna? She did not know. "Why don't you come in?" Zenobie beckoned.

"Sure, thanks," replied Honorée, and suddenly they were in a dazzlingly life-like forest clearing with a group of Zenobie's friends—all chatting and socializing.

"My friend Alfons is a landscape artist. This is his chat-grove."

"It's lovely." Honorée turned to look at Zenobie. For a moment, she was captivated by the virtual scene. It was brilliantly realistic. The crispness of the sunlight and shade, the outlines of the leaves, the silvery fuzz of tiny hairs on Zenobie's perfect arms, their sinews and musculature. Zenobie's skin was magnificent. She flicked aside her hair. The movement was fluid, sensual. Honorée suddenly felt awkward, appearing in this scene with only the headset and her low-resolution holomorph skin—a wooden cartoon character with limited motility in a display of such subtle detail and liquid movement. This was so real, more real than reality itself. She felt a pang of inadequacy. But she fought it. She was not there for socializing or posing. Anyway, she had once seen a photo of Zenobie, and she looked nothing like this. "Zenobie," she began. "Pardon me for dropping in like this, with no warning, but has Sanna been in touch today?"

"No, I haven't heard from her in some time. For days, I think. Why? Has something happened?"

162

"Yes, well… We had a fight last night. Things are a, um, they're strange and I'm not sure where we're headed, but…"

The expression on Barbie-Zenobie's face became one of concern. "I'm sorry," she said. "I thought Sanna was settling down. She's such a wild one. Where is she? Is she all right?"

"I don't know. She left last night. Took our van. You see, we're a couple but we're also in business and things are stressful enough as is…"

"I see." Barbie-Zenobie suddenly held a seashell-formed telephone handset near her head. "Have you called her?" Honorée nodded but then shook her head. "Do you want me to call her?"

"Yes, if you don't mind. I found her for a second, but then she blocked me and I couldn't get through."

"Sure. Wait a minute." Sanna's mother spoke softly into the seashell in Swedish. She nodded, and smiled at Honorée. "I've got her…"

"Ask her if we can talk. I need to speak with her." Honorée watched Zenobie relay this to her. She spoke softly with her for several minutes, nodding, her face grave. Then she de-rezzed the seashell and faced Honorée.

"She said she's sorry she has upset you, but she needs some space, some time to think. She's confused about many things. I know my daughter…"

Honorée felt irritation and anxiety rising inside her. "Yes, yes," she interrupted impatiently. "I'm confused, too. So many feelings. But we have a business we rely on, and Sanna has disappeared, taking both her working self and our van with her. Even if she wants to take time off, I need the van so we can get products to the market to sell. We are losing money for every hour we're not open. We're supposed to be opening very soon, um, today, that is." Her voice shook with irritation. "Oh, Christ, this is really NOT what I had planned for today…"

"I'm sorry for you, Honorée, I really am. Sanna said she'll call you very soon, after a little while to, to get things together…"

"Well, when you speak with her again, tell her I need the van now, and the rest can wait until she is ready. But this is just awful!" Her holomorph fluttered back and forth like a paper cutout, only the expression on her face lifelike. Zenobie saw her distress nonetheless.

"I'll tell her about the van. But Honorée, I am worried about Sanna and I think she is very much affected now by the situation in your country. I

163

want her to come back home to Sweden—I've been telling her this, and with you and the boys, too. Very welcome, all of you. Your life, it is so hard, and we are getting worried about the coming years, about how they will affect you. Anything could happen, and you have no safety!"

This idea was not something Sanna had shared with Honorée. "Is she interested in doing this?" asked Honorée. "Has she talked about it?"

"Yes, every now and then." Zenobie crossed her wiry, honey-tanned arms and shifted her weight to the other hip. "More, recently. I think she very much wants to."

"She's said none of this to me."

Zenobie looked sad, or was it just a programmed-in mournfulness or gravity about her avatar—the grave woman-child? She replied, "She should say how she feels, tell you this…"

"Zenobie, I need to get to work, but tell her to please call me, please, to let me know." Honorée raised her bat to end the conversation.

"For sure. I will." The waifish blond girl in the forest glade smiled and waved her hand, and then, in an instant was gone.

21-AT THE COOLIDGE HOTEL

Wednesday, October 24th

"The Homelanders are going to try to make hay with this." Bill Zeller took a deep gulp from his sweating glass of ice water and wove his thick fingers together, elbows on the table. "Lot of out-of-state money and pressure. Not sure how many they'll sway. There aren't very many of them here. Bart's one of us. But they'll try. Vermont's a test case. You should hear some of the stuff, especially in the VNET soapbox rooms. They're calling it treason, building fear with it."

Wilder knew the chatter. It went on and on, in a million VNET chambers, ten-thousand news feeds, all pretty much alike. Cynical, panting speculation. About politics, personalities, gossip, scandal—global and overwrought. Endless online conversation for its own sake, while in the "RNET"—drab, daily reality—most people spent most of their time grubbing for their food, repairing what was left of their belongings, and maintaining the horses, donkeys, and bicycles that had become their lifelines...

Wilder glanced at Christine. She was listening brightly to Bill's account, a faint smile on her lips. Even after three days of intense campaigning, she did not look especially tired. He wondered where she got her vigor and composure. He felt drained and shaky.

"I was there in Rochester myself," Bill recalled, "right there in town on the common—you know, where Route 100 goes through—and he was up on a small rise by the old war memorial. It was fascinating. I'm looking out across these faces—lot of folks, more than a thousand, a lot down from Montpelier on the bus—and I'm asking myself, how are they taking this? Are they thinking he's committing political suicide? Do they support him? Do they think he's irresponsible? Or that he represents some kind of solution to what's going on?" Zeller himself could go on and on, and he looked like he was about to. He was the chief editor of the Vermont

Clarion, a shrewd observer of state and national politics and a staunch supporter of Greens and progressive Democrats. He had cut his political teeth back before the turn of the century with the likes of Dean, Douglas, Leahy, and Jeffords, back in the newsprint era. Wilder intercepted his gathering monolog.

"Bill, one thing's for sure: Bart's lost all ability to influence the Republicans in the US Senate, which is good for my little party, maybe— they'll go even further to the right, now—but I think it's bad for America and bad for Vermont in the long run."

The arrival of the waiter interrupted the flow of their conversation. As he took orders, Wilder looked around the old-fashioned décor of the Coolidge Hotel's restaurant. The venerable railroad hotel in White River Junction had not changed fundamentally in at least a hundred and fifty years. Oil paintings of important people and pastoral landscapes crowded the faded walls. Wilder's own grandparents had held their wedding reception in this very room. He and Christine had invited Bill Zeller here for lunch and a chat before they headed back down south on the 3:15 train. As always, Zeller was happy to oblige. Conveniently, he lived nearby, in Norwich.

"Jake, my big issue now is how he'll influence voters here in Vermont. DC dynamics come later. Things are now very evenly matched here. You're hearing self-appointed experts saying it's a done deal for the Republicans, the way you Greens and the Democrats and the PGM have fragmented the left, but I don't see this as a left-versus-right election. Bart Ross hasn't turned liberal-progressive in the least... He's a pro-business, old-style conservative. And then there's also the referendum on secession."

"More than one hundred towns have it on the ballot now," breathed Christine.

Bill nodded. "Over a hundred and twenty now, for eighty-five percent of the population." He sipped his beer, which had just arrived. "But anyway, what I was saying was this..." He puffed and inhaled. "So, we're standing there in Rochester, and we had decided to do a live opinion poll. I'm there with Molly and Sandi. When Ross stopped speaking, there was lots of applause, and we started working the crowd, just asking the question, 'What does this mean to you as a voter and as a citizen?' We were recording."

Wilder and Christine leaned forward with curiosity. No hands-off editor, Zeller was always jumping right into the trenches.

"And we got amazing stuff. It's coming out in the next issue, like a whole forum. It was all over the map, but there was one common theme."

"Yeah?" Wilder was tiring of Bill's dramatic running start. "What?"

Bill laughed drily. "OK. Well—no big surprise—most people there clearly felt DC is a runaway train—has been for years and years—and that if Vermont has to choose between a shipwreck and secession, they'll take the latter, whatever the transition involved. And the chances increased if other New England states went the same way. And nobody said they'd emigrate. A lot said their relatives would move here if it happened. Or that they already had…"

Wilder shook his head. "As if it were so clear…This is such a complicated issue, but despite how bad things are getting, how can people ignore the risks?"

"So, yes, right, so in my conversations, I asked a follow-up question: 'How will you know if or when it's time to choose?' And this was interesting. I'd never asked that question before. Some said they already knew it was. Others said the clincher was going to be the foreign loan deal. Several used the term 'abandoned'. They talked about how we were abandoned when the refineries decided to satisfy the national demand for transport diesel rather than our need for heating oil. About how federal laws had been overriding ours across the board for decades. You know, capital punishment, nuclear power, education, the environment, campaign reform, journalistic confidentiality, forests, firewood, and so forth. About how we were paying the price for others' fanaticism. This international loan deal was seen as the final test. Oh, and FORSA, too. And they weren't too worried about opening up the US market to foreign competitors again, lifting trade restrictions. Especially Canadian."

"Don't you think the crowd in Rochester was a little self-selected, a bit biased?" Wilder asked skeptically. "I don't suppose Bart's enemies were there. Hecklers?"

"Ha, you think we're idiots?" Zeller grinned. "We asked them about their political affiliation and positions on several key issues, and a few psycho-demo variables, and they wound up looking like a representative sample of Vermont. Even checked out a control group."

"Well, folks in DC representing most other states don't seem to see things this way at all." Wilder looked at the pizza he had ordered. He suddenly realized how hungry he was. "There's a surprising amount of confidence in our own economy, our own capacity to change. That's the rhetoric, anyway." He paused as he picked up his eating utensils, and continued hopefully, "Although—granted—opinion is split between those who see the loan deal as a good idea, along with all sorts of other progressive policies, and the majority, for whom the loan offer is like deal with the devil."

"That's because the whole mainstream has been herded right where the Homelanders want them, everybody trying to outdo each other by sounding even more patriotic and evangelistic and pro-fossil, pro-Fort McMurray, pro-nuke, pro-let's-just-go-back-to-the old-days. Even though they don't believe it." Bill had an ironic sneer on his face. "It's all symbolism. What kind of confidence do the Homelanders have in our ability to change with the help of good old pluralistic, liberal democracy? Not much!"

"Frankly," said Wilder, trying to ignore the nagging sense that he himself was bluffing, "I think the Homelanders are a mixed bunch, and that—collectively—their bark is worse than their bite. Sure, some clearly are fascists—the old gun-loving, racist survivalists, the Nazis—but from the pretty extensive contact I've had with the state delegations, most seem to be well-meaning religious fundamentalists who want to see the country unite around traditional conservative values, with democracy and the rule of law intact."

"You sound like one yourself!" chuckled Zeller. "Better watch it! You may be talking about the representatives in DC, but what about their base? You trust them? And anyway, since when was democracy a conservative value?!"

"Look, Bill." Wilder knew he was going to sound shrill and frustrated, but he was too tired to suppress it. "I'm a fricking member of the Green Party. I'm Vermont's rep, for God's sake. I'm just saying that it's no good demonizing a label, a whole movement of people. We have to work with them, negotiate a future together. Deadlock and refusal to cooperate is a recipe for disaster. Homelanders aren't infected with some disease! They aren't possessed. They are a reaction to extreme times. I don't trust them, but I trust the Constitution and our basic good will."

Zeller grew sober. "Sure, OK, I know what you're saying. And I hope you're right. I really do." He took a long drink of beer. "What worries me is that ultra-right-wing parties have never made it this far in American history before, and it's not just an artifact of instant-runoff voting— conservative Republicans gone to seed, sort of... There are rumblings that bother me, too many loose ideologies and emotions bouncing around, too much real hardship to fuel the process, bitterness, disappointment, fear of foreign powers. Symbols gain terrible destructive power."

"I agree it's nuts," said Wilder. "This whole decade so far—you know, the past decade— has been all about symbolic posturing, and what should be straightforward logical choices about things like how you heat your house and how you produce enough healthy food and basic civil liberties have gotten lost in it, over and over."

Zeller's face turned more serious. "Old habits die very hard. We're talking about gut values people acquired when they were kids. About the good guys versus the bad guys. The good guys are entrepreneurs, business heroes, the rugged individualists, the tough guys, the cowboys. Daddy. The kick-their-butts guys and gals. Sports heroes. The bad guys are the foreigners, the complainers, the tax-and-spend progressives, the alternative this's and thats, the eggheads, the wimps."

"What has never made sense to me, Bill, is why this red-state, blue-state stuff has never broken down in almost forty years. I mean, that's it, isn't it? This pattern of polarization."

"Why should it break down? Aside from the fact that 'it' is part real, part media construct. And the Civil War almost two hundred years ago was a North-South conflict. Looks pretty stable."

Wilder toyed with his food. "You asked me why? Here's why, in my mind: Science. Just the truth sinking in. The success stories where change worked out well... Realizing there're no free lunches." Zeller glanced at Christine, and then back at Wilder. "I mean, it's not like everyone is brainwashed." Wilder's hands formed an appeal. "You can go all over the world and see how prosperity and quality of life—and democracy, too— are surviving the Emergency. Dogmatism is the last thing we need." He took a bite.

"You're in the right party, dude." Bill Zeller laughed. "And maybe Mama Science is loved in New England, bless her. But there are a lot of tired, poor, frightened, angry people out there in places like Denver and

Dallas and Phoenix and Atlanta—people who lost their houses, their jobs, their self-respect, people who went from real estate agent or database administrator to sharecropper in a couple years - some time ago, now—and they want scalps. Foreigners, terrorists, and people who are just a little too 'noo-anced' are wearing the scalps they want."

He put down his fork, and looked intensely at both of them, his face completely serious for once. "You know, what this country has been going through—really diving deep down into now—is the complete and utter re-ordering of who has, who doesn't, who's listened to, who's ignored, who's believed, and who's not.. And it all begins and ends with the availability of cheap fossil fuels. The world they made possible—the institutions, the infrastructure, the distribution of power—is finally vanishing right in front of us. Been predicted all our lives. We're China when the West arrived. Japan. Cambodia in the 1970s. The Islamic countries when modernity hit. God help us avoid the convulsions they went through when everything stopped making sense. Which it did, years ago..." He took a bite of his omelet and chewed furiously.

"Bill," said Christine carefully. "Why isn't the conventionalist argument making more of a dent?" Zeller looked askance at her. She continued. "You know my own position, but the conventionalists, whenever they promote coal gasification or Alberta oil or nuclear or whatever, always seem to ultimately be saying that American ingenuity and our flexibility—adaptability—will make everything right again, and that no foreign loans and no direct government picking of winners is needed. Or even desirable." She laughed without mirth, and added, "'Course there's no sign of this happening."

"Exactly!" Zeller almost shouted. "Disconnect! Making no dent. No dent! The same mantra over and over, yet no counterpart in reality. Superstition. The Energy Trust is nothing but a winner-picker, of course. Or status-quo-freezer. And the wind barons! Just regular old feudal lords. Bingo!"

Wilder listened carefully, but said nothing.

"Christine," continued Zeller. "You know what we were saying about symbolism? Listen, as far as I can tell, and dredge up from my memories of lectures at Harvard and Chicago way back—and please note that there is woefully little public debate about this—there are two basic reasons. The first is the liquidity trap, the capital shortage. That's not symbolic. It's

170

material. The hyperinflation makes money worthless. All savings are wiped out. All the money vanishes. No products or assets can be sold. Then you get deflation, and the government so far has hesitated to just print money because it will kick off hyperinflation again and make matters even worse. They want the loan package to create solidity, get productivity growing again, not just create speculative bubbles." He gulped his water. "So anyway, good old American dollar-denominated entrepreneurial ingenuity can't exactly thrive in this crisis. It needs help."

Wilder and Christine looked at him expectantly.

"Then there's reason number two." Zeller raised his eyebrows. "This may sound mysterious, or mystical, but this is the way I've come to see it...It's like this: right now, rationality is basically worthless in America. It's got no teeth. Nobody has any use for it beyond immediate, practical things. Reason has capitulated. This is what I meant about convulsions, about stopping making sense. If rationality said, 'It's raining and, logically, we should use an umbrella to stay dry', but you believed right down to the bottom of your heart that rain was technically AND morally impossible—not just you, but you and millions of others, and had all your lives, and your career depended on believing that— then you would ignore your senses and reject that logic and just stand there, and... what?"

"What?" said Wilder and Christine, surprised he had suddenly turned a question at them.

"What would you do?" demanded Zeller.

"Get wet," said Wilder. Christine laughed with a snort.

"Exactamundo!" Zeller smiled. "You'd get soaked. When things that make absolutely no sense start turning your life upside-down, you can't rationally process them until your whole concept of rationality changes. Your paradigm. That doesn't just happen overnight. Takes years, and deep personal crisis. Emotion! Denial. Breakdowns. Ruined lives. Death. Then, from the wreckage, come people who believe in rain. No big deal. Of course. Just a little rain! A little rain never hurt anybody! And when it rains, they just put up an umbrella. So simple. And then they look at the societies that couldn't come to terms with AIDS or with climate change, or that fight the market economy, or democracy, or religious pluralism, or women's rights, or ecological modernization, and ask with big, wide eyes, Why can't they simply accept reality? What's the matter with those people? They must be imbeciles! They don't seem to grasp what any child knows."

Zeller's hand was clasped in a fist on the table. He came up for air, and dove in again. "Well, you know what? We're 'those people' at the moment. And it ain't just a trivial little puzzle, a minor bit of reality-acceptance that's needed. America and the world need to grasp this. Then maybe some of the denial about what's going on might dissipate. All that conventionalist pardon-my-French bullshit in Washington, and all that lend-them-some-money-and everything's-gonna-to-be fine crap in Beijing and Brussels. You mark my words. America's paradigm shift is going to continue being the cover story for the rest of this century, and only God knows what will get knocked down in the process..."

"Take Bart Ross, for example..." Christine managed to wedge an interjection into Zeller's diatribe.

"Precisely. Good. Christine, take Ross. He's a man pinned between rationality and ideology. Or two ideologies. One says, 'America Right or Wrong. Just gotta believe. America creates any reality it likes, and the world accommodates.' The other says, "Vermont can again be that mythical tidy democratic little independent republic it supposedly was way back between 1777 and 1791, doing things the smart and principled way.' That ideology has always been around in Vermont, tucked away like a fairy tale that grownups never admitted made them get a little weepy when they secretly re-read it from time to time. Like *The Hobbit*. Camelot. And—oh, yes—the rationality pinning him, or now pulling him, I guess, is his good common sense saying that what's coming out of both the White House and the opposition parties and all their pundits and think-tankers just doesn't add up. Just doesn't fit the evidence all around us. Stops making sense. And..."

Zeller waved at the waiter for the check, and seemed to be almost physically winching himself out of his own monologue. But, for an instant he froze. He looked at Wilder and Christine, who were listening raptly to this editor who had won prizes far and wide for his editorials and columns, and was now spinning a spoken-word editorial straight at them.

"... And, I happen to agree with him," he said in conclusion. "Just look all around us. This isn't OK. We can't look the other way. We have to see what's coming."

But Wilder wanted to know one more thing. "Bill, where's the Governor in all this?"

"You'll find out soon enough," chuckled Zeller. Wilder's face was a question mark. "Up in the hills."

"Up in the hills?" repeated Christine with a dubious look. Wilder waited. He looked at both of them expectantly.

"You doing anything this weekend, Jake?" Zeller looked at Wilder with a poker face.

"Campaigning for Anna," said Wilder. "Reading."

"Doing something, close to home," said Christine firmly, heading off any distractions.

"Ah, well, there's something else you'll be doing, too." The tone of Zeller's voice became less cagey, more confiding. "I just heard about this myself."

"Heard about what!?" demanded Christine. "We have a major family obligation Friday, by the way."

"Governor Jeanne is calling a meeting. Expanding the guest list of those fall meetings she has every year up in the mountains. Check your email. I know she wants you there, Jake."

"That's news to me," mused Wilder. "Kind of short notice."

"Something's up, anyway," said Zeller. "To answer your question, I've been asking myself the same question all year. She's served since—what— '32, and she's always been moderate and fiscally responsible and stayed out of the limelight. A sort of stern, noncontroversial, boring, remote governor. The Emergency has favored Republicans like her, because it hasn't been possible to expand government because there aren't any resources for new programs – except the police and military, of course. So government's just kept shrinking and she's had to keep fighting fires, which she's pretty good at. She's made it clear she wants nothing to do with either Homelanders or secessionists, and she's always been quietly noncommittal toward Greens and other progressives. Very middle-of-the-road. Good at pitting you all against one another."

"I'm just glad she has steered an independent course," said Christine. "She's a republican with a little 'r', not one of those closet Homelanders. I trust her. She's helped stability."

"Mmmm," replied Zeller. "I think your trust will soon be tested. I think some things are coming that will force her into the limelight. Then you'll find what she really stands for." Zeller looked at his watch. "Oops," he muttered, and then to both of them he announced. "I need to get going. See you in a few days!"

22-PETERSBURG, VA

Thursday, October 25th

"See how Bill's started doing a little skip?" Grandma pointed down toward the horse's right side. As Bill, who was harnessed to the left of the shaft, completed each trot cycle, he skipped almost imperceptibly to the right, jangling the tack and causing Belle to compensate slightly.

"I wouldn't have even noticed that," said Mike, surprised. He rubbed his eyes, feeling washed out from lack of sleep due to his indulgence in Vtopia the night before.

"I'm used to this team. You would if you knew them as well as I did."

"So what's it mean?"

"Bill's back-right shoe is not sitting right. I keep cleaning out the hoof and trying to screw it back in place, but there's a split developing and the bondex won't hold it. Too much lateral shear."

Mike held the reins more gingerly. "Think he'll make it to Petersburg like that?"

"Not sure," said Grandma. "I don't want to push it because you let things like this go and you get infections, sores, all sorts of things. Founder, maybe, although I don't have any first-hand experience with that. Let's slow it down a little."

Mike gave a tiny tug to the rains and called a low 'whoa' as he'd heard Grandma do to decelerate. The speed of the trot dropped and the horses relaxed a bit. She looked at him with approval.

"What's founder?" Mike asked.

"It's when the hoof starts to come apart from the bone underneath, the coffin bone. The hoof is just one massive fingernail, or toenail. You know how people sometimes get infections and lose a fingernail? Well, we don't walk on our toenails, but founder's a disaster if it isn't caught in time. It has something to do with what horses eat, too. Lots of lush, dewy grass apparently can bring it on."

"Horses are vulnerable," said Mike, dwelling on how dependent they were now on this team.

"Mm." Grandma nodded. "But a lot of this comes from the breeding and lifestyles we humans impose on them, the work we make them do. There's a price. I bet wild horses have half the problems."

They drove at the slower pace, warily studying Bill's gait.

"I'm not a farrier," Grandma continued, "and we need to get to one pretty soon. I have a name and address in Petersburg. They'll need to work all the hooves over carefully, so we make it the rest of the way. Ought to get Belle and Sherbet re-shoed as well, for the final push. Did it on the way down in Richmond at a big stable I know. Nice place, wasn't it, Fernando?"

Fernando nodded in agreement.

"We should call ahead," said Mike.

"Yup, Mike. We should." Grandma fished around in the duffel bag she kept up on the bench, and pulled out her little archaic green book. "Douglas. There's the number." She picked up her cell phone and made a call. Mike eavesdropped idly, wondering what other vulnerabilities the horses might suffer from. He thought about the flies. They sprayed the horses every morning and night, and hung repellant bulbs around them, from their harnesses and the shaft. But the flies kept appearing, especially when the sun was high.

"OK," confirmed Grandma. "Said they could see us tomorrow morning at 7:30. Aren't promising to be able to get it all in tomorrow, but it's a start."

"Seems like we ought to get anything like that fixed before this hurricane hits." Mike spoke as he concentrated on keeping the horses at their slower-than-usual trot.

"Mm-hm." Grandma seemed ambivalent about the storm. It had just come ashore in southern Florida after sparing most islands in its path across open ocean, and had turned north.

"Would you mind checking its status again?" Mike was worried by what seemed to be a kind of fatalism on Grandma's part, a blasé acceptance. When he had suggested they drive inland a few days back, she had scoffed and failed to act. When he was posted to Alabama, and worked in Georgia, he had developed great respect for hurricanes. They could be terribly destructive. Perhaps she had just experienced so many hurricanes that one more did not seem like a big deal. He watched Grandma sideways as she navigated her T-pad. Her face tightened as she studied the screen.

"What do you see?" he asked after several minutes of silence.

"Well, they've downgraded it to a Cat-2, and its eye has just exited the Georgia coast, heading northeast. Took the past twenty-four hours to transit Florida from the Keys to the northern state line. They're saying it might intensify back out at sea, closer to the Gulf Stream. Hope it stays out there." She scrolled through pictures, shaking her head. "My God... It just flattened parts of Miami. Hundreds dead in Florida, even in the bunkers. Nearly two feet of rain! They're lucky they're a flat state. Imagine what would happen with so much water dropping onto West Virginia or Virginia..." She studied more photos. "This is hitting agriculture down there very hard. No more oranges for a while. It's a huge storm. Three hundred miles across."

Mike made an is-that-so grunt. "We still have time to head inland, Grandma, away from all these lowland rivers. If it hits us and it's still raining like that, all this will be flooded anyway." He nodded toward the flat, open fields they were passing through.

"Well," said Grandma, "depends on when it overtakes us, if it does. We get on I-95 at Petersburg, so we'll be on higher ground, on a better-built road with better drainage."

"I hope water is the main problem. But the winds in this thing are terrific, too. I saw that the wind gusted to 180 when the eye passed Daytona Beach, and there were tornadoes."

Grandma shrugged. "I hope the wind will have pretty much died down once it gets up this far north."

"When would it get here, if it did?" asked Mike.

Grandma studied the display some more, flicking the controls back and forth with her thumbs. "The most likely track sends it way out into the Atlantic. The next track down—20% likelihood—has it coming right up the coast. Let's see. This is Thursday. So it would be here Saturday sometime... We ought to be in Richmond by then."

* * *

As the afternoon progressed, the air became increasingly still and balmy. A haze filled the atmosphere. It was as if a vast mass of stagnant air was damming up from the north, its movement cut off by the expansive vortex to the south. A premature dusk deepened shadows as they began to pass through the outer hamlets of Petersburg. The traffic increased – mainly bicycles and mopeds, but a growing number of carts and wagons with the odd cell-electric threading its way quietly through them. They already had their lights on.

Mike yawned, his head back against the bench. He had dozed for some time, unaware of how much time had passed. They were on good blacktop pavement, a rarity. Grandma drove, hunched slightly, eyes ahead. Mike took a drink of water from his bottle.

"Wonder what's happening with Hon," he mused aloud.

"Thought I'd give her a call next time you drive," answered Grandma.

"I guess she went to the market alone again today, huh? Hope Mom could help out."

"Yes," said Grandma, "and Hon'll either start running out of pickles and preserves—all high margin – or else not be able to get fresh produce out to the stall, which cuts way down on the traffic."

"If there's no van, how's she getting the produce?" Mike knew the wholesale market was all the way over in Silver Spring, at least an hour from Hon's house and from White Flint, and that something more than a bike with a trailer was needed for a day's stock.

"Oh, I've got Marcus helping her out. He's taking our deliveries to Silver Spring with the Lancaster van, and then moving Hon's things out to White Flint. Then, he's been ghosting passengers and taking them down Wisconsin Avenue."

"Can you really spare him?" asked Mike.

"Yes. We always do deliveries to Silver Spring, and he's not so busy this time of year."

"How come Hon and Sanna have that biodiesel, then? Seems they could save a lot by just doing a deal with you."

"Ah, ha," said Grandma. "Now you're onto something. I have been suggesting this for a year. With a diesel vehicle to maintain and biodiesel at sixty dollars a gallon, you'd think they'd jump at it. Not everyone's granny has a small fleet of delivery wagons. But you don't know Sanna!"

"What about Sanna?" Mike inquired curiously.

"Ohhhh no. Sanna wouldn't have it. Had to have their own van."

"Why?" Mike thought he knew the answer nonetheless.

177

"*You* know," laughed Grandma scornfully. "Status. Style. No horses to worry about. Plus, no dependency on Grandma. Grand, splendid independence! Of course, all a façade, too."

"What did Hon say about this? And what do you mean by 'façade'?"

"In the beginning, she was sort of star-struck with Sanna. Sanna's wild optimism and confidence impressed her. Felt like new hope was on its way, a bright future. But that kind of attitude gets no one anywhere. I think Hon's changing her opinion. At least, I hope so, with what just happened."

"Sound like Sanna's approval rating ain't improving," said Mike, smiling and shaking his head.

Grandma turned toward him, and was about to reply when a sudden commotion just ahead in the oncoming lane diverted their attention. A man in the driver's seat of a shabby, heavily laden open-bed wagon was yelling obscenities and arguing loudly with a small group of pedestrians beside him by the roadside. Beside him were two women and several small children, looking worried and embarrassed. A truck had slowed down behind him and was waiting to maneuver past.

"They couldn't give a rat's ass!" cursed the man, beside himself. "They know me here. I got relatives and spent half my time here as a kid, goddammit!"

Mike and Grandma slowed, the horses now almost opposite the stopped wagon. The desolation on the face of the woman beside him and the tears in the children's eyes were painful to look at.

"Other Triple-C towns let us through no problem, but these..."—his voice rose into a bark—"... these holy bastards wouldn't even check, wouldn't even look at my papers!"

Grandma leaned her head toward Mike's. "You experienced with the Triple-C down where you were with the Corps?" she asked in a low voice.

"Sure." There were hundreds of towns and cities in the Commonwealth of Christian Communities now, with Fort Collins, Colorado as its Queen City. Most were in the South, Midwest, and Mountain states. "But there's a whole spectrum. Some are low-key, just getting started. Others make everyone go to church, forbid evolution in schools, introduced the mandatory Creed everywhere. Everything's a sin."

"Petersburg is one of the real strongholds, Mike. I forgot to mention that."

Mike glanced back at the stopped wagon. The man was not shouting any longer. Maybe he had found sympathetic ears, someone to help. "They gonna give us any trouble?"

"No. I came through here on the way down, said the right things, praised the Lord, and everything was fine. Half the time it's an excuse to keep out the drifting poor, which it looks to be in that situation over there." Grandma sighed. "They see this wagon and the Maryland plates, and they'll be just as pleasant as a peach. It'll be 'Ya'll have a nice visit', no worries." She chuckled again, turned to Mike, and intoned quietly— because they were quite close to the stockade and gate now, and there were many people around them waiting to pass through—"Very, very Christian people. Truly." She winked.

"What about Plain Word towns?" Mike asked. There were none of those down where he had been working.

"I don't believe they're organized in this way. They don't take over entire town governments, civil defense, and all." Grandma paused, watching for movement in the traffic ahead. "Lynchburg is one of their strongholds—Remember that guy back in Columbia?—but Charlotte, Greenville, other places are big Elevener towns, too. Of course, they're completely the opposite. There's a lot of praying and vows of poverty and, yes, maybe it's oppressive, but they do a lot of good works. Built a huge poor farm outside of Lynchburg—nice agricultural land, very productive. Called Grace & Mercy Farm. We're seeing their produce up in the DC markets in the winter." She nodded back at the scene of the altercation. "They'd take those folks, no problem. See 'em as assets, recruits."

Settling back to wait out the time it took to move the remaining fifty or so yards to the crowded gate, they regarded the southern entrance to Petersburg. Remarkable earthworks rose on either side of the road, extending in star formations on both directions. At the top of the earthworks were wooden stockades, with occasional watch towers topped by golden crosses. At this southeastern end of the city, there seemed to be a large expanse of open, intensively farmed land outside the stockade, with small groves of trees here and there well back from the fortifications. There were no buildings in this expanse, aside from barns and garden sheds—not even the empty pads of the original strip-mall development that surrounded to many cities.

"Those are some earthworks," observed Mike.

"I've wondered about them myself," replied Grandma. "Seems to go all around the city."

"Looks like they're getting ready for the Civil War again."

"There was a big Civil War battle here. Maybe these are part of the original fortifications."

Mike looked around and cocked his head. "I've visited some battlefields here and there. These look very new and well-maintained."

"Well, they sure aren't doing it for tourism. Who'd come? Maybe it's historic preservation plus job generation.'

"God knows," answered Mike. His jaw dropped. Just as he uttered those two words, brilliant spotlights were turned on immediately ahead, illuminating a huge statue directly in the middle of the road. Just inside the wide gate, where police were busy processing entering traffic, the road lanes divided fluidly around a head-high stone island topped by a thirty-foot metal statue of a sort of warrior-angel, its feet bristling with replicas of Civil War cannons. The statue was clad in shining armor and chain mail, and a helmet on his head with a nose guard that ended buried in a flowing mustache and beard. He held a massive sword in one huge hand, its point in the ground by his feet, and a tall, narrow shield in the other, propped in front of one impossibly muscular leg. His wings arched and spread above him, adding another twenty feet to the height. His eyes stared sternly down the road—right at them, and beyond.

Mike snapped his gaping mouth shut, and laughed at what he had just said. "Well, I guess he does!" He glanced at Grandma. "Who's that?"

"Who do you think?" she asked dryly.

He wrinkled his brow, and shook his head. "God?"

"Good grief, boy!" Grandma looked genuinely irritated. "What the heck is the name of this city?"

"Petersburg." Then it dawned on him. "Saint Peter. OK. Right. On this rock I will build my church, and all that." He looked at the massive statue. "And this is …. the Pearly Gates?" Then he screwed up his face and turned to his grandmother skeptically. "When I think of Saint Peter, I think of an old, portly angel looking people up in his big book, announcing who can enter heaven and who has to stay outside. This guy looks like a cross between Joan of Arc, King Arthur, and Captain America, on steroids. He's ready for holy war. Plus, what's with the wings?!"

Grandma smiled ruefully. "I suppose he *is* preparing for war. He's guarding the gate, anyway." They peered at the inscription at his feet, which read:

And I say to thee, thou art Peter, and upon this rock I will build my Church, and the gates of hell shall not prevail against it. - Matthew 16:18

"Yes, certainly a warrior," Grandma resumed. "Now, remember what you learned in Sunday school, and follow my cue." They were almost at the gate. Then, the truck ahead was waived through almost casually, and it was their turn. A policeman in a broad-brimmed hat like a state trooper's approached the driver's side from their front, shining his flashlight around the team and under the wagon. He smiled up at Grandma and Mike, and stopped about ten feet from their wagon.

"Ma'am. Sir. How are you doing this evening?" he asked.

"Very well, officer," replied Grandma politely. "Praise God."

He ignored her invocation. "Your destination?"

"Bethesda, Maryland." Not Chevy Chase, Mike noted. Chevy Chase was an incorporated village within Bethesda anyway, but Bethesda connoted something different: larger, more anonymous, less privileged.

"Where're you comin' from, folks?" The municipal policeman held up a retinal scanner for the obligatory glances as he spoke.

"We've been on the road for six days now, hauling our household up from the Outer Banks." Grandma gestured at Mike, in the passenger's seat. "This is my grandson, who joined me in North Carolina." She gestured at Fernando. "Mr. Gomez has been traveling with me the whole time."

"Planning to stay here long?" Mike saw that other police were walking around the wagon, pointing flashlights at the cargo and underneath.

"No, officer. We plan to make a stopover tonight, see a farrier tomorrow, and head on up I-95. Unless that hurricane slows us down."

"Any news on what you're expecting here in Petersburg?" interjected Mike. "From the storm?"

"I believe they're saying it'll be off the coast up here, Captain. Lots of rain here, probably. Projection has it heading out to sea." The policeman turned back toward Grandma. "What parish are you folks members of, up there in Bethesda?"

"Christ Church EA, officer." Grandma smiled sweetly. "I'm on the vestry this year, running charitable giving."

181

The policeman, who appeared to be fairly senior, raised an eyebrow and looked doubtful. "I used to be in the DC police department, and I can't say I recall that one."

"Oh, yes. It's right near Chevy Chase Circle - Western and Connecticut. My grandson was christened there, in fact." Mike wondered what the addition of 'EA' meant.

The policeman's face turned slightly derisory. "Oh, sure, I know where you mean... But that's an Episcopal church," almost spitting out the second syllable of the word "episcopal".

Grandma was unfazed, still smiling sweetly. "You must have retired from the MPDC a long while back, officer. Christ Church has been Evangelical Anglican for years now."

The policeman glanced over at the gatehouse booth. The cargo screen was clear. His expression brightened as he faced Grandma again, adopting a similarly sweet, approving tone. "Oh, why I'm sure that's been appreciated very much up there."

"Oh, yes. It very much has indeed. It was high time." Grandma beamed.

"Well, good. Enjoy Petersburg this evening, get your horses seen to, and have a safe trip. You have a 24-hour pass. Let us know where you're staying." The policeman stepped back to let them pass, and the boom gate ahead rose to admit them to St. Peter's sanctuary.

"Good evening, officer," smiled Grandma. "God bless." She prepared to take up the reins. Mike put his hand on her arm, to stay the start. Her eyes met his in surprise.

"Wait, Grandma." He turned to the policeman. The timing struck him as odd, although his experience with Triple-C towns was limited. "Officer, is that normal? Only twenty-four hours?"

"Normal when a big storm's nearby," said the policeman. "Were you hoping to stay longer? Some special reason?" He sounded suspicious.

"Ah, no," Mike responded. "But is this the way you deal with travelers when there's bad weather coming? You don't want travelers staying around too long?" He pressed his question, slight irritation in his voice. "I'd think this would mean good business for the inns, campgrounds, restaurants, stores. Not to mention charitable and decent."

The policeman narrowed his eyes, his tone stiffening. "You're right, Captain, as far as ordinary bad weather goes, but that Rhiannon's a Cat-

Five, so even if it's far off and not headed this way, we're not taking chances. Not until the danger's past."

Years of accumulated experience in disaster preparedness and response had left their impression on Mike. Minimizing disturbances to life and commerce from all the storms and floods of late had become the primary function—preoccupation, even—of the Corps. Resources were stretched all around, but things always worked best when both Federal agencies and cities and towns provided refuge to the vast populations that could no longer move out of harm's way.

"Sir, I used to work quite a bit with this sort of thing, in the COE, so excuse my curiosity here... Are you saying that travelers passing through need to be out by the time—if, that is—a hurricane hits, but that locals can find refuge?" Mike smiled and tried to look disarming, keeping his ire in check. Grandma's face was impassive.

"Only if they're city residents, Captain. Resident within the city limits."

"Where does everyone else go?" asked Mike. Grandma breathed sharply, betraying her exasperation.

"Wherever they go," said the policeman noncommittally. "There are a few hurricane bunkers around here. One up near Midlothian, for example. Some folks have their own defenses."

"I see," said Mike. "Some sort of city ordinance?"

"Some sort, sir," said the policeman. They stared at each other in stalemated silence for a heartbeat. Then the policeman stepped back, and called impatiently to the cart behind them: "Next vehicle!"

Grandma clucked to the team, and they started rolling. The policeman nodded at them, his expression cold, and fell behind the moving wagon.

When they were clear of the gate, moving past mighty St. Peter, Mike whistled and shook his head. "What the hell is going on these days?! That's just going to make things worse for everybody."

"What I want to know is what the heck you were thinking!" Grandma was irritated with Mike. "I got him sweet about our religious affiliation, and then you have to start asking funny questions."

Mike grimaced at the sting of her criticism. "Well, what Petersburg is doing IS mean, you know—all the control and exclusion—and I couldn't leave that one alone."

183

"Keep the authorities happy in a place like this. You don't want them surly or suspicious. You're not in the Army anymore, for goodness sake. You're just another poor civ driving a wagon. Skip the activism, grandson."

"This stuff is illegal, you know." Mike was angry. "Modest civil defense and controlling crime are one thing, but controlling trade, kicking out the poor, refusing to give people shelter from big storms, and making travelers pass some sort of religious test is definitely against federal law."

Grandma sighed. "Sure, you're right. But is the Federal Government trying to stop it? Uphold the free flow of interstate commerce? Rule the land. No. They've got enough other more basic things to worry about. This is about self-preservation at the local level. You think the Feds provide them with any money, or food, or weapons?" She laughed, and then called to the horses to draw their attention back to the road. "OK, some places go too far. But Petersburg's not unusual, in my experience, for around here."

"That probably explains why that family wasn't let in... Boy, things have really changed up this way. I thought Alabama and Georgia were bad." Mike paused, and then continued with amused indignation, "And that Christ Church business. What was that?"

"Oh, all of that's true. The church did change its name a couple years back, to stay religiously correct." Grandma lowered her voice and smiled at him. "But it's just flying below the radar now. No talking in tongues, healings, or that sort of thing. Very low-key."

"And you're on the vestry?" This seemed very much out of character for his grandmother, seldom given to volunteering or to congregational socializing.

"I joined just before I took this trip, sweetie!" She laughed. "Seemed like the thing to do."

23-A CLUE EMERGES

The phone rang as Honorée was getting out of the Lancaster van. It was just getting light. She glanced at Marcus in the glow of the dashboard with a look of uncertainty on her face. He smiled encouragingly. She took a breath, and answered.

"This is Honorée. Hello?"

It was the police. They had found the van. It was out in Gaithersburg.

"Gaithersburg?! What is it doing out there?" Honorée sat back down in the passenger seat, holding the door frame for support. Marcus pulled up the hand brake and turned on the warning flashers.

There was a major problem. The van had been sold. The buyer—a plumber—had been pulled over by the police on his way to work. He had a valid receipt and bill of sale in his T-pad. The police could verify its VIN number on the spot. He owned the van now. The sale was legal, and there was not much the police could do at this point.

"Jesus Christ!" snapped Honorée. This was now a mess. Sanna's name had been on the title along with hers. The police officer's voice was polite and sympathetic, but this was now a matter she and Sanna had to resolve. He would V-mail her the report. Honorée hung up in shocked disbelief.

And where was the money now, she wondered?

"Marcus, oh God, you are not going to believe this. I haven't seen Sanna in two days—don't know where she is—and I just found out she's sold the van!" Her eyes welled up with tears of exasperation and helplessness. "That was the most valuable thing we owned. She has sold our van. My van!"

Marcus looked a her with concern. He had known her ever since the Chevy Chase Market Garden opened, when he went to work for Grandma. "Your grandmother will be back in town soon. You get her working on this, and all the lawyers she knows, and you'll have your van right back, no problem."

Honorée's heart sank. "Thanks, Marcus." Typical man, she thought, coming up with a nice, practical, stupid solution when her whole existence was falling to pieces: her relationship with Sanna, her household, her business, her livelihood. If Sanna didn't show up with the money and some pretty solid explanations right about now, she was going to have to give up the rental house and move in with Grandma. And her boys would be going through another upheaval in their young lives. She put her head in her hands for a moment, and then straightened up, wiping tears away from her face angrily. She looked at Marcus. "This is going from bad to worse, but we're here, so we might as well get your things unloaded and pick up my order." She sat back in the seat. "I'll ride around to the dock with you." Marcus released the brake, and called the horses into action. They slid back out into the Georgia Avenue traffic, heading for the next turn that would take them around to the loading docks of the wholesale market. They leased a twenty-minute time slot, on Dock G, and it started in only five minutes.

The Silver Spring wholesale market had grown into an enormous scene of commerce and logistics, the primary entry point for food and many other commodities at the north end of the city. Originally a small farmer's market in the parking lot beside the Metro station, it had expanded into nearby buildings all around. The wholesale market opened at 4:00 AM, when the first milk train came in from Western Maryland. Its arrival was followed for hours by the arrival of farmer's trucks, vans, trains, and wagons from near and far, and the simultaneous appearance of grocers and market traders from all over the city and inner Montgomery and Prince Georges Counties. Most trades were conducted over VNET in advance of their arrival, so customers spent the bulk of their time checking cargos, loading vehicles, and doing the odd spot purchasing of other things put out for sale. Thousands of people milled around in the complex of high-ceilinged halls surrounded by loading docks and warehouses. The pace was hectic and accelerated, with the retail markets set to open within the hour.

As Marcus coaxed the team backwards up against the G dock, Honorée jumped out of the Lanc and walked quickly to the dock manager's counter, trying to push aside all thoughts of Sanna and the van. A crew, ready for them, was gliding their first pallet up to the back of the Lanc, its manifest already in the wholesale market's computer system and the contents already sold and destined for other docks.

"Yer starting to be a regular here," said the G dock boss, a short, middle-aged man with a broad, pocked face and wide-set eyes. Honorée felt his leer on her back as she glanced up at the queue board, checking where her cargo was parked. "Aisle 60, babe," he added, his Baltimore accent drawing "aisle" out into "awl". "We'll get a crew on it in a sec."

"I'll take a look," said Honorée curtly, raising her voice over the din. She picked her way the short distance to the aisle, dodging pallet crews, boxes, totes, spilled stock, and roof columns. The warm, moist air was thick with the smell of fruits, vegetables, flowers, sour milk, horse manure and the fried odor of biodiesel. She turned the corner into her aisle, and asked her cellphone to signal the cargo. Down the aisle on the right, about head height, a tote's RFID label flashed green, and her cellphone tinkled. She jogged down to the tote and started poking around, trying to see exactly what was there.

"You want that down?" shouted a truck operator from the other end of the aisle.

"Sure. Thanks." Honorée stood aside as the truck approached with a soft hum, its warning light flashing. The operator swung the forks under the pallet and brought it smoothly down to the floor.

"Crew'll be here in a minute. It's got floor status now." With a smile and a wave, he maneuvered the fork truck around and was gone. She stooped and looked through the crates sitting on the pallet, which was packed shoulder-high. There were pumpkins, squash, nuts, and marigolds, jars of Shenandoah Valley honey, late-season corn, eggplant, garlic, and a variety of other produce. In the muted light, they shone with bright, earthy hues. She smelled the fragrance of farms and harvest.

A shout behind her and the clanking of metal caused her to turn around, and she saw a pallet crew headed straight for her. "Good morning!" boomed the crew boss, T-pad in hand. Two guys followed, one directing a pallet cart. "Chevy Chase Market Garden?"

"Yep. Sure is." She stood up. As the men got nearer, she saw that one was Grackle. He smiled at her and held up his hand in greeting.

"Honorée, madame."

Honorée nodded. As the crew brought the cart's forks under the pallet, Grackle kept looking at her. She sensed something different about his expression: less cocky and sarcastic, more concerned.

"Sanna taking time off?" he asked.

"Haven't seen her for two days. Took off, with the van. Sold it to some plumber. Left me in the shit." She smiled without humor. "So I'm doing both jobs now."

Grackle paused as they turned the corner out of the aisle. "I'm really sorry to hear that. I like you guys." They kept moving as a group toward G-dock, where the Lanc had already been emptied. The third man swung the cart to back it onto the lift, where the pallet would be lowered down to the level of the Lanc's bed. Grackle worked to steady the pallet, holding the Lanc's open door aside, but went on. "You know where she is? She OK?"

"Nope, and I don't know." Honorée waited for the men to finish the job. Marcus came jogging back from a stall with filled tea bottles and fresh donuts, weaving among small carts and motorized vans.

"OK. Look, I hear a lot of stuff and I talk to a lot of people, Vtopians and realos..." Her eyes met Grackle's for an instant, and held them. "I can look into it."

"Get yer butt in gear, Grackle!" interrupted the dock manager. "Customer service is Walid's job." He turned toward the crew boss. "Tractor-trailer down in section three. Two crews."

As Grackle started to turn away, Honorée called to him. "Thanks. See you at the market?"

"Certainly. Don't know much more, but that much I know." He flashed a smile, and hurried away with the crew along the broad walkway connecting the docks. Honorée watched him go for a moment, frozen in thought. Vtopians? It stunk of a pattern. Of course, she should have been paying more attention to it. This was another clue she would have to absorb.

"Ready to go?" called Marcus. "Our time's up."

"OK. I'm coming." She pulled her attention back to the moment, and with a few quick steps she swung herself into the Lanc, and Marcus started the team on its rush-hour walk over to East-West Highway and then toward White Flint beyond.

24-HELP FROM GRACKLE

Friday, October 26th

Grackle stopped by the stall later in the morning, before the early lunchtime rush was noticeable. He had a young, skinny diverse with him.

"Salutations, milady," he called out with a grin, his demeanor bright and cocky again. But a searching look in his eyes reflected a change in his attitude. "This is Ty."

Honorée smiled wanly, wondering what news they bore. She recognized Ty vaguely. He looked like an offliner, with his faded clothes, rumpled rasta hair, and dark eyes.

"Honorée, I brought Ty over 'cuz maybe he can give you some insights into what's been going on. I've been doin' some research. Field research." He laughed, and Ty looked down with a furtive glance, and chuckled nervously.

"OK," she said. She waited, dividing her attention between the two men and the stall in case more customers came. There were gypsies in the market, and she'd already had a brush with a pack of gypsy children.

Ty told a story that confirmed what she now suspected, but would have completely stunned her only days before. Ty was a market bird, but an active Vtopian as well. He practically lived at a V-Tel in Bethesda, when he was not working at the market. (Honorée wondered how he could afford that.) And, for at least a month, he had seen Sanna there frequently. He recognized her from the market, and said hi to her a few times. He had no idea how long she was spending there, but seemed to recall running into her both daytime and evening.

"Was she alone?" wondered Honorée.

"Always seemed to be," answered Ty. "'Course you're never alone in the V," he added, with a faint smirk. Honorée did not return it. She knew about V-tels. Everyone did. They were nondescript, smelly, barrack-like buildings or converted office blocks full of little capsules. There were no common spaces, besides the check-in desks: usually just a counter with a window and security cams. People came and went around the clock, disappearing into the capsules. Sanna herself used to joke about them, calling them "spaceports." With her self-assured attitude and social f2f nature, Sanna never seemed like the type for V-tels. The idea had never crossed Honorée's mind.

"Are you still seeing her there?" Honorée probed.

Ty said he could not confirm whether it was two or more days since he had most recently seen Sanna at the V-Tel. Honorée considered how she might intercept Sanna there, and whether she might need Ty's or Grackle's help.

"You've done me a huge favor, Ty," said Honorée. "Do me one more: please don't say anything to her about this conversation, when you see her again." The two men stood grinning at her. "And help yourselves to one of my products, within reason." Their grins grew larger. They accepted her invitation and started looking through the day's remaining stock.

She stood there, watching, thinking about her next move. The van was gone, and there was no easy way to get it back—no way at all, really. She would have to sue Sanna. With what money? Lawyers were a luxury nobody could afford these days. And it could take years. The courts were overwhelmed and under-funded, awash with the back-log of personal and business litigation from a decade of collapse. And Sanna had nothing to hand over anyway—no assets—besides the proceeds of the van.

Nodding at the men as they departed, she was overcome by a staggering bitterness. There was absolutely nothing she could do to set things straight. Sanna had really screwed her, with no warning. She never should have trusted her, and yet why had she never seen it coming, never detected any signals, however faint, that Sanna was not on her side, that something erratic like this was even possible? Well, she had not, in any case. Maybe it was because she did not want to. What were her prospects, now? One was clear. She would have to give up the apartment, and move with her two boys back to Grandma's house (which fortunately had some spare room). Her attempt at living with some independence had utterly failed—romantically and financially. Maybe she could keep the market stall going, but not without Grandma's and her mother's help, at least until Asa was five and could go to kindergarten, if she could afford it. At worst, she would have to shut down the stall and just work for Grandma. She knew Grandma would offer her that option. She had before. Grandma would just lay off one of the paid staff. Family came first. Grandma did not own the Market Garden—Cumberland Coop did—but she had considerable autonomy to run things, and they trusted her.

Anyway, most people she knew lived with family, and they somehow made it work out... Who could afford the luxury of independence? What was "independence," anyway? Some outmoded fantasy?

She needed to call Grandma.

25-WITH THE ROAD CREW

Friday, October 26th

"These sandbags ain't gonna do shit if the banks get undercut and collapse," said Dee, standing back and surveying the morning's work. A few of the other men grunted or uh-huh'ed in agreement as they gathered together their tools and bags, and headed up the slope to their trucks, parked beside the Route 114 bridge.

"What do you fuckin' know about banks, Dee?" snorted Pierce. "You a civil engineer?"

"I saw what happened to the I-81 bridge down where the New empties into Claytor." He brought his hands together and thrust them away from his chest in illustration. "Bags all fell into the river, bringing it up just enough to start pushing on the bridge, and the whole fuckin' pile o' shit just washed away." He spat. "Hurricane Dwayne."

"'Cane Dwayne," laughed Pierce. "Yeah. Who can forget? My cousins in Lynchburg got their whole neighborhood washed into the James. Couple hundred houses. You remember Dwayne, Daryl? Or were you still suckin' your momma?" He laughed rudely, looking over at where Daryl was coiling the ropes and loading the block and tackle. Pierce was the crew boss, a sun-leathered man in his mid-forties. Taut sinew and veins stood out on his tanned forearms and calves, and a lacework of tattoos swarmed up his neck.

Daryl grinned wryly and tried to joke. "Nope, boss. I was on the bottle by then." He was afraid of Pierce. He also still felt shaky and tired after the trip back from Head Island—all the checkpoints and delays. The morning's early start had not helped. Sleeping in would have been nice. But he had had no choice.

Pierce spat dismissively, and picked up his radio. Dee smirked. They all started walking up toward the State Highways trucks. Their next destination was another bridge down-river, where an overflow spillway needed to be cleared out and reinforced with sandbags and cable.

"When's this hurricane gonna be here?" asked one of the Virginia Tech volunteers, when they reached their truck.

"You in a hurry?" asked Pierce, challenge in his sharp eyes. "Got a date with one of your butt-buddies?"

The student looked glum, but said nothing. Daryl, now the observer instead of the victim, watched the exchange. Pierce had a nasty reputation, and looked like he could do damage. Daryl knew him from the Home Guard, where he was a Master Sergeant. Pierce was also showing up at Homeland Brotherhood meetings as well. He was always on the offensive—goading and provoking with his cutting humor. Daryl had never seen anyone really challenge him. And he had never seen Pierce use any weapons but words. He did not want to, either.

"Take time now for lunch, boys. Don't forget to drink water." Pierce pulled his lunch pack out of the first truck, and the crew of about a dozen volunteers and reservists followed suit. They had been out since 5:00 AM, and they were hungry and thirsty. Pierce was a hard-ass, Daryl reflected, but he was a responsible leader when a job needed doing.

Daryl sat down on the sagging crash barrier beside the bridge, wiping the sweat from his face. It was humid and close. The air reeked of damp soil and pawpaw leaves. Dee, Pierce, and the two guys from Roanoke sat down nearby.

"Unfuckinbelievable what's going on with those Fourth Crossing folks," said Dee.

"You been following it?" asked Pierce.

"Yeah, after all the talk at the Homeland Brotherhood, I decided to take a look myself."

"You been to watch those V-rallies?" asked the short, heavy-set man from Roanoke. Daryl thought his name was Julius but could not recall.

"The Neuronburg Rallies?" Dee chuckled, and nodded. That was their nickname. The real name was something like "The European Destiny Forum," but some British tabloid punster had coined the name in memory of Hitler's rallies in Nürmburg, and it had stuck. Dee continued, "You've gotta get through layers of authentication to see more than the main sessions, or talk to anybody, but a bunch of us have been online in the gallery the last few nights checking it out. It's crazy and getting crazier..."

"They can get as crazy as they want, but make a move in this direction and they're fucked." Pierce had not even a glimmer of humor in his eyes. "Even if they try to pretend it's humanitarian aid or something."

"There's always crazies, but I'm kinda wondering how much real power they have, beyond the VNET rallies," offered Daryl cautiously. He was convinced that America needed the Homelanders' stern discipline and traditional values at the moment, but he became uncomfortable when sensational conspiracy theories were used to argue for the Homelander cause. He did not agree with his father or Lara about politics, but he shared with them a belief in reason and facts, and he feared what could happen when they were ignored.

"Oh, they have a lot of power, boy," countered Dee. "You go in there any time of day or night and there's at least a couple million users online. Twenny-four-seven. That's power. And they got some serious trouble brewing up north bringin' more users in every day."

"What kind of trouble?" asked Wilson, who had just walked up.

"Fourth Crossing trouble," answered Dee. "Climate trouble."

"Where's 'at? We doin' a fourth bridge?" Wilson thought they were talking about another sandbag job.

"Fourth Crossing, Wilson. Neuronburg." Dee looked at him expectantly.

"That near Christiansburg?" Wilson looked puzzled.

The men burst out in hysterical laughter. Christiansburg was up Route 460 about a mile from the Interstate. Even Pierce grinned. Dee was hooting. Wilson stood frozen, a mixture of confused irritation and reluctant amusement on his face.

When they had all calmed down, Dee said, "Oh, man, Wilson, that was good. Man, where you at? This is big stuff. The Neuronburg Rallies, in Europe, on VNET."

"Nope." Wilson shook his head. He was a big farmer in his fifties, with a flat-top and heavy glasses.

"Professor, tell him." Dee nodded his head at Daryl. They teased him at will, but in the Home Guard and Homeland Brotherhood, everyone considered Daryl particularly educated.

Daryl explained. "It's this mass movement. In Europe. You aware of what's going on up in Northern Europe with the climate?"

"Yuh," said Wilson. "Sure. Getting colder." This news was common knowledge now. The reports had been coming for years.

"You hear about the glaciers in, what, Norway?" Dee directed his question at the group. Wilson nodded, waiting.

"I heard one of 'em is going about ten feet a day," said Pierce. "Already wiped out a few towns."

"Scotland has its first three glaciers now. Wales has one." The shorter man from Roanoke spoke up.

"OK," continued Daryl, going into unnecessary detail as he was prone, but everyone listened. "So, there's a lot of talk about population starting to evacuate from Scandinavia and Scotland and Holland and places like that. Just a trickle now – people need money, and don't just walk away from their houses and farms – but the glaciers are all growing, winter's getting really cold and wet, and the growing season's shrinking by days every year. So they figure there's forty, fifty million people who'll eventually have to leave. Maybe more. Maybe a decade or two. That's the mainstream story. The EU. They're talking about where they're going to go. Which explains why they want us to do something about climate. And lend us the money."

"Who believes that bullshit?" asked Dee rhetorically. "'Ere's more to it. That's not all they want. The loan is a smokescreen."

"OK," Daryl continued. "So anyway, there's this Fourth Crossing movement, and they say that the North Atlantic problem is America's fault..."—there were snorts of derision—"... and that we should compensate by letting huge numbers of them come here because our population density is still a lot lower, but the crazy stuff comes in with the Fourth Crossing prophecy."

Pierce entered the explanation with an air of authority. "What they say, is that this is Europe's destiny, and that Europeans first came here thousands of years before Columbus—that's the First Crossing—and then the Vikings came—that's the Second—and then there's the Third Crossing, that brought most of us here, and now they say it's time for the Fourth."

There was silence for a moment. Wilson nodded again, still standing. The others were finishing their lunches. "Well shee," mused Dee, his brows knitted.

"The key is that they're saying it's their right, their destiny. Nothing about negotiating something or that maybe they should ask us first." Daryl shook his head. "Just come on over and take it. Fifty million."

"I taught history for twenty years," the taller guy from Roanoke spoke up. "It makes sense in a weird way. I mean, the US was the world's superpower for a long time, so we thought we ran everything, like we WERE the West. But remember that all this here—most of us, English language, Spanish, our government, the legal system, Christian churches and Jewish synagogues—it's all here because Europe put it here, without asking for anyone's permission, so when you think about it, why would they be asking for anyone's permission now, all of a sudden?"

"Because they fucking need to ask for OUR permission, that's why," snarled Pierce. "We're in charge, not the Indians anymore, and it ain't gonna happen."

The history teacher was unfazed. "I agree. Maybe they should have asked the Indians' permission too. But what I'm saying is, this Fourth Crossing thing is Europe's conversation with itself. We're not part of it. They're making up their own minds."

"And anyway," Daryl cut in, "Fourth Crossing is a fringe group. It's not the government. It's not a major political party. It's just chatter right now."

"Sounds like a bunch of crazy cusses," said Wilson slowly, and they all laughed.

"Yeah, well, take it seriously," ordered Pierce, "because you might think they're wackos but the fuckin' glaciers are nobody's imagination and neither is twenty, thirty million people thinking about moving, all packed up with nowhere to go." He stood up and looked around. "Over there, they're probably saying the Homeland Front is a bunch of fringe wackos too. Are we?" His tone and face were sharp. The men avoided his eyes. Daryl wondered how many of the group were on board, and how many were not.

Pierce went on. "The day is just about over when a bunch of frickin' corrupt politicians and bureaucrats and oligarchs think they can run global thermopolitics the way they want to, just nationalizing everything and getting richer and fatter while everyone else gets poorer and things get worse. Fourth Crossing or something like it is gonna knock down the EU folks we're talking with now about this loan shit—all polite and official—

and something a lot worse than wanting to rebuild America's consumer markets is gonna be number one on the EU agenda. You mark my words, gentlemen. Happy shoppers and exciting new foreign retail chains is about the last thing anybody's gonna be worryin' about anymore. You ever hear of Hitler? Stalin? They got that in their genes." He stopped.

Pierce's pause punctuated the political discussion for the day with a period.

"Now," finished Pierce. "Let's get our butts goin' again. We got a cat-five-plus off the Carolinas and five more sites to reinforce by tonight. We also gotta go back to the Op Center and get ready for at least a week of mobilization. Maybe two."

That was the end of the political briefing, Homeland Front-style. They stood up to move on to the next site.

26-A CHANGE OF TRAVEL PLANS

Friday, October 26th

"Excuse me. Do the earthworks go all the way around the city?" asked Mike from the table where he sat alone. The young woman behind the counter looked at him blankly, shaking her head imperceptibly. He repeated the question. Another woman came up behind her, bringing Mike's tea and breakfast. The first woman muttered something to her.

"Huh?" asked the second woman, older and battered-looking, with mild surprise. "You from outside?"

"We're traveling through, ma'am," he replied reassuringly, snapping easily back into his Corps manner. He had been to a lot of towns across the South that were gradually subsiding into the isolation of the Long Emergency, instinctive suspicions growing stronger among the inhabitants - suspicions of outsiders, Northerners, and people of different races or ethnicities.

"Where're you from?" She rolled an eye at him. He was not sure whether this was asked with hospitality or hostility.

"Maryland, ma'am. Headin' home after six years in the Corps of Engineers."

"Oh, yeah?" She said this with a friendly sort of curiosity now. "I'm from Germantown myself. Used to get up there a lot more than I do nowadays." She starting stacking plates and cups as she spoke. "Used to be a lot cheaper on the train. But it's nice to see some travelers still comin' through." She paused in her stacking. "What was you askin' again?"

"These fortifications," said Mike. "The earth wall with the wooden fence on top. Does it go right around the city?"

"Yeah, most of it. Not where the river goes through, 'course." She laughed. "Pretty much most of it." She frowned and looked up at the buildings across the street. "No, maybe I got that wrong. Don't think they got 'em up around Ettrick and Colonial Heights. But definitely south of the river and around downtown... And the battlefield. Big ones there." She opened the gate in the counter to bring his order out to the table. "You'd best talk with a police officer or Public Works, honey. They-all 'd know."

"Thanks," he replied. "Just curious. Never seen anything like 'em before." She put the tea and pancakes and scrambled eggs down on the table. "That looks good."

"We make 'em good here. Anything else I can get you right now, hun?"

"No, thanks," said Mike. "That's just fine for now." She smiled and went back into the kitchen. The younger woman peered sidelong at Mike from behind the counter. Then another customer called her. Mike took a sip of his tea, swallowed, and leaned back. He looked around the old diner, worn yet cheerful. They had recommended it at the campground across the road. It seemed well-patronized, although the morning rush had ebbed. The food smelled good, over the sweet basement-y smell of coal smoke emanating from the kitchen. He wondered why they were burning coal in a diner. It was usually reserved for big power plants. Then he remembered the rail lines nearby, and the universal way kids everywhere would walk the tracks picking up dropped coal chunks and tossing them into wagons, baby carriages and backpacks for resale, despite the illegality of this practice.

Some old cydub gospel hit from the Twenties pulsed and tinkled over the sound system. He looked at his watch, Army-issue and reliable. It was almost nine. Grandma had been gone for two hours. He wondered what the prognosis was for Bill's hoof. She had not called. They had spent so much time together over the past week that Mike decided not to bother her now with a call. She would call if anything was urgent. Maybe she just wanted some peace while she waited for the farrier to finish. Probably working on the morning produce trades. He dug into his food hungrily, and opened his T-pad flat on the table as he chewed his first bite. The dashboard chimed with various messages and notices. There was the usual Olian V-mail he had to ignore for now. The weather icon pulsed and glowed with urgency. He took another sip of tea and tapped it open, peering at the text and map as they covered the screen. He gulped the tea, and froze.

Out over the blue expanse of the Atlantic, level with Charleston, South Carolina, Hurricane Rhiannon sat like a flawless disc of white, its tiny eye sharp and perfectly centered. The hurricane was big. By the map, it looked

199

like it was four hundred kilometers across. Animations of the preceding forty-eight hours saw it slide eastwards, stall, wobble, and begin progressing steadily toward the northwest.

"Looks like a frisbee," said a voice behind Mike. He glanced around. An older man was getting up from a nearby table, a leather bag over one shoulder. He met Mike's eye with a grave, calm expression, and tilted his head toward Mike's T-pad. "The storm. No whorls—arms—like they usually have."

Mike nodded. "Coming right this way, all of a sudden." The track in the forecast put the hurricane on a path right along the Outer Banks and straight up the western shore of the Chesapeake Bay. Right now, its eye spun more than two-hundred kilometers offshore, its outer fringes not even touching the coast. But that would soon change, and if the eye crossed Norfolk at the Bay's mouth, its rim would already be lacerating Petersburg. Large populated areas lay in its projected path, including Washington.

The two men stared down quietly at the bright colors and hypnotic movements on the T-pad. Mike broke the silence.

"Category five-plus-plus right now." The man grunted in affirmation. Mike read from the National Hurricane Center website. "Sustained winds of seventy-five meters per second. Gusts up to a hundred. Tornadoes radiating from center up to a hundred kilometers. Lowest-ever recorded central barometric pressure…"

"Friggin' monster." The man shook his head. "Heard this morning on the radio that it's sitting on Gulf Stream water that's almost ninety-five degrees. Just sucking up fuel. Like a battery charging. Out in the Atlantic Ocean!"

"You live around here?" Mike sat back. He was already thinking about their emergency plan. This would change everything. He looked up at the man. The man glanced back over his shoulder. Mike followed his line of sight, and saw several other people—adults and teenagers—at the table the man had left. They looked back in silent reaction.

The man turned back toward Mike. "No, came down from Fredericksburg. For a wedding. Bunch of us came, gifts and all, so we took our coach. Planned to head back today."

"How far's Fredericksburg by wagon?" asked Mike.

"Two long days from here, best of conditions with good horses. Where're you headed?" The man paused. "Or are you local?"

200

"Oh, no. We're on our way to just outside DC," answered Mike. "Bethesda. My grandma—she's who I'm traveling with—estimated it would be five more days. We've got a team pulling a pretty heavily loaded wagon. 'Course, now we have hoof problems. Grandma's at a vet's now. Or, a farrier's. So we don't know altogether…"

The man cleared his throat. "We've started thinking through our alternatives." He looked at his companions. "Right, team?" There were some murmurs. A young man spoke up.

"Dad, when's it supposed to get here?"

The man looked back at Mike and shrugged. "What are they saying? About twenty-four hours?"

Mike studied the website more closely, clicking to enlarge the picture of the projected path.

"Much quicker. The eye should hit the coast late this afternoon, but by then Petersburg should be within the area of wind and rain. I'd say things will be very, very bad here by early tomorrow morning. Even late tonight." He squinted at the screen. "It's moving pretty fast, speeding up."

The conversation became more lively. It seemed everyone in the man's party was going all the way to Fredericksburg. They, too, were planning to get onto I-95 here in Petersburg. At the speeds their horse-drawn vehicles permitted, it was not a question of whether the hurricane would overtake them, but rather of when and where. And although Grandma had mainly worried about the effects of heavy rains, it was clear now that fearfully strong winds would also probably strike them.

"My Grandma's going to want to keep going. Maybe try to get to Richmond, where we know folks. If the horse with the bad hoof can take it."

"I think that's a bad idea, if you don't mind my saying so." The man took his bag off his shoulder and put it back on the floor. He had already sat back down. "And since I'm giving you advice, you might as well know who it's coming from." He reached his hand over to Mike. "Ethan Burhans." They shook hands.

"Mike Kendeil," said Mike.

The man gestured. "These are my wife Lena, kids, plus one other member of the wedding party." Mike looked over and they all exchanged nods, brief smiles. The wife was attractive, sweet-faced. The girl was sexy, athletic-looking, late teens or early twenties. The overall impression was of

201

health and capability. These were not poor crackers, not country people living at the subsistence level.

"Who got married?" asked Mike.

"My eldest daughter. Jessie. On Wednesday. We stayed yesterday with her and her new in-laws down in Disputanta. Big hog farm." Mike vaguely recalled riding through there the day before. "Drove up from there this morning. They called a little while ago. They're clearing out this afternoon, heading west in their diesel bus. By tonight, they'll be in West Virginia, where there's kin. Disputanta's in low country. Said it was sure to flood. Pigs'll have to swim. They said we ought to at least get inside the Petersburg berm."

"You mean the earthworks?" Mike's attention rose.

"Sure, you can call it that too."

"What's the story with it?" Mike asked.

"We wondered, too," said Ethan Burhans. A young man—a son?—nodded in curiosity, and pulled his chair closer. The girl slid in behind him and put her arms and head down on the table. "Seems there were already lots of fortifications from the Civil War battles here, but some guy about ten years ago started promoting the reconstruction of berms and stockades for civil defense, storm protection, crime control, protecting the faithful. You know, when a lot of the stockade building started. So they used the old star patterns and forts and tunnels—fit it together with the historic fortifications—and it kept a lot of men working when their jobs started disappearing."

"Do they have any hurricane bunkers here?"

"Not that I know of. My new relatives didn't know of any. But they said that, if any place was secure, Petersburg was. Like one big hurricane bunker. They use some long tunnels as hunkers. Out in the battlefield. They're wet and dank but safe. And they have old concrete parking garages."

"Petersburg, protected by saints and angels," laughed Burhans' wife softly, breaking her shy silence. Mike wondered whether her laugh was ironic, or whether she meant it literally.

"Oh come on, mom," groaned the daughter.

"But there's a few other pieces in this puzzle," continued Burhans. "I'm older than I look, and I was almost grown when my cousins' house

202

was destroyed down in Mississippi by Katrina. Completely obliterated. You remember that one?"

"Yes," answered Mike. "Well, no. I mean, it was some years before I was born, but I just spent the past six or so years with the Army Corps of Engineers down in Vicksburg and around Georgia and Alabama, and Katrina was always the benchmark, the baseline storm for everything down there since. They called it the first greenhouse hurricane."

"Well, wherever you draw the line, I don't know," said Burhans. "But, OK. So, with a storm like that or worse, I learned some key lessons that have served me well ever since. One is, you better have water, food, and other supplies for a couple of weeks. Another is, you never know what's going to happen with civil disorder, especially nowadays. A third is, look carefully at where the transportation routes are going to break down, be cut off."

Mike approved of his methodical approach. "I like your way of thinking," he said. "My grandma and I have been talking about this for the last few days, and she seems to want to just wing it."

"Wing this one," said Burhans with no hint of a smile, "and you're going to be wearing wings when it's all over and done with. Like St. Peter down the road there." He pointed over this shoulder with his thumb toward the garish statue. "Here's what we've been talking over on the way up." He glanced at his companions. His wife and the young man had joined the circle. The other two sat back, listening less intently. "First, you don't want to get stuck in Richmond with a valuable team and cargo, only three of you, when all hell breaks loose. Sure, authorities will crack down again pretty fast, but for that scary day or two or three, it's going to be 'circle the wagons' and shoot to kill. I'm not joking. And you might be the ones killed. You know about what happened during that summer power outage two-three years ago." Mike shook his head. "Thunder storms and a few tornadoes?" Burhans went on. "Bandits robbed almost every truck and wagon on I-64 because it wasn't secure like I-95. Dragged folks off their wagons and just shot them. Then drove off. Quick as lightning. The horses were worth plenty. People, nothing. Richmond's got no stockade, not the whole city. Lots of gated in-urbs, but the main city's wide open. In that storm—lasted about an hour—the police and National Guard had to cover the gated in-urbs, the key infrastructure like the bridges, and the firemen and emergency workers, who got called all over the place and were shot at

203

the whole time." Ethan Burhans took a deep breath, glancing at Mike's empty tea cup and plate. "Not a pretty picture. More than a hundred shot dead. Authorities since then have basically given up trying to secure a big part of the inner city. Bottom line is, you—or we—get stuck in Richmond tonight or tomorrow and we're going to regret it. If we live."

"What's second?" asked Mike.

"OK. Second is that—besides trees and stuff down across the smaller roads—a hurricane like this may well cut I-95—and 295 as well—where the Appomattox, James, and Pamunkey Rivers run under it. Those rivers are going to be wild. So if you're on the road, you may get stuck somewhere less than optimal." He glanced over at his wife. "Rappahannock's probably going to get wild again as well. What do you think, honey?" She nodded. He continued. "Up in Fredericksburg, they've built extra spillways through the town to take the pressure off the Route 1 and I-95 bridges, but the last few hurricanes have seen real damage. Closed Route 1 for a couple of weeks two years ago. I-95 is of absolutely maximum priority for the government. Lose that and they literally lose overland control of the Near South. So they'll put huge resources into keeping it open. But you just never know."

"So I guess you're staying here, then," said Mike, his mind sorting through numerous plans.

Ethan Burhans turned to his whole group. "We staying put here?" Nods and gloomy murmurs of assent were returned. He turned back toward Mike. "Yup. Somewhere safe, if we can find it…"

They were all silent for a moment.

"Sounds like our best bet, too," said Mike. "Civil order is what they seem to have plenty of here, as well, in addition to the earthworks. And food and water…Quite a process getting in last night."

"Did you have to recite the Creed?" asked Lena Burhans. Mike shook his head.

"We all did. It was tricky." She laughed softly. "We're steady churchgoers, but we only know the Apostles'—we're non-liturgicals—and here it's Nicene. Almost threw us off, when the guards started scowling. But they gave it to us. We put on a convincing performance…"

Mike chewed his lip, and nodded slightly. "Anyway, sounds like we should dig in here, but we'll see what my grandma and Fernando think when they get back." He looked at his watch again. It was well after nine now. "Which ought to be soon." He smiled. "Thanks for all the info."

Burhans sat back. "Pleasure. Got to help fellow travelers. And we still have a little time before we have to get ready." He patted the knee of the young man beside him. "What do you think, Nate, my man? Need to get some more supplies, position the wagon and team, talk to the local cops, get a plan together." He looked back at Mike. "Ask your grandma if she wants to team up with us. There's some safety in numbers."

"Ah, there's a problem," said Mike. "We only have a twenty-four-hour pass. It runs out this evening."

Burhans shook his head. "Don't worry about that. That's what they always give you, in case they want to kick you out. Gives them the option. But it often gets automatically extended in case of emergencies. Illness, storms, accidents..."

Mike was skeptical. "Are you sure?"

"Sure. We got 'em too. I asked the police and that's what they said. Although we may have to work for it."

"Work?" asked Mike.

"Dig ditches. Carry sandbags. That kind of thing."

"Mmm. Hope you're right." Mike wondered about this. He recalled the poor family turned away at the gate, and his conversation with the gate-keeper. There might be some fees, some wrangling. He also wondered what was happening with Grandma. He put away his T-pad, set some money on the table for the waitress—they didn't take milscrip here—and stood up. The Burhans party was also stirring, standing and getting ready to leave the diner. Mike sensed attention, and saw from the corner of his eye that the teenage girl was studying him closely. He shifted his head and grinned at her. She jerked her eyes away, cheek muscles taught. Her mother caught the exchange. She stared at Mike coolly. Then the tableau dissolved as everyone began heading toward the door.

Out in the fresh air again, Mike scanned the street. Traffic was moderate. Down to the right he could see the roof of Grandma's wagon over the campground fence, and this reassured him. A creaking noise above him caused him to look up. In the apartments over the diner, the inhabitants were pulling their storm shutters closed. He looked back at the street. Now he noticed what he had missed when he came in. Or maybe it had not started yet. In all directions, shutters were closing, and people were nailing planks over storefronts and preparing in other ways for the oncoming hurricane. In the distance, he heard the engines and back-up horns of trucks or construction equipment.

"Where are you parked?" Mike asked his new acquaintances.

"Right over there," said the younger of the two young men—Jim—who had joined the conversation, pointing down the street a short distance. A large enclosed coach stood parked by the curb. Its team of four brownish-black horses stood in harness, their muzzles in feedbags. A boy sat on the driver's bench, reading. A rifle sat stowed in a holster attached to the bench by his side.

Mike stopped to examine the coach. He had never seen anything quite like it up close. Essentially, it was a stagecoach, 1870's Wild West-style. It sat up on big spoked wheels with rubber tires, the rear wheel bigger than the front wheel. A single door on either side led into the compartment, which looked large. There were curtained windows, carriage lamps, an elaborate roof rack, and a kind of baggage cage on the back. A ladder behind the front wheel led up to the open driver's bench, which was at the level of the horses' heads, with a footboard extending quite far out from the compartment. It was a shiny deep-brown with yellow and red trim, and appeared to be made of a mixture of wood, fiberglass, and aluminum.

"Nice coach," said Mike to Burhans, who had just come abreast. "Did you get it in Fredericksburg?"

"Made it," said Burhans.

"You made it?" repeated Mike. He was impressed.

"That's what I do. Main thing I do these days, anyway. What people are willing to pay me for. Although maybe not always in cash..." Burhans stood admiring his coach. "I used to be a weapons engineer for the US Navy at Dahlgren! Imagine that. I was always messing with old cars. Built a machine shop in my basement. Now I build stagecoaches! Pretty cool, eh?" There was no irony at all in Burhans' voice, just mild self-deprecation and enthusiasm. He appeared to simply like what he did. "That's my youngest, Carl, up there." He nodded his head toward the boy. "Hey Carl." The boy glanced down and smiled.

"Celia's the one who got me into horses." He indicated his daughter with his chin. She was already removing the feed bags, patting the horses' noses with smooth, long strokes. She was a tall, slim girl, dressed in jeans

206

and an oiled cloth coat like her father, despite the sticky warmth of the air. Celia glanced at her father and Mike through her tousled hair, lips serious.

"What breed are those horses?" asked Mike. They were very different from Grandma's hackney crosses, with low bellies and strong-looking necks. He knew he needed to learn more about the seemingly endless variety of breeds and crosses.

"North Swedish," said Burhans. "Great combination for riding and draft. Very low maintenance."

Almost on cue, as they stood there, the clip-clop of a shod horse echoed up the road to their left, and both men turned to seek the sound. Here came Grandma, leading Bill along the curb. Fernando walked beside her. Mike was used to seeing Bill hitched to the wagon, but seeing him loose, just behind his wiry grandmother, reminded Mike how fine and tall Bill actually stood. And he walked with a springy, healthy step. Was this just because he was happy to be free of the wagon and his team mates for a change?

Grandma and Fernando drew closer, and when they reached Mike and Burhans, Grandma deftly tethered Bill to the diner's hitching rail. Bill eyed them through his big, kind left eye.

"Hi, Mike. Morning, mister." She smiled at both of them. Mike saw she was tense.

"Grandma, meet Ethan Burhans, from Fredericksburg." She reached out and gave his hand a hard shake. "This is my grandma." He indicated Fernando. "And this is Fernando, the third member of our crew." Fernando nodded.

"Florence Trudeau." She turned toward Mike, a shoulder to Burhans, and began, "Mike, good news and bad news. We have to get going..."

"Um, Grandma, maybe going's not such a good idea now..." Mike's voice was resolute. "I've been looking into this hurricane, and discussing things with the Burhans family here."

Grandma's face tightened. She did not like what she was hearing. Mike had known this would come. Then he remembered the purpose of her errand.

"And anyway, how's Bill?"

"Oh, he's fine... And, yes, I heard something about the storm at the farrier's. Moving up this way."

"Fine?" asked Mike. "Is that all? It seemed serious yesterday. You were talking about founder!"

"No, it wasn't that. Loose shoe and a stone under it. Uneven. But no gashes, no infection. Farrier seems to have fixed it..." She dismissed that subject altogether. A different note of urgency entered her voice. "But, listen, I got a call from your sister—"

"Hon?" interjected Mike.

"Yes, Hon," said Grandma impatiently, "and, so, well, things are really going from bad to worse. She called from the Lanc on their way from the wholesale mart to White Flint, and you won't believe what's happened now... It really ticks me off..." Her anger and frustration were palpable. Burhans looked away, not sure if he should remain standing there as the conversation turned inward.

"What?"

"That Sanna...She, she sold the van! Sold it legally, for cash, to some plumber. Took the money and vanished."

"She already had vanished," said Mike.

Grandma's voice was strained. "You know what I mean. She's gone, the money's gone—the money I lent her, most of it—and Hon's working like a dog while Claudia has had to drop everything to watch the boys. Hon's scared she'll have to give up the apartment. Poor girl. She works so hard, and doesn't deserve any of this." She looked at the ground and shook her head. "Or at least not most of it."

Mike was almost about to remind her what the sale of the gold could achieve, but remembered Burhans and Fernando, standing there, and bit his tongue.

"We have got to get back to Chevy Chase A-S-A-P. Hon needs us. And if I can catch Sanna I'm going to wring her sassy, mixed-up, Euro-trash neck." Her eyes were livid.

"Grandma," said Mike. "There are some things we need to deal with."

"Like what?" Grandma stood in front of him, looking up at him, her back to the street. She stood with her body braced, like she was preparing for a fight. "Like, can we talk about it while we're driving?"

"Grandma, I don't think we ought to be driving anywhere today."

"Of course we're driving. We can't afford to stay here a moment longer. If we leave now, we'll be in Richmond for an early dinner, and Dwight and Henry are expecting us! They have lighting on the Interstate, if we're delayed." Dwight and Henry were old friends of hers from her government days. They lived together in a fine brick townhouse in Richmond's old town. She had had tea with them on the way down. They had connections. She wanted Mike to talk to them—get work ideas.

Mike's tone became more resolute. It required a conscious effort. This was his grandmother. But she needed to see things in a different light.

"Grandma, Honorée and mom are in a real bad situation, but they have each other, and Marcus, and Lon, and a lot of other people they can rely on for a few days. We have to start thinking right now about our own situation. This storm is a killer. We can't make any mistakes."

And, standing there, in front of the diner, Mike recounted the conversation with Burhans and his companions, while Burhans listened, and at one point signaled to his daughter Celia to bring some of the apples she was giving their team over to Bill. Bill happily crunched up all she could spare.

Grandma listened, her eyes away, face drawn. When Mike was finished, she took a deep breath and blew it back out with a sharp sigh. Her fists were clenched. Even with all the intelligence and impatience and fury and power in her, Mike suddenly saw in his thin, sun-weathered grandmother the shadow of a worried, frightened old woman—an old woman who wanted to right all the wrongs close to her, and ignore the dangers, but who was beginning to see that she no longer had the energy or strength to take on what she easily would have triumphed over once.

"OK, all right. I hear you. Let's wait it out. I'll call Hon and Claudia, and Dwight, and Marcus..." She looked around in exasperation. "Fernando, take Bill back over, will you, please?" Fernando went to untie Bill. Mike and Burhans waited, watching her. Then out of her like spit came some of the sharpest exclamation Mike had ever heard his grandmother utter. "Oh, goodness; oh, DAMN this awful Emergency!" Her eyes were on fire. "For pity's sake, look at this. For most of my life I could have hopped into my car in this holy little city here and been in Chevy Chase in just over two hours." She laughed harshly with humorless irony, her voice rising in pitch. "But no! We have to ride around in wagons and feed horses and hide from storms, and sleep in tents, armed all the time, and waste all this precious God-DAMN time...All this precious, precious time!" She abruptly beat the air with a fist. Mike saw angry tears in her eyes. "Oh, I just don't know. Sometimes, I just don't know anymore."

She fell silent, leaning against the hitching rail. Mike glanced at Burhans. He nodded faintly, and then pointed at his watch. Time was becoming scarce. It was well past nine now. A light wind from the east was stirring the treetops and lifting puffs of dust off the road. The sky was a humid yellow-gray.

27-THE ANNIVERSARY PARTY

Friday, October 26th

Christine terminated the call and pulled off the tiny earset, dropping it in her coat pocket.

"They're already turning off of Route 5."

"Who was that?" Wilder, looking harried, ducked his head around the kitchen door frame so he could see her.

"Gill Challis, at the General Store. I asked him to keep an eye out."

"Smart." He laughed. "We don't want the surprise to be on us!" He raised his eyebrows. "So, that gives us about fifteen or twenty minutes."

"I'll go out back and get everyone to settle down." She ran off, closing doors and tidying minor details as she passed through the old farmhouse. Then Wilder heard a shout. The click of her footsteps returned. "Whose bikes are those?!" she exclaimed, out of breath, pointing out the window toward the road.

"Speranzas', maybe." Wilder was hesitant. "Or Coles'?"

She ran off again, to remove this last suspicious detail from where her sharp-eyed mother might spot it. Wilder finished putting the chilled cider bottles on the tray and glanced out the window. Nothing was visible coming down the road but two girls on horseback and, then, a lone motorcycle. He opened the window. The cool, dry, spicy air of the bright fall day drifted in. He heard a burst of laughter from around back. Spirits were high and it would be hard keeping everyone quiet until they could spring the surprise party on Maryann and Rob. But it was worth a try.

He looked around the kitchen, but he could not see anything obvious that remained to be done. The snacks, bread, cheese, fruits, stew, wine, cider, cake and everything else seemed to be under control. He washed his hands and hung the dish towel back up by the refrigerator. More laughter and a cheer came through the window. Christine did not appear to be having much luck. People needed a party, and they were getting one. He turned back to the window facing the road, opened the sash all the way, and stood leaning on the window sill with his elbows. Still no sign of Rob and Maryann's black phaeton.

The view from the old farmhouse, sitting in its meadow up above the quiet road, was unremarkable for Vermont, but after the toil, tension, and taut politics of Washington, it nearly brought tears to his eyes. Up and down the shallow valley, open fields and meadows clustered around the houses along the road, dotted with sheep, cattle, horses, haystacks, and crops. Behind them, small bumpy hilltops and ravines rose, covered with thick mixed forests. Amidst the lush green cover were hints of fall colors and the dry browns from a long, hot summer. Over Christine's meadow, lawns, and gardens, dragonflies hovered and darted, their wings crackling like old-fashioned plastic wrappers. Golden hazes of small insect swarms drifted above the sunflowers, Echinacea, chrysanthemums, and hostas. The woods and fields jingled with the steady song of late-season crickets. Christine's cat Maddy drowsed on a warm stone below the window, concealed among the lavender.

Wilder felt as though he were falling into a trance, an Indian summer spell, transporting him to a simpler world—a safe, sleepy valley that bigger, badder trends would always overlook. He sighed, and chuckled softly. How false this sense of security was. Yet, as long as he had known Christine – which was all of the time he had been in the House—six years—plus some years before when he was in the State Senate—it was this farmhouse that had always welcomed his retreat from the struggles and nastiness of politics. He still had his apartment up in Montpelier, which was convenient. But, whether in the depths of winter or the abundance of summer, his best times were always spent here.

"Jake! They should be here any second!" Christine came hurrying through the house again. He turned with an easy, relaxed smile toward her, still leaning on the window sill. She surveyed him and the kitchen, eyes flashing. "Well, I'm glad you're having a nice quiet time just hanging out and being very anti-social about it as well—they're asking, 'Where's Jake?' and 'Is Jake all right?'—but when I went back there they hadn't done anything I asked them to, not even my sisters–they think the party's already started—so I had to see to all that as well!" She whirled and fussed at high speed. Wilder laughed. He rarely saw Christine like this. In the permanence of his mind's eye, she was always cool, always calm.

Just then, the whinny of a horse snapped their eyes to the window, and not more than a hundred yards off they saw her parents' sleek black phaeton, pulled proudly by the two young Morgans Rob had recently bought in Swanzey. It smoothly ascended the rising grade. Wilder and Christine looked at each other, grinning. They really had taken the phaeton—not too surprising on such a lovely day, after all—and left Rob's cell-electric at home. This had been Christine's suggestion. She hardly expected him to take it. But his parents had, aiding Christine as a result in her scheming with a long leisurely ride out through Dummerston, rather than a quick drive.

Christine went running out the door to divert them into the front drive so they would pull up in front of the house. "Remember, Jake. The story's they're coming for lunch. Low key. Just relax. And drinks for them!" She slowed and trotted down the flagstone walk, waving. Her mother waved back.

"Hey, mom. Just drive on up here and I'll put them in the meadow."

Christine giggled under her breath at her parents' impending astonishment.

Her father pulled the brake tight, they descended, and for a sweet moment they stood innocently poised on the brink of the impending surprise party, suspecting nothing!

* * *

"... We're seeing more and more of them, too," agreed Sam Miller, who had just come back from the house to get more ciders. He was Christine's neighbor and an old friend of her parents. He sat down in the chair opposite Dean, Christine's brother. "All kinds of folks, drifting by. Wagons, cars. On foot."

"We had a guy stop by the mill a few weeks ago, whole family up in what was basically a covered wagon." Dean worked at the paper mill in Putney. "This guy appeared to be a mechanical genius. He had a team of four, and a huge wagon with a mobile machine shop. Diesel generator, solar array, all kinds of power tools. He said he had just come up from Connecticut, where he'd been contracting for the National Guard, but he said life was getting too risky down there. Bunch of little kids, wife, a few relatives along."

"Where'd he go?" asked Sam. "Shame we couldn't use him around here."

"Well, we had him fix a couple of pumps and the augur in the main boiler. Really nice guy to deal with. He said he was heading for Springfield, where he had relatives. He said he was hoping to set up a business there. A mechanical instrument business. We kept his name. He took payment in allens, too."

"Most of the folks who come by our place don't want cash for their work. They just want food and a place to camp for a couple days. Or, if they'll take cash, they want euros or Canadian. Never heard of allens."

"I wonder how many are headed for Canada?" Dean opened a beer. "If they can get in, that is."

"I think a lot of 'em don't know where they're headed, but they want to get away from the expensive food, high cost of living, crime, and just plain overcrowding wherever they came from..." Sam, laced his fingers together and capped them over his head. "Thing is, and this is the scary thing, the migrants—Rob over there calls them 'settlers'—are the ones who actually CAN pick up and move. They have the wagons, horses, cars, trucks, fuel, whatever. They have the means. Plus, given what they've lost and don't have a stake in anymore, they are the people who at least have the hope and the spunk to start looking for something better. A lot of people just stay where they are, give up, scrape by... I had a long conversation a couple months back with a guy who worked for us with his sons during haying. He was a car dealer in New Haven. Comes up here in the summer with a crew, works for cash, buys a big cargo of food, and goes back down there for the winter to work in a German rebuilt car-parts factory. Still owns a lot of land, but he can't rent it out."

The evening had started off warm, but had cooled substantially since the sun set. A few crickets still sang drowsily. Dean and Sam grew silent. Their eyes scanned the dark dell down beyond the house, the dim lights of the houses and farms in the direction of Putney, the red safety lights of the slack wind turbines on the ridge above it.

The conversation beside them suddenly grew more heated, and they turned their attention to catch it.

"What those buttheads in Washington don't seem to realize is that America has moved on, into something else." Rob Hayes leaned back in his chair, and smiled sweetly at Maryann. She tutted disapprovingly at his language. He went on. "They took over oil, gas, and coal production, refining, transportation, and distribution as soon as the roof blew off—and what was left of nuke—and we got the usual sort of mess you get when the government gets into business. All politics and no performance." Rob was an old-school Republican, a rare breed. "Now you got the government trying get its hands on more fossil fuels – even get going with this OSCIA business... That's its only source of power. Everything else they used to control has fallen to state and local hands. Food, health care, the auto industry, construction...those big corporations are all gone and there's no campaign funding from them anymore. That's what Laugherty ain't saying. He's going for the old values and villains appeal, which most of his Republican base and all of the Homelanders will go for. Scare and hypnotize the superstitious suckers into voting him in... Hitch a ride on their fear... I wish people would grow up. People 'a lost sight of where their prosperity's going to come from now."

"Y'oughtta run, Rob," interjected Sam. "I'd put a sign on my lawn for you." They all chuckled. Sam raised a finger, and added, "About time you got up on your soap box." The laughter was louder and longer, with guffaws of "bad one!" and "keep it clean!"

Christine sighed darkly. "OSCIA's no joke. The Homelanders aren't joking, either."

Rob took another drink of his wheat beer and smiled at the dozen-plus faces around the flagstone patio. "Well, no, but sometimes you gotta laugh at it all anyway. And maybe the darkest hour is the one before dawn...I think there's a lot of opportunity out there. With the weak dollar, low wages, sooner or later this country's gonna be the world's factory, like China once was. Soon as we can settle down politically."

He was in no mood for gloom. This had been a wonderful anniversary celebration. He studied the faces around him. There were Maryann, his wife of forty years, their daughters Christine and Jessamyn, their son Dean, Jessamyn's husband Chris, Rob's cousin Emma, several old friends including Sam, his business associates Hal and Ernie, and Jake Wilder. Their twentieth seemed like it had taken place both a century ago and only yesterday. He remembered every detail of that party in Hinsdale, the weekend in New York, the week in Costa Rica. He was nobody special back then, money was always short, yet the travel and luxury at their disposal in those distant, dreamlike days—much of it on credit—felt unreal now. And now he was really somebody, comfortable beyond his wildest imagination, albeit in a different and hyper-local way.

Rob was a "transpreneur"—one of the originals. When Christine and her siblings were young kids, he had a paint store in Hinsdale just off Route 119 near the dog track. The increasingly hard times motivated Rob and Maryann to move across the Connecticut River to Vermont—where she had grown up—to gain access to the new universal health insurance plan—which New Hampshire did not have. In his struggling, cyclical *and* seasonal business, he could no longer afford private health insurance, but with four kids aged two through ten, he was afraid to operate without it, since he was not poor enough to be eligible for Medicaid, which kept shrinking its coverage anyway. This was a fateful move. It did not make complete economic sense, either, because he left New Hampshire's zero personal income tax and Hinsdale's lower property prices, and took on the overall higher tax burden in Vermont. But better protection against health risks plus the good schools and public services seemed to compensate, and even though the flaky liberalism of his new home drove his personal politics further right, he put up with it.

While Rob would commute the short distance across the river every morning to the paint store, Maryann started a tiny business in her kitchen making scented soaps, cleansers, lotions, and oils. It was just a money-maker on the side. She sold to the various co-ops and gift-shops in the region, and at outdoor markets and craft fairs. It was something she could combine with being a stay-at-home mother. The years passed. There was plenty of competition in this niche, so it developed slowly. Along with revenues, her knowledge about soaps and her sales network grew deep and wide.

Then came the first turbulent indicators of the Emergency in the Twenties. Although no one understood it yet, the Sanderborough bomb in 2021 essentially marked the start of the Third World War. As the decade progressed, abrupt rises in energy prices and geopolitical shocks repeatedly disrupted the retail economy, and even the Wal-Marts and big drugstore chains started periodically running out of merchandise. By late decade, with continuing recession, the falling standard of living, and government rationing and wage-price controls, Rob's business had shrunk to a shadow of what it had been, and he struggled on the brink of ruin with no college education and few alternatives to consider. The winters were especially hard. The only food they could afford was boring and seasonal, and their old wood frame house was very cold, since they could not afford to switch to a decent wood-pellet furnace (heating oil prices had gone through the roof) and had to rely on a used wood stove they bought that only heated the downstairs adequately. They went to bed in rooms hovering above freezing.

It was in the beginning of those trying years, around the time that the kids were beginning to leave the nest and search in vain for ways to start their adult careers or continue their educations, that Rob and Maryann noticed something interesting. Whenever energy prices jumped or something else traumatized the economy, sales of their soaps jumped as well. It was subtle in the beginning, but over a few years became so pronounced that they would be faced with stock-outs and late nights in the kitchen making new batches that were sold before they had even bought the ingredients. It was odd because their soaps were luxury items: little pink sandalwood cakes shaped like fish, red peppers of carbolic hand soap, and blocks of avocado-green facial soap tied together with dried grass. But it quickly became apparent that people just plain needed soap for home use, for schools, for businesses, for washing dishes at restaurants, for hospital operating rooms... And if they could not get the old standbys from Proctor & Gamble, Colgate-Palmolive, and Unilever that had traveled hundreds or thousands of miles to reach their local grocery store or pharmacy, then they would find their equivalents wherever they could.

In this crisis and accompanying realization, out of serendipity, Rob's transpreneurship was born. One snowy night, around midnight, their main blender broke. They had several big orders but needed the cash flow immediately to get their ancient biodiesel Subaru's brakes fixed so Rob could get to work and so Maryann could get down to Northampton for more supplies. (They had recently traded away their other vehicle, a newer pickup, for a couple of cords of wood, six months' rent on the paint store, and enough oils and lye for what they thought would be a few months of soap production.) Rob jumped in the Subaru, and with only the handbrake working, drove over to Hinsdale in low gear and brought back an electric paint mixer, which they set up on the kitchen table. As they mixed and poured through the night, it literally 'dawned' on Rob that this was turning into a big business. With retail supplies of soaps and detergents running low with growing frequency, he suddenly saw that the day might come soon when the big producers could no longer keep recovering—as massive and permanent as the likes of P&G seemed to someone who had grown up in the late Twentieth Century. Yet demand would never let up. Like food and shelter, people needed hygiene, and taking a bath and doing the laundry at home was only the tip of the iceberg. What about the whole health care industry? Slaughterhouses and industrial kitchens? Farms? Restaurants? Schools? Degreasers for machine shops? Mopping the floors of the courthouses and town halls?

From that moment on, Rob Hayes was no longer in the paint business. He closed it down that month, and they moved solid and liquid soap and detergent production to Hinsdale. The first few years were challenging, draining, and full of unexpected lessons, but what Rob had foreseen came to pass, and by 2035, hardly a single national retail chain or mass consumer brand remained in business to compete locally with what was by then named Riverbridge Soaps & Detergents. Many local and regional competitors started springing up, but within a 100-mile radius, Rob and Maryann had first-mover advantage and the best reputation. They prospered. They went into lye production up on Monument Road, integrating backwards into their own and others' supply chains (lye being easy to make from nothing more than water and wood-ash). They helped farmers up and down the valley expand oilseed and oil nut production—rapeseed, linseed, oil corn, safflower, sunflower, hazelnut—to reduce the transportation costs of bringing oil to Hinsdale. They built an oil pressing plant in Bellows Falls, and barged the fresh, pure oil down the river.

Now, the Hayes were truly wealthy. Their cash and credit, when neither were in easy supply, made them kings. All their children worked in some branch of the network of businesses they ran. As the soap business matured, spurred by the children's interests, they had bought orchards and a defunct sugarbush, started raising sheep for wool, and started breeding draft horses. They bought a wind-turbine farm in Franklin County. They now owned part of the paper mill in Putney. They still owned the house down in Brattleboro, but spent most of their time on the farm in Dummerston. They drove a late-model Japanese cell-electric cruiser. They could afford to routinely ride the train up to Burlington and down to New York. Some envious people called them oligarchs, but their success had nothing to do with political pull in DC or prostitution to the state-run fossil-fuel companies.

Rob and Maryann Hayes came to epitomize mid-century transpreneurs in Vermont. The greens and bioregionalists were continually awarding

218

them praise and recognition. Ever a Republican, Rob ignored all that. He was in it for the money, he always told them, not the "crunchy". Being socially responsible for the Hayes meant helping people stay clean, paying taxes, paying decent and regular cash wages, and not breaking the law.

Quietly, though, they still managed to contribute substantially to Jake Wilder's political campaigns. And not only on behalf of Christine…

"Jake, I've told you many times, I swear I don't know how you put up with all that bullshit down there in Washington." Rob grinned, inviting Wilder into a favorite topic of friendly debate they had not shared for quite some time. Wilder chuckled, in the limelight for the first time on a day he had been happy to step into the background. Curiosity rose in many of the faces of their companions on the patio.

"You can put up with just about anything if you're exposed to it long enough."

Rob laughed his trademark haw-haw laugh. "What, ya mean like radiation and lead?"

"DC politics are pretty toxic these days; you're right about that." Wilder's smile was wry.

"Seriously, you travel back and forth, work like a dog, and have to put up with what seems to me like some very nasty characters. And with all the financial shortages and bad news, I just cannot fathom how someone can get up and go to work day after day under those conditions." He took a swig of beer from his bottle. "I sure couldn't. Right, Mare?" His wife nodded.

"I mean," continued Rob, "in my business, you see results sooner or later that tell you whether you're wasting your time or doing the right thing. Nowadays, it looks like you and the other good guys down there are bangin' your heads against a brick wall. Madame President included."

Wilder took a deep breath and a sip of his cider. "It comes down to public service in the end. Representing the people of Vermont. We need all the advocacy down there we can get. I've been doing it for a while, and know a thing or two. I sure don't want to do it forever, but there are some very dangerous, risky twists and turns ahead. I think I make a difference." To his own consternation, Wilder heard a defensiveness, a preachiness in his tone. This isn't the place for this, he chided himself.

"Sure, of course I'm not doubting any of that." Rob reassured him. "You're the best guy we could possibly have down there right now." Everyone nodded in agreement. "What I'm talking about is the difficulty of getting the federal government to do things that make any sense."

"Like this loan deal," interjected Sam Miller.

"Yeah," said Rob. "Where's that now?"

Wilder shrugged and rubbed his eyes. "Well, technically it's in the hands of the White House and Treasury. It's basically about government debt, the way the World Bank has so far presented it. It's not a budget issue. It's like, does the government issue bonds and bills or raise funds this way? The Fed has a say in it as well. Congress gets in when the borrowings are to be appropriated..." He took another drink, and shifted in his seat. "But the whole thing has become politicized way beyond what it should be. Probably has to do with the size of it and the conditions. Foreign governments have been buying T-bills for ever. Nothing new about that. China and a few other Asian governments basically kept the government alive back during and after the Younger Bush administrations, when we started fighting the oil wars and running huge trade deficits..." A few people were saying quiet good-nights and getting up to go. He continued, "But you know, America's credit is pretty much zero now, after the various dollar collapses and defaults. The USG can't go out and borrow on the open market—whatever's left of it. It has to be political, intergovernmental."

"Well, I like the conditions that go along with it," said Christine. "They're sensible. We need to be hearing it. We should have listened years ago."

"Maybe," said Wilder. "I personally agree. There's nothing I'd like better than to see the rail system rebuilt and the kind of energy efficiency they have in the EU, plus all the distributed generation. We don't have the money for anything more than marginal improvements at the moment. But, politically, it's a non-starter. It takes on the Energy Trust head-on. Without the Energy Trust, the government would be completely bankrupt, as would most of the oligarchy. The Energy Trust and its friends want total control of those funds if they come to us. And they want them to mostly go to conventional projects. Coal and oil. And nuke. Even though it's not in the terms and conditions, everybody know the EU and Beijing want the Trust busted up, deregulated. That gets the Homelanders howling. An 'internal affairs' thing..."

Rob yawned deeply, and shook his head. "If the Chinese and the Europeans and the rest of 'em didn't think we were a good bet, they wouldn't want to give us money. And they have to think about their own climate problems, and political stability, and their own economies. The US used to be a huge consumer market. Look what happened to soap, speaking of something dear to my heart! I'm making a decent living because nobody can afford anything. The G-12 want us online again. Open for business."

"Not just consumer, Rob." Sam pulled his chair forward out of the shadows. "You think of all those great makes we used to buy and can't afford now – Kubota, Hilti, Stihl, Husqvarna, Makita... Honda generators... Ridgid and DeWalt were all offshored... It's killing us and it's killing them because we can't buy them foreign brands. If we could even find them, that is."

"Exactly. If we could get them. You know," said Wilder, "I've been thinking a lot about the trade-related conditions, and we're going to have to watch that angle carefully, if we say for the sake of this discussion that the loan goes through, which I'm afraid it won't within the foreseeable future." They looked at him expectantly. He went on, "A basic condition that folks are tending to ignore in most discussions I hear is that all the US trade barriers set up over the last ten years be dismantled, and trade restored to pre-2030 WTO norms. And when the Homelanders bring this up, they act as if it's some kind of plot to destroy the US economy and take American jobs away and given them to foreigners. A Trojan Horse. But we need efficiency desperately, and the capital to invest in it. Our purchasing power may be the pits these days, but even though we're bottom-of-pyramid in global terms, there are a lot of us, and a lot of demand. You know what I read the other day?" A few shook their heads. "I read that Mitra-Shops is now the world's biggest retailer, and in South Asia alone they have ten million retail distributors—employees, with benefits - consisting of a guy with a T-pad on an electric bike with a basket, and two hours' worth of inventory. They make money hand over fist. We need that kind of investment to get the big scale efficiencies we're not getting with all these little, isolated markets."

"I'm glad Mitra-Shops is thinking big," said Rob. "I hope I can still sell my soap when their electric bikes start showin' up. But it seems to me that we've got some big political stability things to straighten out here before that can happen."

"And there's Canada, too." Dean, Christine's younger brother, joined in. "Where does a lot of China's oil come from? And if anything like OSCIA or the Fort Murray movement gets going, it's like, I mean, the rest of the world is GOING to get involved. The Western Hemisphere is not some hidden corner of the world where Americans can do stuff nobody notices... They have a stake in our political stability way before it's about retail trade again."

"McMurray," his sister Jessamyn corrected him.

"Okay, Mc." Dean threw her a sidelong glance and shrugged. "What I'm saying is that the world wins with a stable, prosperous America. Maybe we need some help. It's not the end of the world. Jake, why isn't this idea sinking in in Washington? Laugherty and the right-wing Republicans and the Homeland Front are all talking like the rest of the world doesn't exist, doesn't have legitimate interests or useful know-how, or is up to conspiracies. They're just feeding the feelings of isolation and desperation around the country. But anyone can read about what the world thinks in the VNET. There's no mystery."

Wilder raised his eyebrows. "This idea has already sunk in pretty deep at the highest government levels. They're not dumb. The White House has its eyes wide open. Rationally, almost everyone knows the dangers and the risks of the Conventionalist position. They know the loan conditions are right on target. But this is where politics come into it..."

"Yup," said Rob. "Zactly." Dean wrinkled his brows.

"It's like this," said Wilder. "If the Authoritarian Right can keep people paranoid and scared and blaming someone else, they're hoping that one way or another they'll be able to grab access to most of the Alberta oil, which will buy time against real transformation. SHE-WEBS-style. The real thing. And the Right will get credit for it. Practically nobody anywhere in the political spectrum is so stupid to think that America's prosperity and global military power can be restored to their former glory on the shoulders of oil and gas. Our coal reserves have some potential but they're dirty and expensive. Nuke is problematic but might have a role to play. But SHE-WEBS and much smarter foreign policy are the only really sustainable solutions in the long run. The problem is that the Energy Trust is running scared from this idea, and buying off anybody who will support them. And admitting this would mean the Right's basically handing over the future to what the progressive parties and critics have been saying all along." Wilder laughed drily and shook his head. "Oh, no. They're not going to do that. The country's stretched to the limit with these acute, grinding problems right now that affect everybody, and the time is ripe for scapegoating, and there's no social solidarity, no shared rationale, no prevailing story about why this has happened and why we all have to stick together. The country's coming apart, fragment by fragment. Towns with stockades. Oligarchs sealing themselves off. State secession movements. Evangelical separatist communities like the Triple-C. The Right is trying to manipulate and capitalize on this situation for all they're worth. Especially the Homelanders. They think they have the right story. Authoritarian traditionalists. Benign dictatorship..." He lowered his voice and narrowed his eyes. "The worst thing about them is that they really believe the Conventionalists and the more paranoid Republican assessments. SHE-WEBS et cetera doesn't mean a damn thing."

"I've always felt I was a conservative—morally, socially, financially, politically," said Rob angrily. "But the Homelanders are a whole different ballgame. We ought 'a shut them down. They talk a good conservative line sometimes, but I see them for what they are. They're perfectly happy to let the Energy Trust strangle the economy—Big Government at its worst—but it looks like what really drives them is the openings they're looking for to take away civil rights and property from, you know, everyone who's not white, and turn the clock back a hundred years. Jake, what was that word you said a while back? Like "kryptonite"?

"Crypto?" offered Wilder.

"Yes," said Rob. "Crypto-racists and crypto-fascists..."

"Crypto-petro-feudalists?" offered Dean archly.

Maryann stood up, preparing to start the process of leaving. The talk made her face grow perplexed. Christine noticed her confusion.

"Mom," she said. "Crypto-this and crypto-that means people really believe something but they hide it. Like a pig in a poke."

"Oh," said her mother. "You mean, like, people who secretly side with the separatists but pretend they don't?"

"Don't get me started on that now, too!" Rob let out a groan. There were chuckles.

223

"Mom!" exclaimed Christine. "Are you trying to get us all riled up again?"

"No, hon. No, it's late… Don't know why I said that." Maryann looked like she genuinely did not.

More people stood.

"What are you doing the next few days?" asked Rob, looking at Wilder.

"Tomorrow I leave for the Governor's Overnight," replied Wilder.

"He's not even started packing," remarked Christine, blowing out the candles on the side tables.

"You?" Sam Miller raised his eyebrows. "You been on that before?"

"Nope," said Wilder shaking his head. The Governor was a Republican. For decades, she and her closest handful of advisors, plus fellow Republican members of Vermont's Washington delegation and key state politicians since she became governor eight years before, had gone off on a three-day backpacking trip to talk and relax away from the pressures of Montpelier and the media's eye. The destination and day of departure were always secret, revealed in coded form at the last minute. Only the backpackers or their drivers knew. They traveled alone or in small groups, inconspicuously, hiking in to where a campsite awaited them from different trailheads.

"Guess we're not even supposed to know this!" laughed Rob.

"No, and now I must kill you," intoned Wilder darkly. There were low, mysterious chuckles among the few that remained on the patio.

"Kind of a new thing, letting you in on this," said Sam after a brief silence.

"I guess the times are getting increasingly ripe for real tri-partisanship in Vermont," said Wilder, nodding.

"I wonder what she has up her sleeve," mused Rob. Rob liked the Governor, and he said this with curiosity, not suspicion.

"Well, this is a chance to listen," said Wilder. "It will be interesting to see who else is there. And see whether she wants me in on some sort of deal."

Dean spoke up. "I wonder if Bart Ross will be there, too."

"Good question," answered Wilder. "Up until last week, he definitely would have been."

224

"Can't imagine he's the most popular guy at the prom these days, among Republicans," replied Rob.

"Never know. Maybe he's more popular than some folks let on. Well, it's going to be an adventure," said Wilder. "A real one."

"Hope your weather holds out," offered Sam. "Supposed to be nice a couple days – high pressure should bounce that hurricane down south out to sea."

"When do you leave?" asked Rob. They were all walking toward the back door of the house.

"State trooper's going to pick me up at six."

Rob grunted. "Better you than me, young man." He looked at his watch. "Already ten-thirty now." He stood back to let Wilder and Dean pass through the door ahead of him. His voice rose. "Darn it all, too!" They looked back at him, surprised. He regained his composure. "Oh, it's nothing. Just remembered we have to ride home in the phaeton."

"You want a ride home?" Sam held up the keys already in his hand. "We came in the cell."

Rob looked askance at Dean. Dean grinned. "OK, Sam. Sure. We'll send someone over tomorrow to drive it back." There was relief in Rob's voice. He wanted to be in bed sooner than a carriage ride through the dark, forested hills could give him.

People gathered their coats and other loose items, and left together. Christine and Wilder stood just outside the main door, arm in arm, looking down across the dooryard. Jessamyn and her husband had already left. Dean fired up his biodiesel motorcycle and started down the drive. Rob and Maryann turned, silhouetted by the dome light of Sam's car just beyond them.

"It was a wonderful surprise, you two," called Christine's mother. Rob added his agreement.

"Nothing any less would do," laughed Christine.

"Good night," said her parents. Her mother added, "And take care of my new babies."

"Your Morgans will be just fine here, Mom," smiled Christine. "With Jake running off tomorrow, I'll need company. I might take them for a drive down to the river."

Sam's car moved silently off into the cooling darkness. Christine and Wilder stepped inside, and closed the heavy oak door behind them.

225

28-RHIANNON ARRIVES

Friday, October 26th - Saturday, October 27th

"Somebody's coming," motioned Grandma with her flashlight. The beam illuminated a wild spray of wind-blown raindrops in the pitch-darkness. It had already been raining for about two hours. Although gusty and wet, it was hot, like a Turkish bath.

Carl sat up expectantly. Mike looked in the direction Grandma indicated, up the sunken road. Another light was bouncing along toward them. He crawled out from under the wagon, zipping up his Army-issue raincoat tighter as he stood up straight. Around him in the agitated night were the occasional bleats of sheep and lowing of cattle that had been driven into the shelter of the fortifications.

"Hope it's one of us. The rest of these horses need to get out of the weather immediately." He peered at the dark shapes of their horses, tethered to the side of the wagon. They were stamping nervously, tossing their heads. The steep, high berm rising beside them afforded considerable shelter from the gradually strengthening wind, but the rain was repeatedly flung into their faces.

Lena Burhans appeared beside him from the coach, where she had been trying to better secure the crazily flapping tarp they had pulled over it earlier. "Hey!" she called, raising her voice to be heard over the noise. A faint high-pitched cry could be heard: Celia's reply. Lena turned to Mike and Grandma behind him, sitting with Carl under the wagon in the relative shelter of the stacked sandbags. "I'll help you. We can each take one horse," she offered. The Burhans' four North Swedes were already down in the tunnel. Ethan, Nate, Jim, and Celia had left with them half an hour before, with Fernando bringing up the rear. The entrance to the restored Civil War tunnel was not far—perhaps a hundred meters—but the process of bringing more horses into the tunnel had been slow. There were already many local horses down there—the tunnels were part of the city's civil

226

defense and emergency preparedness system—and it had taken negotiation and a day of filling sandbags and nailing up shutters for the city by all of them except Grandma to give them access to the shelter they needed. For the time it took for the hurricane to pass—about eight hours was the estimate (it was moving fast now)—the horses would be entirely out of the wind. This part of the battlefield was above the floodplain, so there was little danger that the tunnels—with their system of drains—would get more than damp and muddy. It was a real stroke of luck. Given the strength of this storm, they would have had no hope in an open field, on the road, or hitched in an ordinary stable.

The situation was less certain for the wagons. It had been impossible to find space in the city's concrete parking garages or more heavily constructed buildings. The locals had filled every available nook and cranny with cars, trucks, wagons, and animals, and there was not even enough room for them. The visitors would have to fend for themselves. Mike's credibility as a Corps of Engineers officer and a Civ.E. had prevailed: the best option was to find a sheltered corner behind the earthworks. Full of doubt, the Burhans had followed suit.

Doing the best they could, Mike, Grandma, Fernando, and the Burhans had parked the wagon and coach together, end-to-end, in a narrow sunken side-road off Siege Road, partially enclosed by the pointed wings of an artillery fort along the main wall of the fortifications. With ropes and cables attached to tree-trunks and stakes, they had tied down the vehicles, and had banked sandbags they had filled themselves against the wheels and sides. The upper cabs were exposed, but loose details had been removed or secured. The area they chose was very sheltered. As the hurricane moved over them, moving north by northwest, it would first slam them with winds from the northeast. They would feel none of this directly, just side currents and rolling turbulence in the wind-shadow of the berm. Then, after the eye passed over, the wind direction would reverse, creating somewhat of a problem. It was a compromise solution. There was also some chance that the wind would weaken as the enormous vortex moved inland.

They planned to spend the night under Grandma's larger, more heavily weighted wagon, with about a foot and a half more clearance between the bottom and the ground. It was going to be a hard, wet, sleepless night. They prayed that the ropes would hold, that the sandbags would have their desired effect, and that the winds would not shred the cabs and cargoes above them. A stone cellar would have been safest, but this was better than an ordinary wooden building.

The positioning and securing of the wagons was completed by five. An hour passed. They waited for the rain to start and the winds to pick up. For what seemed like a long while, the evening remained languid. An oppressive summertime mugginess built up. Most of them were withdrawn, subdued. They ate a light supper of shared snacks, swatting at a rising swarm of biting flies driven by some unfelt signal into a pre-storm frenzy. Lena sat in the compartment of the stagecoach, lost in some VNET religious service, occasionally singing softly, muttering prayers and responses to the preacher. Celia, Jim, and Nate sat in a semicircle at the foot of the berm, chatting in low voices. Ethan, Mike, Fernando, and Grandma sat together on the wagon's bench, the cab open to the elements. The punk smudges smoked continuously. They talked of storms, floods, the hurricanes they had experienced. There was hushed speculation about what this would bring. Others drifted by with comments and news – the farmers and shepherds whose livestock was gathered along the fortifications, the occasional policeman, a group of children on their way to a cellar. Trains rumbled along the nearby railroad track as the better-heeled inhabitants of Richmond and Petersburg fled southwards out of the storm's expected track.

Carl updated them with news about Rhiannon's swath of destruction as it reached the coast. The eye had made landfall just south of Virginia Beach around six that evening, at which point its outer bands were just starting to ruffle Petersburg with a stiff breeze. There had been a fifteen-meter storm surge which traveled five kilometers inland, winds over one hundred meters per second, and massive dumps of rain. The angry eye was tiny—only a few kilometers across—compared to a storm diameter of over three hundred kilometers. Passing over Norfolk, the winds close to the eye were especially catastrophic. Carl's attempts to access local news and video footage yielded nothing as power and telecommunications vanished from the areas the advancing storm enveloped. National and international sites repeated the same satellite images of the storm, conveying sketchy stories of flattened towns, deep water, and death. Storm preparations rose to a feverish level of activity in Washington, Baltimore, Philadelphia and beyond. The roads were clogged with vehicles slowly heading west, out of its path. Forecasters predicted an arc that would take Rhiannon back out to sea somewhere in New Jersey. Moving about fifteen kilometers an hour, its eye was expected to reach Petersburg at around four in the morning.

* * *

Celia and Jim came jogging up. Celia had tied her long blond hair back in a ponytail, to keep it from whipping around her face. It was drenched. Her face seemed thinner, more childlike than before. Jim had his raincoat hood cinched tight around his face.

Lena put her hooded face up close to Celia's. "You feel like taking another horse down, honey?"

"Sure." Celia rubbed the water away from her eyes with the back of her wrist. "It's crowded down there."

"They better still have room!" Lena sounded shrill, worried.

"Uh-huh," answered Celia. "Little bit."

With this, Grandma, who had been watching and listening from a crouched position in the opening between the sandbags, grabbed a wheel and pulled herself to a standing position, grunting with the effort. Whistling between breaths, she started untying Bill, who stood nearest. Mike followed with Sherbet, who stood uncertainly where the two wagons almost touched, and Lena and Celia went to work on Belle. In seconds, they had all three horses ready for the transfer.

"I can take your horse down," offered Lena.

"Oh, it's all right," said Mike. "I'll go with Jim and Celia here. You stay with my granny and Carl." A thought occurred to him. "Hey, why don't y'all ditch the area around our wagon?" He pointed at the gravel road surface. "Dig a ditch around so deep." He indicated a shallow depth with the fingers of one hand. "So the rain won't run under our wagon. We can stay a little drier. There's a shovel under the seat." Lena smiled and nodded, but Carl gave him a gloomy look.

The walk to the tunnel was gusty and soaking, but brief. Across a small field, with the main line of fortifications to their backs, the approach to the tunnel ramped downwards at a shallow angle until they were in a trench about eight feet wide that was paved with slippery bricks. The iron gates of the tunnel entrance were open, and they could see lights in the tunnel. Horses were tied up to support posts and improvised stakes along the right-hand side of the narrow tunnel, nose to tail, with enough space between them to disarm kicks. Their heads almost bumped against the wooden roof of the tunnel. There was barely enough room left for two horses.

229

Ethan and Fernando were near the entrance, waiting. "You'll have to leave one outside."

Mike felt irritation rising, but held back. How were they supposed to know this? But they were lucky to be getting real shelter for most of their animals. This was not the time for arguments. "You sure?" he asked them.

"Yeah, I'm afraid so," said Ethan. "I've been way in there, and it's really full. There's more horses coming, so he won't be the only one on the ramp."

"OK." He looked at Bill. "Bill, old man. Looks like you get wet." He started tying Bill to the gate. Celia had already gone in with Belle, and Jim stood waiting to pass with Sherbet. At least it was sheltered here, Mike reflected. The sides rose at least twelve feet to reach the level of the field. There was almost no wind down here. Bill would get wet, but the air temperature was at least ninety degrees, so he would not catch a chill.

In about ten minutes, the horses were tied up and settled. Jim, Nathan, and Fernando would stay with them. About a hundred feet into the tunnel was an open room, with a deeper floor, located at a junction. They could sit there, with plenty of company.

After a quick farewell, and an agreement to check in when the eye passed over, Ethan, Mike, and Celia headed quickly back to the wagons. The speed and strength of the wind had risen noticeably. It was gusting less, holding a steadier direction. The trees dotting the battlefield roared and thrashed, starting to shed their still-green leaves.

"You know about that tunnel before?" shouted Ethan over the rush, when they were about half-way.

"No." Mike shook his head. "Kinda convenient." That was an understatement. Where to protect the horses had been a major concern all morning, and with the violence of Hurricane Rhiannon, they doubted whether any structure like a barn or stable would be safe. Then, in town, when they started asking about underground parking garages, they quickly learned that these were already spoken for.

"You ever see that old movie *Cold Mountain*, with Nicole Kidman?" asked Ethan. Mike shook his head. "The movie sort of starts here, during the battle. There were all kinds of trenches and excavations and bunkers. They even tunneled under the battle lines to blow up the other side."

"Nice that they kept them maintained," shouted Mike. "I never knew about this place. We'll be saved again by Nineteenth Century technology."

"I've been here before," said Ethan. "We've got battlefields like this up in Fredericksburg, too. They've done more than rebuild here. They've expanded the fortifications. Dug them deeper."

In minutes they were all back under Grandma's wagon, out of the wind behind the fifty-odd sandbags they had filled with gravel from the road and banked up against the wheels and sides, along with rocks from a stone wall and logs they had rolled across a field. It was dark and close. Sitting, their heads almost touched the underside of the wagon. But it was dry, and sheltered. They tried chatting, telling stories of other storms, but eventually, after Lena led them in a prayer, they fell silent.

Beside his grandma, who remained sitting, Mike stretched out on a horse blanket. He was weary beyond weary from the day's work and the stress of the wind and rain. Wrapped in his rain jacket, he dozed off.

Some time later—minutes, an hour?—he was abruptly awakened by shouting and commotion. The thundering din of the wind outside had grown to the likes of nothing he had ever heard before. It sounded like a huge waterfall, like a train passing at full speed. Was it a tornado? This storm would probably bring them. He glanced at his watch. It was just past midnight. Grandma had her flashlight on. The wagon was shaking, vibrating. Mike heard dull thuds and crashes, things flapping around. Grandma yelled something but he could not understand. At one end, sandbags had blown down and rain was whipping through the opening, filling the space under the wagon with a crazily dancing mist. Leaves and other debris flew through the opening. Grandma's face and the faces of the others were taut with fear.

Impossibly, as the time passed, the roaring continued growing in both pitch and intensity, shrieking like some massive power tool about to grind them up. Mike instinctively knew that no human would survive even a run across the field. The wind would simply pick them up and fling them. The wagon continued shaking, bouncing on its shock absorbers. It began to shudder, as if being pounded by collisions. Several times he thought he saw the wheels on the east side straining to lift, but the ropes and cables held. The ground began to flood—trickles of water driven under and through the up-wind sandbags, despite the ditching.

Suddenly, without warning, more sandbags collapsed. Several shrieked. The air under the wagon carried droplets, dirt, gravel, and larger pieces of debris driven by the shrill wind. Mike, Ethan, and Celia – mud and grit stinging their faces and hands - managed to drag several sandbags back into place to create a partial barrier.

Then, just as they finished this, above the roar, there was an enormous crash and the yelping of twisting metal.

"The coach!" screamed Lena. Ethan scrambled to the end nearest the coach and tried to peer through a small gap in the sandbags, shining his light. He squinted into the blast but he could not discern what was happening out there. He crawled back to them, shaking his head. They would have to wait.

Carl had been fiddling with his PDA. "Cell network's gone!" he shouted. "I'm on satellite." Up in the windless tranquility of space, far from any hurricane, the telecom satellites followed their routines undisturbed. Carl browsed news sites looking for information. Mike crawled over to where he sat, peering at the bright, colorful display in the pitch darkness under the wagon. Banners and stories danced past as Carl scrolled and toggled. "Apocalyptic storm races toward Nation's Capital," they read. "Thousands already feared dead." "Winds scour path of buildings, bridges, trees, vehicles." The BBC was especially ominous. "Leviathan hurricane threatens coming elections, political stability."

Mike moved back to Grandma, and sat beside her. Several centimeters of water now ran across the gravel road surface. He took her hand and gave her a smile. She glanced at him, wincing at the dazzle of his headlamp, but gave no other reaction. She bowed her head, staring down at the silty water. Seated together, they waited with a kind of dazed apathy in the deafening din. Mike struggled to stay sharp and clear-minded. But the storm was overpowering, relentless.

Imperceptibly at first, and then almost as if a giant hand was turning a volume control, the wind fell off. In the span of a few minutes, it became eerily still. The silence was almost as disturbing as the roaring wind.

"The eye!" Ethan broke the sudden silence. Lena and Grandma started, as if they had been asleep. "It'll be short. Ten, fifteen minutes!" Celia and Carl leapt toward the entrance, in front of which they had piled sandbags, splashing wavelets of water across the ground. Mike followed, ignoring the cold water on his knees and hands. It was a relief to stand up and stretch. Ethan crawled out right behind him. They all had their headlamps on in an instant, flashing them in all directions to assess the damage.

It was still completely dark—a few hours before dawn—but they knew instantly that the scene had changed profoundly from what they had seen before the storm arrived. The ground was covered in a flotsam of debris—branches, splintered lumber, tatters of plastic and fabric. Stepping over and around it, Ethan went immediately to his coach. The tarp had been completely ripped clear. Brush and a metal sign had become caught in the roof rack and luggage cage. A side window was broken. But it still stood where they had parked it. What had caused the enormous, metallic crashing noise? They trained their lights around, peering into the night. Mike glimpsed something light-colored nearby. It was a large aluminum rowboat that must have blown over the berm, wrapped around a fallen tree. He shot a glance back at their own wagon. The cab and cargo (in its wooden crates) were also covered in branches and other debris, but appeared intact, except for one door, which had been bent forward and nearly ripped from its hinges.

"Hey, somebody," Mike called. "Help me get this back so it doesn't break anything." Celia came over. They pushed and pulled urgently, forcing the bent door back into position. "I'm going to have to tie this in place." He smiled in thanks at her, and started undoing the latch of the seat box to get a length of rope.

"Sure," she breathed, stepping back. A look of surprise and then horror twisted her face. Mike turned and looked up to where she was pointing. Ethan, who was nearby, also looked up. In the faint glow of their lights, a dismal scene greeted them. A huge, indistinct shape loomed above the berm, most of it lying on the other side, but with its tip hanging over where the wagons were parked. A dozen partial explanations flashed through Mike's mind as he tried to make sense of it. Was it the wing of a jet? Another boat?

"A steeple!" yelled Carl. That was it. A wooden steeple, with some of its aluminum siding still attached and other sections with only the framing joists remaining, lay flopped over the berm. A twisted metal cross was still fastened to its peak, festooned with wires or cables. Then, Mike realized another detail. The tree beside the coach, below the steeple's tip, was full of sheep—dead sheep—from the flock that had taken shelter not far from the wagons. Three or four sheep's corpses were entangled in the tree's branches, wedged in odd positions. No other sheep were to be seen, nor bleating heard. Then, in the silence, Mike heard Celia start sobbing. Over on the other side of the coach, Ethan was already talking on his cellphone. Grandma and Lena emerged from underneath, holding each other for support.

"Mike," said Ethan. He had already hung up. "We need to decide right this second if we want to stay here for the second half or make a run for the tunnels. Nate says there's room for all of us in the junction gallery, although it will be tight."

"They OK down there," asked Mike.

"Nate said it's wet—they got more than a foot of water in the tunnel—but there's no wind."

"What if we stay here?" The question was mainly rhetorical. Mike knew the wind would be stronger, more direct.

"If this sucker can pull a steeple off a church and blow it, what, a quarter mile, then I don't want to see what it can do to a stagecoach." Ethan sounded disgusted, but determined.

"Oh, Jesus," said Lena with a sob. She put her hand to her face. Grandma, Celia, and Carl stood frozen, faces pale. Mike realized they were all on the edge of shock. But he agreed with Ethan. On the way into the battleground park, he had not even noticed a church anywhere nearby. When the wind came back from the opposite direction, it would be an entirely different storm. In two quick steps, he stood beside Ethan.

"OK, you're right. Good call." He turned to the others, clapping. "Let's go. Fast! We can't stay here." He quickly went to Grandma, taking her by the shoulders. "Let's go down to the tunnel, with the horses. We'll be safer." He raced to the seat box and pulled out the backpack with his valuables, the weapons, and the pomme d'or. He spotted Grandma's yellow canvas duffel and grabbed it, too. The Burhans were also lunging for light bags and other items they did not want to leave behind.

"OK, we all here?" Burhans looked around, counting. "Stay together. Let's go!"

When they started off, it was still calm. Proceeding cautiously, they followed the contours of the sunken road, and then the path that led to the tunnel. What had been an open field before now looked more like a clear-cut forest with the slash left behind, or the aftermath of a building demolition. There were tree branches everywhere, pieces of framed wall with insulation and gypsum board hanging loose, appliances, clothes, parts of vehicles. They passed a human body, and then the corpse of a cow. A stiff breeze abruptly began blowing as if a fan had been switched on, rising sharply before they had walked for another thirty seconds. They saw lights ahead, at the tunnel entrance. "Here, here!" shouted a voice. It was Fernando, expecting them. They started running. The wind gained in strength, pushing at their backs. Things started flying around in the air. They ran, stumbling over wreckage. Mike held his right arm around Grandma, the bags in his left. Something bumped his headlamp, which then started working its way down over his brow. He batted at it with his clenched, weighted left fist. The entrance grew closer. They were going down the ramp into the trench. Above the rush of the rising gale, he heard the roar returning. The opposite eyewall was looming overhead. They stumbled and sloshed into the tunnel only minutes ahead of the full force of the storm. Jim reached forward to take Grandma's hand. Mike followed, entering last.

Mike glanced at Bill as he passed. The horse looked sideways at him, seeming to nod in recognition. Bill's head was low. Mike patted Bill's vast flank. He looked no worse for the wear. "Hey, Billy Boy," he said softly. He wondered if the horse needed water, and then remembered he was standing in rainwater up to his shins. The tunnel was starting to flood, despite its drains.

Into the dim light they filed, passing along the row of uneasy horses. Celia and Grandma spoke to all of them as they passed, reassuring them, calming them. Mike hoped none would suddenly get the idea to kick him in the narrow, confined space. He thought of the ponies that were once used in mines, long ago. They kept moving for what seemed like a considerable distance. The sounds were muffled, filled with the dull slap of the water they walked through. Cool water dripped through the gaps in the planks that reinforced the ceiling. Finally, they came to the junction gallery, which was more like a cloverleaf of alcoves off the main tunnels. There were simple benches along the walls and more benches in the few open areas. Dozens of people sat there quietly, some dozing with their backs against the walls. It was like an air-raid shelter. There were a few battery-powered lamps hanging on the walls, and deeply shadowed recesses. Mike thought of old World War II movies. Nate and Jim showed them a narrow place where they could sit down. Grandma took a quick drink of water from a bottle Fernando offered her, and then sat stiffly beside Mike, her hands clasped tightly, looking into space.

"God only knows what this storm is going to do to the market garden and my house," she finally muttered, gloomily.

"It's bad now, but it may be a lot weaker when it hits DC."

She looked askance at him, and replied dryly. "It already is hitting DC. Look at your T-pad. We're the same distance from Washington we are from Norfolk."

"Ah, no, Grandma," said Mike gently. "It's almost twice as far. I checked it. The eye has to travel more than 200 kilometers." He shivered from the cooler temperature in the tunnel. "Things might slow down by then—Category Four, Three, lower, even. It's still completely quiet up there."

"Might. Maybe. That's not much to have your whole future hanging from." Her tone was resigned. Mike found this disturbing. Grandma had always been such a cheerful, determined figure in his world.

She took his hand, and patted their clasped hands with her other, trying to muster some reassurance. "No sense letting your imagination run wild, eh? Things might be just fine when we eventually get home." She chuckled without humor. "Whenever that is."

Grandma grew silent. Mike felt a very slight relaxation of her body as she started to lean against his side. He let his eyes wander around the several dozen people in their alcove. This tight, clammy space was certainly not designed for this. Anyone with claustrophobia would find it nightmarish.

He brought out his T-pad and rolled open the display. It was Army-issue and Army-grade. He inspected its cool green case and black controls. It was barely scratched—still in excellent condition after almost a year. Now that he was out among civilians most of the time, he had become aware of how beat-up most people's T-pads and PDAs were, purchased years ago or traded through the open-air markets and maintained by freelancers. He thought about Grandma's, scratched and faded, dating to back before he joined the Corps.

"No link" read the network icon. For a moment he was puzzled, but then recalled the thickness of earth above his head. Ordinary satellite signals would not penetrate the earth, he realized. And there were no base stations in the primitive tunnels. This meant they were cut off as long as they sat in the tunnel. No weather picture, and no communication with Hon or anyone else. Mike looked at his watch. They had four, five, even six hours now to just wait.

Mike's ears popped, and he glanced up. He swallowed, clearing the pressure in his inner ear. Across the narrow aisle, Nate's eyes met his. Nate raised his eyebrows and shook his head faintly. Mike nodded back. He studied the Burhans family, most with their eyes closed, slumped together. They were decent people, strong people. He missed the rest of his family. He would see them soon, but under what circumstances? After several years of providing relief to others in need, he was finding he could not imagine the roles reversed. He was taking each moment as it came, not daring to think ahead now.

Mike then became aware of a distant droning. The wind was back up to its full strength. Perhaps some odd effect was causing the pressure in the tunnel to fluctuate; hence, the pop in his ears. He sat for a moment, Grandma's head on his shoulder, the droning wavering. Suddenly, his ears popped again. The droning grew into a roar. Mike thought about Bill out there in the tempest. He wanted to go check on him. Gently shifting Grandma's weight from his shoulder to the wall, he stood up. A wooden support beam nearly touched his head. He remembered the small, heavy pack was still on his shoulder, and shifted its strap. He turned and headed back up the main tunnel, carrying the pack with him. He realized there was a slight uphill incline toward the iron gate, continuing up the ramp that had brought them down here, because the water became shallower as he walked along the line of horses. Ahead, he saw several headlamps. There was a small cluster of people just inside the entrance.

When he reached them, the roaring only a short distance beyond them was so loud that normal conversation in the tunnel was impossible. Puffs and gusts of wind caught them as the hurricane's blast found its way underground. There were three men by the gate. They nodded in greeting, moving to give him space. Mike peered out at Bill, playing his flashlight beam around and near the horse. One of the men yelled something. Mike shook his head and pointed at his ear. The man leaned closer, and shouted, "Horse yours!?" Mike nodded. The man nodded, and looked sympathetic. He shouted again, "He'll do OK, the Good Lord willing." Mike looked more closely at Bill. The horse stood still, his head close against the wall and down, his ears flat against his head. From above, rain was driven hard against the opposite wall, but Bill seemed well-sheltered. Above was darkness. Mike squinted up, visualizing the torrent of air, water, and debris rushing like a river over them.

29-HON AND JENNY

Friday, October 26th - Saturday, October 27th

Jenny's avatar was a holomorph caricature of Jenny herself when she was younger: big head, bigger eyes, button nose, brown hair pulled back in an exaggerated 1950s ponytail. She floated with Honorée in a vast bed of flowers—red, pink, orange, white, yellow—borrowed from some Bollywood romance. Jenny called it her 'floral room'. They had been chatting for hours, or so it seemed. It was getting really late. Despite all the tensions of late, Honorée found herself relaxing again, laughing and talking about small, normal things with her little sister. But the approaching hurricane started to make its arrival known.

"Oh, I'm starting to hear the wind now," said Jenny with a nervous laugh. "Um, this is starting to get scary now."

"I think it's done its worst down south, Jenn," lied Honorée. "You're up on a hill there, in a brick house. We've been in lots of hurricanes before!"

"Do you have any wind yet?" asked Jenny.

Honorée briefly removed her headset, pulled aside the blind, and looked out. The street was dark and silent, and the air still. The flashing lights of an emergency vehicle sped by. Stillness returned. She heard her mother's raspy breath as she slept upright on the sofa in front of the switched-off 3V.

"Nope, nothing. They said the storm's shrinking a little and slowing down. 'Course we're a hundred kilometers north of y'all. No strong winds are expected here until mid-morning…" Honorée saw Jenny turn her head, and the avatar froze. She heard some conversation in the background. A small "BRB" icon bobbed and blinked over the avatar. In an instant, Jenny was back, and the avatar breathed life again.

"Sorry. Portia just got home. All wet and scared. It's starting to rain. She said it's worse outside than it looks. Hey Porsh!" Jenny turned to her left. A green sphere suddenly started expanding and contracting, flashing the text, 'Admit PortiaP19?" Jenny waved at it. The sphere morphed fluidly into Portia's avatar, a shimmering little animé action-hero girl.

"Whew, I think I'm gonna stay in here until that hurricane's finished and gone by!" They all laughed.

"You were out late!" scolded Jenny.

"Julius' family just headed out of town in their cell. They waited for the roads to clear. We helped them get packed up."

"Where's Julius?" asked Honorée.

"Oh, he's coming," answered Portia. "He's putting his paint down in the parking garage. They're bringing all the horses down, until tomorrow."

"He didn't *leave*?" joked Honorée. "And take *you*? To safety?"

"What a rude sister!" Jenny rezzed an oversized mallet and swatted at Honorée. "Don't mind her, Porsh. She's down on relationships at the moment."

"That's not very funny either, Jenn." Honorée's voice was sharp. But it felt good to gently spar about Sanna's disappearance, after days of taking it deadly seriously.

Portia's av pulled open a weather-map window. "Look. The eye's still a few hours from Richmond. This map says we should be getting some light wind right now. Wait a sec." Her avatar froze as Portia went to open the door to check again. Honorée heard it slam shut. In a moment, she was back and the avatar jumped up. "It's suddenly breezier than a few minutes ago when I came in. The trash cans and gates are blowing around!"

"I'm going to go see!" Jenny repeated the procedure. "Mmmmm, it is getting fairly windy all of a sudden. No longer just rain. I'm not a *little* glad the landlord closed our shutters!"

"I'm starting to get worried about y'all," said Honorée with concern. "Not sure why you had to stay there."

Jenny shrugged. "Excitement, sort of. And we can't leave Julius and all the pretty horses behind to fend for themselves." Jenny and Portia had their own riding horses, and Julius had a logging team and a striking paint he rode.

Suddenly, Portia screamed and her avatar flailed around before abruptly freezing. They heard her nervously giggling, chastising her boyfriend. "Julius! How many times have I told you NEVER to sneak up on me when I've got the bodyset on! I can't see you. I'm gonna have a heart attack one day!"

Julius' voice addressed them, although he did not appear in the floral room. "Hi ladies." He just had the phones on.

"Hi," answered Jenny and Honorée.

"It's weird outside. Calm before the storm. Nothing to joke about." He sounded sober, out of breath.

"Don't worry, Jenn," replied Honorée. "I'll stay up with you through this, and then you can stay up with me."

"Where are you anyway, Hon?" Jenny had never inquired whether Honorée was at her own apartment or at Grandma's house.

"My place," answered Honorée. "Bottom floors of a brick building in town seemed a little safer than Grandma's place."

"Is Grandma's house all empty?" Jenny sounded dismayed.

Avatar-Honorée shook her virtual head. "Mom's here with me, but Marcus and his family live in the cottage at Grandma's, so they're keeping an eye on the house. Marcus and his brother-in-law have been boarding up Grandma's windows all afternoon. The brother-in-law has moved in temporarily. They live down near Rock Creek and of course it's going to flood."

Without warning, Honorée found herself out in the vast multicolored spaces of Menu Mode. The floral room and its inhabitants had vanished from cyberspace. She tried teleporting, but could only get a busy signal.

"I wonder if they lost power?" said Honorée aloud. For a moment, there was silence. She was about to pull off her VRI set when the audiophone rang. "Hello?"

Jenny's voice sounded tense and low. "The power's gone. I'm on satnet now. Can't stay for long." In the hands of hard-currency foreign operators like Oranja and T-Virtual and RealAsia, the satellite network's billing rate was a hundred times what the cellular land network cost.

"You OK, Jenn? What's happening? I can't believe the power's gone already." Honorée heard the worry in her own voice.

"Kinda windy now, and just tons and tons of rain against the roof and shutters."

"I'll call you every hour, honey. It's going to be OK." She longed to have her little sister with her in the safety of her apartment.

"Portia's got some candles lit now," said Jenny. "Oh!"

240

"What?!" exclaimed Honorée.

"Oh, nothing. Just lightning, a big blast of thunder." Jenny laughed nervously. "That's weird. Lightning in a hurricane!"

"I guess so…" Honorée tried to visualize the scene. Maybe she'd try to find some live cams in Fredericksburg after they hung up. After all, the same storm would be upon them in a few hours.

"Jenn, this is expensive," Honorée continued. "Call me if you need to, and I'll check in with you in an hour."

"Right. Bye for now."

"Love you!"

"Love you. Love you, Sis!"

The call ended.

30-AN EVACUATION COMPANION

Saturday, October 27th

The five-minute warning chimed. Vulk took off his headset and peered through the windshield to see where they were, which was unnecessary because the warning chime always occurred at the same spot: the Herndon exit. Vulk chided himself for wasted effort as he put the glasses away. He folded the work table back into its slot and pulled the driver's seat forward into drive position again—not that he was planning to drive, but because it would be easier to open the door and get out.

It was late: after midnight. The staff meetings and then the meet-and-greet with the Senate caucus leaders had kept him on Capitol Hill longer than planned, and with the evacuation, there had been cancellations, double-bookings, and last-minute briefings crammed into every available slot. This hurricane was turning into a damned nuisance. Vulk had wanted to stay in town, but as senior staff he was under orders to relocate to Mount Weather until the all-clear was given. Which he hoped would be in a day or two. And which he believed would be seen as completely unnecessary in hindsight. It was one thing for a bunch of peasants down in Hootenanny County to have their pig pens, hen houses, and pipe-smoking grannies blown away by Hurricane Rhiannon, but another thing entirely for a weakening hurricane to have any real impact on the capital city. A bit of flooding, some lost shingles, and things would be back to normal by Wednesday, Vulk figured. Isn't that what the labor force was for? Clean-up? Anyway, like most hurricanes, it would probably veer out to sea and miss DC. There were hurricanes every year.

The car slowed down and entered the streets of Herndon, automatically seeking the gate to his complex. There was unusual activity along the broad avenues beneath the gated blocks of apartments: people packing cars and carrying bags out from building exits. So a lot of people were taking this seriously. He would not be the only one evacuating. All these people

242

would be driving somewhere, though, whereas he would be conveniently whisked away by helicopter. He glanced at his watch. It was almost twelve-twenty. He had over an hour to get to the Congressional terminal at Dulles Airport. That would be easy. Dulles was only a few minutes away. His car would drop him off and just drive back to his own garage, where it would be safe underground. Laugherty would be on the same flight, with Joyce. Sharon Denny, Bob Peyton, and other staff were traveling on a different chopper, straight from Reagan National.

The gate opened and Vulk's car glided silently down the ramp into the underground parking garage. The guards waved scanners and did a visual check. He gathered together his few things as the car came to a stop in its numbered spot. Something shiny rolled on the carpeted floor of the passenger side. He glanced over. It was a gold lipstick cylinder. Shit. Suzanna. He had been so wrapped up in work all day and evening that he had neglected to think about Suzanna and the evacuation. Well, she could stay in his place. That would be OK. She had the authorization, and her card account. Or maybe she would just go home to, well, wherever it was—some shabby outer suburb where her mother and God-knew what other relatives, dogs, cats, chickens, and goats lived. Olney? PG County? Fred-neck? He had never asked her about that. He didn't want to know. The agency had done all the placement work. He had used them before without any problem. He told them what he wanted, and they delivered. Particularly well, this time, in fact. It was amazing how such a delicious girl could emerge from some drab, impoverished setting—at least, that was how he imagined it.

Still sitting in the car, Vulk saw Suzanna in his mind's eye. He hoped she was waiting upstairs. She was supposed to be. He hadn't given her the night off. He resisted the urge to call her and check. That would betray weakness, dependence. He wanted to stay in control with this one. Suzanna had a spark in her, an authority of her own. Suzanna Teacher. Funny name for someone who had probably barely been to school. What was she, maybe twenty? What could she teach him? Well…Vulk became aware how horny he was starting to feel. He looked at his watch again. Twelve-thirty. Did they have time to play around? No, not really. Damn. Vulk then started wondering whether he could bring her with him. She wasn't family. It might be harder to get her into the chopper than into the Mount Weather complex, ironically. If he handed over her profile, which the agency had done very thoroughly, they would process her in. No, this was getting too complicated. His mind was tired. This was exactly why he didn't have a family in the first place! Compromises and dilemmas at every turn. Yet here he was. And would she be safe, left behind? What if the storm was as bad as some meteorologists were predicting? How would he like to have that on his conscience? Or, maybe he could drop her off somewhere safe, with family? But then he'd have to miss the helicopter flight, and who wants to be wandering around in a luxury cell-electric in the sticks, in the early hours of the morning? He might get attacked. There were plenty of stories about people who made that mistake once too often.

With no solution, Vulk still needed to get moving, so he got out of the car and rode the elevator up to his floor. It was now almost a quarter-to-one. Where did the time go? He walked down the short corridor and opened his door. The lights were on. Two bags were standing in the entrance hall: his own black wheeled bag, and a smaller blue bag. "Hello?" he called.

"I'm in here," came Suzanna's distinct contralto from the kitchen. He went to find her. She was leaning back against a counter, watching weather news on a wallscreen. Vulk caught his breath, and coughed to conceal this fact. She turned away from the wallscreen with a smile to greet him, but remained leaning back in her relaxed pose for a moment so he could view her. She was dressed in a black burner, but he could only see little glimpses of her body under the dark blue maxicoat she wore over it. On her feet were black ankle boots.

"Sorry it's so late," he muttered.

"Are you tired?" she asked.

"Well, yeah, but that's not important right now." He adopted a more assertive tone.

"I packed our bags," she said. "But come see what I laid out on the bed in case you wanna take it, too."

"How did you know I was leaving?"

She pushed off the counter and stood upright. "It's been on the news all day," she said simply. "'Specially your Congress channel."

"Oh, yeah, well that makes sense," he said, nonplussed.

"I'm coming with you," she said. "Are we flying?"

"Um, look, Suzanna…" He set his jaw and looked her in the face. She stared right back at him with the clearest, most feral, calculating, and

244

impassive green eyes he had ever seen. "It's not gonna…" He trailed off. She waited silently. "You can stay."

She took a step toward him. She was half-a-head shorter than he was, with thick, wavy brown hair hanging down her back; pale, unblemished skin; and a pretty, angular face. He looked at her, weighing the alternatives. She smiled sweetly and placed an index finger on his lips.

"I'm coming. End of story."

He pulled his head back, liking the touch but not the tone.

"I'm not sure they'll let you on the flight," he said tentatively.

"They will," she said.

He laughed with a disorienting mixture of disbelief and relief. "What?"

"I called and checked," she said. "Why do you think the agency sent me so quickly after you saw me online? Why do you think I can go anywhere?"

"Um, OK, why?" He studied her confidence, frowning.

"I already had the clearances before I met you, Mister Vulk. I was in the SIF for four years."

He laughed again, this time with amusement. "You never said that."

"You never asked."

He nodded. He'd give her that.

"Just another pretty ass, right?"

"Honestly, Suzanna, you know I wanted more than that." He meant it, sort of.

She laughed. "Yeah, sure. But the ass didn't hurt, did it?" And she struck a sultry pose and let her maxicoat fall open a little.

"No." He looked her up and down. "Nope, it didn't hurt." They both laughed. "But, after SIF, why this?"

She put her finger on his lips again. "Shush. We can talk about that later. We have to hurry!"

It was nearly one-o'clock.

"You know, I could just fire you for that kind of attitude," he said as they went to the bedroom. "Wouldn't be the first time."

"But you won't," she said.

"Anyway, how do I know you're not still working for SIF?"

"I'm not," she said. "You can check."

"Jesus, you're confident," he smiled reluctantly.

"Well, you keep telling me how good I am," she smiled coolly back. "I believe you."

"OK," he said. "You are good." Vulk was feeling very disappointed that they had no time to dally. But they didn't, and were out the door moments later, on the way to Dulles just ahead of the first faint harbingers of much more wind to come.

31-AN EARLY START

Saturday, October 27th

The roasted okra-seed coffee filled the kitchen with a pleasant, earthy odor as it brewed. Wilder cut thick slices of bread and spread butter and honey on them as he waited for the coffee, gloomily contemplating the enormity of the hurricane's destruction unfolding eight hundred kilometers to the south. His T-pad lay on the massive kitchen table, several newstapes running across from right to left. The Global Centrum audio feed murmured quietly. It was the big story of the day, the week, and potentially the year, depending on what happened in the next few hours.

Hurricane Rhiannon's winds were already being felt in Washington, and the rain had started. It remained on track to pass immediately to the east of the District of Columbia. Early, confused reports indicated that Richmond was in ruins. The eye had just crossed the old southern city. More than fifty centimeters of rain had fallen, swelling the rivers to mad torrents and flooding all low-lying areas. The winds, still at Category Five strength, had ripped wooden structures to shreds and shattered brick walls. Steel-frame buildings were reported to have had not only windows but internal walls blown out. The low-built communities along and in the Chesapeake Bay and its brackish tributaries had all but vanished. Wilder ached from the human tragedy, but he also started to worry about his own office and apartment, which were next in line to receive the fury. Washington, D.C. had been his home for the past six years, and most of his few belongings were there. And many friends and colleagues.

An animal anxiety paced restlessly inside him. He stood up for no conscious reason. It was, he reflected, the fight-or-flight reflex. Rhiannon was like a monster, an enemy army. Just thinking about it brought this impulse. There was something outrageous about the fact that a transient storm of this magnitude could wander along, unstoppable, indiscriminately altering human plans and conditions in its wake. Wilder was angry. Angry, too, at the fact that human irresponsibility had created an atmosphere in which such storms had become so common. And this storm in particular was the storm many had been dreading for years. The counterpart to California's "Big One" earthquake (which had so far failed to materialize), a hypothetical storm dubbed "The Leveler" had been sketched out in stories and weather scenarios – a top-strength hurricane that would draw energy from the heated Gulf Stream until it drew even with Norfolk, and then wreak havoc with the densely populated megalopolis from Richmond to New York City, killing thousands, displacing millions, punishing the regional economy, knocking out food production, and potentially hampering the Federal Government's ability to function normally. It was rapidly becoming clear that Rhiannon was The Leveler. What lay ahead was less clear.

Headlights flashed down on the road. Wilder poured his okra coffee into his ancient travel mug and quickly put things away. In a moment, he quietly let himself out into the dooryard, his battered old backpack on one shoulder, and waited for the state police cruiser to pull up. Everything was covered with a heavy dew. The air offered cool scents. A rosy dawn filled the east.

"Morning, Mr. Wilder," said the Vermont state trooper from the open window of the powerful road/rough hybrid.

"Morning, Archer," said Wilder.

Archer jumped out and opened a rear passenger door for Wilder, taking the backpack from him as Wilder moved to get in. The trunk clicked shut and the uniformed trooper hopped nimbly back into the driver's seat and started the car. They silently glided down the driveway toward the hard-top road.

"This new?" asked Wilder. He had been acquainted with Bill for years. Archer's kids had gone to school with Wilder's nieces in Bellows Falls.

"The cruiser, sir?" queried Archer.

"Yup."

"Brand new."

"Smells like it." Wilder looked around at the clean, sleek interior.

"Something that doesn't smell like horse manure, for a change." Both men smiled.

"Toyota?"

Archer nodded. "Yes, sir. Turbo biodiesel hybrid. Sun-charged thin-films. Gets over 200 to the liter."

"Nice. You guys occupy the Statehouse?"

"No, sir. This is a reward from the taxpayers, for hard work." He was not kidding. The state police had their hands full, but their reputation seemed to only get better in an age when many public servants either burned out quickly or went crooked.

"That's well-deserved," chuckled Wilder. There were not many police forces in the country besides federal agencies that could afford advanced imported equipment and vehicles like this. But, in the past year, the Montréal banks had started accepting allens, selling the State of Vermont Canadian dollars and euros it could use for procurement like this. And that was thanks to Vermont's steady exports to Québec of food. The summer droughts across Canada were worse than ever, and the large population around Montréal needed every calorie Vermont could sell them. And they paid hard currency. Vermont's location along a hard-currency border had become a solid advantage.

"Where we headed, Archer?" asked Wilder. He noted Archer was signaling a right turn at the Route 5 intersection.

"Classified, sir," said Archer.

"Just a hint?" asked Wilder.

"OK. It's off Route 100, and it's going to take about three hours."

"Route 100 and three, four hours...Camel's Hump?"

"No sir. OK, a bit less than four hours."

"You coming?"

Archer frowned. "It'd be nice, if I were invited, sir. But I've got highway duty today and we're closing down a border crossing tomorrow. May be trouble."

"Which one?" Wilder knew there were still about a dozen minor crossings left to close or restrict.

"Route 142, down south. Although that's classified, between you and me."

"I guess 'cuz that's next to the Interstate."

Archer nodded. "That's right. Redundant. We share the checkpoint on I-91 with the Feds. And more and more people keep trying to barge through on Route 5, when it gets backed up."

"Smugglers?" Wilder asked.

249

"Nope. Smuggling is still huge, but mostly over into New York. This is more about refugees. Desperate folks. They have their families and belongings and all, and they get hung up at the border and need to be processed, inspected. They get in line and they have to wait. Overnight, days even, a lot of the time. There's a lot of weapons, and people get talking around the campfires and start getting this fantasy that it's frontier times again. Especially the urban folks. As if we didn't have a government and law and order in Vermont." Archer slowed down as they approached a major intersection. "Pretty sad, all of it. But we have to keep it orderly."

Within a minute, they entered I-91 itself. They slowed as they approached the Exit 4 ramp, but the trooper waved them through. They picked up speed again, heading north in the motorized lane. At this time of the morning, there was little traffic. A few hay wagons crawled along in the right lane. On the southbound side, greater numbers of market carts and trucks rumbled toward the Brattleboro railhead and the bigger markets in Massachusetts beyond. Archer steered expertly around the cracks and potholes in the blacktop. Radio traffic crackled quietly from the dashboard.

"Some storm down there," commented Archer.

"Awful." Wilder shook his head. "Just awful."

"I heard on the way to your place that there may be five to twenty thousand dead in Virginia alone."

"Whose numbers?" With the insights he had, he instantly grew suspicious of government facts for public release these days. Especially after his conversation with that Princeton professor the previous week.

"The CBC's, apparently straight from the Red Cross."

"Those may be accurate, then." Such numbers were beyond grasp. How could random death on that scale be comprehended?

They drove on, rising and falling with the swells of the Green Mountains' foothills, the Connecticut River below on their right. Up on the high ridges of Mount Ascutney, a faint, dry brown heralded the autumn, but the valleys were still a deep summer green. Smoke rose in hazy curls around the steeples of the towns along the river.

On long straight-aways, they accelerated to eighty, ninety, even one hundred kilometers an hour, but the motorized traffic eventually backed up into a long convoy of several dozen vehicles moving together—cell-electrics, hybrids, biodiesel trucks—held back by the slowest at the head of the column. They zipped by the slower right-lane traffic: wagons and carts plodding along, bunching together as they climbed the inclines once reserved for fossil-fuel-powered vehicles alone.

On the opposite side of the highway, framed by granite outcuts festooned with kudzu vines and the rising slopes of birch and white pine, military convoys passed them, moving south. They were a mix of Army and Guard units—trucks, JEX's, APC's, and a group of light motorized guns. The vehicles looked the same, but the Guard units flew the Green Mountain Boys flag and bore the characteristic light-green half-chevron on their sides. The US Army vehicles had white markings, and flew the Stars and Stripes. Wilder wondered where they were going. Perhaps they were moving into position in case the hurricane kept coming all the way to Vermont. Maybe they were mobilizing to assist with the recovery in the devastated areas. Maybe they were needed for the border-crossing changes.

Wilder leaned forward. "Archer, know where the convoys are headed?"

"No, sir. I just know we were instructed to facilitate passage for an unusually high number of units on the move this week." Archer glanced at Wilder in the rear-view mirror. "Governor's orders."

Wilder mused about how security and civil defense had evolved differently across the country as the Emergency had worn on. Since Sanderborough nineteen years before, there had been little significant terrorism on US soil. In ways that completely dwarfed the first decade of the century, the Pentagon had eventually taken the Long War to nearly every other part of the globe, but the militarization of US society and the steady drop in resources flowing to Islamic terror networks meant that terrorism on a grand scale faded away from the American domestic agenda. Nevertheless, crime, contraband, economic dislocation, and migrations driven by economic collapse in certain regions had led to a radical change in security concerns at home. The pattern that emerged intrigued Wilder. Here in Vermont, the state government had asserted considerable control, with the National Guard and State Police as its instruments. They were in evidence everywhere. Certain other states like Massachusetts, Maine, Washington, and Minnesota had gone the same way. They acted increasingly like nation-states. This may have had something to do, reflected Wilder, with the ability of the state governments to obtain hard-currency revenues, and also with two other key factors:

there were limited or non-existent fossil fuel resources in those states, and they were not being routinely pummeled by hurricanes or drought.

In contrast, the two other models that had emerged were fragmentation, on one hand, and Federal control, on the other. In places like New York and vast stretches of the South and West, cities and towns had assumed responsibility for security, with stockades, checkpoints, and open regions without regular security in-between. The Federal Government maintained an active law-enforcement presence along the major interstate highways and railroad lines, because these were essential for moving fossil fuels and military power. People traveled in armed convoys along the uncontrolled roads. Law and order was maintained to varying degrees within the stockades.

In the major fossil-resource states, from the Gulf Coast to West Virginia, Wyoming, and Alaska, the Federal Government ran everything. They were like armed colonies, thought Wilder. At the National Legislators' Conference he had attended in Cheyenne, he could hardly believe the Pentagon's visibility. Tanks were positioned at major highway interchanges and the drone of military aircraft could always be heard in some quarter of the sky. Half the population seemed to be wearing a uniform. The Feds couldn't be everywhere, thought Wilder. With limited resources, they needed to concentrate force where it mattered, which meant the sources of the natural resources to support what had become the USG's main public justification for its existence: protecting the nation from attack. But was this really the main priority they needed to be worrying about now, and was it even true? Morales spoke about economic recovery and alternative energy and international cooperation, but how much could she really change? Against the background of a nation traumatized by war, economic decay, disrupted private lives, and the chaotic weather, the Pentagon and the Energy Trust and their oligarch clients had other convictions and priorities, and strong allies in Congress.

The rhythm of the journey changed. They were getting very close to the I-89 interchange. Traffic in both directions became heavy: more military vehicles, a few state police, VTrans construction vehicles, and convoys of ragged refugee wagons pulled over on the shoulder, horses grazing, children playing by the wheels. The congestion was surprising, this early in the day. Wilder surveyed the scene as they idled along in the motorized lane. He had a fleeting impression of people waiting, of uncertainty. A few men and women standing by a carriage met his gaze with searching looks, and then were left behind.

From I-91, they spiraled down the bumpy, pitted ramp onto I-89 below, to head northwest along the White River, cutting into the main chain of the Green Mountains. As they came around, the car momentarily pointed east, and Wilder caught a glimpse of a pall of black smoke drifting above the river valley in the direction of Hanover, New Hampshire. It struck his attention for a moment—burning crop waste, possibly, or a house fire, or a large boiler being fired up for the first time of the season—and then it left his mind as he set his thoughts on the day ahead.

Some time later, Archer left the interstate, and they began weaving their way deeper into the mountains through cheerful little valleys and villages of faded white and red clapboard houses, their commons full of sheep and their main streets lined with vendors' stalls and hitching posts. Rural life was awakening. Fog in the valleys was beginning to burn off, and the sky above was a deep blue. They passed a defunct ski area, where the hoof-trails of cattle and sheep crisscrossed the high, green slopes above.

"Looks like you'll have a nice day for a hike," remarked Archer.

"A nice hike is about the last thing I have time for, unfortunately." Wilder yawned and shook his head. "Maybe after the election, when we're in recess. And after the relief and recovery this storm's going to require." That dark feeling of dismay pulled at him, momentarily overwhelming him. "And all these other political crises…"

Archer responded with a polite silence. They slowed down to let a herd of cattle cross the road, bells clanking from their collars. Boys whose experience with motorized vehicles was limited to old biodiesel trucks and tractors looked with rapt curiosity at the shiny green cruiser idling in the country lane.

"Looks like you guys probably don't have much trouble with recruiting!" joked Wilder, pushing the dismay into the back of his mind.

"We don't now, sir. Everyone wants to be a trooper."

"Well," replied Wilder, "it's an honorable profession, isn't it?"

Archer's reply was cryptic. "Yessir, plenty of good work to do. As long as the right guys are giving us orders."

Wilder was struck. "Is that ever in doubt?"

"Oh, no sir. Not in this state." Archer grinned back at Wilder in the rear-view mirror. "And we get about the best salary and benefits you can find these days."

* * *

The cruiser slowed down and turned left. Wilder's awareness returned, and he realized he had been dozing. He rubbed his eyes and looked around. They were slowly driving up a gravel road in a mature forest. A small, wild river cascaded through rocky pools in the ravine to their left.

"So where are we?" he queried Archer.

"We just drove through Granville, sir."

"It looks like we're almost there, eh?"

"Yessir. I'm just taking you up to the trailhead. After that, you're on your own." Archer glanced back at him darkly through the rearview mirror.

"Do I get a map or something?"

"No, sir. You get a compass and that's all."

Wilder knew the trooper was messing with him. He would wait and see. "Who needs a compass?" he laughed, shrugging and sitting back. The trooper chuckled, his attention reabsorbed by the steep, winding road. The forest around them was cool and dark, choked with knotweed and vines under its thick canopy. Streams trickled down from many smaller gullies into the rocky, bubbling river below the road. They skirted several washouts. Finally, the car slowed, and ahead Wilder saw a small group of people gathered where the road ended. They had packs, and were variously dressed for the outdoors. A few cars and wagons were parked nearby. He scanned the figures and faces. Bart Ross was there. That would make for some discussion! Rosen was there, as were Bill Zeller and Roy Kapp, and there were others he did not recognize. It looked like a scene from a summer camp or hiking club outing in days gone by, but their serious faces and watchful eyes betrayed something else.

What did Governor Remington have planned?

32-OUT OF THE TUNNEL

Saturday, October 27th

While the storm still raged, before dawn, a section of the roof had started collapsing as the soil above the tunnel turned to mud. Someone had spotted it, and a whole group including Wilder had been roused to action to prevent it from getting worse. They pushed and hammered boards and jack-posts into place, rank water and red mud streaming down their necks and arms. That problem contained, Mike sat down again beside his dozing grandmother, and drifted off into an uneasy sleep.

"It's over," said a voice to the tired, motionless figures huddled on the gallery benches, water now risen to mid-calf. In the darkness of the tunnel, there was nothing to indicate that daylight had broken, nor that the hurricane had moved on, save a deeper silence. Mike and Grandma stirred. Cold and stiff, Mike forced himself to stand up, shivering as he stretched. His neck ached, and he had a strong need to urinate. He looked down at his rumpled, muddy grandmother. A memory came back to him of a book he had once read while serving in the Army about the siege of Stalingrad. Civilians and soldiers had had to bear many nights of conditions like these, and worse. They had languished in tunnels for months, the cold and hunger gnawing at them, their bodies covered with lice. This was nothing in comparison. But it felt dire, nonetheless.

Behind him, the Burhans started awakening as well. Ethan and Nate were absent. They must have already gone out.

"Grandma, let's get up there and see how things are." She shivered and smiled back at her grandson—a tired, lost, warm smile.

"Yes," she answered, and with his steadying hand stood up with a groan.

Hanging their backpack and duffel over one shoulder, steadied by his hooked thumb, Wilder led the way. Some of the horses were already out—including the Burhans', they noticed. They continued along the narrow, flooded passage. The bright light of the opening burst upon them as they rounded the curve in the tunnel. Reflections of the water danced on the planked ceiling. Belle and Sherbet huffed and twitched as they recognized Grandma and Mike approaching. Grandma ran her hand along their heads and sides as she passed, talking and cooing to them. "Just a moment, girls. Just a moment." She raised her voice to Mike, walking just ahead of her. "Lord knows what standing in cold, muddy water for half the night is doing to their hoofs."

Then they were passing through the gate's opening, into the ramped trench. The sky was a happy, clear blue above them, and the sunshine warm. The bottom of the trench was full of branches and other plant debris over which they stepped carefully. They saw Fernando, Jim, and Lena standing at the top of the ramp with a small group, talking quietly and looking around in awed surprise. And then, they reached ground level.

The severity of the sight that assaulted their eyes was not lessened by the bright sunshine and cheerful sky. The landscape of the battlefield had changed completely since the night before. Where tranquil green fields and meadows had existed before, there was now a scene of cluttered destruction. As far as the eye could see, the fields were piled and draped with broken-off trees and branches, building materials, cars, roofs, animal carcasses, and objects of uncertain origin. The broken trees were hung with the tatters of plastic sheeting and fabrics. There was hardly any open space left. Where all the debris had come from was a more worrisome question than what it had covered. Near them, there were pieces of what looked like a silo. Out in the center of the field between the tunnel entrance and the berm was an upside-down cart. And everywhere: snapped lumber, tattered plastic, and shredded leaves.

"Oh, merciful God," said Grandma, her teeth chattering, and she sat down on a low brick wall by the ramp and hugged her hunched frame. Mike looked at her in the clear light, and a mixture of empathy and worry rose in him. His grandmother did not look well. From the tough, salty traveler of a few days ago, she had become pale, bent, thin. He looked over toward where the wagon should be, and began wondering if Grandma could survive the destruction of the wagon and its cargo, if the worst had indeed happened. He sat down beside her.

"Grandma, we need to get some warm drink and food in us, get our strength back." He put his arm around her, her back all sharp struts and sinews.

"Mike," she said slowly, in a faint voice, "the wagon, where is it?"

"It's over where we left it, I think. Let's get over there and take a look..." Mike sat up and looked around, and continued, "... after we get the horses above ground and let them graze and dry out a little." Standing in the water could not be good for them.

"I'll come down and help you," she replied.

"Why don't you sit here in the sun for a little while. I can get Fernando to give me a hand." He rummaged around in the backpack, feeling the solid heft of the pomme d'or. Finding a bag of raisins and some apples, he pulled them out to share. "Let's get some food in us right now. Energy. And some water. We have a lot of work ahead of us." They sat there methodically chewing, taking in the unreal transformation of their surroundings. Others emerged from the tunnel, some leading horses, and stood around with expressions ranging from tearful anguish to numb inscrutability.

"Hey, y'all!!" Ethan Burhans' voice called from the direction of the berm. Mike looked over. Ethan was climbing over debris, moving toward them, accompanied by Nate. Mike stood up.

"God *damn* this hurricane!" swore Ethan. His face was sweating, ashen. "Tipped both our wagons over, but the berm held 'em from getting flipped or blown around. Stuff all over the place. I think they'll both still pull, with some fixing." He caught his hand on an upended branch, and leaned over to catch his breath. "Jee-sus H. Christ, did this damn storm give us a whupping. I hate to think what it's done from here to Fredericksburg and on up north. Carl's been in the Satnet finding out. Just destruction, destruction everywhere. People don't know where to begin." He squinted at Mike, his blue eyes intense. "So, what d'you think things would be like right now up on the road somewhere outside Richmond? If we were there?"

Mike slowly nodded his head, and stood up. Grandma looked at the horizon and said nothing. "Looks like we ought to travel together from here on up, as far as we can. Strength in numbers."

"Deal," said Ethan. "Although I guess it's going to be some time before we can even get moving, with all the trees down and bridges out."

257

At that moment, Celia came up the ramp leading Sherbet, who pranced and skittered after the dank confinement of the tunnel.

"Hey Celie," said Nate.

"Hey," said Celia. She handed Sherbet's halter-line to Mike, and smiled shyly at him as she ran her hand up and down Sherbet's nose. Mike smiled, and found himself blushing, and wondering how a young girl could look so fresh and normal in a setting of such utter destruction, exhaustion, and shock. He glanced down at her trousers, which were wet to her thighs from the horse's splashing. She wrinkled her face up and looked at her father, and then pulled off her boots and emptied about a liter of water from each one.

"Yuck," Celia said.

Mike laughed, and realized his own feet were sodden, his socks squishy. Even Grandma cracked a weary smile.

"We're alive," said Lena Burhans. "Our horses are alive. It's a sunny, warm day." She looked around at them all, and put her arm around Carl, standing beside her. "Praise be to God for delivering us from the tempest."

33-INTO THE WOODS

Saturday, October 27th

"I'm not really in shape for this," puffed Bill Zeller after they had walked for about a minute and the knot of new companions had spread out into a single file. "I tell you, the things I do for a good story…"

"What *are* you in shape for, Bill?" Roy Kapp furrowed his brow, and threw a raised eyebrow at the newspaper man laboring up the trail behind him.

"Resting," replied Zeller. "Sleeping. Dining out."

"No time for that now," grunted Bart Ross, leading their column.

"No. Not with loose cannons like you around!" snorted Zeller faintly. His face was turning red, and sweat was already beginning to gather on his face.

"Without folks like me and young Jake Wilder here—" Ross jerked his thumb toward Wilder, who was following closely behind him "—you'd have nothing interesting to write about." There were low, breathless chuckles. These men had known one another for a long time.

The overgrown, eroded trail pitched up more steeply, and the hikers kept their thoughts to themselves as they struggled to catch their breaths and navigate the rocks and roots. The trail was clearly seldom used, and not maintained. A stream had commandeered it, cutting down into a v-shaped cross-section. Loose round stones made footing difficult. Wilder steadied himself by grabbing the branches of bushes and saplings growing out over the trail. Sweat started building up on his back under the pack and straps. The cool morning started to feel like a hot summer day.

This went on a little longer, the trail alternately leveling off and rising as it cut up the grade of the small valley, followed the contours. They crossed small brooks, some dry, some with weak trickles of water flowing. A broken footbridge took them across a larger stream, dark with moss, pools full of black leaves. They hurried past the stream, leaving behind clouds of mosquitoes that had risen to greet them. Ascending from the valley bottom, the light level gradually increased and the vegetation became thinner and less rank.

After about thirty minutes of slow, steady progress, the state guardsman who led them signaled a rest-stop. The dozen-odd hikers dropped their packs, and pulled out water bottles. Wilder surveyed his companions. Most seemed relatively comfortable in this environment, from the years they had spent in camps, hunting, and similar outdoor activities. Zeller was clearly an exception, a die-hard urbanist in a radically rural state.

"… About a mile," Wilder overheard the guardsman saying. He walked over to him. A petite dark-haired woman whose name he could not recall was talking with the guardsman. She flashed a smile at Wilder as he joined them. Kapp was there, too, fishing around in his pack.

"We'll leave the trail here," continued the guardsman. He was a lieutenant, Wilder saw. "The Governor's camp is not on a trail."

"She always does this," said Kapp. "Like a secret hideout."

"You been to one of these before?" asked Wilder, anticipating an affirmative answer.

"No, actually." Kapp shrugged and shook his head. Wilder's and the dark-haired woman's faces both revealed their surprise. "No, I know. Same party. But we pretty much kept to our own separate constituencies. Different circles. This is the first time."

"It this your first time, too?" asked Wilder, turning toward the woman. "And I'm truly sorry, but could you tell me your name again?"

"Oh, no, Mr. Wilder. I've been doing this for years. And, yes, it's Cindy." She smiled in a cool, professional way. Wilder considered his impression of her for a second: forties or fifties, fit, neat hair, Latina or Italian, possibly. An old friend of the Governor's? A Republican, too?

"Are you with her administration, Cindy?" Wilder was drawing a complete blank for this woman. He thought he knew just about everyone in the state.

Cindy laughed. "We were college roommates, at Middlebury. Very old friends."

So these gatherings were pretty eclectic, then, thought Wilder. "What kind of work do you do now?" He glanced at Roy Kapp. Kapp's expression was hintless.

260

"Oh, I'm a lawyer. Law school professor. At VLS."

"I see. Sure. That fits the pattern." Governor Remington had a circle of experts on whom she informally relied, from campaign strategists to lawyers and academics. "What's your field?"

"A whole lot of land claims and property rights, recently. So many changes going on in who owns what, foreclosures, eminent domain, land trusts, and all." She inserted her water container back into the top of her backpack. "But my main specialty is, or at least was, state constitutional law and Federal jurisdiction."

Kapp's eyes lit up. "Oh, now, that's interesting," he interjected. He hoisted his pack onto his back. "How come I don't know you?"

Cindy's demeanor became more reserved. "Well, now you do. I've heard and read a great deal about you, Mr. Kapp." She gestured vaguely with her head toward where Bart Ross stood. "And your fellow autonomists."

Kapp's eyes remained full of curiosity, but he only nodded silently. Their guide the lieutenant strode out into the middle of the group arrayed along the trail.

"If I could have your attention for a minute," he announced in a loud, crisp voice. The talk quickly died down, and he went on. "We will continue off-trail from here to the camp. We'll stay together, moving up that slope over there—" (he gestured with two straight fingers) "—until it levels off and we come to an old clearing up in a pocket in the shadow of the ridge. That's where the Governor has established camp." He swung his narrow pack up onto one shoulder and pushed his other arm under the strap. "Watch your footing, folks."

And then they were moving again, carefully switchbacking up the forested slope, hanging onto tree-trunks and rocks, helping each other, waiting as those ahead in the column scrambled over obstacles. Most were silent now, concentrating, panting with exertion. What exactly was the point of this, wondered Wilder? These were busy people, during a packed time of year, with several crises looming. They could be in a meeting room in Montpelier, two hours into the conference by now. Instead, here they were, a group of key leaders from across their state, slipping on moss and clutching at moose maple and hobblebush, with no idea where they were headed. Or the knowledge to escape, unless they were seasoned orienteers.

261

"Ha!" laughed Bart Ross, with his trademark joviality. He stood leaning against a large tree where the column halted to re-group, puffing and wiping his face with a bandana. "This is a blast." He suddenly started poking at the leaves among the tree's roots, and held up a small, red salamander. "Red eft," he said.

A few of the group bent over to look. They stood around as the last caught up. Zeller brought up the rear. His lip curled in mock scorn. "I bet you haven't had so much fun since you went to hand in your party membership card to Laugherty!" There were several cautious laughs.

"Oh, this is just good clean fun," replied Ross. "That was scary as hell, along with being hysterically funny."

"You, scared?" His fellow member of the Washington delegation, Senator Rosen, raised his brows and stared at him. From rival parties, their communication of late had been limited, Wilder knew.

"Of Laugherty? Martin *Laugherty*? You kidding?" Bart Ross looked around at expectant faces. His grin vanished as he put the red eft back down among the moss and ferns. "Of course I was," he said, abruptly soft-spoken. "Martin Laugherty is one of the most terrifying people I have ever encountered." Standing together in the calm, sun-dappled forest, his listeners looked back at him, saying nothing. "Ever," repeated Ross, with emphasis. "And so is that Vulk guy, his COT." His eyes glanced across their faces, meeting their eyes. Rosen looked down. Kapp looked back, intensely. Then, it was Cindy who broke the spell with a private little "hmmm". They all started moving again, following the guardsman up the slope.

As promised, the incline started to level off, and before long they were walking through terrain and vegetation of an entirely different character. Instead of the tall, mature hemlock and broadleaf trees, they were in a more open forest of scrubby pine and juniper, with deep mats of blueberries around their feet, and rock outcroppings and boulders. They followed a faint trail. On it, Wilder noticed the droppings of a large animal – was it moose or horse? Around them, they could see the landscape better, with a long, high ridge directly ahead, clothed in dark stands of spruce. Above it was the blue vault of sky, streaked with cirrus and sprinkled with ravens.

"Halt!" A voice shot up from nowhere. They stopped in surprise, looking around in disarray. The guardsman grinned. Wilder suddenly realized they had come to a camouflage net, and that there were eyes looking out at them. Ahead, from around the bend in the trace of a trail, strode Governor Remington. Everyone relaxed, and Bill Zeller clapped and let out a cheer.

"Well done, Governor! High drama!"

Jeanne Remington drew herself up, and spreading her arms wide, quoted the famous words of Revolutionary Vermont patriot Ethan Allen: "I am as resolutely determined to defend the independence of Vermont as Congress is that of the United States; and, rather than fail, I will retire with the hardy Green Mountain Boys into the desolate caverns of the mountains and wage war with human nature at large!"

She finished with a laugh and a bow, and her little audience clapped.

"What an ice-breaker," said Wilder under his breath to Cindy, who stood next to him.

"Jeanne always does that," she whispered, wrinkling her nose in amusement. "Same routine for about thirty years. We used to come up the other side of the ridge, from Middlebury, right to this same spot."

The Governor was moving through the group, greeting everyone personally. More guardsmen appeared from the shadows of the trees and camo nets, offering to carry packs and ushering everyone into the camp. She came to Wilder and Cindy.

"Hi, Cin!" She gave her old friend a quick hug, and then turned to Wilder, taking his hand. "Congressman Wilder! This is wonderful. I was afraid you'd be too busy with the campaigns." She laughed a kind, entirely genuine laugh. "I'm so glad your comrade Anna could spare you for two days."

Wilder was nonplussed for a heartbeat, and then recovered his ease, aiming for a balance between sounding rude and sounding obsequious. "I guess that if you can spare two days up here, she can give me two days off."

Jeanne Remington laughed again, and gave him a friendly poke in the arm. "Oh, this is work! We're not going to take any breaks. Don't get too comfortable." For that instant, Wilder studied her. The Governor was a wide-faced, pale-skinned, slightly plump woman in her late fifties, with wispy reddish-blonde hair and dark-rimmed glasses. Normally attired in gray suits and long raincoats, she now appeared in a completely unexpected guise, in green fatigues and a gray biofleece jacket, a broad-brimmed hat on her head, its brim snapped up against the crown on one side.

Her countenance changed. She took his hand again, and looked him in the eye. "This is very important and I am so grateful you've come. We've got some important business that's a lot more urgent than politics, I'm afraid. I'll forget you're a Green and you forget I'm a Republican." She shot a smile at Cindy. "And Anna's here, too, anyway."

Wilder nodded. "I'm happy to oblige, Governor," he said carefully.

"Oh, say Jeanne, for goodness' sake. We're not in a 3V debate right now."

Wilder smiled and nodded. "Jeanne." He turned to Cindy, and Bill Zeller, who was listening in. "We used to be Jake and Jeanne in the Legislature, but since Jeanne was elected Governor, I don't think I've addressed her as anything but 'Madam Governor'." He turned back to her. "And I'm still Jake, too."

"Good, good to get that straightened out. Enough of all that." Jeanne Remington motioned them all to follow her, and turned back up the trail. "This is Captain Lafontaine." She gestured toward an officer coming to meet them. "He'll get you moved in and set up. There are lunch boxes, in case you're hungry yet. The meeting starts in 45 minutes. You're the last group. Everyone's here now."

In the mossy shade among the pines, under camo nets, Wilder saw low sleeping tents, a huge high-slung meeting tent that was mostly fly mesh, ATVs, gear, grazing horses, and dozens of people sitting in camp chairs – some at tables - working with T-pads or wearing VNET headsets. There was a low, orderly cacophony of cooking sounds and the crackle of radios. It looked more military than anything else, although civilians seemed to outnumber the Guardsmen. Seated in a fold in the ridge, protected on three sides, the encampment's view to the east was grand and sweeping, if you stood up on a rock and looked between the nets and tree branches. Rank upon rank of the Green Mountains vanished off into the humid, hazy October air. No human feature could be seen—not even a wind turbine.

So this was the setting of the Governor's Overnights...

34-MORNING ON THE BATTLEFIELD

Saturday, October 27th

For an indeterminate while, they all just walked around, looking in a daze at the wagon and the coach, at the soggy, splintered debris spread across their campsite. They hugged their arms, poking at objects with their feet, probing to understand what was theirs, and what had appeared from nowhere. A vast dampened stillness filled the littered field, broken only by the distant sound of a chainsaw, and the closer chop of an axe somewhere nearby.

Mike had to sit down several times, take a deep breath, and fight the RDD. This happened sometimes in RL when he found himself in highly abnormal situations, like accidents and natural disasters. He'd struggle with unreasonable impulses to teleport, fly, or rezz something. People would look at him oddly as his focus momentarily shifted to a HUD that was not there, or a bat that was not in his hand. This was happening now, in the dramatically changed landscape around the wagon. He shook his head and kneaded his temples and forehead with the tips of his fingers.

"I'm going up there," said Nate, looking up at the berm.

"I'll join you," said Mike, grateful for something that would help ground him in RL. Together, they scrambled up the muddy, slippery pitch until they reached the crest. Mike had not been up there until now. On the other side, the elevation was higher: the raised plateau of the old artillery fort. In the distance to the north was the main part of Petersburg. Just below them were the toppled wagon and coach, and the small huddle of their companions. To the south, they had a commanding view of the battlefield park and the countryside beyond. Spread out as far as they could see was what looked like a junkyard—a tangled, multicolored sea of natural and human-made wreckage. The roads had vanished. The railroad line had disappeared, buried. No trees were standing. Destruction was total.

"Where's that steeple?!" Mike suddenly asked, recalling the dark apparition hanging above their camp the previous night. He searched around. It was nowhere to be seen. Then, far off along the front of the main earthworks, he thought he could see something long and angular that matched his memory of the steeple. Now, it was just another misplaced item in an ocean of detritus.

"I've seen enough, Nate," said Mike. "Listen." The younger man looked at him alertly. "We just met yesterday, and until now everything's been about taking care of our own business and getting along with our own family members and caring for the horses. You know, normal stuff." Nate nodded, wondering where Mike was going with this. "Now, nothing's normal. This storm has changed everything in its path. Richmond, Fredericksburg, DC…we don't know how much of these cities are even there, now." They looked down at the others. Terry had his T-pad out. Ethan was pulling branches off the coach. Celia stood looking up at them, her body language indicating she was preparing to climb up to where they stood.

Mike went on: "And we're stuck here behind I don't know how many miles of blocked roads, broken bridges, snapped power lines, and all. We might be here days, maybe weeks. We have to think about water, food, security, and not getting sick." He looked closely at Nate. Nate's serious eyes flashed back and forth between Mike's look and his sister's precarious ascent toward them.

"Hear what I'm saying?" asked Mike. "I'm talking from years of military duty down near the Gulf, where the hurricanes hit all the time, although not like this, usually. What I'm saying is that, if we don't cooperate and if we make some bad mistakes now, right at the beginning, we might end up dead, or at least seeing our family members suffer." He let the words settle. "This is RL, not some sim," he added, perhaps unnecessarily, but Nate caught his glance and nodded thoughtfully. "With what has happened, there isn't going to be a quick response by DRR. We can assume that huge numbers of folks out there for hundreds and hundreds of kilometers around are dead or injured or homeless. Their houses are gone, kids missing, horses and herds loose. Clean drinking water's gonna be a big issue. People are going to be desperate." Nate nodded, and then gave his sister a hand for the final lunge to the top. She

266

shook back her hair and stood up, looking out with wide eyes across the ruination.

"Isn't it horrible?!" she burst out with lingering amazement. She shaded her eyes with her hand, and peered back toward the tunnel entrance. "I can't believe we climbed over all that stuff down there."

Mike returned to the subject, to make sure Nate had gotten his point. "So, you hear what I'm saying?" He peered at Nate, and then widened his aspect to include Celia. Nate nodded again, slightly impatiently. "If we all want to get home, and get through this safely and efficiently, we're going to have to work together. Really work together."

Nate smiled. He was a team player, a pack dog. "I got ya. Not a sim." He jerked his head sideways, indicating the site below. "Your grandma doesn't look like she's doing too good." She sat by herself on a fallen tree, motionless.

"She's a tough lady," answered Mike. "She'll pull through – she's been pretty much running my whole family as long as I've been around – but she's been dealing with a lot of issues recently and having to do some inside work." He took a deep breath and let it slowly out. "Getting used to all of this is hard for her. She's from the Old Days."

Nate and Celia nodded in agreement. "Our granddaddy was like that," said Celia. "He hated horses."

"Oh, Celie, that's kinda harsh!" Nate chided her.

"No, he hated them, for no reason. But I forgave him. It wasn't his fault. Nanna said it was because he was a car lover and didn't like having to give them up."

"Mm," said Nate. "Well, you were pretty little then, if that's how you remember him."

Mike cut into their sibling banter. "Let's go down and talk to your dad, get a plan going. We have to get the wagons upright again, deal with any broken parts and cargo, get a hot meal going, and plan for some perimeter defense. And inventory our food, water, water containers, and filtration pumps."

"Aye aye, Captain," mumbled Nate. His sister stared in cool surprise at both of them. As the men half-climbed and half-slid back down, she remained standing atop the berm, looking toward the flat tidewater horizon and jumbled foreground around her, letting the hot sun bake into her shoulders and back, still stiff and chilled from the damp night underground. A cloud of small flies began to accumulate close to her head. She waved at them irritably, and started down.

35-THE BREADLOAF WILDERNESS COUNCIL

Saturday, October 27th

In their mountain redoubt, they pulled their chairs and pads into several concentric circles around a raised spot on the hidden meadow—state legislators, State Supreme Court judges, the Adjutant General of the Vermont National Guard, a couple of media editors, the mayor of Burlington, the Governor's cabinet, select board members from a variety of towns. The senior civil servants of all the state departments were there as well, and the president of the state university, and the list went on. They were quiet, subdued, expectant, and—in a few cases—mildly irate. Some chatted, while others studied T-pads and sent email. Wilder did a quick count and reached about sixty, in addition to the Guardsmen around the camp. It was a mixed group—multipartisan—but conspicuous by their absence were the few prominent Homelander politicians in the state.

Into their midst walked the Governor and Lieutenant-Governor. Wilder knew they had a good working relationship, despite their party differences. Anna remained standing, off to one side. The Governor held out her hands in welcome.

"Folks, fellow Vermonters, thank you so much for coming. I am humbly grateful you accepted my invitation." She looked at the sky. "Thank you, Weather Gods, for cooperating." This brief display of humor aside, Jeanne Remington was formal, serious. "In past times, this might have been fun and festive. It was, originally." She turned as she spoke, studying their faces and choosing her words carefully. "I have been organizing—or at least, helping to organize—gatherings up here longer than I've had a political career. They always used to be social get-togethers, to relax, recharge, do some new thinking about things, plan campaigns... Those meetings were quite a bit smaller. Most of you by definition would *not* have been invited." There were a handful of sudden, soft chuckles, but the Governor met them with a neutral pause. "No, those were in political days, when you were either allies or opponents, when we worried about energy bills and health care reform and what to do about Social Security, as if we had the luxury to do something about such issues at our own pace. We planned campaigns and legislative strategies." These last words she pronounced with irony. She took a deep breath. Her audience waited silently.

"The past few years have been years of continual crisis and compromise. We've had to drop policy agendas we pursued for decades – in Vermont and in Washington—and fight one fire after another. We've had to cut budgets again and again, and deal with public dissatisfaction no one was ready for. The state's finances have been at rock bottom for five years. Infrastructure is crumbling before our eyes. The state university system and health-care system are both out of money. Keeping the terrestrial wireless network up has taken enormous resources. You know all these things. Without everyone stepping in at the local level, without all the mutual aid groups and volunteers, without private foreign aid, without the remittances, we never could have kept things together... You know all this." She looked around at the stony, reflective faces of her listeners, and went on.

"It's been said many times that the world changed after Sanderborough, and again after the Panic of '35. But, in a way, at least here in our state's politics and public administration, some things did not change. Old habits have a way of dying hard, or refusing to die. We've still run our town meetings, and passed our budgets, and conducted our elections. We've kept the agencies and departments functioning, even if they had to be staffed by volunteers more and more. We've sent our delegation to Washington in good order—an excellent group of representatives, regardless of party affiliation. We've collected taxes, and made sure some of that went to Washington, too." She smiled faintly at Senators Rosen and Ross, and her eyes briefly met Wilder's. "We, ah...," she paused, and seemed for an instant to be laboring to breathe. Wilder watched her closely, in some surprise. Jeanne Remington was known for her iron composure, for what some saw as coldness. She had been compared to old Margaret Thatcher. Was she struggling to contain her emotions? Glancing around, he saw others watching her. The silence was complete.

Then, with a slight raggedness in her voice, but clear eyes, she started again: "We have faithfully abided by the Constitution of the United States, together with the other forty-nine states, and, in most areas, federal jurisdiction—the law of the land—has continued to hold sway as it has for centuries. In recent times, this has not always been easy…," She stopped. The audience quietly let out its breath. There were a few low mutterings. Faces were full of curiosity, surprise, other emotions.

She resumed, agitated, meeting everyone's look eye-to-eye. "Events are now moving very quickly. VERY quickly. I want to share what I can see with you, share my sense of urgency. Crisis has become normal for us all, but a number of calamities are now interacting with longer-term trends, posing the most serious sorts of threats to the people of Vermont. As your Governor, with your counsel—which we will spend the rest of today hearing and examining—new kinds of actions will have to be taken."

"What new kinds of actions, Governor?" Howard Rosen leaned forward abruptly, firing out the words. He was ashen, trembling very slightly. In that moment, Wilder reflected that Rosen was in his seventies now, and that he had been under tremendous pressure recently. It showed.

Jeanne Remington's self-control was firm again, icy. "Senator, we will go through this all in due course. But," she looked around at everyone, "the Senator, our elected representative to the US Senate but not to any deliberative body in Vermont, has cued me to make a major request—no, requirement… that I have to make of you." She then turned to Rosen, and looked at him in silence until he sat back again, tensely. She continued: "You are a hand-picked group. I did not invite everyone I could have invited, and there are certain areas of state government where I did not see fit to include a representative. My advisors and I thought long and hard about whom to ask to this meeting. You are here because I believe you are committed to the integrity and security of Vermont, and because you will play key leadership roles in the months ahead. However, I must ask you this: everyone who remains to take part in this meeting must swear an oath, before me and all assembled here." She let the words linger, weigh on her audience. A few whispered conversations broke out. Rosen was looking skywards, shaking his head. Anna Cleary looked at Wilder. She smiled calmly, encouragingly. He reflexively scratched his head and took a deep breath, meeting her eyes with a look of caution.

270

"And if we don't take this oath?" asked Roy Kapp with a wave of his hand.

"Then you will be escorted right back down the mountain, immediately, Representative Kapp." Governor Remington then addressed the whole group again. "I must, absolutely must, obtain this oath from all who take part in the discussion we need to have. There is just too much at stake now. I think you all know what I am concerned about. The timing of public information will never be more critical than it is now. Your responsibility as public servants has never been greater." She turned to Kapp again, and added cryptically, "And I think you're going to like this, actually."

"Governor, let's hear what this oath is about," said Ross pleasantly. "I can't decide without hearing a little more detail."

Jeanne Remington laughed. "Of course, of course. I wouldn't expect you to. You all need to make an informed decision." She raised the volume of her voice over the many conversations that had broken out. "Everyone, please, save the chatting. Let me get to the point." People quieted down instantly. Wilder noticed that the associate justices of the Supreme Court were sitting together, whispering and looking at a T-pad.

"This will be called the Breadloaf Wilderness Oath," said the Governor with emphasis, "and it will most likely be of historic importance, and I'm not just saying that to flatter myself. It was partly to emphasize its importance that I brought you here, away from the office, although, conveniently, this is the time of year we organize the Overnights anyway. We're in the Breadloaf Wilderness right now. Here is what you will swear, if you agree to: you will affirm your allegiance to the State, the Constitution, and the Government of Vermont, and you will swear to keep everything we discuss here absolutely secret from anyone who was not also here, unless or until I personally give you permission to do otherwise." She looked around. Anna started passing out small cards with the oath printed on them. "Is there anyone," the Governor went on, "who does not wish to take this oath?" At first, no one moved. Then, Howard Rosen spoke out again, and rose. He stood stiffly, hands at his sides, a veteran of almost fifty years of rivalry with the Governor's party, his earliest political career started in the staffs of Bernie Sanders and Peter Clavelle.

"Governor, I'm sorry but I cannot go along with this. It's, it's... irregular..., ah..." He groped for the right phrase, at a rare loss for words.

"It's inappropriate. Swearing loyalty to the State Constitution is completely redundant... I mean, of course we support it. We—that is, most of us—have already been sworn in anyway for the offices we hold. Where are you going with this?" He looked around, hands out, his face a mixture of worry and demand.

The Governor responded respectfully. "Senator, I know you are no friend of even our more moderate Republicans here at home, your antipathy toward Mr. Laugherty notwithstanding. But I refer you to Section 20 of the Second Chapter of the Vermont Constitution, regarding my executive powers. I am among other things the Captain-General and the Commander-in-Chief of the forces of this state, and as you know very well—and as we will soon be discussing in detail—the forces of the state are going to have to be put to unaccustomed uses, very quickly and decisively, to preserve what may turn out to not only be the civil order of Vermont, but its very liberty." She clipped her phrases, her face tense and slightly flushed. "I need to know without a doubt that every person here is with me on this, bound to support our common cause. This is not a time for partisan politics or opt-outs. If you cannot swear this oath, then I don't want you here and I won't be calling on you as things heat up." She stood very still, her head hanging slightly like a fighter's, scanning the faces around her. People were silent, uncomfortable.

"I think this is inappropriate, bringing us up here like this, herding us into a circle with armed Guardsmen all around. We came because we trusted you, but...this isn't exactly what I expected." The speaker, an elderly man, was Chief Justice Morris Patek of the Vermont Supreme Court. He stood up from his chair angrily and addressed the gathering. "Times may be hard, but there's no need for this sort of secretive behavior by the Governor. I swore my oath to serve the State Constitution years ago, and once is sufficient. I will not take any oaths up here at this camp, and frankly do not think I belong at a meeting of this type."

"I'll have to ask you to leave, Judge Patek, if you cannot take the oath, even if you already took it once before, or one similar. My office may need to take some decisive measures, and it would be very dangerous for the word to get out in advance. But we need consensus and absolute loyalty—everyone from this group informed and on board. Freedom and Unity, Mr. Patek." The Governor paused, and then repeated the state's motto. "Freedom and Unity."

"Count me out. This shouldn't be taking place." Patek raised a finger of warning. "A governor ought not to be going about business in this collusive, irregular way. And a judge, of all people, needs some distance from it. The Judiciary determines constitutionality and legality, but we don't legislate or execute." The other justices stood up, and made ready to leave together. "You do what you need to do, Governor Remington. We'll advise and opine—just give us a call—but not in a forum like this."

"Then a guide will drive you back down, Justice Patek. Thank you for your time." She bowed almost imperceptibly, and turned back toward the circle, waiting, looking impatient but not embarrassed. Patek stiffly strode off when the Guard officer arrived, followed by his colleagues. Then they were gone, and a few moments later they heard an ATV starting up somewhere off in the woods.

"Any others?" asked Jeanne Remington. Heads shook. There apparently were not.

"I'll swear the oath, Jeanne," Wilder spoke up. "The situation in Washington is untenable, we've been muddling along for too many years, this storm has thrown all bets off, and I want to work with the Governor and hear what she has to say." He shrugged and raised one finger. "Anyway, if you look at Section 20, you'll see that the Governor can only take extraordinary powers with the consent of the Senate. We'll be OK; right, senators?" Several people signaled their agreement. He grinned at them. "Let's get moving, then." What else could they do? Refuse and leave? Years ago, in the Legislature, he had had his differences with Jeanne Remington, but they were simple matters of policy, and she was from the north of the state while he was from the south. Otherwise, he knew her to be an ethical, conscientious politician. A bit full of herself, sometimes, but honest. Besides, reflected Wilder, though the atmosphere was contentious and uncertain, the levels of decorum and mutual trust in this meeting were enormously refreshing after the stark tension, intimidation, and fear in Washington politics.

With the Lieutenant-Governor and the Adjutant-General beside her, Jeanne Remington administered the oath to groups of several people at a time, who repeated together, standing at the foot of the squat white pine tree, with their right hands on the Vermont Constitution and left hands raised, the following oath:

I, [name], do solemnly swear that I will be true and faithful to the State of Vermont and that I will not, directly or indirectly, do any act or thing injurious to the Constitution or Government thereof, under the pains and penalties of perjury. I also swear that I will keep all information about this meeting secret, unless otherwise personally instructed by the Governor, likewise under the pains and penalties of perjury.

This procedure took approximately fifteen minutes. Participants milled around, ate from the lunchboxes provided, spoke among themselves, or reflected quietly. After taking the oath, to Wilder it seemed as if some sort of catharsis, some unburdening, had taken place. There was an odd relaxation of tension. Everyone seemed to display this. He discovered a new sense of admiration for the Governor. It had all seemed incongruous—artificial—but out of this group of busy, doubtful, inconvenienced people, a kind of symbolic pact was already forming.

Waiting for the meeting to be called back to order, Wilder had a brief conversation with Bill Zeller about a column article that was due the following week, and then scanned his T-pad for mail and news. Reports from Virginia were getting worse and worse. Strong winds had reached Washington, DC. Rhiannon was still a Category Five. Rivers were rising rapidly from the relentless rain. Morales and her cabinet had been evacuated to Dayton Air Force Base. Government facilities were being secured. Millions of people were stuck, unable to move away quickly enough from the path. Highways and roads leading away from the Nation's Capital were packed with stalled queues of low-speed vehicles. Morales had just declared all of Virginia, Maryland, Delaware, DC, eastern Pennsylvania, and New Jersey federal disaster areas. The military and DRR were fully mobilized. Concerns were rising that New York City might also lie in Rhiannon's path. Looting and carjackings were reported. Foreign governments were making pledges of aid. Stories were confused, conflicting. An immense human tragedy was unfolding.

Closing the T-pad and taking off his headset, Wilder leaned back in his low camp chair, and rubbed his eyes. He stretched his neck with a rotating motion, his glance panning across the deep blue sky above. This crystal-clear Canadian high was promising to keep Rhiannon from traveling very far north. The point where it would nudge Rhiannon out into Atlantic was still uncertain.

His attention returned to the oath-taking. It was the last group. Together with the President Pro Tem of the Senate and a group of Legislators, Howard Rosen stood awkwardly, his left hand raised. Rosen, the patrician academic from Burlington, eternal opponent of Remington's party, profoundly skeptical of the Governor's motives, even more outraged by the direction of national politics, was getting with the program. Wilder laughed to himself. Wherever this Breadloaf camp-out was going, Rosen didn't want to miss it after all.

* * *

"The Lieutenant-Governor will lead off with a situation update," said the Governor crisply when everyone was seated again. "Anna?"

Anna Cleary, with her soft voice and intense brown eyes, moved gracefully around the circle as she spoke, referring occasionally to notes, speaking quickly and urgently. First, she thanked the Legislative Commission on Trade, Migration, and State Sovereignty, at whose weekly meetings she had been gathering and comparing information for months. A few moments were then spent on the hurricane, but too little was known to be drawing many conclusions, yet. How devastated the big Mid-Atlantic cities would soon be was still a matter of speculation. Large numbers of people might evacuate as long-term refugees, but how many was still unknowable. Whether it might affect the election in ten days was uncertain. Morales had made no statements about this. Her critics on the right had already been calling for her to resign and step aside for a "Government of National Recovery." As the hurricane approached Washington, some voices had started calling for a postponement of the November election. No US presidential election had ever been postponed, and numerous congressional resolutions had reaffirmed the principle that no federal agency or official had the authority to do this. The Homeland Front and many other politicians on the right argued heatedly in favor of "staying the course" and remaining on schedule with the election. Confused debate about this had erupted. State election commissions outside the region affected by Hurricane Rhiannon were saying that elections would go ahead as planned. The US Constitution, Anna informed the group, contained no guidance about the scheduling of general elections. "However, we all know that high concentrations of progressive voters are located in the area affected by the hurricane," she noted dryly. "We can only guess at this point how the storm will affect their turnout."

Closer to home, an incident had occurred on Vermont's border during the night that demanded careful attention. Months of anti-government student protests at Dartmouth College in Hanover, New Hampshire had led to an uprising, the burning of several federal courthouses and other facilities in New Hampshire, and a call for Hanover and surrounding towns to secede from New Hampshire and join with Vermont in a "Connecticut Valley Republic". This, realized Wilder, might explain the smoke he had noticed as they left Interstate 91 earlier that morning, and the military vehicles. The upcoming independence referendum in Vermont was having a strong influence on sentiments among the students.

The protesters were being reinforced continually by students arriving from across the Northeast every day, although federal forces were now trying to stem the flow through their control of interstate highway access. There was a tense standoff in Hanover. Students were occupying university buildings and barricading roads. College leaders and New Hampshire politicians were attempting to negotiate. Students, reflected Wilder, must be stressed beyond the breaking point these days. The oligarchy could always send their children to the elite universities abroad, but ordinary students had no ability to pay tuitions, and university administrators and faculty had gradually slid into poverty as well, so the alumni of many universities had stepped in to resist complete take-over by the oligarchy. Radicalization was a result, and Dartmouth was a case in point. It had only been a matter of time before something like this would boil over. For a few years now, a collectivist community called the Free Academic Village had organized student housing, grown food, distributed firewood, produced biofuels, and helped support faculty, staff, and the College through these activities in lieu of paying tuition. The Free Village was in fact one of the main reasons the College was still in business because it had solved many local food and energy problems. Homelander groups, oligarchs, and others were vehemently opposed to the left-wing politics of the Free Village movement, which was spreading to other universities and colleges. In Hanover, the Free Village had become a breeding ground for revolutionaries, focusing young people's frustration on the vision of radical change they hungered for.

Jeanne Remington stepped back into the center of the circle, and said she had several things to add before Anna Cleary continued.

"What's happening in Hanover and Lebanon is a reminder of our own approaching independence referendum. The referendum will be on the ballot in the vast majority of towns around Vermont. As most of you know, it calls for a representative State Secession Convention to be held within 90 days of November 2nd, to deliberate about Vermont secession and draft Articles of Secession for ratification by the Legislature and my signature. We've been through this process four times already, and the votes in favor reached 32% in '36. Now, I know this is 'merely'"—she made little bunny-ear quotation marks with her fingers—"a non-binding, advisory referendum, but I'm curious...who here thinks the referendum will pass this time?" Bart Ross and Roy Kapp raised their hands without hesitation, along with several others, but an embarrassed hesitation seemed to grip most present. Jeanne Remington waited in silence for several heartbeats. She aimed a sour look at Ross and Kapp, and resumed. "Well, this is obviously a contentious issue. You may not know where you stand yet, or want to reveal your position in public. Wise, perhaps. I respect that. But you know where I stand. One-hundred-plus percent against! Economic suicide, and the wrong sort of provocation at a time when—yes, you are hearing this from me—at a time when, unhappily, the nation's leadership and many states are or will soon be in the hands of fascists." There was a murmured reaction. "You know Hedges has a snowball's chance in hell now. Nobody can recreate Morales' early momentum. Here's me saying I wish the Democrats still had a chance of winning, but no. No way. Let's be frank. Things are too far gone, overall, for that kind of governance and policy to succeed. Within four months, Alberta will be applying to become the fifty-first state, we'll be at war with Canada, global pressure will be excruciating (but of course it will remain economic and diplomatic, not military), and the Aztlan movement and Cascadians and other secessionists around the country will be expanding from strength to strength. Things will happen fast, we'll have to make some hard and quick decisions, and it may be a long time before common sense rules this country again."

We may even see states secede and then get re-annexed because they have coal deposits or timber, thought Wilder to himself grimly.

She waited for a moment, letting her words sink in. Her listeners sat with downcast faces and averted eyes. Wilder's and Anna's eyes met again. She frowned.

"So," continued the Governor, "I'll turn things over to Anna again in a moment, but take note of what I just predicted. We'll return to that. As for the Vermont secession referendum, it's going to pass. You know it is. Vermonters know what I just said. They've had three decades of painful education about secession and the dysfunction of American democracy. The Green Teens and the New Energy Plan was a nice time, lots of hope and enthusiasm. We were going to do away with fossil fuels and build an ecotopia. But for twenty years the policy base and wealth for building a sane future have been slipping away, and we are now on the steep downward slope of the oil peak as well, and climate change is accelerating. Getting worse every day. The instincts of the majority – and every poll shows this now – are to simplify, break free of the federal structure, become more flexible, more local, and escape the worsening legacies of many aspects of Third-Century America that, frankly, most Vermonters feel they are not responsible for. Like the Energy Trust, for example, and OSCIA and Forsa. This is basically why I think—and my cabinet thinks—that the majority will go for secession. Talk to each individual and they'll have varying lists of reasons, but so it will go. So it will go." She paused for breath.

Bart Ross, who had very publicly taken the separatist position little more than a week before, raised his hand. He sat in a folding chair at the foot of an ancient, gnarled birch, his legs crossed. The Governor nodded at him.

"Governor Jeanne, I'm assuming we can raise some questions and have some discussion at points in this briefing?"

"I'd prefer to keep that for the end, and focus on developing an action plan in smaller groups—yes, I should have already mentioned this—we'll be breaking up into working groups when we have some sort of consensus about the situation and its highest priorities."

"Well," resumed Bart Ross, "can I ask for a clarification before you and the Lieutenant-Governor continue?"

"Certainly," said Jeanne Remington curtly.

"I'd like to ask you why, if you understand why most Vermonters want secession, and you see national events going in such a dire direction, you are still totally opposed to it? Aren't you worried about how these events might compromise and disrupt us further, if we remain a state of the Union? For instance, if this Fort McMurray business goes ahead and the US under Laugherty does annex or absorb Alberta and forces oil exports to China to end, and Canada objects, our border with Québec will become a war front. Wouldn't neutrality serve us a lot better?" Ross said all this in his eternally affable, sensible manner, without a trace of stridency or provocation. Jeanne Remington seemed to take it this way, as well. Her body language changed, and softened.

"Bart, thanks for raising this. I suppose I should have left my personal preference out of this. My preference is for us to remain a US state, for complicated reasons. That's that. At the same time, Vermont is a unitary constitutional democracy and we have to listen to our constituents. As Governor, I cannot stand against the will of the people, constantly vetoing or publicly criticizing things most people want. They'll throw me out next chance they get, or recall me. But even more important than this, I—we—must do what is best for the lives, safety, and liberty of the people under our jurisdiction, and that includes being realistic about what's going to happen, and about the implications. There's no room for wishful thinking. Which gets us to the matter of how we must act when this referendum passes, perhaps sooner..."

She took a long drink from a water bottle she had been passing back and forth from hand to hand as she spoke. Bart Ross nodded thoughtfully, and thanked her. No one else spoke. No one challenged her. Almost everyone, it seemed, essentially agreed with the forecast, whether they liked it or not. They wanted to hear more. Where was she going with this?

"So one of the strategies we will develop today is an immediate action plan for this probability. My administration will have to be proactive and act fast, with the total support of the Legislature and Judiciary. A lot of other crazy things may unfold in the next two weeks, made suddenly worse by Rhiannon. More on that in a second. But the election on November 6th will be a "shot heard 'round the world" and even if the non-binding resolution is to schedule a conference for January or February at a nice leisurely pace, we won't have time on our side. Events will decide. Fast-moving events." She took another drink. "Which brings us to migrants and refugees. Anna, please forgive my interruption. Tell us what you and Ed know." She smiled wearily at the Lieutenant-Governor. Anna spoke up, introducing Ed Schoonemaker, director of Vermont Emergency Management.

Wilder sat back, listening carefully, with his eyes searching the sky and upper ridges. Turkey vultures swept upwards in great spirals among the breezes cresting the higher ground. Two ravens darted aggressively toward a lone vulture, and it flapped twice and sailed away lazily, accelerating down into the valley and out of sight. His fingers played with a piece of birch bark they had fished out of the pine needles. But his mind was focused on her words. This was the central piece, where politics and ideologies and policy and procedures became hostage to more pedestrian events, literally: people on the move. Anna and Ed revealed statistics that were entirely new to him, statistics that the state governments were not releasing. But they matched his first-hand impressions.

Over the past ten years, more than one hundred and fifty thousand migrants—net—had settled in Vermont. This was epochal for a state with less than 800,000 inhabitants. Most had moved in with family or friends—or been absorbed into the expanding Mennonite and other plain-living communities. But there were still more than fifty thousand in refugee camps scattered around the state, as well as an uncertain number of squatters. The newcomers added to the food and biofuels farming workforce—now about a third of total employment—and brought all sorts of skills and trades with them. Most had come up from southern New England and New York. Many towns and villages had seen a homespun, low-income renaissance because of the new arrivals. Houses were being fixed up, barns raised, new gardens laid out, fire ponds dug, timber cut. Schools were full and health clinics overtaxed.

However, since late summer, the trend had changed sharply. Ten thousand migrants were now arriving at Vermont's borders every week: whole families and convoys of families were on the move - entire communities - in every type of vehicle imaginable, driving herds of horses, cattle, and sheep along with them. The majority were passing through, heading for the open country in Upstate New York and Maine, or to Ontario, Québec, and New Brunswick, if they could get visas. The roads and campgrounds could not handle the peaks of traffic, and Vermont authorities needed to know whether people intended to stay, and where, so entry was regulated at the border crossings, and many crossings were in the process of being closed so State Police and Guard resources could be concentrated. The Police and Guard were overwhelmed, deputizing hundreds of border guards to meet the crush. There were tensions: fights, protests, attempts to crash the barricades. Landowners were complaining of squatters, poaching, trash, human waste, fouled watercourses, and accidental fires. All the border towns were increasing their armed militias, and many were now moving to build stockades. There were charges that the measures being taken by Vermont officials were unconstitutional according to US law—that they amounted to restraint of mobility and trade. No one in Washington was bothering to listen at the moment, but they might. Meanwhile, neighboring states were equally overwhelmed. The migrant situation was in crisis. All the New England governors were in constant contact about this dilemma, caught between humanitarian concerns, America's tradition of open travel, and the need to maintain order and protect private property.

Now, the prospect of secession and the hurricane meant a vastly greater migration crisis could be anticipated. If it truly appeared that Vermont was leaving the USA, many people might make a dash for it, hoping for a slightly brighter future if they could get in 'under the wire.' Ed estimated that this alone might mean up to several hundred thousand additional people, or more. With its small population and overtaxed capacity for accommodating refugees, this had the makings of chaos for Vermont, of the undoing of all the painstaking gains in food production, energy conservation and production, and preservation of public welfare that Vermonters had achieved against the odds.

But an increase in immigration in response to the prospect of secession would be nothing compared to what the administration and its advisors now saw as practically inevitable: a wave of refugees from Hurricane Rhiannon. As many as sixty million people lived in or near the storm's track. With the collapse of the economy and public services over the past decade, few of these people and communities had it within their own means to easily recover from the hurricane, and rebuild. Homes would be destroyed, food production through next year devastated, jobs lost, schools closed. Energy would be scarce. Public safety would be endangered. Even worse, the risk of insect-borne epidemics would be severe. And all this would be coming on top of years of worry, disappointment, political tension, ongoing economic dislocation, and other hurricanes. People were already fed up, and migration *somewhere* was already on many minds.

Experts foresaw as many as ten million refugees leaving the affected zone, with most starting their journeys within two months, especially if serious epidemics arose. Two to three million might head north, for New England, where food was relatively plentiful, hurricanes rare, and law and order still the norm. This obviously would be a cataclysm for Vermont, stressed Anna Cleary, humanitarian concerns aside. Winter was only two months away. Wherever the refugees settled for the winter, massive food and medical relief would be needed, as well as energy supplies the state did not have. Federal help could not be guaranteed, as disaster assistance was up to Congress and the politics would be convoluted. Along with neighboring states, Vermont would have to seek assistance from Canada and overseas. Timing would be critical. Under the threat of immense deprivation—starvation, even—desperate refugees would destabilize wherever they were concentrated. As much as they wanted to offer kindness and humanitarian aid, Vermont's public servants, military, and emergency workers would be sorely pressed.

The state's choices were stark.

The briefing continued through the lunch hour. Others shared information they possessed. Long-term matters were ignored. Politics and ideology were kept at bay. The mode was practical and immediate. Cindy, the law-school professor, was revealed in a new and apparently planned role: facilitator. When the briefing ended, working groups were formed around counties and topics. Their assignment was to come up with one-hundred-day action plans to stave off a refugee crisis, migrant unrest, and the other interconnected disruptions that the hurricane, independence referendum, and national election would precipitate. Wilder joined the Southern Counties group and the working group on energy supply.

As they worked, they saw that ripples would quickly expand out from their working groups to include many others around the state, leading to total mobilization. Thousands more would be called in to assist with the planning and execution. The communication with neighboring states and provinces would be intense. A feverishly busy, uncertain time lay ahead. And the Governor was taking no chances, and certainly not trying to monopolize the management of perhaps the greatest crisis ever to face the state.

They worked late into the evening. By dinnertime, they were naturally calling themselves the Breadloaf Council. Detailed action plans to meet the swelling crisis began falling into place.

*   *   *

It was pitch dark. Wilder awoke in the close confines of his tent, his senses tingling. He lay still, his breathing suspended, listening to identify what had awakened him. There was a vast, brooding silence on the mountainside. The summer insects had quieted down. Then, in close proximity, he heard the call tones and static hiss of a radio. A low voice—presumably a Guardsman's—said something indistinct. Footsteps crackled quietly on the forest floor, moving away. He heard some more radio sounds further off, and an engine in the distance. Far, far away, he heard shouts, and what might have been a rifle shot. Then Wilder heard no more, and after waiting and listening for some indeterminate while, he eventually drifted back into a deep sleep.

ABOUT THE AUTHOR

Ralph Meima, MA/MBA, PhD, consults, writes, and pursues activism in renewable energy, sustainability, and community resilience. Born in the United States, he has lived in six countries and intermingled corporate, higher-education, and small business careers. He holds degrees in economics, engineering, international relations, and management. Ralph Meima lives in Vermont. *Fossil Nation* is his first novel.

>cal author ction-111

(Ralph meima's son)